Bastion

Book Three of
the Outsider series.

by
Aiden Phoenix

D1528029

Bastion

ISBN: 9798395986795

Cover created by Aiden Phoenix.

This book is a work of fiction. Names, characters, locations, and events are products of the author's imagination. Any resemblance to any persons living or dead, locations, or events are coincidental and unintended by the author.

Table of Contents

Welcome to Collisa!

Collisa is a new world brimming with opportunities for adventure and growth. It is also brimming with chances for romance and fun. This is the story of Dare and the life he builds for himself with the women he meets and falls in love with.

As you can guess, it is a harem tale, with all that includes. Be aware that it features varied and explicit erotic scenes between multiple partners. It is intended to be enjoyed by adults. All characters involved in adult scenes are over the age of 18.

Prologue
Balance

Dare finished piling the small rocks around Zuri, covering every part of her body but her head, which was protected by not only her leather helmet but the hood of her cloak. Then he paused to check on her. "Are you sure about this?"

She looked up at him impatiently. "This was your idea."

Yeah, but now that they were actually trying it he wished he hadn't thought it up. After all, the explosion of the mana barrier from her spell Sheltering Embrace had done enough damage to the chimera they'd fought several days ago to outright kill two or three even level monsters.

He wasn't really comfortable with the woman he loved being in the center of that force. Especially since his goblin lover barely came up to his belly button, small and beautiful and looking delicate and vulnerable.

Dare knew her appearance belied her strength, had seen proof of it time and again, but he still felt protective of her. Although honestly he wouldn't be any happier to put Pella, their dog girl companion who was larger and stronger than Zuri, not to mention higher level, in that kind of danger either.

He wished he could be the one to test whether it was possible to turn the explosive force generated by Sheltering Embrace's detonation into a weapon. Or more of a weapon, that was, in the same way a firecracker blowing up on your open palm barely stung your skin, while one blowing up in your closed fist would blow your hand off.

The tiny goblin saw his doubtful expression and shook her head irritably, which was pretty much all she could do in her current position. "Look, it'll be fine. Sheltering Embrace wouldn't have any effect that could harm me . . . that would go against its intended purpose."

"Well turning a spell that's primarily meant to save your life, and in some circumstances do a little damage, into a giant fragmentation grenade that could potentially kill weak monsters en masse, also seems against its intended purpose."

She rolled her eyes. "My mate, I had a chimera that had to weigh at least a few tons land right on top of me, then I was in the middle of an explosion that shredded the thing's legs and I walked away with no injury. This is just a few rocks."

Pella nodded in enthusiastic encouragement, golden-furred tail wagging. "Remember how much more damage it did to the chimera? Think how much faster our farming will be if this works!"

Dare still didn't like it, but when he'd initially thought up this idea he'd reasoned through all this and determined it would probably be safe for Zuri. And it *was* just a few rocks; at worst she might have to heal herself of some bumps and bruises.

He sighed. "All right, let's get this over with."

His lover happily settled into the pile of rocks, and he reluctantly piled up smaller stones around her head. Then he and Pella retreated back to where they'd made a barricade of rocks and fallen logs around the sturdy trunk of a large tree.

"Okay, cast Sheltering Embrace!" he called.

Down near the tiny goblin's legs there was a hole among the piled rocks just large enough for an arrow to get through. Within it he saw the shimmering transparent green surface of her mana barrier appear.

Please let this not end in a disaster, he thought as he raised his bow. He would've liked to craft a Level 1 basic bow, something that would so little damage to Zuri at her level it would feel like a mosquito bite. But he had to do enough to make the barrier blow up, and he could only do that with his Exceptional short bow and quality arrows.

While shooting at his lover's delicate, beautiful little calf; he was really starting to hate this idea.

Just before loosing the arrow he paused. *You'd warn me if this was going to hurt Zuri, right?* he asked his unseen benefactor, the entity or perhaps deity who'd brought him to Collisa months ago. *I mean, just a hint at least?*

There was no response.

"Come on!" Zuri's muffled voice reached them. "Sheltering Embrace doesn't last forever!"

Dare grit his teeth, took aim, and loosed. Then he ducked down behind the barrier, throwing himself protectively atop Pella.

Almost immediately he heard a sharp *crack*. It wasn't the sound of an explosion, but the tree and barricade they hid behind began shuddering with the powerful impacts of flying rocks, and he heard deafening crashing and clattering noises from all around as the stony shrapnel pelted everything in the area.

"Zuri!" he shouted as the noise died down. "You okay?" He risked raising his head, looking anxiously at where she'd been buried in rocks.

His tiny lover waved cheerfully from the center of a ring of devastation, completely unharmed and looking triumphant. Meanwhile around her the improvised fragmentation grenade had shredded foliage, shattered branches, and gouged deep holes into the trunks of trees. Not to mention tearing up the ground for a dozen feet in all directions.

Dare hated to think what it would do to anyone standing in that area. Although that was entirely the point.

"It worked!" Zuri shouted, bolting towards them with an excited expression. "You're a genius, Dare! Now we can pull entire spawn points of weak enemies and mow them down like wheat!"

He vaulted the barricade and wrapped her in his arms, just relieved that he'd been right and it had worked out okay. Yes, he was gratified his idea had worked, and excited about the potential of this new weapon. But that was a smaller consideration right now.

"You sure you're all right?" he asked, brushing strands of soft, shimmering black hair out of Zuri's face as he looked her over anxiously. Pella joined them, exuberantly hugging them both with her tail wagging.

Then they all jumped as a tone sounded. Text appeared across the center of Dare's vision, accompanied by the soothing, pleasant voice of his benefactor.

"Worldwide alert: To preserve class balance, explosive force has been removed from the Healer spell "Sheltering Embrace". It is otherwise unchanged and damage remains the same. End worldwide alert."

Dare stared at the text in disbelief, while his companions looked at him in confusion. "Dare, did they just . . ." Zuri asked uncertainly.

He leapt to his feet, staring up at the sky. "Come on!" he shouted. "A hotfix as soon as we discover something cool?"

His benefactor's voice replied without text. "Would you rather be facing hordes of Healers all turning themselves into living bombs? I advised you against introducing gunpowder to this world for the same reason . . . class balance matters, *world* balance matters, and some things would cause so much disruption they can't be allowed to exist."

It was hard to argue against that. "You couldn't have at least let us use it until someone else saw us and tried to spread the tactic?" he grumbled.

She laughed. "It's been a pleasure, my lover. Until we speak again."

"Yeah, because you've been so helpful lately."

His benefactor just laughed again. "Really, a "what have you done for me lately?" from you?"

Dare flushed in embarrassment. "Thanks again for everything, but I won't complain if you decide to help some more in the future."

There was no response.

His lovers were both staring at him. "Dare," Zuri said quietly. "Did you just invent something so powerful that the gods themselves stepped in to remove it?"

He shrugged awkwardly at their expressions, which ranged from confusion to awe. "Not so much invent as discover an exploit," he said. "Or an unintended utilization, or whatever. They definitely hurried to balance it."

Pella frowned at the devastation around them. "So what now?"

Dare sighed. "Get back to leveling, I guess." He looked up at the sky. "This was certainly a fun diversion."

His unseen benefactor's voice drifted to him as if from a distance. "It was, my lover. You always offer such pleasant surprises. And I'm not the only one who thinks so."

He jumped as more text abruptly appeared in front of him. "You have gained Noticed."

Dare looked at Zuri and Pella, who were watching his one-sided conversation with the sort of blank curiosity he probably would've shown in their shoes. "Did you guys get that?" he asked.

Their brows furrowed. "Get what?" Pella asked.

"That's the question." He looked upward again. "What the hell is Noticed? What does it do?"

His benefactor giggled. "Nothing."

Dare frowned. "No, seriously. Is it an ability? An effect? What does it mean?"

"It means you've been Noticed." She made a kissing sound. "This was fun, my lover. May I visit you tonight?"

The prospect of a nocturnal visit from his unseen lover was almost enough to distract him; last time she'd come as a shadow figure in a dream/not dream. One of the strangest and hottest sexual encounters he'd ever had.

Which was saying something, considering the experiences he'd had since coming to Collisa.

"Are you going to tell me what Noticed means?" he demanded.

The disembodied voice just laughed. "Save some energy for tonight, my lover. Until then."

Sighing, Dare turned to his lovers. "Well, I guess Benefactor's going to be paying me a booty call tonight. Should we head to the next monster spawn point?"

"Okay." Zuri grinned as she held up her arms for him to pick her up. "Even if the test didn't work out, it was fun."

9

He picked up his lover and she held him tight as he took off at a run. With his elite athletic body gifted him by his benefactor, and Fleetfoot which increased his speed by 34%, not even most other humans could keep up with him, let alone a goblin with much shorter legs.

Pella, on the other hand, could. The tall, athletic dog girl might not have been able to match his top speed, or his usual running pace for an entire day, but she got close enough that he only had to slow down a little and they still covered an insane amount of ground when traveling.

They'd left Jarn's Holdout on the southern border of the Bastion region yesterday morning, and had traveled north far enough to find monster spawn points at their level they could farm, then spent the day farming. Dare was content with hanging around in a good area to focus on leveling up for a while, but his preference was to keep moving.

He wanted to explore. Find new places, fight new monsters, and meet new people. And thankfully Collisa, which had inexplicably been designed by its creators to in many ways resemble the games he'd loved so much in his previous life, generated its spawn points in a way that accommodated his love of exploration.

If an intelligent race created a settlement of sufficient size, it had an effect on the world that caused the monsters that spawned near them to be weak Level 1s, with the monsters getting progressively stronger until, theoretically, they reached maximum level. Or raid rated difficulty for max level or whatever the limit was.

In practice, as long as settlements were close enough you'd get monsters getting stronger up to a midpoint, then weaker again. Most of the towns in Kovana, the region they'd recently left, had been close enough that between them the monsters hadn't gotten much higher than Level 30. That essentially created two bands of spawn points between each town that were in a good level range for hunting.

In less populous regions like Bastion the spawn points got more wild. Literally. And beyond Bastion's northern border, which also served as the border for the larger Kingdom of Haraldar that included the two regions, were even more dangerous wilds that no kingdom claimed, teeming with monsters of random difficulty and loot just waiting to be found.

Monsters that were beginning to threaten the border.

A spawn point left alone for long enough began letting loose roaming monsters in greater and greater numbers, until eventually all the monsters it spawned were roamers. To make matters worse, they gradually got higher and higher level, and increased the level of the spawn points around them. Those monsters began spreading into the nearby kingdoms and causing all sorts of chaos, eventually escalating to a full-on monster horde that could wipe out every living thing on a continent if they weren't stopped.

In other words, hunting spawn points wasn't just a matter of gaining experience and loot. It also ensured the safety of the people in the area. A constant battle to keep chaos and death at bay.

"You're looking awfully serious," Zuri said, kissing his neck. "What are you thinking about?"

Dare smiled down at her. "The company of heroes who went north to clear the spawn points in the wild and stabilize the area."

"Oh." His lover's eyes danced. "And maybe also thinking of the cute catgirl who went with them?"

His smile broadened as he thought of Linia, the beautiful orange cream felid he'd spent an incredible night with in Jarn's Holdout. Hopefully he'd get a chance to see her again.

And who knew, maybe in the future as their circumstances changed he might even be in a position to convince her to join his harem. Felids were free spirited wanderers, but the orange catgirl might be inclined to settle down, or at least choose his home as the place where she returned from her wanderings each time.

Maybe it was the hope of spotting the company of heroes that her mercenary company had been hired to assist that made him veer off and begin climbing up a taller hill in the area. They'd been steadily circling a large lake north of Jarn's Holdout as they farmed, but his lovers didn't complain about the detour.

In fact, when they reached the top they both seemed more than happy to pause for a rest and to admire the view, murmuring appreciatively as they breathed in deeply of the cool, fresh air.

Bastion was a wilder region than Kovana, where he'd first been placed on Collisa. But it was also more starkly beautiful, with a rugged landscape of plains, forests, low hills, and mountains. There was also at least that one large lake to their west, which formed a glittering dark blue expanse that stretched almost as far as the eye could see in that direction.

Dare loved it here. Not only was it more beautiful, and with more opportunities to level and make a name for himself and his loved ones, but it was also very much a frontier land that provided numerous opportunities.

Most important of which was freedom.

In Kovana it had been almost impossible to find a non-human who wasn't a slave or pet, and he'd had to keep up the ruse that Zuri and Pella were his property for their own safety, so they wouldn't be taken from him and enslaved again.

He'd also had to pay a tax for them in every town and city they visited, which had eaten into their earnings. Although that was a far lesser consideration than the hurtful reminder of their past lives endured by the women he loved.

Dare had been forced to witness cruelty and inhumanity everywhere he turned, powerless to do anything about it. He was still determined to change things for the better when he could, but at the moment he was just grateful to be somewhere that was safer and offered more opportunities for Zuri and Pella.

That was because Bastion was desperate for adventurers and other fighters willing to go out and hunt monsters, bandits, and wild invading tribes, bringing stability to the region and gradually taming it for more settlers. That desperation, combined with the lawlessness of the region, meant that they were more willing to offer freedom and opportunities to members of other races as long as they were keeping the peace and paying their taxes.

Especially if those non-humans happened to be willing to fight monsters and improve the region's currently tenuous situation.

Pella pressed close to Dare's side, resting her head on his shoulder, and he wrapped an arm around her waist and hugged Zuri closer.

Here he was, in a new land with new opportunities, with two beautiful women who loved him and who he loved just as deeply fighting by his side. A life he couldn't even have imagined back on Earth, stuck in a dead end manual labor job with romantic opportunities few, far between, and always fleeting.

A cool breeze sprang up, making Zuri shiver in spite of her leather armor and fur-lined cloak, and he kissed her head and gave Pella an affectionate squeeze.

He saw no sign of Linia, her mercenary company, or the kingdom's heroes heading north. And much as he enjoyed taking in the view, there were monsters to hunt, levels to gain, and loot to earn.

"Come on," he said, motioning to a nearby spawn point. "That looks like a good place to start for the day."

Chapter One
Nocturnal Suggestion

Dare jumped in shock and cursed as he became aware he was standing on a stark white surface in a stark white space with no discernible source of light.

The last thing he remembered he'd been in his tent beneath the blankets on his bedroll, in a sweaty, contented tangle of limbs with Zuri and Pella after a comparatively brief but enjoyable session of lovemaking before bedtime.

And now he was here. Apparently in a small room, judging by the nearly imperceptible lines where the white walls around him met each other and the floor and ceiling. He was naked but not uncomfortable, the still air around him the perfect temperature to not be noticeable.

Well, his unseen benefactor had told him she'd be paying him a visit tonight. And this was certainly unsettling and surreal, which seemed to fit the theme.

Dare shuddered, thinking of last time he'd made love to her. When her shadow had done a sexy dance for him on a wall, then slid onto the floor and towards him in a way that could've been straight out of a horror moving in different circumstances.

"Is it going to be creepy as fuck every time you pull me into one of these dreams, Benefactor?" he asked wryly.

As if in answer the white wall across the room rippled, then a shape began to emerge, making him stumble backwards with another curse of surprise.

The shape was white like the wall, perhaps even more brilliantly so, and quickly defined itself into the nude form of a physically perfect woman with long hair falling down to just above her waist. The details of her alabaster figure were formed by shadows and contours, but even so he could see her face was strikingly beautiful.

14

Flawless, delicate features that somehow conveyed strength and openness at the same time, expressive eyes that seemed to laugh and exude warm empathy and show knowing familiarity all at once.

The effect was somewhat marred, however, by the fact that she was basically a white mannequin. And although her motions were more fluid and graceful than the most skilled dancer, there was something distinctly off-putting about the entire situation.

Dare took a tentative step towards her, taking in her perky breasts and medium sized nipples, the slope of her flat stomach down to a narrow waist, wide hips, slender legs and a gorgeous slit pouting open slightly at the top around her clitoris.

He felt his face flush as his cock began to stir and grow in spite of the surreal situation, and laughed wryly. "I'm still trying to decide if you do it this way because it's the best you can manage, or because you've got a weird sense of humor and enjoy freaking me out and turning me on at the same time."

The white mannequin smiled warmly, then twirled as if to show off her body. Her curves were just as perfect from behind, arched back and shapely ass just begging him to run his hands over them.

Was she taking these different forms to tease him? Or was there some constraint on what forms she could take? Was she getting better each time, going from a two-dimensional shadow to a three-dimensional mannequin, and possibly even closer to a realistic woman next time?

And why didn't she ever *say* anything?

The alabaster woman turned back to him, sensually running her hands down her sides before cupping a pert breast with one, teasing the white nipple until it began to stiffen, and trailing the other down between her legs. With a playful smile she spread apart the delicate white lips of her pussy, revealing an equally white interior glistening with arousal.

Dare felt his jaw go slack at the sight, rock hard cock throbbing eagerly.

The mannequin glided forward, slender arms lifting to wrap around his neck and tease the hair at its nape. In spite of the fact that she looked like she was made of plaster or plastic, her skin was softer than anything he'd ever felt, although still cool to the touch. He was just grateful there was at least some friction now so he could actually feel her.

He lifted his hands to wrap around her small waist, looking down into white on white eyes that somehow managed to be lively and expressive. Then he leaned down and kissed her full, sensuous lips.

To his surprise, in spite of the fact that the shadow had had no taste or smell to her, now he tasted something like sweet strawberries as he kissed the mannequin.

His benefactor melted against him, bare white flesh indescribably soft and even its coolness soothing, pressing his cock between them. She kissed him back hungrily, lips cool and wet.

Dare wrapped his arms tighter around her, pulling her closer, and her mouth opened invitingly to let his tongue in. He had no doubts now about whatever wetness took the place of her saliva, and eagerly slipped his tongue into her mouth, savoring the sweet taste of it.

Her own tongue, small and cool and soft, found his and swirled around it teasingly, before darting forward into his mouth to playfully run along his front teeth. Dare groaned as her tongue sought its way deeper into his mouth, letting his own retreat to welcome and play with hers.

Although his lover remained utterly silent, he had a feeling of pleasure from her as she backed away and stood on tiptoes, guiding his cock between her thighs. She again pressed her body against his, hips undulating so the slick lips of her pussy slid along the top of his erection from tip to base.

Then to his further surprise his nostrils caught an impossibly compelling, heady scent as her nectar coated his throbbing shaft. His hand reflexively dropped, and his benefactor opened her mouth in a silent moan of pleasure as his fingers accidentally brushed the velvety lips of her pussy.

They came away soaked with her arousal, and he briefly broke the kiss so he could bring them up to his face. They smelled heavenly, more rich with pheromones than Zuri or Linia by far, sweeter than any bunny girl, and with a richer feeling that spoke of something divine.

Dare looked down at his benefactor's face and saw she was grinning at him in amusement. "I have to taste you," he said.

He jumped again when another shape began to ripple across the floor, then a full king-sized bed complete with bedding, all stark white, began to rise into view.

Grinning impishly, his lover scrambled backwards onto it until she was in the middle. Then, biting her lower lip in mock coyness, she swayed her pressed together knees shyly from side to side before opening them wide, revealing the glistening petals of her perfect pussy.

The heavenly scent wafted from her, and Dare scrambled up onto the bed in pursuit of it.

He lovingly kissed his way up one perfect foot, tasting a hint of sweet perspiration on her skin as he did, and marveled at how much sensory detail she was able to put into this blank white mannequin. He practically salivated at the thought of reaching his destination and lapping at her arousal.

But he held onto his restraint, patiently kissing his way up her calf and knee, trailing his lips along her inner thigh.

Apparently his benefactor was feeling impatient, because at that point she grabbed his head and yanked him forward into her crotch, thrusting her hips at the same time so his mouth met her nether lips in a fierce, erotic kiss. Her cool, slick nectar coated his lips, overwhelming his senses with her scent, and he slipped his tongue out to lap some up.

It was impossible to describe her flavor. Deeper than the superficial sweetness of strawberries and honey, he felt like he was tasting love and raw passion while simultaneously getting a glimpse into the mysteries of the universe. It expanded his senses, then overwhelmed them, like visiting a too-loud rock concert and eventually the volume of sound just becoming a ringing in his ears.

From that first moment of savoring her ambrosia, the experience became hazy and dreamlike. He didn't know if his mind was overpowered by the raw strength of the pheromones she exuded, or if the sheer bliss of it took him to another place where it was all a vague delight.

Either way, he floated in a dream as he licked, fingered, and toyed with the clit of the alabaster woman, pushing her towards orgasm as he relished his opportunity to savor the constant stream of paradise that flowed from within her perfect sex.

Everything became a hazy bliss after that.

Dare was vaguely aware of devouring her heavenly pussy for what felt like a very long time as she writhed beneath him, occasionally arching her back and going rigid as her delicate lips winked in orgasm and ambrosia gushed from her. He eagerly sought to bring her to climax again and again so he could drink more of her perfection.

Then at some point he found himself being pushed onto the bed, the alabaster woman climbing atop him and positioning herself over his rock hard cock.

His surprisingly intense disappointment and longing at no longer being able to taste her faded in the wake of the intense pleasure her impossibly soft, delicate folds gave him as she briefly kissed his tip with her perfect white lips, then took him inside her and began sliding down his shaft. The juices flowing down his length made it easier to push between those almost painfully tight, cool walls.

Dare felt resistance and his mysterious lover paused, flawless white face twisting in sudden discomfort. Then her expression became determined and she gave a firm push, and the resistance inside her melted away as she continued to lower herself down his shaft.

He looked at where their hips joined, and to his shock saw that the arousal flowing from her heavenly depths was tinged with pink. The only color in this entire white room, it seemed. Besides him of course.

Even as he watched, the pink darkened to pale red as what could only be blood joined with her sexual fluids and flowed out of her.

"Shit," he groaned, cock twitching wildly inside her, "you're a virgin?'"

The alabaster woman gave him an almost shy smile in reply.

Dare wasn't sure how that fit with him making love with her shadow, or if it even made sense that a mannequin in a dreamspace could have a hymen, but in his blissful haze he didn't care.

Between her crushing walls and the knowledge that he'd just deflowered this divine beauty, it was all he could do to avoid spurting right then and there. He grit his teeth and tried to lose himself in the pleasant haze of her nectar again, and somehow staved off his climax as his lover continued moving slowly down on his cock.

Then he had another shock as, around the point where he bottomed out in even the deepest woman he'd been inside, the mermaid Trissela thanks to the extra space of the watertight pouch protecting her pussy, his mysterious lover kept right on going.

And going, until she was fully impaled on his length and her dripping white pussy lips were pressed against his base.

"Oh gods!" Dare gasped. This was the first time he'd been able to be balls deep inside a real woman's vagina (not counting her shadow form and slime girls, that is) with his new cock, and the sensation was incredible. Especially with her impossibly tight virgin walls practically strangling him from tip to base.

It seemed impossible any real woman of her size could take his full length like that, but he supposed that the mannequin-like construct that had come out of the wall could do whatever she wanted with her insides.

He looked at the alabaster woman's flat belly and saw the bulge his thickness made. The sight made him curse quietly again, struggling with all his strength not to climax and cut this incredible experience short.

This was too much . . . he sank back into the ambrosia haze, letting its warmth engulf him as the slickness of his lover's soft core did the same. He bit his lip as she began to ride him, lost in a world of pure contentment.

His mysterious lover smiled down at him, white eyes somehow

sparkling, and then she pushed down harder than she ever had before.

Just for a moment, as Dare's fully engulfed cock strained in her depths, he felt himself press against the end of her tunnel.

Holy shit. He was in that magical, impossible zone where he was simultaneously balls deep and bottoming out inside this divine woman's pussy. As if her perfect sex had been made for his cock.

The alabaster woman's smile widened as she slammed herself down again and fought to hold herself there, and as his tip pressed against her cervix his self-discipline finally crumbled.

With a groan, Dare pulled her perfect hips down to hold himself against her deepest depths and began emptying himself inside her.

The normally intense sensation was magnified by his lover's ambrosia haze, and he cried out in pleasure as his orgasm stretched longer than seemed physically possible, shooting spurt after powerful spurt until he felt the very real sensation of the pressure of their combined fluids beginning to push him out.

Finally his climax ended, but he wasn't done there. In fact, it didn't seem like he *could* be done. He flipped his perfect alabaster lover around to lie beneath him and continued to thrust inside her, not so much pushing through his refractory period like he often did but more like it didn't even exist. There was no discomfort, only pleasure that grew greater and greater as he continued to thrust until finally he came again.

Then again, and again. Over and over.

Lost in the ambrosia haze Dare mounted her more times than he could remember. In every hole, in every position, enjoying her body in a wild frenzy and emptying load after pulsing load into every pristine alabaster orifice. And the longer he went, the deeper into the haze he fell, pleasure reaching heights he didn't realize were possible.

It was almost like he had electrodes attached directly to his brain that could trigger sexual pleasure over and over, with no physical limits. Although he felt like he was approaching some sort of limit as deep in his mind he started to get worried at this endless sexual frenzy.

His benefactor fucked him back with equal intensity, body

quivering in nearly constant orgasm and luscious lips parted in a endless cry of pleasure. Her arousal flowed and squirted from her in such quantities that it soaked the bed beneath them, until both of their bodies were coated in the slick nectar as if they were wrestling in oil.

That flood of ambrosia just deepened the haze he was in, increasing his frenzy.

Until finally, with startling abruptness, Dare felt the alabaster woman's arousal beginning to dissipate, evaporating away with startling speed similar to how the shadow woman's had in his previous encounter with her.

He cried out in protest as he felt his skin drying, the silky skin of his gorgeous alabaster lover drying, the bed drying. All of it fading away without even leaving a trace of residue, as if it had never been.

Then clarity finally pierced his haze and exhaustion deeper than any he'd ever felt before washed over him. Dare bonelessly flopped to the bed, gasping like a fish, every movement a herculean struggle.

He felt his lover cuddle up behind him and hold him gently, stroking his forehead as if he was sick and she was soothing him. To his startlement she suddenly spoke, although the words didn't come from her mouth near his ear but from some impossible to pinpoint source, her usual disembodied voice.

"I'm sorry, my lover," she murmured, sounding genuinely chagrined. "I got a bit carried away there."

Still exhausted and wrung out and gasping to catch his breath, Dare tried to remember the lovemaking he'd just experienced. Much of it was like a half-remembered dream of indescribable wonder already fading away, aside from the lingering memory of overwhelming passion and all-encompassing pleasure. "Holy . . . fuck."

His benefactor giggled. "Pretty much." She stroked his chest with her other hand, voice contented. "It was just so intense. Such amazingly powerful sensations. I couldn't bring myself to let it end." She kissed his neck. "Don't worry, your exhaustion is only mental and spiritual, not physical . . . a good night's rest and you'll be right as rain."

He chuckled, breathing slowing. "It seems silly to ask but you're okay too, right?"

"Mmmm," she murmured playfully, pinching his nipple and making him jump. "Is there a metaphysical equivalent to being fucked bowlegged?" She laughed again. "Don't worry, I'm doing great. Thank you for this wonderful experience."

"Any time," he said, grinning. "You going to manage even more details next time?"

She giggled again. "Oh, I definitely have a surprise planned. One I think you're going to like."

They lay entwined together for a while, peaceful and spent. Dare was wondering why the dream/not dream hadn't already ended, the way the previous one with his shadow lover had, when she spoke as if she'd read his mind.

Which of course she probably had.

"By the way, I didn't just come for the fantastic sex."

Dare smirked. "Although you came more times than I could count from the fantastic sex."

His benefactor giggled and playfully slapped his arm, then pushed and prodded him until he rolled around to face her, white on white eyes intent as they stared into his. "Listen, this is important. It's about a dream you've had from the beginning."

He met her gaze soberly. "All right, what is it?"

"Something very important will come about if you heed my advice." She fell silent.

An uncomfortably long time passed with her just lying there staring at him, making him more and more aware that she was basically an animated mannequin with every passing second. It reminded him of when they'd first met and she'd often needed him to prompt her, even if just with some inane acknowledgement he'd heard what she said, before she'd go on.

Was that was this was?

"What advice?" Dare finally asked.

His benefactor giggled and sprang off the bed. "That was it! Until next time, dearest lover!" She took off at a sprint and slammed into the wall.

It made him think of when his cousin had tried to trick him when he was a little kid, telling him that if he ran at a wall fast enough he'd be able to go right through it. Except while he'd been too smart to fall for the prank because it obviously wouldn't work, for the alabaster woman it *did*.

She disappeared through the barrier with barely a ripple, leaving him alone in the room.

"What the hell?" he asked, just in time to realize he was back in his tent, Zuri cuddled in his arms and Pella pressed against his back with an arm wrapped around him.

The dog girl started awake. "What is it, Dare?" she asked anxiously.

"Nothing, sorry for waking you," he said, settling back against her firm breasts. "Go back to sleep."

"From the sounds of it you're very bothered by something." She stroked his arm. "You can tell me."

Dare sighed and cursed softly. "My benefactor. She said she had important advice, then said that was the advice and disappeared."

They'd woken Zuri up by this point too. "What?" she mumbled.

"She said something very important would come about if I heeded her advice. Then she said that was the advice and ran into a wall."

"She . . . ran into a wall?" Pella asked hesitantly.

Zuri, bless her heart, didn't get sidetracked. "Maybe it was a code," she said. "We should write it down exactly as you remember it and see if we can find any hidden clues."

The dog girl, with her weak skill at writing and (something he and Zuri were working with her on), didn't seem to like that idea. "I bet it's just a prank," she said. "If she really wanted you to know she would've been more clear."

Dare shook his head irritably. "My guess is she thinks she knows me so well that just planting the suggestion will get me to do whatever it is she wants. And it fits with her being reluctant to help me too much."

"Oh." His goblin lover nestled closer to him. "Well in that case what do you think we should do?"

He gave it some thought, then shook his head. "Fuck it. We've been farming spawn points while making our way around the lake and then northwest to Redoubt. We'll keep doing that."

"What about Polan's Folly?" Zuri asked. "It's closer than Redoubt."

Dare stared at her. His goblin lover liked to study his map, even though it didn't have much more information on it than terrain features and a few larger towns in each region and the capitols. Dare had been adding all the information he'd learned about the areas he'd traveled through, on the map as well as in a journal he'd purchased in Jarn's Holdout so he'd have more room to write, and Zuri liked to study them.

Maybe trying to figure out how his mind worked, since many of the things he said still seemed to baffle her.

The shoe was on the other foot now, though, as he gave her a puzzled look. "It's in like the opposite direction, to the northeast."

"Yeah." She giggled. "But this entire thing about her giving advice by not giving advice is stupid, and the town's name fits the situation, right?"

Pella laughed too. "You know what, that works for me."

Dare joined the laughter, rolling onto his back so he could hold both his beautiful lovers close. "Polan's Folly it is, then. We'll start that direction in the morning." He paused. "While still leveling, of course . . . if she's not going to be more clear I'm not changing my behavior too much to accommodate her. For all we know rushing up there is the wrong choice too."

"All right." Pella rubbed her soft floppy ears against his cheek as she settled into a more comfortable position. "Good night, honey."

Zuri didn't say anything, just affectionately patted his chest and went back to sleep.

24

Chapter Two
Caravan

More by coincidence and good luck than planning, Pella reached Level 29 the same day Dare and Zuri reached Level 25.

It had been six days since they'd changed direction for Polan's Folly, focusing on leveling and only making progress towards the town by heading northeast with each new spawn point they visited. At least until they were out of the band of monsters within their level range, at which point they'd run through the higher level zones on the safety of a road they'd found leading to the town.

They probably could've cut through the wilds between the higher level spawn points, since he could see enemy levels with his Adventurer's Eye and also sense when he was inside a spawn point's boundary. But that would've exposed them to danger from roaming monsters and animal predators, both of which likely would've been higher level as well.

So they'd followed the road until they found spawn points they could safely farm, then set to work clearing them as they continued towards Polan's Folly.

Until finally they'd all gotten their next level.

It was a more humble level for Pella, giving her some ability points she could put into improving abilities she already had but not offering anything too exciting. Her next level, 30, would make up for it though, giving at least one new ability and probably a lot of other cool stuff.

At least, they assumed so going by the awesome stuff they'd gotten at Level 20, and to a lesser extent at Level 10. Which if anything indicated that Level 30 would be even better than the previous two.

As for Dare and Zuri, at 25 they got some stuff to be excited about, not just for that level but for levels to come.

Every ten levels starting from Level 5 was when they got free abilities, which didn't cost a point. For Dare it had been Roll and Shoot at 5 and Prey's Vigilance at 15. This level, though, instead of a free ability he unlocked an entire new ability tree, which was even more exciting.

The tree was called "Student of the Wild". It allowed him to spend a point to learn abilities animals were capable of using, with some specific animals he killed in the past unlocking a specific ability. From the looks of things it was only abilities appropriate to his class, and there were less of them than he would've hoped (although that might've been because he just hadn't found the animals he needed for more options).

Most disappointing of all, though, was that he could only learn a new ability in the Student of the Wild tree every 5 levels. So he had to be picky about what he chose, and carefully consider his options. Luckily it seemed he immediately became aware of a new ability unlocking when he killed the animal that gave it, even if he couldn't get it yet, and he could see the abilities that were available at any time so he could prepare for his next pick.

At the moment Dare had three choices: Pounce, Escape Bonds, and Claw. Claw was a melee attack he could use with dagger or axe, Escape Bonds allowed him to instantly get out of a snare or root effect, and Pounce was the one he ultimately picked.

Claw was something he'd probably never choose if he had a better option, since his priorities were anything using his bow, anything that gave him mobility, and any crowd control that could help him against enemies.

Escape Bonds was tempting, and had almost been his immediate grab. Escaping a snare or root effect could save his life in a fight. But its cooldown was 5 minutes, one of the longest cooldowns he'd seen, and it was more situational than something that offered sheer mobility.

Pounce, on the other hand, had a 1 minute cooldown and allowed him to leap to a valid target within 10 yards at 200% of his max speed (based on his current speed stats, which meant with Fleetfoot it felt like he practically teleported). On striking his target he tackled it and applied the Tackle effect, rendering it incapable of movement or attacking for 1 second and returning him instantly to his feet. It also had a 1% chance to stun for 5 seconds if he landed on his target's head.

The mobility offered by the ability was incredible, and while as a Hunter he didn't really want to be going *towards* an enemy, there were times when it could be useful.

But what was even better was that Pounce let Dare leap to a *valid target*. In this case valid was any living creature, which meant he could Pounce to a random forest critter or prey animal. Or in a pinch Pella or Zuri, with no downside other than inconveniencing them for a second as long as he didn't land on their heads.

In fact, the dog girl got a huge kick out of the ability when he tested it with her. She laughed in delight when he leapt towards her at close to 60 miles an hour, and after he tackled her she playfully used her Subdue ability to pin him while Zuri tickled him mercilessly.

It turned into wrestling which eventually devolved into groping, kissing, and finally enthusiastic lovemaking.

As for Zuri's Level 25 ability, it also involved unlocking a new ability tree. One that was just as incredible as his in its own way. And in fact one Dare was even more excited about when it came to their lives outside of combat.

That was because her new ability tree was Craft Scroll. It allowed her to spend ability points to learn how to make one time use scrolls for her utility spells. Which anyone could use to cast that spell, consuming the scroll in the process.

At the moment her utility spells were Cleanse Target, Prevent Conception, and something called Nature's Purity.

"What's Nature's Purity?" Dare interrupted as she was explaining her new Craft Scroll ability tree. "I've never heard of that before."

His goblin lover blushed dark green, and Pella snickered. "Forget I said that," Zuri said hastily. "It's nothing." At his curious stare she shifted uncomfortably. "Okay fine, all you need to know is that it's for, um, women's issues."

Ah. "Say no more," he said. "As an understanding and supportive mate I'm happy to talk to you about anything, but I understand that there are some things-"

"I don't want to talk about!" she finished firmly.

"I'm okay with discussing it," Pella said cheerfully. "Anything you want to know-"

"That's fine!" Dare said hastily, face heating. "Go ahead and keep going, Zuri."

The scrolls required parchment or vellum, which could be made with pulped wood in a laborious process, or animal skins in a somewhat less laborious process. Since he produced so many animal skins anyway with hunting and trapping, they decided to go with vellum. Although first Zuri had to collect limestone and process it to make lime.

Thankfully, like with most abilities on Collisa, making vellum took far less time than it would on Earth.

It might've been a bit selfish, but Dare was so overjoyed at the prospect of being able to bring Prevent Conception scrolls with him in case Zuri wasn't around that he pampered his tiny lover outrageously as they continued leveling. Pella seemed equally eager about being able to have all three scrolls available in case of an emergency, and similarly lavished praise and affection on her fellow mate.

As usually, they cleared every spawn point they found. At the moment those were in the range of 27-29, closer to Pella's level than his and Zuri's. They were dangerous, but with careful coordination Dare and his companions took them out without any disasters.

And it was nice to see the dog girl finally getting real experience, after she'd spent so long helping them level with almost no gains herself.

In the last week since leaving Jarn's Holdout they'd ventured deep into the region of Bastion, on their way to Polan's Folly. And while Dare still intended to head to the town, if for no other reason than to sell the loot they'd accumulated along the way, he had half a mind to come back to this area afterwards.

It was actually a surprisingly ideal one for leveling, not just currently but possibly even for weeks or even months to come. It was between three towns, Jarn's Holdout to the southwest, Redoubt to the west, and Polan's Folly still a bit to the northeast. That put a lot of variance in the levels of the spawn points, and also offered multiple locations to sell loot from in multiple directions, so they could keep moving.

In fact, it was more properly four towns they were between; going south and a little southeast they would eventually reach Terana on the southeastern border of Bastion, near the Gadris Mountains and the goblin ravine they'd taken to get into the region. Although in the opposite direction from Jarn's Holdout.

And if they moved from here in any direction besides a town, they'd find higher level spawn points for when they got strong enough. It was a great area, and a part of him really wanted to linger even if it meant gathering more loot than they could carry.

They could always cache some of it, like Pella had her cache of loot near Hamalis back in Kovana. Someone might stumble across it, but not even adventurers tended to just wander around in the wilds; the smart ones followed monster compendiums written by more experienced adventurers, and stuck to known spawn points.

Something Dare and his lovers didn't have to worry about, thanks to his Adventurer's Eye.

But tempting as it was to stay, his benefactor's "advice" was weighing on him more and more. So he'd keep them moving in the direction of Polan's Folly and leave the monsters in their level range behind, with no idea whether it was the right call or not.

Sometimes his interactions with his benefactor were maddening. And the fact that they were lovers didn't make things any less complicated.

After getting back to hunting they took out a spawn point of monsters called Gaunt Fiends, hideous creatures with four limbs that bent unnaturally and moved just as eerily. Along with dropping small amounts of silver coins, junk loot, and the occasional item, the fiends dropped tattered silk that would make good clothing. And would probably fetch a fair price after Zuri used her Tailoring subclass ability to make bolts of cloth with it.

Although the little goblin insisted on making them all nice clothes first, before she'd agree to sell any. She seemed eager at the prospect of seeing what she could make.

Dare had his reservations about wearing something made from cloth those freakish fiends had worn, and had to remind himself it was loot and there was objectively no difference than if it had dropped from, say, cute furry rabbit monsters.

The only corpses that didn't let you just grab the loot via the Loot Target ability, and actually had to be searched or harvested, were non-monster animals and intelligent creatures. Although even with the animals you used abilities to skin them, harvest meat, and collect things like claws, horns, and teeth.

And thankfully Dare hadn't had to loot intelligent creatures often. Only the bandits he and Zuri had helped stop near Lone Ox, although the grisly task still made him shudder when he remembered it.

After finishing off the last of the Gaunt Fiends they moved on to the next spawn point, which was slightly lower at 25-28. Although if the monsters they'd just been hunting were creepy, the ones here were truly nightmarish.

Giant Spiders.

They looked like brown recluses, although the size of small livestock like sheep or goats. And while he wasn't close enough to see their abilities, even as he watched one snagged a passing bird out of the air with an expertly shot strand of webbing, then got to work wrapping its prey. The nearby spiders pressed closer in interest, at least until the one with the prize reared up threateningly, fangs bared. The other spiders retreated, some also rearing up as if to show they weren't intimidated.

Dare watched the giant arachnids skitter around with disgusted fascination.

Small spiders were terrifying enough to watch move around with their jerky, too-fast movements that made them look like they'd come straight out of a horror movie. Or the way they'd just sit there perfectly still for what felt like forever, and then suddenly move or simply disappear when you looked away for a second.

Spiders the size of sheep were a million times worse. The motion that looked so unnatural on a small scale looked downright nightmarish when they were big enough to see more clearly. And all the godawful details you couldn't usually see without a magnifying glass were writ large and easily discernible.

For the first time since getting the Eagle Eye ability he regretted his improved vision.

"Nope," Pella said the moment she saw them. "I don't care if they drop gold bars, I don't want to get within a hundred yards of those things."

"I'm with her," Zuri said, shuddering. "I'm the perfect size to be a snack for those nightmares."

Dare chuckled. "I'm not arguing. Back in my old home people used to joke that spiders were proof that the gods didn't exist."

"Well we have solid proof that they do," his goblin lover said. "And you yourself have one as a patron."

Pella shook her head. "Still, it's at least proof that whatever deity made them hates us."

He laughed outright. *You want to weigh in on this?* he asked his unseen benefactor.

Her warm, disembodied voice replied like a whisper in his ear, sounding on the verge of laughter as well. "Oh no, I'm with you. Those things give me the creeps."

They quickly bypassed the spawn point and moved on, although Dare couldn't help but pause to give it one last look. He knew giant spiders were a common monster in games, and honestly he'd killed more of them than he could count through the years.

But in real life they were awful.

Were there going to be other monsters like this, where on the other side of the screen they were creepy and cool, but in real life they made him want to run the other way? What if it was a monster he had to kill, like enemies in a dungeon he was clearing, or a party or raid rated world monster?

31

Zuri stepped up beside him, slipping her hand into his. "You know there are humanoid arachnids, right? They're called arachnii."

Dare perked up. "Oh yeah?"

Pella glared at him. "You better not be thinking spider girls, Dare."

His goblin lover laughed and shuddered at the same time. "Nature's bounty, seriously? No, just no. Keep it in your pants . . . whatever you're imagining is nothing like reality."

Oookay. "So no sexy spider girls trapping you in their web and sucking you dry?" he asked wryly.

They both stared at him flatly. "Arachnii are the opposite of sexy," Pella said, ears low and tail stiff. "Their similarity to humanoid features just makes them even more hideous. But more importantly they're monsters in the vilest sense of the word, because they're intelligent but still monstrous. There's a long standing extermination order on them from all the races, and it's not a misunderstanding or prejudice."

Zuri nodded, shuddering again. "You wouldn't be happy if you fell into the fangs of a female. They hunt and capture a male, of their race or any other, and force him to mate. Then they devour him. And the males are worse."

"Worse than raping and murdering people?" Dare asked incredulously.

"Yes," she said, then fell silent. When he stared at her curiously she grimaced. "I'd rather not talk about it at all, but if you really need to know then think of it this way . . . most women facing capture by arachnii choose to take their own lives instead. And the few successfully rescued from an arachnii's dark underground lair are so physically and mentally broken that they usually never recover."

He felt sick as his imagination supplied unbidden the details she was reluctant to go into; he regretted asking now. "Okay, I can understand an extermination order," he said, swallowing his rising gorge. "And none of them try to go against their vile nature?"

"Not even ones raised in civilized society," Pella said. "Whatever god created them didn't seem to make them capable of anything but acting on their basest impulses."

"They're right," his unseen benefactor supplied. "And their creator is a real piece of work too . . . not a fan of that guy."

"Well, let's hope we never run into them then." Dare motioned to a hill up ahead. "Let's climb that and check for a better spawn point."

As it turned out, before they even reached the top of the hill they became aware of shouts, screams, the harsh clang of blades, and what sounded like the roar of flames coming from somewhere in the distance over the far side. Along with roiling clouds of black smoke rising into view.

Pella was first to hear, of course. With a whine of concern she bent low and sprinted the remaining distance to the hilltop, cautiously peering over. "Dare!" she called anxiously.

He was right behind her with Zuri, and his first view of the sight beyond made him curse.

Up ahead the road to Polan's Folly curved around a large copse of trees. Near the beginning of that woods a caravan of a few dozen wagons, most covered and many with walls and roofs to make moving homes, was under attack by around a score of men.

A couple of the wagons were already ablaze, courtesy of one of the attackers shooting fire arrows. A few of the attacking men were ablaze as well, courtesy of a man in robes beside the lead wagon who was in the midst of forming a fireball in his hands.

Thanks to Eagle Eye Dare could see that the caravan's defenders, as well as the noncombatants huddled near the wagons, had pale gray skin, bone white hair, and long, slender ears.

Elves, although not one of the more common types he was familiar with.

Even though he didn't know the specifics of the confrontation, at a glance it was a safe guess the attackers were ambushing the caravan from the woods. And if he had to pick one side to be the good guys, he'd tend to go with the people traveling on the road minding their own business. The ones who weren't setting fire to wagons full of innocent women and children.

"Come on!" he snapped, bolting down the far side of the hill.

If he'd had any worries that his kindhearted companions might protest them coming to the aid of strangers in need, it was dispelled when Zuri held him tight to help him run more smoothly, expression determined, and Pella caught up with effort to sprint by his side.

He felt a sort of sick dread as they ran, wondering what would happen when they reached the caravan. He didn't like the idea of harming people unless there was no other choice, but he'd fight to defend innocents.

Even so, he couldn't help but think of the bandits he and Zuri had cleared out of the forests outside of Lone Ox. Those had been monsters, murdering innocent people and taking two girls to abuse, and for the most part he slept easy about killing them.

But he couldn't ignore the fact that those bandits had been the first people he'd ever killed, and the act had affected him deeply.

He'd kill the people attacking that caravan if he had to, but no doubt it would also affect him. His only consolation was that if he didn't act, the innocents who'd surely be hurt would haunt him more.

"Think we're dealing with bandits?" Zuri asked, holding Dare tighter.

"Maybe," Pella said, panting as she struggled to keep up with his sprint. "Or slavers . . . they're going after non-humans, after all."

Zuri made a growling noise in his ear. "Slavers are scum," she spat. "All the depravity of bandits, but their actions are smiled on by the kingdom because they commit their atrocities against non-humans who aren't under Haraldar's protection."

She would know, given her experience with them. Although she'd told Dare almost nothing of when her tribe was captured and enslaved, other than that they'd surrendered willingly to avoid losing lives in a fight they couldn't win.

And that even so the slavers hadn't been gentle with them.

"Anyway it's probably not slavers," Pella said, panting so hard her words were hard to make out. "Or at least, not ones acting with official sanction from Haraldar. All elves are protected by our agreement with Elaivar to the east, even dusk elves."

Dusk elves, huh? He wasn't sure he'd ever heard of those from games or stories on Earth. Some kind of dark elf, maybe? "Any idea how they'll react to us jumping into the fi-"

A piercing scream shivered through the air, and Dare watched as a young elf woman twenty or so yards from the embattled caravan broke from hiding and bolted for the forest, a bit to one side of directly in the direction Dare and his companions were coming from. The four bandits who'd discovered her hiding place shouted gleefully as they took up the chase.

She had a good lead on them, but the bandits seemed to be running faster and closing the lead fast; she might be able to keep ahead in the dense undergrowth of the forest, but not forever.

Dare swore and broke into a flat out run; he could reach the elf faster than the caravan, and he wasn't about to let her get hurt if he could do anything about it.

"Dare, wait!" Pella shouted, falling behind in spite of her best efforts. "We should face them together!"

"Use Run Down on me!" he shouted back at her.

The dog girl's Tracker class ability allowed her to increase her speed by up to 50%, and reduce the amount of stamina used by the same amount, as long as she was pursuing her target, for a maximum duration of 5 minutes. When she finally caught up she would tackle her target, applying the Tackle effect that kept her target from moving or attacking for 1 second.

They hadn't thought to have her use Run Down on critters or friendly targets to move more swiftly before, but with what he'd discovered with Pounce earlier it was basically the same principle.

"Hey, you're right!" the dog girl shouted eagerly. A moment later he heard her panting breaths getting closer again, until she was directly behind him. "I can choose not to catch up and stay behind you as long as I want, too, and I can cancel it at any time so I don't even have to worry about applying the Tackle effect."

That was great to hear, but at the moment Dare was focused on getting to the dusk elf girl before the bandits did.

He reached the woods and his speed increased thanks to the small boost from Forest Perception. Although it became a battle to maintain that speed in the dense foliage and with all the obstacles found in a forest, even with the ability improving his movement through undergrowth.

He ducked branches and wove between tree trunks at a reckless pace, nearly impaling himself on a fallen log and numerous times having to push off from something he was about to crash against. Without his speed and reflexes from Fleetfoot he probably would've knocked himself out on a low-hanging branch, running the natural obstacle course at better than 25 miles an hour.

Behind him he heard crashes and whimpering from Pella as she wasn't quite as lucky, even though she was doing her best to follow his path. But through determination and a bit of luck she kept up.

Up ahead the forest lit up with a *whoosh* as a fireball detonated, and he heard the horrifying scream of someone who'd been immolated. Then he heard the shouts of the pursuing bandits ahead become snarls of fury.

The dusk elf must be a magic user of some sort.

Up ahead the trees opened into a large clearing. He saw the young woman standing at one end of it, hands engulfed in blue flames as she cast another spell. At the other end of the clearing a bandit was rolling on the ground, continuing to scream as he burned. Although the fire wasn't doing as much damage as it should've, and a quick check of his health bar showed he had only lost 10% or so.

The elf girl was weaker than her attackers, only Level 13, while the bandits were all in their low 20s.

The remaining three men had left their companion behind and were halfway across the clearing, howling in fury. The spellcaster flung her fireball at the man in the lead, but he managed to dodge and the spell hit the man behind him instead. That bandit also dropped to the ground screaming, desperately rolling to put himself out.

The lucky bandit in the lead waved his spear, lips pulled back in a snarl. "That was my brother, you gray slut!" he screamed. "I'll fuck your bloody corpse!"

Phoenix

Paling, the elf began frantically casting. At least until the bandit flung his spear.

It slammed into her stomach and twisted her around to crumple to the ground, the flames around her hands dissipating. She lost over half her health with that one attack, but in the desperation of survival mode she still managed to claw to her feet and stagger toward the trees.

Dare finally reached a spot where the trees didn't obscure his aim, just a few feet from the edge of the clearing. He dropped Zuri and unslung his bow as his tiny companion began casting a healing spell.

Pella zoomed past both of them, still sprinting, and burst into the clearing in pursuit of the bandits.

The lead bandit rushed forward unnaturally quick in some sort of Charge ability and tackled the mortally wounded woman, viciously stomping her face with a heavy boot as he grabbed his spear and yanked it free. "Give me a death scream to get me hard, cunt!" he snarled, raising the weapon over her.

Dare activated Rapid Shot and loosed his first arrow.

The bandit started a vicious downward thrust at his victim just as the arrow slammed into his throat. It sent him stumbling to one side, his spear burying harmlessly in the dirt instead of the woman's chest.

The shot was a critical hit and applied a severe bleed effect, but the man was only a few levels lower than Dare and only lost about 20% of his health.

Dare was already loosing his other three arrows in quick succession, Rapid Shot increasing the speed of each attack by 50%. The repeated impacts of the barbed shafts slammed into the bandit's chest, further throwing him off balance away from the wounded woman.

The elf was huddled on the ground writhing in agony, but the horrific wound in her gut was gradually closing as Zuri continued to cast her Plea to Nature, draining her mana pool healing the spellcaster.

Pella slammed into the second bandit, who'd turned toward Dare when he realized the danger. The man went down and the dog girl

37

used Subdue, using her full body to trap him in a hold he couldn't escape for up to 10 seconds.

Dare loosed a final arrow at the lead bandit, dropping him for good, then briefly checked on the burning men. The flames on both of them were almost out and they were still high health, but they seemed too disoriented by the pain to do anything and were still out of the fight.

So he began loosing arrows at the man Pella held, hitting the bandit with two before Pella had to disengage.

The bandit stumbled to his feet with a snarl and stumbled towards the dog girl, sword in hand. But Pella already had her lasso out, and with an expert throw she caught one of the man's legs, yanking powerfully and sending him tumbling back to the ground.

The dog girl leapt forward, long knife rising and falling as she stabbed the dazed man. Dare's next arrow slammed into the bandit's head, and he went still.

With a *whoosh* a fireball the size of his head roared across the clearing and hit one of the burned bandits, sending him back to the ground screaming. The elf woman was screaming as well, face twisted in pain and fury as she stood hunched around her still-bleeding wound, casting another fireball.

In spite of their comparable levels the two remaining bandits were in no shape for a fight. They quickly went down as arrows, Mana Thorns, and fireballs rained on them, Pella's lasso flicking in to trip the last man as he tried to flee.

Finally that bandit went still, clearly dead, and Dare and his companions ceased their attacks, the clearing falling unnaturally silent in the aftermath of battle.

Chapter Three
In Gratitude

With the danger momentarily over, and Zuri working quickly to heal the injured Mage, Dare finally got a chance to get a closer look at the dusk elf.

His Eye identified her as: "Dusk elf, adult female. Humanoid, intelligent. Class: Mage Level 13. Attacks: Fireball, Wind Slash, Ring of Fire, Manipulate Breeze. Gale."

As he got a better look at her figure, it became more clear why the bandits had been able to catch up with her so easily.

Pretty much all elves Dare had seen before in games and other media were either skinny to the point of looking like an underfed supermodel, or at the other end of the spectrum had the figure of a fit human woman. Elves and slender grace went hand in hand, and he couldn't remember ever seeing an exception.

The Mage in front of him, however, was toeing the line between curvy and plump. Which wasn't to say she was unattractive, actually the exact opposite: she had the fabled elvish beauty, and her fine pink riding dress hugged the sort of body that would make any man's heart beat faster.

She was simply an elf who happened to have big tits, wide hips, a thick ass, and the kind of plump thighs you wished you could get smothered by. She looked like a goddess of fertility.

He judged she was medium height, a few inches shorter than Pella. Her silky hair was bone white and so fine it nearly floated, pulled into a tight braid that hung to the small of her back, and her flawless skin was the soft light gray of ashes in a campfire. Her eyes were such a pale red they were closer to dark pink, large and mysterious.

The dusk elf's ruby red lips were almost obscenely plump, the sort that tended to make your mind picture things unbidden. Her oval face gave her a regal beauty, with high cheekbones, a small aquiline nose, and fine white eyebrows.

In spite of the urgency of the situation Dare couldn't help but stare; he'd fantasized about romancing an elf ever since coming to Collisa, and while she wasn't what he'd pictured if anything she was even more incredible. Like a dream come true.

She caught him gawking and glared for a moment, then brushed her irritation aside. "Quickly!" she cried, bolting across the clearing and beckoning to them desperately. "The caravan!"

Zuri had finished healing her, but even at full health the curvy Mage was obviously no sprinter. Even with her shorter legs the goblin Healer kept up with her easily, while Dare and Pella burst ahead. Although this time he didn't pick up Zuri to come with them, in spite of her obvious irritation at being left behind.

"Keep an eye on her in case more bandits are out there!" he called to his goblin lover, speeding into the woods with Pella hot on his heels.

"Hurry!" the dusk elf called urgently after them, spurring them to greater speeds as she fell behind.

Dare moved almost as recklessly as he had before, but made sure Pella was able to keep up this time. Although it turned out their haste was unnecessary.

To his relief, when they reached the edge of the woods he saw that the rest of the dusk elves seemed to have fought off the bandits attacking their caravan. There were no enemies in sight, apparently fled aside from the several dead being poked over by surviving elves.

From the looks of things they'd lost a few people themselves, with surviving family members grieving over the bodies, and one of the wagons had completely burned while a couple more were seriously damaged. But otherwise the caravan seemed to have weathered the attack well.

Pella also looked relieved that the other elves were safe, as was Zuri when she and the Mage caught up to them. But to all of their shock, the dusk elf wasn't pleased at all.

"The attack's over?" she said in disbelief. "Fuck!"

"It looks like most of your companions are okay," Pella said, hesitantly stepping closer as if to rest a hand on the furious elf's shoulder.

The Mage didn't seem to hear, stomping around just inside the treeline. "Fuck! Fuck fuck fuck! They couldn't have pressed the attack for a few more minutes?"

Dare stared at her blankly. "What's going on? Are you rooting for the bandits?"

She whirled on him with an expression of fury. "How dare you insult me like that? Of course not, I just wanted them to be ineffective at attacking and die slowly!"

Pella scratched one of her floppy ears. "Okay, I genuinely don't get it."

"There's nothing to get!" the Mage shouted. "If you'd helped the caravan then we'd all be in your debt, and that would be okay! But you just saved me, Immortal Ascendants damn me to the Abyss!"

Dare's confusion was losing the battle with annoyance. "Look, if you're not grateful that's fine, but you don't have to be a jerk about it."

"Of course I'm grateful, you stupid human chode!" she snarled, stomping around some more. "Fuck my life. Fuck!"

Okay, forget this. He motioned to his companions. "Come on, let's go see if they need help."

"Don't bother!" the Mage snapped, getting in their way and holding out her hands. "They won't be glad to see you, especially now that you've snaked their Mage from them." She spat in fury. "And they won't talk to me at all. Fuck!" She whirled and kicked a tree, then screeched in pain and hopped around clutching her foot.

Dare sighed. "Can you heal her again, Zuri? I'll go talk to the other elves and see if they're not completely insane. And Pella . . ." He nodded towards the furious woman.

The Mage tried to intercept him again as he left the trees, but the dog girl tackled her and used Subdue, putting her in a full body bind. Leaving the curvy elf no choice but to thrash against the unbreakable hold and screech furiously.

He left them to it and made his way to the caravan.

The elves' levels were all in the single digits or 10s, aside from the elderly elf Spellsurger who seemed to be the leader, who was Level 20. They all paused their efforts and bunched up warily as Dare approached, and he stopped and raised his hands. "Easy, I'm not with the bandits!" he called.

The leader stepped forward to within 10 feet. "Yes, some of my number saw you and your companions in pursuit of the bandits chasing our Mage," he shook his head with a sigh. "A pity she was caught away from the wagons during the attack . . . her spells would've turned the tide and perhaps saved lives."

Dare motioned towards the caravan. "I'm sorry for your losses, but glad you were able to repel the attack. Is there any assistance we can offer?"

"No." The old elf's eyes darted towards the trees, where the elf Mage's furious shouts could still be heard as Pella continued to restrain her. "I hear young Leilanna there, none too happy it seems. She survived, then?"

Dare nodded. "She was gravely wounded, but we were able to heal her and kill the bandits pursuing her."

"Ah." The elf leader suddenly looked even more weary and sad. "That explains her temper . . . she wasn't able to flee the bandits and you saved her life?"

"Yes. And in the nick of time too."

The old elf's shoulders sagged, and he sighed heavily. "A pity."

What the fuck? Dare grit his teeth. "Sorry, but did you want her to die or something?"

The leader turned away. "Please leave us be, human. We've lost loved ones today, and not all to violence."

"Well can you at least come and grab your Mage? She's freaking out and I don't know why."

"I'm afraid that won't be possible." The elf started back for the caravan.

"You're not going to tell me what the hell is going on, are you?" Dare called after him.

The caravan's leader paused and looked back. "As you seem a decent sort, I pray you'll be good to young Leilanna. She only recently reached womanhood, and regrettably remains very immature, temperamental, and ignorant about the harsh realities of the world. Particularly since we may have spoiled her. Hard not to after the losses she's suffered, and given her potential as a Mage."

He shook his head and sighed again. "Poor girl . . . no luck at all. With her birthright traits she could've gone far. Immortal Ascendants give she at least holds to her honor."

Dare flushed. Okay seriously, what the actual fuck? "I have no idea what the hell is going on, but if you're suggesting I intend to dishonor her, I can assure you I would never-"

"It isn't about you at all, human!" the leader snapped. "I speak only of a spoiled girl's willingness to do her duty and not dishonor herself and her people."

"Well if you'd actually tell me what's going on-"

Again the elf interrupted him, sighing heavily. "If you really wish to help, go and finish off the bandits who attacked us. They've been hounding us for days, picking us off from afar, sneaking in to cut our throats in our sleep. We've already lost a dozen of our strongest fighters and even more innocent travelers in our caravan to them, and they only committed to a full scale attack now because they thought they'd weakened us enough that they'd win. But even after today's defeat, they'll likely come back to persecute us further. Or if not us then other innocents."

Text appeared in front of Dare. "Quest offered. Knives in the Dark: Slay the remaining bandits and ensure the future safety of the dusk elf caravan."

The elf was already turning away, striding purposefully back to his caravan. Dare watched him go, scowling, then with a quiet curse accepted the quest for himself and his party members and stormed back to the trees.

The dusk elf, Leilanna apparently, seemed to have calmed down slightly. She was seated with her back to a tree, arms crossed, scowling in the direction of the caravan. Although to his surprise, as he got closer he saw tears streaming down her ashen gray cheeks.

Some of his annoyance faded at the sight of the girl's obvious misery. "Leilanna, is it?" he asked gently. "Are you all right?"

She didn't look at him. "No."

"Well maybe you'd feel better if you rejoin your people-" he began, then cut off when she broke into sobs.

Dare and his companions exchanged helpless looks, then Zuri tentatively approached and settled down beside the Mage, putting her small arms around her.

He expected the elf to push the little goblin away, but surprisingly Leilanna hugged Zuri back and sobbed even harder into her shoulder.

Whatever was going on, he didn't want to interrupt the fragile elf. He would've been willing to set up camp here, or wait around until the Mage got her shit together and went back to the caravan.

But there were still bandits out there and he felt like he should deal with them. With or without a quest from the elves.

"Pella," he said quietly, pulling her aside. "Keep an eye on Leilanna and Zuri. I'm going to go track the bandits."

The dog girl hesitated. "It should be safe here, so close to the caravan. Besides, I'm the one with the tracking abilities so I should help you." She frowned. "Especially since the bandits we faced were in their 20s . . . you might not be able to take them alone."

Dare opened his mouth to answer, but before he could Leilanna surged to her feet, making Zuri tumble onto her back with a surprised squeak. "If you're going after the bandits I'm going with you!" she snapped. "I'll help you kill them."

"Absolutely not," he said. "You're too low level, and anyway you're not in any condition emotionally to go into a fight."

The Mage's eyes flashed, and her hands briefly glowed with dangerous blue flames. "No need to insult me, human," she snarled. "You're never too low level to set someone on fire. And I'm not your average Mage."

Well, she certainly had taken those two bandits out of the fight, even with her comparatively weaker spells. But it was still out of the question. "Go back to your people," he said sternly. "You can tell them we'll take care of the bandits so you won't have to worry about another attack."

"Don't talk to me like I'm a child, human, I'm the same age as you!" The dusk elf stubbornly crossed her arms beneath her large breasts, lifting them and making them even more attention-grabbing. "I either go with you or go on my own."

Dare chuckled; she seemed to have recovered some of her spirit, which meant she probably didn't need Zuri to comfort her. "Yeah, have fun with that." He picked up his goblin lover and nodded at Pella. "Lead the way."

The dog girl grinned, tail wagging, and shot off like an arrow. He held Zuri close and followed.

Behind them Leilanna shouted in furious protest, sounding as if she was trying to chase them, but the racket quickly grew fainter as they easily outdistanced the less than athletic elf. "Should we really leave her alone?" Zuri asked worriedly. "I have the feeling she might be in trouble or something."

Honestly, a less generous part of him wouldn't have been sad to leave the ungrateful, foul-mouthed, ill-tempered woman behind. Beautiful or not, she wasn't pleasant to be around. But he sighed. "We can come back and check on her after this."

"Got them!" Pella shouted from ahead, veering off.

Dare was able to catch some of the tracks she was seeing, but only by sight; unlike Pella's Find Prey, which allowed her to track anything, his own Find Prey ability was more literal. As in it only worked on prey animals and critters. Not even predators, aside from some omnivores that counted.

The bandits must've been running for their lives, because even at his and his dog girl companion's fast pace it took them almost fifteen minutes to catch up. Although when they did, it was more because the remaining five men from the caravan attack were facing an attack of their own.

They'd inadvertently stumbled into a spawn point where the monsters had Stealth and were all in the 24-27 level range. In their headlong flight from the elves they'd inadvertently aggroed two of them, and the nightmarish lizard-octopus hybrid creatures were currently standing over the corpse of one and ripping another apart with their tentacles.

The remaining three had scattered back to either side to try to get out of the spawn point boundary, splitting up, and Dare pointed. "Get the straggler, Pella. Me and Zuri will get the other two."

"On it!" the dog girl said just loud enough for them to hear, her voice grim and focused. She unspooled her lasso from her belt in one hand and drew her long knife in the other, and her pace sped up as if she'd turned on afterburners as she activated Run Down and broke into a sprint.

Dare bolted the other way, getting close enough to the two bandits so they wouldn't run out of range as he shot them. Then he set down Zuri and used Rapid Shot, loosing arrows at the farther away one. At his side his goblin lover began casting Mana Thorn on the nearer one, sending out small shards of dark green energy to slice at the running man.

It almost wasn't fair, with both of them fleeing with their backs turned, but it was hard to feel much pity when his ears were still ringing with the vile things that other bandit had said as he tried to kill Leilanna.

His first arrow knocked his target off his feet and sent him rolling awkwardly, giving Dare time to hit him with two more arrows before the bandit managed to stumble back to his feet. At which point he dropped again with the next arrow, which hit his leg in the critical crippling spot, and finally the fifth arrow finished him off.

Zuri's target was still at over half health, and had turned back with a snarl and activated a Charge ability as he rushed the tiny Healer. That didn't help him much as Dare and Zuri's combined attacks dropped him before he'd gotten halfway to them.

"Quest Completed. Daggers in the Night: Slay the remaining

bandits and ensure the future safety of the dusk elf caravan. 10,000 experience gained. This quest has no turn in."

A quick glance confirmed Pella had dispatched her target, and the two lizard-octopus monsters had finished off the last surviving bandit. Dare hadn't expected the no turn in thing; apparently the elves really didn't want to see them again.

With a sigh he got his companions' attention and motioned to where the monsters that had killed the two men were beginning to fade away into Stealth again. The bandits had been kind enough to reveal the monsters, so they might as well take them out so they could loot the two men's corpses.

The octolizards turned out to be fairly weak once they were out of Stealth, taking one less arrow than other monsters their level. Dare and his companions quickly took them out with no mishap, although Pella nearly got pelted by a spray of blinding ink and had to back away, yelping.

The monsters dropped some of that ink as loot, along with something called Chameleon Oil, which looked as if it could be valuable. That was more than he could say for the bandits; aside from their weapons and a few pieces of lower quality armor, they only had a few silver between them.

Dare finished stuffing the loot into his pack and stood. "All right, I think we're done here. Let's head back to the woods and loot those other four bandits we killed." He grimaced. "Assuming the elves didn't already take the stuff."

"And go back for Leilanna too, right?" Pella asked, looking worried.

He stared at her. "Why the hell would we do that? She's probably already rejoined her people."

She shifted uncomfortably. "You don't know anything about dusk elves. I don't know much either, just what I've heard, but I think she can't go back. At least, that's the sense I got from how she was acting and what the caravan's leader said."

Dare frowned. "What, some sort of punishment for nearly dying and needing to be saved? An honor thing?"

"An honor thing, yes," the dog girl said. "But not quite like that, I don't think. I just know dusk elves are very prickly about their honor and have some weird customs."

Well, maybe they'd finally get some answers now that the bandit threat was dealt with. Dare picked Zuri up and they started back to the caravan, although at a less frantic pace.

The elves were still where they'd stopped during the attack, moving things from the burned wagons and digging graves. Dare and his companions circumvented the line of wagons, since they had no business there and the elves didn't seem inclined to welcome them, and made for where they'd left Leilanna.

To his disappointment and annoyance she was still there, although now there was a pile of items beside her.

The dusk elf tried to put on a cool front, but it was obvious she was relieved to see them. Almost desperately so. "You came back to me," she called. "I figured I'd have to chase you down when you returned to the caravan for your reward."

"I'm wondering why *you* haven't returned to them," Dare shot back. He motioned to the loot. "Helped yourself to the bandits' stuff while we were gone?"

Leilanna flushed. "How dare you insult me like that?" she spat. "I collected it for *you*. And it was a super gross task, so you're welcome." She paused, then added under her breath loud enough he didn't need to be a canid to hear her, "Jerk."

"Well no wonder it was gross," Zuri said, wrinkling her nose. "You took their clothes?"

Pella snickered. "Not just their clothes. She took their *underwear*. Even I think that's disgusting."

The Mage's pale ash skin flushed a darker gray in a mixture of anger and embarrassment. "How was I supposed to know what to take?" she demanded. "I've never pawed over a corpse like some sort of undertaker before . . . I've only looted monsters. I was afraid I'd leave something valuable behind if I wasn't thorough."

She shuddered. "And you're right, it was super disgusting. So again, you're welcome."

Dare scratched his jaw. "Is used underwear typically seen as valuable to dusk elves?"

"Not men's underwear, at least," Pella deadpanned, and Zuri giggled.

Leilanna flushed further. "Of course not, don't be stupid. But how do I know what vendors want? I've never sold anything before, all my skill is with shopping."

His initial impression of her as a spoiled brat wasn't getting any better. Although he supposed he had to admire her for at least going to the effort to loot the bandits for them. And while he couldn't admire her . . . thoroughness, the fact that she was willing to go that far in spite of her obvious disgust suggested she might have some redeeming qualities.

"Well then, thank you for looting the bandits," Dare said. "After Zuri uses Cleanse Target we'll sort through what's worth taking."

"I'll cast it on you, too," the little goblin said, patting Leilanna's arm.

"What are you still doing here, anyway?" he asked as Zuri got to work casting spells, using water from their waterskins.

The dusk elf grimaced and straightened, throwing her shoulders back proudly. Which did very nice things to her generous bosom. "To begin, human, let me clarify a misconception. My current circumstances notwithstanding, you and your servants have my gratitude for saving my life."

Dare bit back a frown. "They're not my servants, they're my companions."

She sneered at Zuri and Pella. "You're traveling with a goblin and a dog girl. You're definitely the master here."

He sighed; he hated having to explain this to everyone he met. And it wasn't doing anything for his opinion of Leilanna, either. "At best I'd be willing to claim the title of party leader. But they're my party members and equal companions."

"And lovers," Pella added, tail wagging.

The dusk elf's dark pink eyes widened in disbelief and disgust.

"The canid I can understand, knowing how you humans love your pets, but you're fucking a *goblin*? What, you couldn't find any rats to shove your dick inside?"

Okay, he was done with this conversation. "You're welcome for rescuing you," he said with forced politeness. "I hope you fare well from here. Safe travels." Without waiting for a response he turned to rejoin his lovers at the loot.

"Alethorinel mel'aline," Leilanna muttered behind him, her tone suggesting she was cursing. She caught his shoulder. "I'm afraid it's not quite that simple, human," she snapped. "You saved my life."

"You're welcome, happy to help," he said, shaking free of her and turning away. Hopefully she'd get the hint and leave.

She sucked in a breath as if struggling to contain her fury and grabbed his arm, yanking him around to face her. Then she squared her shoulders and her tone became formal. "I, Leilanna Aleneladris, of the exalted Aleneladris lineage, do formally acknowledge that my life has been saved by . . ." She trailed off pointedly.

"Dare," Pella said helpfully.

"By Dare, which is a stupid name but that's beside the point." Leilanna took an even deeper breath, wearing an expression like she was about to give a viper an openmouthed kiss. "As my honor demands, I swear that my life now belongs to him, to do with as he sees fit. I will serve him to the end of his days, or mine. May my shame be boundless in this life and all those to come should I break this oath."

Dare stared at her, a leaden weight sinking in his gut; this explained why she'd been so pissed off that he'd saved her, and the elf leader so sad about it. "Stop, don't make promises like that!" he snapped. "What the hell are you doing?"

"I'm giving you a *Lifesworn Oath*," she said through gritted teeth. "It means my honor compels me to serve you for the remainder of my life." She paused, brightening. "Or yours I suppose, since I'm longer-lived than you."

He wondered if that was true, given the longevity his benefactor had given him with this improved body. Then again, in a lot of fantasy worlds elves were immortal or lived for up to a thousand years. On the other hand, his benefactor had told him nobody had ever reached the level cap, and if elves were immortal they realistically would've by now.

Although that was the least important consideration at the moment.

Dare bit back a sigh. Godsdamnit, what was he supposed to do about this? "I free you from your Lifesworn Oath," he said firmly. "I don't believe in slavery or any other binds."

He kind of doubted it would be that easy, and sure enough the dusk elf bridled in outrage. "A Lifesworn Oath is *not* slavery!" she snapped. "It's an honorable servitude to a deserving master. One that I cannot weasel out of without utterly destroying my honor, and you cannot refuse."

Of course. He turned to Zuri and Pella. "Is that true? Are Lifesworn Oaths a thing?"

The dog girl shrugged, while the timid goblin hesitated before also shrugging.

"Of course it's a thing, human who never misses a chance to insult me," Leilanna said stiffly. "In spite of our current nomadic ways, my people have a very noble heritage. All other races of elves are descended from us."

Pella scratched at a floppy ear. "I thought dusk elves were the offspring of dark elves and wood elves or high elves."

"Oh, so you're joining in on your master's insults?" the dusk elf demanded. "That's vile slander, perpetuated by the other races to claim we're lesser when in reality we have the most noble birthright." She straightened again; if nothing else, she sure knew how to strike a proud pose. "For instance, the Aleneladris family carries the elite bloodline trait Fiery Disposition, which gives me greater casting speed and damage for Fire eleme-"

Dare couldn't help it, he burst out laughing. "You, one of the most foul-mouthed, ill-tempered people I've ever met, have a trait called Fiery Disposition? That seems a little too perfect."

Her hands caught fire, balled into fists at her sides. "Every time you open your mouth," she seethed. "*Every time*. One insult after another! Have you no respect?"

"Respect grows as it is given, and withers as it is withheld," Zuri said sagely.

"Shut up, goblin! The others are bad enough, but I won't hear insults from a pukeskin-"

Before Dare could even begin to be angry at the insult Pella growled and grabbed the curvy elf by the front of her fine dress with both hands, lifting her onto her tiptoes with a squeak.

"Call her that again," the golden-haired woman said quietly, ears flat and tail stiff. "Insult my friend again, I fucking *dare* you."

They all stared in shock at the normally gentle, happy-go-lucky dog girl. Although he'd seen proof of the fierceness of her loyalty before; she might be a big sweetheart, but if you went after the people she loved she showed her teeth.

And he loved her for it.

Leilanna tried to maintain her arrogant front, but visibly gulped and shot a glance at Dare. From anyone else it might've been pleading.

He wasn't inclined to give her a break, given how she'd been acting. "Say what you want about me, treat me how you will, but you'll be civil to the women I love or we *will* leave you behind, whatever oath you've sworn."

The beautiful dusk elf opened her mouth, then snapped it shut, and her pale skin turned a darker shade of gray in a furious flush. "I spoke in anger, I didn't mean it," she said reluctantly.

Pella glared at her for another second, then released her dress and stepped back.

"Now, I suppose we should do this properly," Dare continued. "I'm Dare, this is Zuri, and this is Pella." He motioned to each of his lovers in turn.

"Charmed," the Mage said, not quite sounding sarcastic.

Dare did his best not to scowl. "So, Leilanna, let's say I refused to acknowledge your Lifesworn Oath and simply continued on my way, ignoring you. What would happen?"

The Mage didn't even try to hide her scowl. "My honor would compel me to skulk after you like a thief in the night, haunting your steps and attempting any service I could get away with or you would allow. Only by crippling or killing me could you escape, and then I would be honor bound to seek you for the remainder of my days, even after I was certain you should be long dead."

Damnit. "And exactly what does the servitude entail? Would you become my servant? An armswoman?"

She grit her teeth. "It entails whatever you desire it does. You may have me fight for you, or do menial tasks. My life is yours, and I cannot honorably refuse any command save to kill myself, since that would be robbing you of my life, or anything that would dishonor myself."

Fantastic. "So I can't free you from your Lifesworn Oath," he said as patiently as he could. "What if you were to save my life in turn. Would that nullify the debt?"

Leilanna sneered at him. "Don't be stupid, human. I'm your servant, and a servant's duty is to protect the life of her master. You can't nullify a Lifesworn Oath by doing your duty."

He sighed, feeling a hopeless weight in his gut. "And there's no other way?" She grudgingly shook her head; obviously she wanted out of this as much as he did. "So this is happening, even if forced servitude goes against my personal beliefs?"

Her dark pink eyes flashed. "Again you insult me, human! This is *not* forced servitude, it is honorable servitude." She sniffed. "In any case my honor and what I am duty bound to do is not affected by your beliefs."

Dare threw up his hands in defeat. "All right, then. We'll sort this out somehow." Maybe he could command her to take up a profession she wanted to do and life a good life, or something. But until then, the poor woman had been attacked, exiled from her people and thrust into the company of strangers, and bound to a life she didn't want.

"All right, let's sort this loot and get back to leveling," he said. "We'll head over to those octolizard things next . . . they're pretty weak once you get them out of Stealth, and Pella can do that since she'll be crowd controlling them anyway."

Leilanna cleared her throat. "If you don't mind me asking, what exactly is it you're doing out here?"

He stared at her. "Leveling. I just told you that."

Her eyes flashed; was she ever *not* pissed off? "Yes, but what's your end goal? Are you traveling somewhere? Do you have a home? Are you following a monster compendium? Are you part of a guild?"

"No, no, no, no, and my end goal is to become very high level and have a harem full of beautiful women of every race," Dare said, smiling tightly. "Also I'd like to have the influence to change the things about Collisa that make it such a cruel place, like slavery and owning people as pets." *And Lifesworn Oaths*, he didn't add.

The dusk elf laughed harshly. "Wow, you've set realistic goals, haven't you? And people call my kind arrogant."

"Wait, you said no to whether we're traveling somewhere?" Pella asked, frowning. "We're headed to Polan's Folly, aren't we?"

He shrugged. "Well I was going to talk to you guys about that, but since we don't have any pressing reason to anymore I figured we'd stay here and finally put some real focus into leveling after all the traveling we've done."

The dog girl's frown deepened. "But we were going that way because of Benefacto-" She cut off, glancing at Leilanna.

Zuri nodded in realization. "You think this was what her advice was about?"

"It seems likely," Dare said. *And thanks for being so keen to saddle me with a spoiled, arrogant princess*, he added silently to his benefactor.

"You're welcome," she said, sounding slightly smug.

Well, that confirmed this was what she'd given the advice to achieve. And also likely meant she'd be pissed if he left Leilanna behind and forced her to tag along after him and his friends until the pampered Mage most likely starved to death or got eaten by some monster.

Not that he'd been planning to do any such thing.

Dare sighed; looked as if they had a new member of their group, whether he liked it or not. "Welcome to the group I guess, Leilanna." He didn't bother inviting her to the party, pretty sure she'd refuse and not wanting to invite more of her abuse. Besides, she was too low level to get any benefit. "Do you need your things from the caravan?"

The curvy elf's shoulders slumped with obvious embarrassment and hints of sadness. "I don't have anything," she muttered. "All of it was a gift from Elder Nirol, and from the looks of things he doesn't seem inclined to share any of it now that I'm honor bound to you."

Fantastic. Well, he was no stranger to outfitting new companions. He'd make her a tent and bedroll, and he and Zuri could make her more suitable clothes for travel and fighting than that ridiculous (if undeniably sexy) dress she was wearing.

Which meant he'd have to hunt more animals and set his snares tonight. And maybe they should go back to those Gaunt Fiends when they respawned for more silk tatters.

Speaking of loot, he quickly sorted through the pile of stuff Leilanna had collected. As he'd expected, most of it wasn't fit for much but to be left behind even after Zuri had cleaned it.

Grimacing, he tucked the weapons, a chainmail chestpiece, and the few other things worth taking into his pack. Then he turned to their new companion.

"All right," he said, motioning towards the octolizard spawn point. "Let's set out. We'll start with an easy pace to see how well you can keep up."

Chapter Four
In Tolerance

As it turned out, how well Leilanna could keep up was not well at all.

She managed what felt to Dare like an agonizingly slow run of maybe 6 miles an hour for a few minutes, then had to slow down and catch her breath for almost the same amount of time before she could go again. At which point she lasted even less time before again slowing to a walk, panting.

At this rate he estimated they *might* manage 4 miles an hour if they wanted to go all day.

As he watched the out of shape Mage continue to struggle to catch her breath he grew impatient with the situation. He called a halt and turned to Leilanna. "This isn't going to work."

She glared at him as she hunched over, hands on her knees, breathing like a bellows. "It's not my fault I mostly rode in a wagon with the caravan," she whined.

"It kind of is," Pella said. "You could've at least done a bit of physical conditioning. After all, aren't dusk elves nomadic? Seems like you would've wanted to be able to keep up if needed."

The Mage flushed. "Okay, I'll admit I don't have the best endurance," she snapped. "But give me a few weeks and I'll be able to keep up."

"No, you won't," Dare said bluntly.

The curvy elf struggled to straighten, expression fierce. "Again and again you insult-"

"It's not an insult, it's a statement of fact," he interrupted. "And it's not just you, it's Zuri, which is why I carry her. I can easily manage a pace of 25 miles an hour at a sprint, and 10 or so miles an hour at a run I can maintain all day. And thanks to a use of Pella's Run Down that we just discovered, she can match whatever pace I can set."

Leilanna sneered at him in open disbelief. "25 miles an hour? You think I'm stupid?"

Instead of answering Dare grinned at Zuri. "Want to go for a run?"

"Zoom!" she agreed with a laugh, holding up her arms.

He picked her up and bolted away, running faster and faster until he was going all out, in a way he usually didn't. He was moving fast enough that the wind stung his eyes, forcing him to squint, and in his arms his goblin lover squealed in delight.

He loved running with her.

Light, thumping footfalls came up behind him, and he risked a quick glance over his shoulder in spite of his breakneck pace. Pella was at his heels, keeping pace with ease thanks to her ability. By her huge grin she was enjoying this as much as they were.

She'd only be able to maintain it for 5 minutes, then have to wait another 5 minutes for the cooldown, but even so it should let them set a rotating pace that tested both their limits without one coming ahead of the other.

"This is fun!" the dog girl shouted. "Can I Tackle you at the end of it?"

Come to think of it, with the mechanics of Tackle that might be a good way to stop quickly without getting torn up by crashing at high speeds. Although now wasn't the time or the best way to test it.

Dare shook his head. "Maybe when I'm not holding Zuri," he called back. Looping around, he made his way back to where Leilanna waited.

The dusk elf was staring at them, jaw slack. "Okay," she said grudgingly as Dare and Pella stopped, panting. "There's no way I could match that pace, short term or long term." She put her hands on her hips. "But what can we do about it? I'm bound to follow you, no matter how fast you go or how far behind I get. So you have the choice of either matching my pace or leaving me."

"I can think of another option," Pella said with a smirk, tail wagging. "Dare can give you a piggyback ride."

The dusk elf laughed. "Yeah, sure."

"Actually, that's exactly what I was thinking," Dare said. "Pella's fine carrying Zuri, we've done it before, but since I'm stronger and faster I should carry you."

Leilanna's eyes narrowed. "What's that supposed to mean?"

Dare wasn't about to reference a woman's weight, even in comparison to a goblin over a foot and a half shorter and around 70 pounds lighter than her. "It means I'll carry you. I'll need to build up my strength to do it for long distances, and we won't be able to maintain the same speed as before. And you'll regularly have to get down and run. But we can make it work."

Her cheeks flushed a darker gray, with anger or embarrassment he wasn't sure. "You, carry me," she repeated.

"It's that or leave you behind." He smiled thinly. "I'm not dropping my pace to 5 miles an hour at best if I don't have to."

The dusk elf looked as if she was about to explode, and Pella cut in hastily. "We can save up for a horse for you as a priority. That'll be the best solution all around."

That was a good suggestion. Dare had intended to get them all mounts when they could afford it, but from what he'd seen in the towns they'd passed, horses tended to cost at least 50 gold for a packhorse, and between 100 and 200 gold for a fine riding mount. No doubt the best bred and well trained ones were even more expensive, but he was a long time away from even considering those.

They were making enough with their farming now to be able to afford a horse, even though it would make a huge dent in their savings. But there was the question of whether it was worth it for a prickly Level 13 Mage who'd joined their group without his agreement or even the chance to offer her an invitation.

And although it probably made him a dick to admit it, if she wasn't a useful and contributing member of the group, he'd still be happy to have her along if she was a romantic partner, or seemed interested in becoming one in the future. But from what he could see she found him detestable and his presence barely tolerable.

Case in point, how obviously opposed to the idea of riding on his back she was.

To be fair, he wasn't exactly thrilled about it either. Sure, under most circumstances the prospect of giving a beautiful, voluptuous elf a piggyback ride would've been awesome, but with her so clearly not into it he couldn't really enjoy it either.

And beautiful or not, friendly or not, carrying her long distances was going to suck purely from the standpoint of effort required. And he doubted she'd be doing her best to make the ordeal any easier.

Dare sighed. "We'll worry about that when we're traveling long distances again. For now, going from spawn point to spawn point, Leilanna can work on her cardio."

"My what?" she demanded suspiciously, as if she thought he was being vulgar.

"Your endurance." He motioned curtly. "Break's over, let's go."

They set off again, and whether because she was miffed or she was trying to conserve her strength the dusk elf immediately fell behind. Zuri, kindhearted as always, fell back to keep her company, and while Dare and Pella slowed to Leilanna's pace he let her keep her distance if she wanted.

Which apparently she did. As they ran along, getting closer to the octolizard spawn points, Pella abruptly cocked her head and smiled. "Oh, that's sweet," she said.

He glanced over at her. "What?"

"Oh, Leilanna's apologizing to Zuri. She sounds sincere too, although it would be nice to be able to smell her and hear her heartbeat to be sure." The dog girl's ears abruptly drooped. "Oh, the poor dear. No wonder she's such a mess."

"What?" Dare asked again.

His golden-haired lover gave a start, flushing as she glanced at him. "It's not really our business, I shouldn't be listening. I just can't help it."

He supposed she had a point and dropped the subject.

When they reached the spawn point he set his snares in a nearby patch of forest, hoping they'd be full by the time they set up camp. He planned to do that a little early to make sure Leilanna had what she needed and give her a chance to rest after what had been such a challenging day for her.

They situated the Mage far back from where they'd be farming so she didn't accidentally aggro the monsters with her lower level, leaving her to observe as they got to farming.

Pella took care of aggroing, finding the Stealthed monsters with her keen senses and higher level and snagging them with her lasso to break them from stealth. That also snared the octolizards, giving Dare and Zuri time to start damaging them down before the dog girl had to break away and start kiting.

These monsters didn't pull adds, which was nice, and the process was pretty smooth. Although Dare couldn't help but think that he was probably going to have to replace his Level 20 short bow, even with its Exceptional quality. It was getting to the point where a lower quality bow of his level would be far superior.

To Leilanna's credit, every time he checked on her he found her attentively watching them, studying their teamwork and tactics. She might have been a spoiled hothead, but it was obvious she was smart. As a Mage and solid damage dealer she could potentially be a good addition to their group, especially if she was telling the truth about her bloodline giving her a boost.

Of course, first they'd have to get her 12 levels without slowing their own leveling down too much.

Dare spent the rest of the day, as they cleared the spawn point and moved on to others, working through the best way to make that happen for their new companion. With his knowledge of Zuri's mana regeneration and spell rotations he had a good idea of what could be done, although he'd have to talk to Leilanna specifically to find out how Mages differed from Healers.

Wouldn't that be fun.

He broached the topic as they were taking a break after looting the most recent spawn point, and predictably the dusk elf puffed up like a peacock. "You need not worry about my mana," she said haughtily. "All elves are gifted with 10% increased mana capacity and regeneration."

She hesitated. "Although with the cost of my spells I can usually only manage to go for a few hours of constant spellcasting every day. Maybe five at best." She flushed. "And, um, I have a great deal of difficulty leveling on my own. Especially if there are adds. Thankfully I've never been required to attempt it."

A few hours sounded fairly consistent with what Zuri had been able to manage casting Mana Thorns, back when they'd first been working out the kinks in their leveling methods. The increased damage of the fireballs probably made up for their lack of mana efficiency, not to mention that a pure damage dealer's spells would do better overall than a healing class's attack spells.

"All right, thanks for letting me know." He turned to the others. "Let's head back to where I placed the snares and make camp."

In spite of the relatively early day nobody complained about stopping. They headed back to the forest, where Dare got a fire built and food cooking, then got to work turning the hides he'd collected that day through hunting and trapping into items for their new companion.

After equipping himself and his companions all this time he was getting pretty practiced at it.

Zuri also got to work, making clothes for all three women out of the silk scraps they'd farmed. Judging by how she forced him to turn around during part of the process, he had the feeling at least a few of those items were underwear.

Hopefully she'd also thought to make some socks for Leilanna; if the Mage was going to be running a lot from now on, preventing blisters was a priority.

Leilanna lounged by the fire in his collapsible chair the entire time, occasionally leaning forward to eagerly sniff the pot bubbling over the flames and the skewers roasting on the rack. Given how she'd complained about pretty much everything today, he was surprised when she had no criticism to offer about his cooking.

Dare finished a one-person tent and tossed it at the dusk elf's feet, then rooted in his pack for the one he shared with Zuri and Pella and also tossed it over. "Here, make yourself useful and set these up."

"Sure," she mumbled absently, still staring into the flames and showing no sign of getting to work.

Well, it wasn't like it needed to get done immediately, given that night was still hours away.

Zuri finished the clothes, then led the other two women down the stream to a secluded spot so she could cast Cleanse Object on everyone and they could try them on.

Dare spent that time finishing a tunic, breeches, boots, and a fur-lined hooded cloak for the dusk elf, as well as a fur-lined bedroll and collapsible chair. So he could reclaim his own from her. Also a hide pack to hold it all.

Then, since the girls were taking their time, he began experimenting with the honey and maple syrup he'd collected and processed, trying to make desserts. So far all he'd been able to manage was candied fruits and herbs like mint, which Zuri liked just fine but didn't love. Also adding some sweetness to the dishes he cooked for contrast.

Although he sort of wondered if he should maybe scale back a bit on the desserts; his goblin lover had a definite sweet tooth and she continued to put on weight. Although nothing more than a thickening around her middle and a bit of a tummy at the moment. Not to mention adding a bit more gravity to her already glorious breasts.

Actually, he thought it made her more sexy. Although he didn't want to end up feeding her unhealthy food in excess.

Since the girls were still gone Dare gave in and set up the tents himself. He was torn about setting up Leilanna's for her, but decided that she probably didn't even know how and he'd probably end up doing it anyway.

Still, he might've been a bit irked about it.

His mood didn't improve when the girls finally returned, all looking freshly washed and gorgeous in clinging silk gowns that showed their figures to best effect, and the Mage saw her set up tent.

She smiled almost smugly and turned to him. "Oh good, you set up my tent. Thank you."

"No need to thank me," Dare said flatly. "When you don't do the work you're supposed to, somebody has to do it."

Her gray skin darkened slightly, in anger or embarrassment. "Even so," she said, obviously trying to hold her temper, "I'm grateful."

He ignored her. "Of course, if someone has to keep picking up your slack, eventually they're going decide to ditch your useless ass." He snorted. "So much for your so-called Lifesworn Oath."

"Your insults are endless, human!" she shouted, stamping her foot. "I'm sworn to serve you, not wash your dishes and chop your firewood."

"What do you think serving means?" Pella asked, sounding genuinely curious. As if she thought the dusk elf didn't know.

"It means to fight valiantly at his side!" Leilanna said confidently. "A sworn sword."

Zuri frowned. "Do the rules about the Lifesworn Oath say that? Because you made it sound like indentured servitude."

"I am *not* his servant!" the elf shouted furiously. "If you want to wait on him hand and foot, when you're not walking face first into his cock that is, then you go ri-"

Dare, who'd been stirring the food, loudly clattered his spoon against the pot, cutting her off and getting her attention. "This isn't even an issue of service or the duties of your customs." He motioned around the camp. "There are things we need to do if we want to enjoy the comforts of a camp. If you don't want to help with those tasks then you are not entitled to enjoy the comforts."

He kicked at the pile of leather goods he'd made for her. "Including this stuff you'll probably need if you want to have a pleasant night."

Leilanna's lip curled. "A bunch of woodsman's trash still stinking of the animals it came from? I'd rather shiver next to the fire."

"If you're not pulling your weight even the fire is more than you've earned." His voice hardened. "Also, whatever *you* may believe about your Lifesworn Oath, bear in mind that to the rest of us you are a guest. Currently a barely tolerated one due to your attitude and behavior."

He paused significantly. "If you want to continue to be welcome in this camp, you might consider doing your fair share. And it wouldn't hurt if you tried to be more agreeable, either."

"You think I *want* to be here?" Leilanna snapped. She turned and stormed off into the woods.

Pella sighed and started to stand. "I'll go after her. I don't like people to be sad, and she's really not as bad as she seems."

Dare caught her hand, gently tugging her back down. "I don't want her to be sad either, but remember that her misery is currently self-inflicted. And I'm not talking about her culture's pressure to uphold the Lifesworn Oath if she wants to remain honorable, either. I'm talking about the way she treats us, and whether we want to put up with it."

The dog girl's tail drooped. "But I don't want her to think we hate her. She's all alone out there, probably curled up in a ball crying. She acts like she has a hard shell and nothing touches her, but I know she's hurting."

He sighed and patted his lover's hand. "I think it would be good to go and try to keep her company, but maybe give her some time to calm down first. Otherwise she might just end up shouting at you next."

They waited a few tense minutes, none of them particularly happy about the thought of Leilanna out there. Especially given that there might be high level predators or more bandits around.

Finally Dare motioned to the food. "This is almost done. How about you go talk to Leilanna, keep her company for a few minutes, then bring her back for dinner?"

Pella grinned and bolted away, tail wagging.

Smiling slightly at his lover's enthusiasm, he turned to Zuri. "How about you? Do you think Leilanna might be able to fit in with our group and become a useful party member?"

"I think it would help if you put her over your knee and spanked her until she learned to keep a civil tongue and do her part, but that's just the less kind part of me speaking." His little lover stared into the flames, large eyes sad. "Pampered as she may act, she hasn't had nearly as easy of a life as it might seem. Thanks for being patient with her."

Dare snorted. "I just threatened to kick her out of camp because she wouldn't set up a tent."

Zuri gave him a blank look. "Well yeah, she needs to learn to do her part. *I'm* not planning on doing everything for her."

Pella and Leilanna finally came back, the dusk elf's eyes as red as her irises from tears. She quietly ate her meal, actually thanked him for it, then without a word got to work washing the dishes. Dare let her, even though usually Zuri took care of the laborious task in a few seconds with a spell.

Their new companion took the pile of leather items he'd made for her, thanked him for those as well, then disappeared into her tent. A few minutes later Dare heard the sounds of muffled crying.

He wasn't the only one who heard it. Zuri took his hand and led him towards their own tent. "Come on," she said quietly. "I think we could all use an early night."

"Although I hope we're not planning to sleep just yet," Pella said, tail wagging as she ran her hands over her gorgeous athletic curves in her new green dress. "Zuri went to all the effort of making this, so the least you could do is be so overcome by desire you tear it off and ravish me."

She playfully leaned down to swat the goblin's small ass in her own pale yellow dress. "And her too, for that matter."

Dare grinned. "All right, let's get in some good rest and relaxation." He put his arms around his two lovers as they made for the tent. "Starting with me giving you two the massages you've earned for being so amazing."

* * * * *

The next morning at the crack of dawn Dare slapped the hide

wall of Leilanna's tent. "Wakey wakey, eggs and bakey!" he called cheerfully. "Come on, let's go!"

From inside he heard a snort, then her groggy voice. "Huh? Wha?"

"Wakey wakey, eggs and bakey!"

"The fuck does that mean?"

It sounded like the fiery Mage's spirits had recovered somewhat from last night. And surprising as it seemed, Dare was relieved to hear it; abrasive as the hot-tempered, rude Leilanna could be, he preferred her to the miserable, haunted woman he'd seen last night.

Maybe, with a bit of work, they could coax out a personality that was actually tolerable.

"It means there isn't actually eggs or bacon," he replied, grinning. "What there *is* is your three companions already prepared to set out. You have fifteen minutes to change into the sturdy clothes I made you, take down your tent, and pack up your gear. You can eat dried meat and herb greens as we travel."

"Prepared to . . ." Leilanna's head burst out of the tent, stark white hair mussed. She looked around and spoke in disbelief. "It's still so dark I can barely see! Which means *you're* probably blind as a bat, human."

Okay true, Dare didn't usually get his party up and moving this early. But he wanted to put their new companion through a sort of trial by fire, get her to push her limits.

Besides, after the early night an early morning couldn't hurt.

He turned away, grinning. "Fourteen minutes now. We leave whether you're ready or not."

"Motherf-" the Mage's hands burst alight, and he watched with some trepidation as she cast a fireball.

Thankfully her target was the extinguished campfire, not him, setting it alight again as she disappeared inside her tent. He heard the rustle of cloth as she scrambled to dress.

It was actually closer to twenty minutes before Leilanna, fumbling in her haste, managed to finish awkwardly navigating the unfamiliar task of taking down her tent, then hurriedly stuffed her gifted items in her pack and shrugged it onto her shoulders.

Dare had to admit that her curvy figure actually managed to fill out her leather tunic and pants fairly nicely, making the utilitarian clothing almost sexy. She looked like she could be on the cover of a RPG game or fantasy book, the beautiful adventurer about to head out into the wilds.

"Well?" the Mage snapped, glaring back at him. "Now what?"

He bit back a grimace. Now for the part neither of them were going to like. "Now we let Pella carry our packs and Zuri and you hop on my back so we can set a reasonable pace."

Leilanna made a displeased sound and put her hands on her hips. "This again? I thought you'd given that up when you let me show I could run from one spawn point to the next."

"No, if anything it just showed that we're all going to go crazy trying to stay at your pace." Dare pointed towards Polan's Folly to the northeast. "If you want to be a useful member of the party we need to level you up, which means traveling to where the monsters are ones you can kill on your own. That trip will take hours even if I carry you, and all day if we go at your speed."

"On my own? But I already told you-"

"You'll be killing them on your own, but you won't be *fighting* them on your own," Zuri said impatiently. She began pushing the dusk elf towards him. "Come on, let's go."

"Yeah," Pella agreed in the face of Leilanna's obvious reluctance. "I don't see why you're complaining . . . I'd love a piggyback ride from Dare."

The Mage muttered something under her breath that Dare didn't catch, although from the way the dog girl's cheeks heated in obvious embarrassment he thought he could guess.

"Look, it's fine," he told Leilanna. "I used to give my bratty younger sister back rides all the time. They're fun."

"Bratty?" she said furiously. "Why is it just *me* you're always so insulting to?"

67

Because you're insulting to me, so tit for tat. Also because it's so easy to get a rise out of you.

With some help from the others they got Leilanna comfortably settled on his back, into the harness he'd rigged up that morning to carry her more easily. Unfortunately, easier was a relative term; the taller and more curvy dusk elf weighed close to twice what Zuri did.

And as any weightlifter could tell you, twice the weight was vastly more than twice as difficult. Thankfully with his enhanced body and the more lenient rules of carry weight on Collisa, he thought carrying her at a reasonably fast pace would be manageable over long distances.

Honestly, she didn't weigh too much more than Zuri and a pack full of loot combined.

They set off, Leilanna bouncing on his back as he ran at what for him was a relaxed jog but for most would be a fast run, Pella using Run Down as much as possible to keep up, as well as to reduce the stamina loss of carrying Zuri and all their packs.

Dare thought they'd be able to manage this until they reached a good leveling spot for their new companion. But even so he resolved to get the Mage a horse, ideally all of them horses, as soon as possible.

If he was being honest, he'd admit that carrying Leilanna wasn't the most unpleasant thing in the world. She was soft and felt nice, especially her thighs gripping his waist and her breasts pressed against his back. Although she would've felt nicer if she wasn't constantly complaining in his ear and trying to shift around for a better position, regularly throwing off his balance and tiring him out more than necessary.

He missed Zuri, and not just because she was lighter; she also knew how to be a good passenger, and was cuddly and pleasant company.

The trip got even less pleasant as he worked up a sweat, and Leilanna began screeching furiously about him getting it all over her. Not that he could do anything about that. He finally forced her to get down and run for a while, doing her best to match their pace. Zuri ran for a while as well to give Pella a break.

A few minutes later Leilanna practically begged him to carry her again. At which point *she* got her sweat all over *him* as she perspired heavily from even that brief exertion.

Actually, the only thing he could really complain about with that was that her womanly scent was a lot more noticeable, distractingly so. It didn't help that she smelled nice even while soaked in sweat. She even *felt* nice, clammy or no.

Too bad she hated his guts.

Over the next few hours they rotated between carrying and running, maintaining a pace that ground them all down steadily towards exhaustion. Dare was a bit frustrated to finally have to admit that he needed to call a break; running with a lot of weight was brutal, and he was afraid if he got to the point where he was stumbling from fatigue he'd trip and break an ankle.

Sure, Zuri could just heal him, but it would be a painful delay. Besides, Pella also seemed grateful for the rest; even with Run Down the extra weight was taking a heavy toll on her.

Finally, though, they reached a spawn point for level 16-18 monsters. Dare called a halt and, after they all collapsed for another few minutes of rest, picked out Leilanna's first target.

"There we go," he said, pointing. "Level 16 Juggernaut Beetle. Slow, no ranged attacks. The strengths it has to compensate for its weaknesses shouldn't be a problem for you. Let's see what you can do against it."

She glared at him suspiciously. "How the fuck do you know that?"

"Dare has the Adventurer's Eye," Pella said, tail wagging eagerly. "He uses it to help us level. It's amazing!"

"Like fuck he does," the dusk elf said, laughing. "Nobody gets that before 50."

"He's got a benefactor," Zuri said. "A mysterious deity."

"Who's also his lover," the dog girl added, grinning even wider. "He has wet dreams with her."

Leilanna laughed even harder. "Yeah, he's dreaming all right."

Dare glowered at her. "Kill the beetle," he growled. "If you run into trouble we'll step in."

She put a hand on her hip. "What exactly is the plan here? You all just stand around and watch me fight monsters, then once I'm out of mana I stand around and watch you the rest of the time?"

"I need to know the specifics of your abilities, including mana expenditure, so I can plan the best leveling rotation to get you the most experience every day." He pointed. "Kill it already . . . we're doing you a favor, stop wasting our time."

"I'll favor you with a fireball up the ass," the curvy elf muttered. But her hands whooshed into flame, and a few seconds later she threw a fireball at the target Juggernaut Beetle.

"Holy shit!" Dare said as her spell chunked off almost half of the monster's health. She was already casting, and as her enemy trundled towards her she released a second fireball, then finally a faster casting but lower damage and less mana efficient Wind Slash, finishing it off.

And it had been an enemy three levels above her.

It was obvious a mage was designed to do more damage than other classes, with the weaknesses of low defensive capability and having few options when an enemy reached them. And a limited mana pool, of course.

Still, watching Leilanna blast that monster, her spells flashy and hugely destructive and leaving her enemy charred in her wake, he had to admit that part of him regretted not choosing Mage himself.

Of course, it would've been a lot more of a pain in the ass when he was first starting out, with no survival abilities to keep him fed and clothed and to provide shelter. Not to mention he would've had a lot harder time solo leveling.

The grass was greener on the other side, he supposed. He liked being a Hunter, and he appreciated its strengths.

Besides, if it turned out he really wanted to be a Mage he could always switch classes at the cost of 10% of his total accumulated experience. Which, assuming his math was correct, would only bring him down two and a half levels.

Not bad. And better to do it now if he really wanted to do it, rather than waiting until he was high enough level that dropping a couple would mean weeks, months, or even years of farming, instead of days.

Although honestly if he really wanted to switch classes he'd pick a tank class, since his party didn't have one and could really use someone in that role. Maybe a Flanker like Linia, the catgirl he'd met in Jarn's Holdout.

"Well, human?" Leilanna said, looking smug. "Still think it's a waste of time leveling me up?"

"I never thought it was a waste of time," he replied. "I just wondered if it was worth the bother for *us*, specifically, since it seems like you hate our guts and don't want to be around us."

"Dare," Pella said reprovingly.

The dusk elf looked surprisingly hurt by his comment. "I don't hate you," she said, her attempt at anger more feeble than usual. Without another word she turned away and furiously began blasting the next nearest beetle.

Unfortunately, this one was Level 18. The level difference not only meant more health, but that a lower level enemy would do less damage against them. Something that thankfully was only the case for monsters and animals, not intelligent creatures.

Getting curb stomped by a higher level person you couldn't even try to defend yourself against would suck.

Leilanna squeaked when her fireball didn't even take a quarter of the monster's health, in her panic fumbling her next spell and taking longer with it. "Relax," Dare told her, bow out. He motioned to Pella.

The dog girl rushed forward and tackled the beetle, using Subdue. Which looked a bit ridiculous on a creature with six legs, but was still effective.

The Mage had got off a fireball just before Pella got to the monster and was now casting her next one. At that point Dare began to worry that fireballs would do splash or area of effect damage, hurting his lover.

Leilanna didn't seem worried about that, which could just mean she was a psycho. But Pella and Zuri didn't seem worried either. Come to think of it, when he shot arrows at targets the dog girl was holding some of them should've pierced through and hurt her, but none ever did.

Apparently single target attacks in this game were balanced around not hurting allies in melee range, even if that wouldn't be entirely realistic. Which was a relief.

It was possible that wouldn't be the case if the attack missed and hit the ally, but as long as it hit the enemy it would be fine. He hoped.

Sure enough, the Mage's fireball washed over the beetle and burned it badly, but Pella wasn't so much as singed by it. Looking a bit calmer now that she saw the threat neutralized, Leilanna cast one last fireball and finished the beetle off.

Dare clapped her on the back, making her jump. "Good job. Let's keep going and get the rest of the information I need. Some of it will involve doing odd or even counterproductive things, but it's all in the name of science."

"I've never heard of Science," Leilanna said, plump lip stuck out in a pout. "But he must be a poor god if he demands his people do stupid things in his name."

He laughed at the unintentional joke. "Science isn't a god, it's a process for understanding how the world around us works." He waved at the view around them of rolling plains, hills, and forests. "We observe the world. We make predictions about what will happen in specific instances. We test those predictions to see what happens. Then we test again, many times, to make sure that the results are accurate and repeatable. And then we look at those results to understand not only how it happened, but why. What deeper principle governs it."

"You're stupid," she said with a condescending sneer. "I already know why . . . because the gods will it."

Dare laughed again. "Funny, being called stupid by the person who isn't even interested in trying to figure out why things happen the way they do. I thought Mages had a reputation as scholars."

The dusk elf sucked in a sharp breath. "Throw your barbs, human! I grow more resistant to them every day!"

If so he'd seen little evidence of it. He changed the subject. "By the way, what sort of weapon can you use in case of emergencies? It may suck, but when you're out of mana you may be reduced to bashing enemies with a staff or stabbing them with a dagger, just to keep the experience flowing in. Although once you get higher level you'll be able to join our party for shared experience."

"What?" She laughed incredulously, looking at the other two women. "He says the most ludicrous things . . . is he serious? He's talking like he thinks I can catch up to you guys in no time at all." She waved at Pella. "It would take me *years* to reach that level, maybe decades even. Elder Nirol's 83 and only Level 20, and while he might not be really trying that should say something."

Leilanna's shoulders slumped, as if she was just hearing what she was saying. "Besides, even when I do reach your level, you'll have risen even higher. I'll never catch up."

Zuri smiled wide, revealing her delicate pointy teeth. "What if I told you me and Dare were under Level 10 a few months ago, and thanks to him we've already reached 25?"

"I'd say you're a fucking liar," she said flatly. Then she hesitated. "Although you're both much higher level than most people our age would be. Normally the only way that would be possible is if you'd been started on a strict leveling regimen as soon as you turned 12 years old and got your class. Usually as part of some elite military or guard program or as the scion of a noble house."

Her lip curled. "But no offense, you two don't look very noble, and you definitely don't look like you've had that sort of discipline and professionalism ingrained in you."

Dare knew from experience that the phrase "no offense" could usually be ignored, or even taken to mean the opposite. But their new companion's usage seemed particularly intended to be offensive.

Or maybe that was just thanks to her abrasive personality.

"Don't believe us if you want," he said. "It won't take long to prove our words." He motioned sternly at the Juggernaut Beetle spawn point. "Now, go kill that Level 16 over there. But this time only use Wind Slash so I can observe your mana usage."

"How the hell can you observe-" the Mage broke off abruptly, throwing her hands in the air. "You know what, whatever. I'll just shut up and do it."

But in spite of her sour tone there was the faintest hint of hope in her words.

Chapter Five
Routine

Dare compared the damage done to the Juggernaut Beetle by Leilanna's Ring of Fire spell to the cast time and mana cost, then did some quick calculations.

The disgusting inefficiency of the spell in cast time and mana cost, added to the low damage, wasn't promising. Especially since it was a point blank area of effect, meaning she'd have to be standing in the middle of her enemies, and it did decreasing damage with range from the center until it petered out at 10 yards.

The spell became comparable to a fireball in its damage to mana cost ratio if it hit three enemies standing right next to her. Which theoretically meant that if they could find a way to have it hit more it might be viable.

Unfortunately, he had no idea how they'd manage that without getting themselves killed, even with Leilanna so much lower level than them. Or more likely, getting her killed.

If he wanted to get cute he could dig a hole and kite an entire spawn point's worth of monsters to it, then use his new Pounce ability to jump over the hole to one of his friends and see if the mob of monsters would follow him and fall in. Or if they only came up to the edge of the hole, if Leilanna could use her Gale spell, which blew targets in a cone in front of her and slowed, stopped, or pushed them back.

It would be kind of funny to get thirty or forty monsters crammed in a pit and have her cast Ring of Fire over and over until she killed them all, giving her a huge experience bump in a ridiculously short time with insane mana efficiency.

Unfortunately, the system that governed Collisa didn't allow that sort of cheesing. He'd already proven for himself that you couldn't, for example, stand up on a cliff and shoot down at melee enemies that were helpless to get up to you. Something would happen to prevent it, and usually not to your benefit as a reward for trying to get clever.

If they had a sturdy enough tank that was about Pella's level, they could probably have the tank gather up a spawn point's monsters and then just sit there while they clumped up and wailed on him, soaking up not only their attacks but also Leilanna's spells when she killed the monsters.

But there was no guarantee the monsters wouldn't immediately turn on her the moment she began doing damage to them, killing her before she could finish them off. And that was just one of the problems with the plan.

So yeah, for now Ring of Fire would stay in the back pocket until they found a use for it.

"Well?" the Mage demanded as she finished looting the beetle. "What wise insights did you gain from my tremendous waste of mana, oh glorious leader?"

"Good job," Dare told her absently. "I think I've got all the information I need. Aside from getting back to you using weapons to damage enemies when you run out of mana."

"I haven't increased my proficiency with daggers at all," she protested. "I don't even *have* one. And I don't get access to staffs, spears, and wands until Level 20."

That would explain why she'd been so unenthusiastic about the option. Aside from the fact that it would require her to get right up close to a monster and stab it, trusting to her companions to keep it from going after her.

Dare sighed. "I'll craft you one of my shitty survival ones, and when we visit Polan's Folly to sell loot we'll find you a dagger for every few levels up to 20, then spears up to our level. We need to get better gear for ourselves anyway." He paused. "At least, spears unless staffs give some sort of bonus to casting?"

"Actually they do," Leilanna said. "Based on quality of the staff, the focus runes on them reduce cast time at the tradeoff of lower damage and mana cost. Most mages agree it's worth it."

"Absolutely," Dare agreed; he'd be the first to say speed was one of the most important considerations in most circumstances. "Do you make your own staff, like in a lot of . . ." He trailed off, cheeks flushing as he realized he'd been about to reference games and stories from Earth.

"Of course," she said with a huff. "We need to purchase a staff, of course, the higher quality the better, and then we carve runes. It can be a very laborious process, although most Mages only bother with spells they intend to use often."

Interesting. "I'm guessing that would be Fireball and Gale for you, right?"

"My defensive spell?" The Mage nodded thoughtfully. "Yeah, that probably would be a good one to have on hand in an emergency. And Manipulate Breeze of course." At his blank look she sighed. "It allows me to use wind to pick up and move things at a distance."

"Like Telekinesis?" he asked, brightening. "That's badass."

"No, not *at all* like Telekinesis!" she snapped. "That's an entirely different class, and they use the mind. Manipulate Breeze is wind magic that allows us to move things at a distance, and while it's cheap in mana it can only lift a certain amount of weight, up to 20 pounds depending on a mage's level and strength. Also it requires a tremendous amount of skill and concentration, which is why focus runes on a staff help so much."

That was still amazing. "Can you show me?"

"Yeah, show us!" Pella said, clapping her hands. Zuri nodded eagerly.

Leilanna sighed, but a small, pleased smile toyed at the edges of her plump lips. "Fine." Her hand began glowing storm cloud gray, and she held it out. A rock twenty feet away glowed gray as well and began moving in slow, jerky movements.

"That's amazing!" Zuri said, grinning.

"It has its uses," the Mage agreed, looking satisfied. Then her face tightened as if with remembered pain. "It saved my life, once."

A slightly uncomfortable silence fell, and Pella wrapped a supportive arm around the curvy elf.

Dare cleared his throat awkwardly. "So do other spellcasters have items that do that sort of thing for them? Zuri hasn't found anything like that so far."

Leilanna shrugged. "A few, I guess. I mostly studied my own class and a few other elemental magic variant classes with similar spells. Some of them use staffs too."

"Speaking of elemental magic classes," he said, "if Mages use fire and air then are there other classes that use earth and water?"

The dusk elf sneered at him. "You claim to be a genius, but you don't even know basic facts about the most common magic class?"

"Nope," Dare replied simply, refusing to rise to the bait.

She huffed. "Well Mages can potentially use any of the four elements, it just depends on what one we choose to attune ourselves to. I chose fire as my major attunement, with a minor attunement to air."

At their blank looks the curvy Mage sighed. "Think of it like a wheel, with the four elements on each of the four sides. Air and earth are opposite each other, and water and fire are opposite as well. You can't choose a minor attunement element opposite to your major attuncement, so since fire has air and earth on either side, someone who chooses fire for their major attunement could choose air or earth as their minor attunement. And same with the other elements. I chose air to go with my fire since it seems more useful, and at later levels there are combo spells where air increases the power of fire spells."

"So once you choose your attunements you only get spells for those elements?" Zuri asked.

Leilanna nodded. "You choose your major attunement right away, then at Level 10 can choose your minor attunement."

Pella glanced over at the Juggernaut Beetles in their spawn point, dancing slightly in place and looking bored. "This is interesting and all, but shouldn't we keep going? I thought we were trying to get Leilanna caught up to us."

"Right." Dare nodded to his three companions, getting down to business. "I've thought it over, and the best way for us to level up from here is to split up."

He motioned to Leilanna and Pella. "Pella, you're great at helping people level up. If you're willing to put off getting experience for a bit longer and go with Leilanna, you can give her a hand fighting higher level enemies, 15-17. I'll help you find enough spawn points to last her for a full day of leveling. If mana becomes an issue for her, remember that if she does 30% of the damage she'll get 40% of the experience, which will still be good enough and help the damage dealing go faster."

"I think that would be fun," the dog girl said, tail wagging. Then she glanced at the dusk elf and smiled mischievously. "After she asks me nicely and says "please", of course."

Leilanna predictably exploded, although at Dare and not at Pella. "Why should I have to do that? I'm leveling up because *you* want me to in the first place!"

Dare frowned. "Are you saying you don't want to level?" Her obstinate silence was answer enough. "Also you were the one who wanted to be my sworn sword. Hard to protect me when you're 12 levels lower than me."

"Okay fine!" She turned to Pella and spoke through gritted teeth in a barely civil tone. "Would you help me level up quickly, *please?*"

The dog girl's tail wagged harder, and she spontaneously gave the curvy elf a hug. "Of course! This'll be so much fun!"

"Speaking of fun," Dare cut in, "you'll need to switch to sleeping four hours at a time."

Leilanna stared at him, aghast. "Why? What did I do that you want to punish me like that? I asked nicely and said please, and I've been doing all the weird and nonsensical tests you tell me to do for your Science, and-"

Zuri cut in calmly. "It's not a punishment. Dare's trying to maximize your leveling speed, and that's dependent on mana unless you want to rely on using your dagger to kill monsters."

"How the hell does sleeping for four hours a night help me level?" the dusk elf snapped, speaking over the little goblin. "With passive mana regen I'd only get a couple dozen more spells anyway with that extra time."

"You'd know if you let me keep talking," Zuri said, looking irritated. "Dare discovered that your mana pool completely fills after four hours of sleep. If you sleep four hours, wake up and empty your mana pool killing monsters, then sleep again, you'll be able to level up a lot faster."

She put her hands on her hips. "And he's thought of other ways to maximize the experience spellcasters can gain in a day, with someone helping them."

"Oh." Leilanna's face turned a darker gray in obvious embarrassment. "Well of course I knew that about your mana pool. Elves are the preeminent magic users on Collisa, after all." She pointed accusingly at Dare. "I just thought *you* didn't know that and were being mean!"

Dare held back a derisive snort. "If you guys want to stay around here for the next week or so after I've scouted out all the spawn points, me and Zuri will go a bit farther out to find Level 24-27 monsters. We'll meet back here every night to see how it went, or if there's a problem we can find each other."

Everyone seemed to agree with that plan, so they set up a permanent camp for the next week or so, where they could keep their loot and return to every night.

At the same time Dare also made Leilanna a stone knife using his crafting ability. He hadn't been gaining proficiency in it since near the beginning of his time on Collisa, so he couldn't make a very high level one. And it was complete shit and would probably break after a few uses, so he made several spares just in case to make sure she had enough for the day.

Too bad he'd sold all their lower level daggers once they no longer needed them. But he hadn't expected a circumstance like this.

Leilanna, predictably, absolutely loathed the crude weapons. "I'd rather punch the things," she spat, glaring down at the ugly stone blade with its leather-wrapped handle.

"That's an option, but it'll go slower," Dare told her. "Up to you." He motioned to Pella. "Come on, let's go scout the spawn points. I'll give you my map and we can jot down all the information for them."

80

Speaking of which, he needed to get more maps for the others. He'd been going on the assumption they wouldn't need them since they were all together, but better to have them for situations like this. Or emergencies.

Translation stones too, for that matter.

He took off, happy to let loose in a sprint, and his dog girl lover kept up with him easily, laughing delightedly as the wind whipped past them. He wished they could run side by side, but unfortunately with Run Down she had to stay behind him, never to catch up.

Unless she wanted to.

They were barely out of view of the camp when Dare abruptly found himself on the ground, helpless for 1 second in the Tackle effect, while his beautiful golden-haired lover stood over him, grinning playfully.

"Been wanting to try that out, huh?" he teased.

She giggled. "Mostly I just wanted to get your attention." Smiling coyly, she pushed her leather leggings and pants down around her knees, leaving her in her silky green panties. She was already wet, the cloth clinging to her delicate folds.

Dare stared, cock stirring eagerly. "You've got it," he said.

"Good." Pella dropped to her hands and knees, presenting her perfect round ass to him, fluffy tail wagging. She looked over her shoulder at him with a pout. "I won't get to spend much time with you at all for a while, so you need to make it up to me."

Smiling coyly again, she skinned down her panties to reveal her plump petals, glistening with her dew. "I think you know exactly how."

He sure did. Freeing his rock hard cock, he positioned himself behind her and in one smooth motion plunged into her velvety soft depths.

The dog girl squealed and pushed back against him, tail thumping furiously as her warm walls lovingly caressed his length. "Oh Goddess of Fertility, every time. You stretch me out so good."

Dare began to move in her with long, slow thrusts, his head

kissing her cervix every time, making her whine with pleasure. Her nectar, always copious, flowed freely around him, squelching with every thrust.

Finally, after only a few minutes, he felt her clench down on him and squirt all over his leather leggings. "Yeeesssss," she moaned as her climax took her. Her arms gave out and she buried her face in the grass, desperately lifting her ass higher to compensate as he continued to thrust down into her.

The excitement of mounting his dog girl lover out in the open, with nature all around, was too much, and her orgasm pushed him over the edge. Dare grabbed her hips and gave one last, powerful thrust, mashing himself against her deepest depths, and with a grunt released inside her in shuddering pulses of pleasure.

He was ready to keep going, and was almost disappointed when as soon as Pella came down from her peak she squirmed away from him. He tried to catch her hips and pull her back, but she giggled and playfully slapped at his hands.

"That's enough for now," she said, sounding a bit regretful. "The others are waiting for us." She pushed gracefully to her feet, his seed spilling out to run down her thighs, and pulled her various layers of clothing back into place.

Although first she cracked one of Zuri's scrolls and, as her hands began glowing, pressed them to her belly.

Prevent Conception; glad she was staying on top of it, because in the moment he'd almost forgotten. Although realistically they made love often enough that Zuri cast it on them pretty much every day, so it would've been fine if they missed this one.

Dare laced up his pants, ruefully aware of his lover's arousal beading the leather, then wrapped her in a tight hug. "I love you," he said.

She hugged him back, face buried in his neck. "I love you too. Even though we'll see each other every night, I'll still miss you."

He grinned at her as he stepped back. "I'll make it up to you as many times as you like."

"I'll hold you to that." Laughing, Pella took off to continue their scouting task.

About an hour later they returned to the camp. Dare was pleased to find that the time hadn't been wasted; Zuri had been showing Leilanna the techniques they'd developed for maximizing experience gains and minimizing mana usage. The Mage looked surprisingly enthusiastic about the prospect, eager to get started.

Which meant it was time for him and Zuri to head off and get back to their own leveling.

He walked over to Pella and pulled her into a tight hug, kissing her firmly. "You be safe, and take good care of Leilanna," he told her, giving her ass a playful squeeze. "I'll miss you."

She giggled and rubbed against him affectionately. And a little provocatively. "I'll miss you too," she murmured, pouting. "But don't worry, I'll make it a race and keep Leilanna on task, so we can start leveling together again soon."

She turned and mock glared at Zuri. "And you better not have too much fun with him while I'm stuck babysitting!"

"Hey, I'm the same age he is!" Leilanna protested.

Technically that wasn't true, since he'd been 27 when he died on Earth. Around the same age as Pella, actually.

Dare turned to the Mage solemnly. "And you be safe, too. I expect to see real progress when we get back tonight."

"Ascendant Ancients, you're a patronizing ass," she muttered. "Can we go, Pella?"

"Yep!" Pella started off at a jog even Leilanna would have no trouble keeping up with. "Let's goooo!"

The curvy elf hurried to catch up.

Once they were out of sight Zuri came and wrapped her arms around him. "So it's back to the two of us again," she said, yellow eyes sparkling.

Dare arched an eyebrow. "You won't miss Pella holding monsters down while we kill them?"

She giggled. "Of course I will. But since Leilanna joined us I haven't been able to do this whenever I want." She boldly buried her face in his crotch, inhaling deeply. Then she eagerly untied his laces and freed his cock, taking him into her mouth.

He groaned at the pleasurable sensation. "Okay yeah, this is always fun."

His goblin lover pulled back enough to look up at him, narrow eyebrow arched. "Speaking of fun, you taste like Pella." She smirked. "She had the same idea I did as soon as she got you by yourself mapping spawn points, didn't she?"

Dare laughed. "Caught us."

"Mmm, I sure did." She took him into her mouth again, effortlessly pushing her head down his shaft until he was balls deep in her throat. Not wasting any time, she began humming and bobbing up and down on his cock, tongue working furiously.

"Holy shit," he moaned, grabbing her head. "I'm not going to last long if you go at it that hard."

Zuri's contented noises grew louder. She reached one hand up to begin stroking his shaft when it wasn't buried in her throat, and began fondling his balls with the other.

After a few minutes of enjoying her expert deep throating Dare grabbed her head tighter and began thrusting his hips, gently fucking her tight esophagus. His little lover made a pleased sound and looked up at him adoringly, eyes watering as she furiously swallowed through her gag reflex.

She grabbed his ass and pulled him impatiently, an unspoken signal for him to speed up. He thrust faster, watching the bulge of his massive cock moving up and down her slender throat as she gagged and coughed even more violently. Tears streamed down her face and saliva and mucus streamed from her mouth, but when he tried to pull back she held on furiously.

The pleasure was indescribable, and he grit his teeth and yanked her head down until her pointy little nose was buried in his pubic hair. She eagerly squeezed his balls, and with a groan he emptied them down her slender throat until they were completely drained.

Zuri swallowed with happy sounds of enjoyment, but as soon as he was done she gratefully pulled her head free with a gasping breath. Hacking and coughing, she spit a glob of mucus off to one side and wiped tears from her flushed cheeks, all the while beaming at him with watering eyes.

"Did you like that?" she asked, voice husky.

"That was incredible," he said, pulling her into his arms. Then he paused guiltily. "Although it seemed like it might've been a bit much."

His goblin lover beamed at him with that same loving expression. "That's for me to decide, my mate. And I say it was perfect." Suddenly businesslike, she laced up his pants again, then wrapped her arms around his neck and buried her head in his shoulder. "Come on, let's go hunt some monsters. Just the two of us again for a while."

Dare picked her up and turned south, starting off at his familiar, and welcome, usual ground-eating run. "And the four of us once Leilanna's high enough level."

"I can't wait," she murmured contentedly. "I love Pella so much, and I think we might eventually be able to get through to Leilanna." She lifted her eyes and looked at him tenderly. "And I love you, my mate."

"I love you too." He kissed her forehead, eyes on the terrain ahead so he didn't trip. "I love Pella and I'll love all the women who join our harem. Love you all equally. But you'll always be my first."

"And the mother of your firstborn?" Zuri said, half statement, half question.

Dare chuckled. "When we get there."

She buried her face in his chest again, but not before he caught a hint of a troubled expression. "Soon, I hope," she mumbled, barely loud enough for him to hear.

It seemed like she really wanted his babies, which he could admit was a nice feeling. A really nice one. He hugged her tighter. "Well, the faster we level up and farm gold, the sooner we'll be able to afford a proper home and can start thinking about what the future will look like."

His goblin lover didn't answer, just hugged him tighter.

* * * * *

The day's hunting went well.

Sure, it was harder without Pella there to control adds and keep monsters from reaching them. More dangerous, too, so they had to go back to cautious pulls, and walk away from spawn points with monsters that would bring too many adds or had unfavorable abilities.

They even dropped down to fighting lower level monsters, something they hadn't done often since the dog girl Tracker joined them.

Dare really needed to get a new bow soon.

All in all they would've made faster progress with Pella, but it was balanced somewhat by the fact that they were splitting experience two ways. And it was nice to spend some quality time with Zuri again.

He'd have to try to get some time like this with Pella, too. His beautiful golden-haired lover had been so patient and selfless in helping them level, she deserved some special attention.

When they returned to camp that evening near sundown, Dare was pleasantly surprised to see that Leilanna had gained a level. "That was quick," he said. "Congratulations."

The curvy Mage flushed slightly. "I was close to a level anyway. But I'll admit I got experience much faster than I expected. Faster than I ever have before." She patted Pella's knee. "It certainly helped to have Pella there to make things much safer and easier."

"Just remember you're only sleeping four hours tonight," he told her as he got started making dinner. "You and Pella will set out at first light again to empty your mana pool, then you can catch up on sleep and fight monsters the rest of the day."

"It'll help to run and exercise as much as possible, to make sure you're tired enough to get four hours the second time," Zuri added.

Leilanna scowled. "This is going to suck so much. Only you would think up such a torturous way to efficiently gain experience, human."

"You'll get used to it," Pella assured her. "And if it makes you feel better, I'm going to need to hold to the same schedule for the best results. But I don't mind, really."

"I do," the dusk elf muttered. "I'm going to get huge bags under my eyes and my skin will get all pallid and splotchy."

Dare chuckled. "Don't worry, none of us will mind. Besides, with your elvish beauty I doubt you could ever be anything less than stunning."

Predictably, she bridled at that. "As if I care what *you* think, human!" she snapped. "Will you let me go back to sleeping normally when I catch up to you?"

"Much sooner than that, probably," he said. "When you're within 5 levels of us we can invite you to the party." His smile widened as he thought of it. "It's going to be amazing once you're with us. We'll be able to hunt monsters so fast, and more easily take on party rated monsters and maybe even dungeons."

Zuri nodded eagerly. "All we need is to get Linia to join us so we have a tank!" She giggled. "And another lover for our harem."

Leilanna made a disgusted noise. "I hope you're not including *me* in that," she snapped at Dare, as always her fury turned on him. "Never in your wildest dreams, human."

He hastily held up his hands. "I'm not assuming anything. You're a friend and a companion, and anything more would be up to you."

"So you *would* like me to join your harem!" she said, leaping out of her collapsible chair and pointing at him accusingly.

Dare sighed. "Honestly, if it puts you at ease, with your attitude it's not seeming like the most appealing prospect."

"Insult after insult!" the dusk elf raged, fists clenched at her sides. "I'll have you know I'd be an *incredible* lover and an excellent addition to any harem!" She paused, seeming to realize what she'd just said, and her cheeks flushed a darker gray. "Except yours, of course, which would be the worst, just like you!"

He stood stiffly. "Well if my company offends you so much, I'll give you a break while I go set snares and Forage. Zuri, can you keep an eye on the food?"

"Can I add more honey to the steaks?" she asked eagerly.

Dare couldn't help but chuckle in spite of his irritation at Leilanna. "Your own, sure. I've already put plenty on the rest of ours." He patted his goblin lover's head. "You know you're going to get cavities if you eat too much sugar, right?"

They all stared at him blankly. "We're going to get holes?" the dusk elf asked suspiciously. "Is that some sort of lewd joke?"

"Everything goes to lewd with you, huh," he said, smirking. "Back where I'm from we'd call that accusing others of what you yourself are guilty of. Or we'd say the lady doth protest too much."

She flushed. "Fuck you."

"Seriously though, what are cavities?" Pella asked.

"They're holes in your teeth from not taking good care of them, which rot from within and grow until you have a professional drill out the rot and fill it in with something, or they eventually kill the tooth, or you get your root drilled out."

Speaking of which, he hadn't considered the health of his teeth since coming here; he hoped Collisa had something like dentists. Ideally of the spellcaster variety that could magic away the discomfort and general awfulness of anything to do with bad teeth.

Or not.

His companions' expressions had gone from confusion to horror. "Good gods, is that some sort of Disease or Curse?" Pella asked. "Maybe a parasitic attack?"

"Seriously," Leilanna said. "What sort of nightmarish hardships did you suffer in your home?"

Zuri ran a nervous finger over her pointy little teeth. "They rot from *inside*?" she asked. "And someone takes a *drill* to them? What sort of barbaric place did you live in?"

Dare felt like he was inadvertently maligning the noble and important profession of dentistry. "They have ways to numb the pain, and they do us a service," he said, quickly getting back to the point. "Hold on a second, are you saying people don't have problems with their teeth here?"

The girls exchanged cautious glances, still shaken by what had to sound to them like a horror story. "Sometimes people lose teeth to an accident or combat," Pella said slowly.

"A healing class can sometimes put them back in," Zuri added. "I've never heard anything like you describe, unless it's a more general ailment that affects all the bones of a body."

No cavities or other similar problems on Collisa. And as he'd learned from Ellui back in Lone Ox, no STDs either.

This world was fucking awesome!

"Well that just made my day," Dare said. "I'm going to go set those snares now." He headed out whistling cheerfully.

"That's the man at the center of your harem," Leilanna said flatly as he left the circle of firelight.

"I know, isn't he amazing?" Pella asked.

"He's got an enormous cock, too," Zuri added cheerfully. "Have we told you that yet?"

The dusk elf made a strangled noise. "What the hell, Zuri? I don't want to hear about that!"

Dare found himself pausing among the trees to listen. He didn't like to spy, but this was all too interesting to just walk away from.

"You know," Pella said happily. "It's funny to watch you playing games with Dare."

Leilanna sounded angry and defensive when she answered. "What games?"

The dog girl giggled naughtily. "You pretend you don't like him and don't want to be around him, but I can tell you really think differently. When me and Zuri made too much noise while making love to him last night I could smell your arousal all the way from your tent. And the same when he carried you this morning."

Dare blinked. Wait, what?

There was a frosty silence before the dusk elf answered in tones of barely restrained wrath. "You must be mistaken. I didn't hear any of the very loud and obscene noises you made while screwing like bunny girls, and even if I had I'd be disgusted by them, not aroused."

Pella laughed. "You can say what you want, but I know what I'm smelling. And I don't blame you, since you have eyes so obviously you've seen Dare's sexy face and body. Even by elvish standards he's a catch."

"And you've seen for yourself how kind he is," Zuri added. "Not to mention clever and powerful and favored by an actual goddess."

"I've seen nothing of the sort," Leilanna growled.

The dog girl snickered. "Oooh, you say that but just talking about this has got you all hot and bothered, hasn't it?" Her voice turned teasing. "By the way, elvish arousal is very tantalizing. I'm dying to get a lick of it."

He heard the rattle of a collapsible chair falling over, probably as the dusk elf stood. "You're as degenerate as your lover, dog girl," she snapped. Moments later he saw her storm away from the camp. "And I did *not* get turned on while he was carrying me!" she furiously shouted over her shoulder.

After half a minute of listening to her crashing through the trees, Pella called out cheerfully. "You can stop hiding now, Dare."

Dare gave a guilty start and stepped into view, smiling sheepishly. "Sorry, didn't mean to spy on you."

The dog girl grinned at him, tail wagging. "It's okay. If Leilanna was as mean to me as she is to you, I'd avoid her too. Although I think she doesn't really mean most of the things she says."

He cleared his throat. "She did have one good point. We should try to be more considerate in our lovemaking, and not disturb her with loud noises."

Pella's ears drooped. "I'm trying," she said sheepishly. "But it's so hard when you do all those wonderful things to me."

Dare coughed, feeling his face flush. "Also, don't call attention to anything she might be feeling when I'm carrying her. It's embarrassing for both of us and just makes the experience even more difficult."

"But it should be enjoyable!" his dog girl lover protested. "I'd *love* to have you carry me. And I weigh less than her!"

"That's fine, we can do that sometime. But Leilanna's obviously not romantically interested in me, and teasing her about it just makes it harder for her to fit in."

Pella gave him a weird look. "Didn't you just hear me tell you about her arousal?"

He had, unfortunately. "She can be aroused while still hating my guts and wanting nothing to do with me. The body's weird like that. Try to be more accommodating when she's obviously having such a hard time."

"I'm not sure why we should be," Zuri cut in. "I like Leilanna and I think we could be friends, but I hate how she talks to you. You're a great man, clever and knowledgeable and powerful, and on top of all that you saved her life. But even so she has nothing but unkind words."

Dare shook his head. "Well, maybe by offering her the companionship of fighting alongside one another we can turn her from a bitch into a friend." He paused sheepishly. "Sorry, Pella, habit from my old home."

Pella grinned. "It's fine, since she should be proud to be compared to a dog girl." She tapped her full lips thoughtfully. "She actually reminds me a bit of my master's daughter Ama when I first met her. Pampered and lonely, desperate for a friend. And you saw what a sweetheart Ama turned out to be."

"I did," he agreed, feeling a brief surge of guilt for how he'd scared the poor girl by threatening her brother. It had been a bluff to get the family on Pella's side, but his acting had been convincing and he'd genuinely frightened Amalisa.

Pella had assured him that she'd cleared things up with the young noblewoman as the two parted, but he still wished he could personally ask for her forgiveness and find a way to make it up to her.

Although given the circumstances, going back to the Kinnran estate anytime soon probably wasn't a good idea.

Dare sighed. "Pella, could you go check and make sure she didn't run right into a wolf's jaws? I still need to go set those snares." As she nodded and chased off after the dusk elf he made his way back into the woods as well.

Hopefully his relationship with Leilanna would get less rocky the longer they spent together. Especially when they were finally able to fight side by side and forge bonds in combat.

He had a feeling he'd have to rely on time to fix things, since everything he said and did just seemed to make their new companion dislike him even more.

Chapter Six
Demon Eyes

Polan's Folly wasn't the largest town Dare had visited.

In fact, it was probably smaller than Driftwain, the first town he'd seen on Collisa, which had been a backwater. But in spite of its size it offered a lot more possibilities than Driftwain had, since it was in the rugged frontier region of Bastion and so many of its services catered to hunters, trappers, settlers, and above all adventurers.

Unsurprisingly, it also had far more quests available than most towns, everything from fetch quests to messages and deliveries to monster hunting, animal regulation, and even acting as an ambassador to an encroaching orc tribe.

Although that last one was higher level than them, and also not the sort of thing Dare wanted to just blindly stumble into.

It had been two days since they'd split up, and Pella and Leilanna were still back near the camp leveling as fast as they could. But since their loot was stacking up to the point where they needed to either sell or cache it, Dare had suggested to Zuri that they take a trip to town.

Besides, it would give them a chance to buy Leilanna a proper dagger and all of them better gear.

So here they were, dragging loaded sleds once again. These ones he intended to sell rather than break down, since they were easy to make and slightly increased the value of the component materials.

The loot sold for a surprising amount. Apparently Bastion's governor, in his determination to encourage adventurers and those who supported them in whatever way possible, levied almost zero taxes for trade. That meant traders came in from the other regions and even other kingdoms, drawn by good rates and the plentiful loot being brought in by active adventurers, and they all competed for the best price.

Ironically, it also not only caused a boom in prosperity for the region but likely provided even more taxes through sheer volume. And it certainly made for a happy populace.

Even with aggressive haggling, though, they didn't make anywhere near enough to buy Leilanna a horse. Especially since there were other purchases to make.

In the interests of making sure the Mage got the best possible experience over time, Dare sprung for a Level 15 Journeyman quality dagger. That should see her most of the way to 20, and they could discuss getting her an upgrade the next time they came into town to trade.

"It's a good dagger," Dare allowed as he handed it back to the vendor. "But it's mostly a matter of convenience for me, not necessity."

"I'm sure we can settle on a reasonable amount," the woman said. She seemed eager to make a trade, perhaps because she'd seen him eyeing a couple of Level 26 Good quality spears for him and Zuri to replace their current ones.

Or maybe because she'd been surreptitiously ogling him ever since he approached her stall.

"I'll tell you what," he said, offering her his best smile and noting how her cheeks flushed. "I think you've noticed that I've had my eye on those spears. If you want to buy our old ones, what say I offer you 15 gold for the whole deal and we shake?"

That was one or two gold less than he thought they were worth, a good starting place to begin haggling, but to his surprise she didn't hesitate to offer her hand. "Deal."

Not wanting to miss the opportunity dwelling on his good luck, Dare took her hand and shook firmly. It was warm and slightly clammy, and she held on for a few seconds longer than was strictly necessary.

"I'll tell you what," she said as he counted out the payment and Zuri stowed their new weapons. She was coyly biting her lip, blushing even harder. "I, um, think I might have something in back you'd be interested in, if you want to come take a look. It should only take a few minutes."

That seemed suspiciously like a come-on, and he gave the woman a closer look. She was older, maybe mid-30s, plump and somewhat on the plain side but with pleasant, honest features.

It wouldn't be the first time he'd gotten an invitation to fool around from a woman on Collisa. He could thank the body his benefactor had given him for that. And maybe, in some small part, his own charm.

But mostly his body.

"Maybe next time," he told the vendor with another smile as he handed over the coins and concluded the trade. "I've got a lot of stuff to take care of here, and people waiting for me back at our base camp." He winked. "But I might be more in the mood to browse special wares next time I pass through."

"Okay," she said, looking a bit disappointed. "Next time, then."

Next stop was the bowyer. Dare had been pleasantly surprised at the weapons vendor to find that she had a wide variety of weapons in most levels and with a range of quality up to Journeyman with a few Exceptional pieces. He was hoping to find the same with other vendors.

His hope wasn't in vain, and he found a Good quality Level 25 recurve bow that the vendor was willing to swap straight up for his Exceptional short bow. It was a fair trade since recurves were the most expensive type of bow, with the best overall stats.

Dare was a bit sad to part with the bow that had served him so well, but the replacement would be a huge boost in damage. Besides, given how cheap he'd gotten the short bow since he'd needed to repair it himself, he actually made a profit on the trade in.

He bought a few dozen higher quality arrows as well, and briefly browsed the Level 20 staffs the vendor had on offer. There was an Exceptional quality one that gave small bonuses to intellect and constitution that would be perfect for Leilanna, but given the price he decided to wait until she was closer to reaching that level before making a choice one way or another.

After a bit of browsing he bought a few luxury items for the girls, things that might make their stay in camp more comfortable. Then they left the market behind.

Given the high number of quests on offer Dare went around and collected them all. Most of them were basically rewards for doing what he'd been planning to do anyway, and many of them would be perfect for Leilanna at her level if she wanted to come into town at some point.

It would mean a lot of running around the surrounding area if they wanted to complete every quest, but since he planned to be in this area for a while leveling up anyway that was fine.

Before they headed back to camp, Zuri insisted on treating him to dinner with her share of the earnings. Although her own "dinner" mostly seemed to consist of desserts. Which she'd obviously been looking forward to ever since he'd suggested they make a run into town.

Dare didn't comment on it since it was a special occasion. Also he'd noticed his goblin lover had seemed a bit worried about something for a while now, and he was happy for anything that would lift her spirits.

Leaving Polan's Folly behind, he was pleasantly surprised to see groups of adventurers returning from fighting monsters. They were all in their 10s, and some looked battered from the encounters they'd had that day, their hit points low and only slowly regenerating. Especially the ones with bleed effects, which most serious wounds had.

Zuri healed a few who needed it most, to the sincere gratitude of the adventurers. Tempered a bit for some by the fact that it was a goblin helping them. Dare didn't linger with those jerks, but for the more polite groups he offered information on the monsters around their level that he and Zuri had passed along the road on the way to town.

The young men and women seemed absurdly grateful for the advice, no surprise since leveling without Adventurer's Eye could be terrifying. None asked him how he'd learned his information, maybe assuming he had a monster compendium or simply too eager to have some concrete facts to go on for further monster hunting.

A few of the groups invited him and Zuri back into town to share some drinks, and more than a few of the women gave Dare bedroom eyes and hinted they'd be interested in sharing more. But he politely refused them all, insisting he and Zuri needed to get back to camp and taking a raincheck.

He wasn't sure whether he regretted or was grateful for declining the offers a half hour or so later.

To save time they'd cut straight from town to where Pella and Leilanna were leveling, leaving the road behind and circling around spawn points. It was a safe enough choice, given the level of the enemies in the areas they were passing through, and it allowed him to check out more monster spawn points and make more notes on his map and in his logbook.

At least until they cut through a forest; Dare's perception circle barely had time to warn him that he was running directly towards an intelligent creature in the clearing ahead before he found himself paralyzed.

The next thing he knew he was crashing to the ground mid-stride, at a fast enough speed to injure himself and unable to do anything to break his fall. Even worse he couldn't shelter Zuri, either, and only his arms wrapped protectively around her offered some protection as they went tumbling and crashing through the underbrush.

She was ripped from his embrace with a squeak of dismay, and seconds later he grunted as he slammed into a log at the edge of the clearing, stopping his roll.

He ended up facing his attacker, eyes traveling blearily up a scantily-clad body to finally meet two eyes that glowed with the sullen light of flames.

* * * * *

The woman in front of him was definitely not human. Or any other species he'd met, for that matter. In fact, going by his knowledge of games, and basic common sense, he was 100% sure she was a demon.

Her skin was the mottled orange and red of livid flames, a jarring color, while her hair was jet black with highlights of the same pale orange. For some reason the combination sent warning bells ringing in his head, like the coloring of a poisonous animal.

And yet her curves were so perfect that she seemed like seduction incarnate; he found himself becoming aroused in spite of the dangerous situation he and Zuri were in.

The demon had small horns curled closely around her head, and small, delicate fangs protruding past her lower lip, as well as a whiplike tail with a razor tip that lashed as she stared at him with those eyes that literally smoldered with a sullen fire.

Everything about her terrified him, and yet he found himself unable to stop staring at her flawless curves. Her perfectly sized breasts were covered by a red cloth bound loosely about her chest, thin enough that he could see two eraser-sized nipples tantalizingly poking through. Her pussy was covered by panties of the same material, and due to their thinness clung to her plump mound and disappeared between her lush lips in a mouth-watering cameltoe he just wanted to bury his tongue inside.

He somehow found himself hard as a rock without being aware of becoming erect, struck by a desperate urge to throw the woman to the ground and take her in a wild frenzy.

Which would be somewhat hard to do, considering he was still paralyzed aside from his mouth. And his cock apparently.

He still had use of his Adventurer's Eye, though, and what he saw terrified him even more. "Demon, adult female. Humanoid, intelligent. Class: Succubus Level 51. Attacks: Seduce, Charm, Sleep, Paralyze, Drain Vitality, Drain Mana, Drain Essence, Torment, Dominate, Sadist."

"Dare," the demon purred. "Ooh, you're even sexier than I thought you'd be, and I was given high expectations." She looked down at the bulge in his pants and licked her lips with a small pink tongue. "Lord Master, that looks delicious. I've never seen one so glorious on a human."

Dare abruptly found himself able to move, although not of his own volition. He rose as jerkily as a marionette and walked towards her with a halting gait; the desire to rush her and ravage her perfect body was overpowering, and maddeningly he couldn't act on it.

"Dare!" Zuri screamed. He couldn't see her, only hear her panic. "Dare, we have to get away. This is-"

"That's not necessary, little one," the demon said. She waved a hand and Zuri's cries trailed off to silence.

"What did you do to her?" Dare demanded, straining frantically against the force that had control of him. The thought of his lover helpless and possibly hurt broke through his arousal, terrifying and infuriating him.

He came to a stop within arm's reach of the Succubus, still unable to control his limbs. "Rest easy, Dare," she said gently. "Your little friend sleeps peacefully."

That was small comfort, given the peril they were in. Even at Level 51, a class with so many powerful crowd control abilities was terrifying; was it a special class of demons?

For that matter, what was she doing here, in Bastion, so close to a town? How had she made it here without drawing some sort of alarm? And more importantly, how did she know his name and what did she want with him?

"Who are you?" he rasped.

The demon laughed, low and throaty. "Ashkalla Krisnakha. A faithful servant of my master, Demon Lord Ahzgolrun. Here to deliver a message and a gift."

Dare swallowed with effort. "What message? What gift?"

The flame-skinned woman's smoldering eyes suddenly blazed with lust, and her sultry voice lowered to a throaty purr. "Me."

He blinked. "What?"

Ashkalla slinked forward, every motion oozing sex and making his mouth go dry and his cock pound with urgent need. Her fiery eyes caught his and held them hypnotically as she trailed a clawed finger along his jawline. "You have been Noticed, human. My master sent me to get my pleasure from you." She paused, then added reluctantly, "And to give you pleasure in turn."

Holy shit, seriously? "So you're here to . . . fuck me?"

Her tail suddenly lashed like a whip, making a sharp *crack* loud enough to make him jump. "I am here to make you *mine*, pitiful worm!" she said harshly. "You will feel pain as intense as the pleasure, and at the end will beg me for more while begging me to let you escape."

Well that wasn't terrifying at all. Dare swallowed. "What happens to me and my friend if I refuse?"

The succubus scowled, although it didn't seem to be directed at him. Or at least not entirely. "You'll incur my master's displeasure."

"And what exactly does that mean?" he dared ask.

She looked even more displeased, fiery eyes promising retribution for his audacity. "It means he extended the hand of friendship and the services of one of his most precious handmaidens, and you spurned him. What lord would be pleased at that?"

Dare stared, mind trying to sort through what was happening, and Ashkalla huffed impatiently. "Demon Lord Ahzgolrun bade me do no harm to you or your companions. He also bade me not to dominate you or take my pleasure of you without your express and willing permission. He also insisted I make the experience enjoyable for you and curb my sadistic impulses."

Ashkalla's lips twisted, obviously especially reluctant on this last point, then finished, "And lastly, he informed me that at any time you may end our session by speaking the phrase "Hail Lord Ahzgolrun", and I will depart."

Hold on a second . . . this was sounding a whole lot like some sort of BDSM thing.

Dare had never done anything like that before, but like any cultured man of the internet he knew something about it. And honestly the thought of being dominated by a Succubus was less terrifying than the thought of her planning to torture and abuse him for her pleasure.

She'd even given him a safe word.

Maybe it was insane, but he couldn't help but look at the succubus's sinful body, just oozing sexiness and promises of pleasure to come, and consider that maybe her Demon Lord master really had given him a gift in sending her.

And hold on a second, hadn't she said he'd been Noticed at some point? As in, the thing that had happened after he'd tried to weaponize Zuri's Sheltering Embrace ability? Was this what it meant?

Dare took a breath. "A few last things, Mistress, with your permission," he said; if she wanted to do the dominatrix thing, he might as well play along.

Ashkalla looked surprised, then her sexy, cruelly curved lips curled upward slightly. "Very well."

"First off, I'd like you to wake up my companion so I can make sure she's safe and tell her what's going on. Then you'll release her to return to our camp. But before she goes she'll cast Prevent Conception on me."

"Afraid of knocking me up?" the Succubus asked, sounding amused. Her razor-tipped tail looped around to flick impatiently at one of her small curling horns. "Very well." She waved, and Dare heard Zuri murmur sleepily and the rustle of her sitting up.

"Say nothing, toy," the demoness told her harshly. "You have my leave to approach and join your lover."

The little goblin moved up to stand beside Dare, pressing against him in obvious fright. He was still bound by the Succubus's ability, but he did his best to smile down at her. "Are you all right? That was quite the fall."

She nodded, frightened yellow eyes asking the same question of him.

"It's all right," he assured her. "This is just negotiation. I need you to cast Prevent Conception on me, then head back to camp. I'll be back soon."

Zuri looked up at him in alarmed warning, but held to the Succubus's command not to speak.

102

"Calm yourself, worm," Ashkalla said with a sneer. "Upon my name, I give you my oath I won't harm you, or him, or your friends. And while my kind may tend to be deceitful, manipulative, and capricious, we are bound by our oaths."

"It's all right," he told his lover, hoping he was right. "Go ahead."

"You heard your mate, worm!" Ashkalla snapped, making the goblin woman jump. "Cast your spell then return to your camp without delay, as he bids."

Zuri hesitantly cupped his balls with her glowing green hand, then gave him a last pleading look before hugging him tight.

He smiled at her. "I'll be fine, don't worry. Head back to camp and make sure Leilanna and Pella are okay."

She nodded and reluctantly departed.

Once Dare judged she was safely away he immediately began to breathe easier. "Thank you, Mistress. Second, if I end our session early will I still incur your master's pleasure?"

"If you terminate it too early, yes," the Succubus said. Her voice became a purr. "I've been instructed to sate you sexually, and by definition that means you must spend your seed at least once." She smiled wickedly. "Anything we do after that is just added pleasure."

He swallowed, not sure whether to be delighted or terrified by that prospect. "Okay. And finally, Mistress, I need to know that you consent to this, and you aren't doing it because you've been compelled to."

"Compelled . . ." Ashkalla said blankly. "Are you fucking insane, you pitiful worm? I'm offering a lowly creature such as you sex, what do you care the circumstances?"

"I do care, Mistress," he said firmly.

She thoughtfully tapped her chin with her whip-like tail. "I cannot comprehend the thought processes that compel such a question, slug, but very well." Her lips curled upward again, exposing her sharp teeth, and her tongue flicked out to moisten them. "Yes, human, I am here of my own volition, and had I not been commanded would've happily volunteered. I like nothing more than putting someone under my heel and sating my lusts for pain and pleasure on their cowering body."

That shouldn't have sounded hot, but it did.

The demoness's tail abruptly whipped again, making a deafening *crack*. "Now, filth!" she said, seductive voice harsh and commanding. "You will answer! Do you consent to letting me have you, or will you incur the wrath of Demon Lord Ahzgolrun?"

Dare swallowed, hoping he wasn't making a mistake; this was either going to be glorious or it was going to suck. "I consent to letting you have me."

He cried out as her tail whipped out, lashing his back right through his leather armor and clothing as if they weren't there. It felt like a line of fire scoring across his skin, and he felt a trickle of blood slowly seep out.

"What the fuck?" he shouted. "I thought you said you were ordered not to harm me!"

Ashkalla smiled cruelly. "You have a Healer. Therefore anything I do to you isn't lasting, and does not qualify as harm."

That was the most bullshit thing he'd ever heard. But when he opened his mouth to protest she lashed him a second time, making him cry out again.

His obvious pain just as obviously turned on the dominatrix. "Count yourself lucky I've also been ordered to curb my sadistic impulses, pitiful wretch," she sneered. "A little pain can be a wonderful spice for pleasure, and I've been ordered to pleasure you. So let's get started."

Dare found himself undressing. It was a bizarre and terrifying sensation to have his body moving on its own, similar to the autonomous actions he took when he used an ability but far worse because he hadn't initiated them.

Ashkalla's eyes burned with lust as she watched him bare himself. "For an inferior creature you have a pleasing form," she said in a throaty purr. "Yes, worm, I believe I'll have you. I'll have you again and again until I'm sated. And you'll feel pleasure beyond your wildest dreams."

Her tail lashed him again, this time across his chest, leaving a line of red in its wake, and he grit his teeth around another bellow of pain.

The Succubus stepped forward, small pink tongue flicking out to lick her blood red lips again. She kissed him passionately, then slid her lips along his jaw to his ear, breath tickling him as she whispered, "But first you must prove your devotion to your mistress, worm."

Dare abruptly realized he was in control of his body again. But before he could so much as shake out his arms Ashkalla's small, deceptively strong hands grabbed his shoulders and forced him to his knees in front of her, putting him at eye level with her thin, clingy panties, with a perfect view of her little cameltoe.

She was wet. Not much, just a hint of darker cloth at the base of her luscious slit. But enough to tantalize. As was the scent of her arousal, a smoky, earthy, cloyingly sweet smell that was simultaneously right and wrong in all the right ways.

Just the sort of aroma to send alarm bells ringing in his mind while simultaneously driving him mad with desire.

He ducked his head and swallowed. "Forgive this lowly creature's unworthiness, Mistress. I must be punished for my failure."

There was a long silence. "Yessss," the demoness whispered, pleased. "Yes, you must be. Very good, plaything."

Dare grunted as she pushed him down onto his stomach. She thrust a foot into his face, teasing his lips with her big toe.

It was a lovely foot, petite and perfectly shaped, the mottled orange and red skin soft and perhaps a touch too warm. It was also bare, and after walking around the forest was streaked with dust and grass stains.

"Lick it, filth," she said sharply. "Clean my feet with your dirty tongue."

"Yes, Mistress," he said.

Dare bit back a yelp as the Succubus's tail sliced across his back again. "Obey silently, plaything!" she snapped. "Do not speak unless I ask you a question or bid you to." She paused, as if waiting for a response, but he kept his silence.

"Good." Her foot teased his lips again. "I believe I gave you an order."

Although he would've been perfectly happy to lick a woman's foot if it was clean, as it was he had to show his best acting as he pretended to be eager and servile while playing his tongue over the soft, warm skin.

He started with the top side, lapping at the cleanest part, and was pleasantly surprised that the succubus's skin was slightly salty from dried sweat, but not foul in any way. He worked his way around to the sides, then reluctantly probed between her toes, dislodging some caked dirt and forest debris.

The succubus abruptly pressed her foot against his face and shoved him onto his back. "Good, worm," she cooed, raising her foot over his mouth. "Now finish the job." Her voice turned slightly teasing. "If you do, I may decide you deserve a reward."

Dare's eyes trailed up her shapely leg to the thin, clingy panties molded to her perfect pussy; the damp spot around the cameltoe had grown from when he last looked. He had an idea of what that reward might be, and hoped he was right.

Her sole wasn't as dirty as he thought, cleaned by the grass of the clearing. It wasn't as unpleasant as he'd expected to lick her foot clean, occasionally spitting the taste of dirt and grass out of his mouth. In fact, the pleased moans Ashkalla released made his cock throb.

As did his view up her perfectly shaped leg to her silky red panties, which grew more and more wet as he continued to worship her feet with his tongue.

"Very good, plaything," she purred when he was finished. "You have pleased your mistress, and will receive a reward." She playfully skinned off her panties and tossed them aside to reveal a gorgeous pink slit, her meaty inner labia pouting open like a flower to reveal her glistening hole. "Let's wash the taste of earth from your mouth with something more pleasant."

The Succubus gracefully dropped down on his face, pushing her sex into his lips and her little rosebud into his squashed nose. Her silky skin was feverishly hot on his tongue as he tasted her smoky, sinful musk.

"Yeessss," she moaned, grinding against him eagerly. "Worship your mistress, worm."

Dare was only too happy to comply. Even when the demoness's tail began lashing his chest with light, stinging slaps, making him yelp and squirm, he continued to lap at her scalding opening.

His cock throbbed painfully, on the verge of exploding at the juxtaposition of pain and pleasure. It would have, too, when her thin whip-like tail abruptly wrapped around his base. The surprise of her strangling hold triggered a crushing orgasm, but she closed him off with her tail and didn't allow it until the agonizingly pleasurable sensation faded.

Ashkalla gracefully rose to her feet again, giving him a glorious view of her sexy body from below. At some point she'd tossed aside the wrap around her round breasts, revealing their perky bounce and prominent, rubbery nipples in all their glory.

She stepped on his chest with surprising force, delicate foot shoving him into the ground. "What do you wish of me, plaything?" she demanded harshly. "What pleasure do you crave?"

Dare swallowed, navigating the obvious trap. "Whatever pleasure my mistress desires of me," he said.

The Succubus laughed throatily. "Worm. Saying what I wish to hear? Or too timid to express your desires?" She abruptly dropped down on her back on the ground facing him him, spreading her curvy legs wide to expose her flushed, glistening slit. "Your mistress will give you a chance to redeem yourself."

She reached down with delicate clawed fingers and parted her petals, revealing her dark pink interior. "Take me as forcefully as you're able, worm. Hold nothing back. See if you can give me the pleasure I crave, even with that adequate tool of yours."

That was a challenge he was more than happy to accept. Climbing on top of the demoness, he positioned himself at her entrance, teasing her meaty labia with his tip until it glistened with her smoky nectar.

Then, with a grunt of effort, he slammed into her, going balls deep with no sign of the end of her tunnel.

The demoness's pussy was so hot it was almost painful, a furnace no human body could maintain. Her molten arousal ran down his shaft like lava, nearly scorching his crotch as it flowed and splashed over it, only slowly cooling.

"Yeeesssss," she hissed, undulating her hips beneath him. "Good, plaything. Finally a cock that can satisfy me."

The feeling was mutual; now that Dare had some time to adjust to her intense heat, the pleasurable sensation of her soft, slick walls was intense. Her tight tunnel had hard ridges all along it almost like buttons that pressed and stimulated his shaft, bringing him to a new height of pleasure.

Almost like her cunt was a sex toy deliberately designed to maximize enjoyment.

He pulled back and slammed in again, even harder, and Ashkalla flung her arms and legs around him as she heaved back against him violently. And not in time with his thrust, either; the violent, asynchronous movements made this feel less like lovemaking and more like raw rutting, savage and primal.

Between his massive cock and the powerful body his benefactor had given him, his wild thrusts would've broken most women in two. But the demoness's sinfully curvy body seemed impervious to pain or physical damage. If anything, she just spurred him on.

"Yes, ravage me with your filthy inferior cock," she snarled, thrashing against him. "Show me you can tear me open even without spines or ridges, worm. I've taken demons twice your size, so you'll have to do better than that."

Dare was certainly doing his best, even shifting angles to try to stimulate her more.

Apparently that wasn't enough, because Ashkalla began tearing at his back with her small but wicked claws, her tail lashing cruelly at his thighs and calves.

He thrashed wildly, as much to escape the pain as to increase his pleasure inside her. But the sudden surprise of her cruel sadism brought on the orgasm she'd staved off earlier in an overwhelming surge.

With a last snarl he shoved balls deep in her seemingly bottomless tunnel, then rolled them both over so he was on his back in an attempt to escape her claws and tail.

He erupted up into the Succubus with a violence he'd never experienced before, stars flashing in his vision. She cried out as well in shuddering climax, thighs gripping him with crushing strength as her walls rippled along his length and she squirted molten arousal all over his crotch.

Dare had no time to recover from his incredible orgasm as she began riding him viciously, not seeming to care that he was limp and exhausted beneath her. She either knew about his ability to fuck through his refractory period or didn't care, because she continued mercilessly, seeking more pleasure regardless of the cost to him.

The demoness's wild motions bent his cock painfully and at times nearly broke it, making him cry out. At least until her tail whipped around his head and forced several sinewy loops into his mouth, gagging him.

She rode him faster and faster, claws scraping over his chest as she panted and snarled in pleasure, until finally he gasped and erupted in another powerful orgasm inside her.

Even then Ashkalla didn't let up. She rose up off his cock, but before it could begin to wilt she lined him up with her pucker and slammed back down on him, driving his length deep into her bowels with no apparent effort or discomfort.

Although Dare felt some; her ass was even hotter than her pussy, scalding his skin as she began riding him again, just as violently as before. His tip, already super sensitive, throbbed in protest.

The ring of the demoness's straining sphincter was painfully tight, a strangling clasp running up and down his shaft as she rose up and slammed back down on him, milking the remaining seed from his previous orgasm while trying to force him to another one.

He'd fucked through two orgasms before, but never this forcefully and never in such quick succession. The discomfort and pleasure both rose towards peaks he hadn't experienced before, holding off his next orgasm.

Dare wasn't sure how long he lasted like that, as her tail writhed and steadily tightened in his mouth, and she raked his chest with her claws. Minutes, maybe. But finally with a strangled grunt he again released, spraying her molten bowels with his seed.

"Good, plaything," she purred. "Just a bit more and I'll reach another crescendo." Her tail finally freed his mouth, the tip playing teasingly across his cheek as she continued to fuck him through his third orgasm.

"Hail Lord Ahzgolrun!" he shouted desperately.

For a moment Ashkalla stared at him, perplexed, as if she'd forgotten that was the safe word. Then her flushed face darkened with displeasure and she instantly climbed off him.

Her mottled red and orange skin was dripping with sweat, drool glistening on her chin, and their mingled juices flowed from her well used holes. She looked wanton and sexy as fuck, but all Dare could feel was relief that it was done.

"I suppose all good things must come to an end, plaything," the demoness purred, licking her lips as she stared down at him. "But I know you'll remember me forever, won't you?" When he was slow to answer her tail shot up, hovering menacingly over him. *"Won't you?"*

"Yes, Mistress," he gasped weakly.

"Good." She slid a finger over her sopping labia, tasting their mingled juices, then with a cruel smirk rested a hand on her lower belly. "Rest assured that our child will be a prince among demons, favored above all others. The Master himself will guide his upbringing."

Dare stared at her with shock. In a panic, he double checked and confirmed that Zuri's Prevent Conception was still active on him.

Ashkalla guessed what he was doing and laughed at him. "You put too much faith in your little friend's spell, to the point you're blind to what's right in front of your eyes. I find it delicious that *I'm* the one who finally gets to tell you. When others really should have."

110

"What the fuck are you talking about?" he demanded, angry and worried. "You're not pregnant."

"Of course not." Her cruel lips curved, mocking him. "I'm not, she's not, none of them are."

With a throaty laugh she gathered up her things and sauntered towards the edge of the clearing, voluptuous backside swaying teasingly and tail lashing in contentment like a cat's. "This was fun, Dare. Maybe I'll seek you out again sometime." She turned to give him a wicked grin. "Next time without any commands to hold me back, so we can *really* have fun."

She slipped into the woods, and with a final *crack* of her whiplike tail disappeared from view.

Chapter Seven
Realization

Dare lay in the clearing for several minutes as he recovered from his experience, mind whirling.

Finally, though, the thought of Zuri frantic with worry for him spurred him to his feet with a groan. He gingerly pulled on his underwear, but the various scratches and cuts all over his body made the prospect of putting on any more clothing an uncomfortable one.

So instead he gathered up the rest of his gear, then broke into a painful run back towards camp.

"Noticed," he growled under his breath, glaring up at the sky. "Doesn't do anything, huh. Just draws the attention of demon lords so they send handmaidens to come have rough sex and get knocked up by me."

To his surprise, there was no response.

"Well?" he demanded. "This isn't a good thing, is it? It's never good when powerful people know you exist. You end up a pawn, or eliminated as a potential threat. I'm guessing the gods knowing about me isn't any better."

Still nothing.

"Okay fine," he snapped. "Go ahead, sit back and enjoy. You're just an observer of The Dare Show, aren't you?"

Dare would've thought that would get her attention if nothing did, but there was still no response. "Hey," he said, irritation giving way to concern. "You're there, right? You okay?"

He was still waiting for a response when he caught sight of Zuri up ahead, to his vast relief.

It was obvious she'd been dragging her feet, obeying his request to go back to camp but not happy about it. She was also looking back with every step, expression sick with worry and guilt, no doubt from leaving him behind.

As soon as his goblin lover saw him she whirled around and bolted towards him as fast as her little legs could carry her. "Dare!" she screamed. She skidded to a stop and began casting her Plea to Nature to begin healing his wounds, tears streaming down her cheeks.

Dare swept her into his arms and hugged her tight. "It's okay," he said. "I'm fine." He laughed shakily. "Just a bit of rough sex."

"I was so afraid," Zuri said, clutching him with desperate strength. "Demons are never so merciful. Even with the oath she gave me I was sure she'd find some loophole." She dropped a hand to her belly, looking sick with guilt. "I would've gone back, I should've. But I couldn't risk . . ."

He took in her expression, followed her gaze to her round little stomach, and it all came crashing home.

I'm not, she's not, none of them are.

Holy shit, he was a moron. And it explained what she'd been worrying about all this time. Dare gently stroked her back while lifting her chin to meet his gaze. "You're pregnant?" he whispered.

His goblin lover stiffened, eyes widening with panic. "I-I . . ."

She abruptly wrenched free of his arms and dropped onto her hands and knees, in the submissive pose she'd used when they'd first met.

"It should've worked!" she wailed, pressing her face to the ground. "I used it every time, and it has an almost negligible failure rate! And it's high enough rank to even work on the races with highest fertility, like goblins and cunids and apids."

"Hey, hey," Dare said, gently gathering her into his arms again. "It's okay, it's fine. There's no reason to get so upset." He hesitated. "I mean, I wish you would've told me earlier, but I'm sure you had your reasons."

"It's not that I didn't trust you." She began bawling on his shoulder. "I trust you more than anything. You were just so intent on making sure we leveled up and had a better situation before we had babies. I was hoping we could get there before I had to tell you."

"It's fine, it's fine," he soothed, rubbing her back. "This is good news. Happy news. It'll work out great."

He was still getting his head around the idea he was going to be a father, and he was beset by a host of sudden worries for the welfare of Zuri and the baby, and how he was going to protect and provide for them. But in spite of all that he still meant what he'd told her.

"I know it will," his goblin lover said, hiccuping. "I just feel so guilty. I must've done something wrong with the spell, and now we have to speed up our plans and disrupt all your hard work."

"You didn't do anything wrong," Dare told her firmly. "We must've just got really unlucky with the failure rate. Unless there's some other reason why it wouldn't work."

Zuri hesitated, sniffling. "I-I mean sometimes if both of the mating pair are close to the fertility cap, their combined numbers somehow go above the cap and render the spell ineffective. And of course if one of them is over the cap then it will always fail. But almost nobody has a fertility stat of over 50, aside from Succubi and monsters that specialize in seduction attacks."

Dare didn't hear anything after "50", feeling a sudden sinking in the pit of his stomach. "Zuri," he said hoarsely. "What fertility stat do humans usually have?"

She looked up just long enough to shoot him an uncertain glance, as if wondering what that had to do with their situation. "Um, usually high 20s to low 30s from what I've heard. Goblins are in the low 40s, canids in the mid 30s, elves in the low 10s. Even cunids, one of the highest natural fertility ratings, are only in the mid to high 40s." She clenched her tiny fists in her lap. "It should've *worked*."

He only heard the odd word she said here and there as he silently cursed himself for a fool.

He knew all his stats, of course. In fact, he'd studied them so often that even as they increased from levels or ability rank ups he still had a good handle on where they were at. He hadn't paid much attention to his fertility stat, though, not knowing its purpose and assuming it was in the normal range.

But of course he should've considered the chance that if his

114

unseen benefactor had given him high stats in so many other areas, she might've done the same for fertility.

Fuck. Fuck fuck fuck!

Dare closed his eyes and braced himself for the storm. "I'm so sorry, honey, this is my fault. My fertility rating is 51."

Zuri slowly raised her head, expression blank. "That's impossible," she said.

He shook his head bleakly. "As impossible as having Adventurer's Eye or Fleetfoot."

She sat up in his lap, face blinking through a variety of expressions before settling on alarm. "But that sort of fertility is unheard of. Even in cunids it would be super rare. I mean, at that number my Prevent Conception would do nothing."

Her hands flew to her mouth, eyes huge. "That means Pella is pregnant too. And Linia, and Trissela. Every single woman you've ever been with . . ."

Dare groaned and scrubbed his hands through his hair, his shock turning to the sinking feeling of being in a nightmare.

Gods, what the hell was he going to do?

He really, really should've paid better attention to what the fertility stat did. His was even higher than a godsdamn *bunny girl's*, and Ellui had told him they get pregnant if a man so much as touched the entrance to their pussies with his dick. It would be even more likely for him.

Speaking of which . . . if this was all true it meant he'd guaranteed knocked up the farmwife by fucking her, even if he'd pulled out and come on her ass.

At the moment, though, he had bigger worries than some unfaithful woman in another region.

Dare tenderly rubbed Zuri's growing tummy. "A baby," he said quietly. "That's amazing." He kissed her head. "How long has it been since we first made love, about two months? From what I've been told about goblins, if you're showing this much already then that means-"

"A goblin child," she whispered, trembling. "I'm sorry."

He looked at her in confusion. "Why?" He gently rubbed her stomach again. "Whether our child is a goblin, hobgoblin, or human, it'll still be our child and I'll love it with all my heart, and do my best to give it a happy life."

The tearful goblin looked up, expression torn between hope and doubt. "You'd raise a goblin or hybrid the same as a human?"

"Happily." He leaned down and kissed her soft mouth. "I can't wait to meet our child."

She began sobbing again and burrowed her face in his shoulder, clutching him tightly. "I love you, Dare. I'll be a good mother and mate, I promise."

In spite of the situation he couldn't help but chuckle. "Of course you will be," he said. "The very best, because you're amazing." He rested his cheek on her head, hand on her stomach protectively cupping their child. "I love you too. Thank you for making my life here so wonderful."

They cuddled out in the middle of the wilds for several minutes, then with a sigh Dare kissed her head again. "We should probably get back to camp," he said reluctantly. "We need to tell Pella that she's pregnant, too."

Zuri giggled. She looked as if an enormous weight had lifted off her shoulders now that her secret was finally out. "She's going to be so happy."

He wasn't so sure about that, given that this pregnancy was unexpected and all his fault. But hopefully she would forgive him for messing up.

* * * * *

As it turned out Zuri was right after all; Pella was over the moon when they explained the situation.

"I thought I might be pregnant!" she squealed, tail waging furiously as she hugged them both and practically jumped up and down. "My moon blood is a few weeks late." She giggled giddily and began licking Dare's face, practically bowling him over with her

116

enthusiasm. "We're going to have puppies!"

Come to think of it, Dare should've noticed something was up since he hadn't seen either Zuri or Pella have their periods since he'd met them. And given how often they made love he definitely would've.

In his defense, though, what guy paid undue attention to that sort of thing? Especially since he didn't know, and wasn't inclined to ask, if dog girls and goblins had the same monthly cycles as humans.

With another squeal Pella jumped on him and wrapped her legs around his waist, still fiercely kissing and licking his face. "Isn't this great, Dare? I've wanted this for so long . . . I can't wait to be a mommy!"

Dare couldn't help but laugh at her enthusiasm, even though he still felt guilty about putting her in this situation so unexpectedly. "I'm excited too," he admitted. "We'll have to figure out what we're going to do, but I'm happy we're having children, Pella." He managed to keep her head still long enough to kiss her back, long and tenderly. "I love you."

"Well I think you're an irresponsible moron," Leilanna said, throwing cold water on the celebratory mood.

"Hey shut up!" Pella said. "Even if he made a mistake, it's fine since we're happy having his babies."

"How is it fine?" the Mage demanded. "How are you two going to level when you have babies? And what about all the other women this walking dick has probably knocked up without realizing it?"

Dare cut in before an argument could break out. "She's not wrong . . . I have to consider everyone I've been with since coming here."

"And back wherever you came from, too," Leilanna insisted. "If you were as much of a stud there as you are here."

He felt his face flushing. "That won't be a problem," he said; a silver lining on the cloud. He reluctantly set Pella down. "Still, I should probably go sort this out."

Zuri perked up. "Are you going to go talk to Benefactor?" He nodded. "Well you can talk to her here if you want," she insisted.

"She's not a secret or anything."

Dare sighed. "This is probably going to be a lovers' quarrel, so I'd best have it in private."

Assuming his benefactor actually bothered to answer this time.

He wandered out into the woods until he was out of earshot of the elf's and dog girl's keen hearing, then pulled up the system commands. "That was a dirty trick you played on me," he told his benefactor.

When she replied she sounded suspiciously impassive, almost robotic. "You expressed a desire to have sex with many women of different races, so I helped you."

"How is guaranteeing I knock up every single one of them *helping?*" Dare demanded incredulously. "That's the opposite of helping! It's going to make my goal impossible unless I want to leave dozens of bastards out there, faced with the dilemma of either struggling to support them all and give them proper care and attention, or abandoning them like complete scum."

The disembodied woman's voice remained impassive as she answered. "Fertility affects more than pregnancy chance. It also increases your libido, your attractiveness to potential mates, the arousal you both feel during sex, and the pleasure you both receive from it. In addition, it increases your stamina and prowess in lovemaking, and allows you to continue to have sex even after multiple ejaculations. Far past the point where most men, as the saying from your world goes, would be "pushing rope". You also ejaculate more copious amounts of semen."

Wow. That was . . . a lot of good stuff. The problem was . . . "It could make lovers orgasm at the slightest touch and let me fuck until I drop dead from exhaustion and I still wouldn't take it because of the pregnancy thing."

He raised his voice. "And that's why you shouldn't have done this to me, or at least should've warned me that you had. What, were you just sitting back giggling to yourself as I had sex with all of these women, thinking we were being safe with Prevent Conception? Laughing at what a gullible fool I am?"

118

"You yourself acknowledged that it was your fault you didn't pay more attention to the fertility stat-"

"You should've told me!" Dare roared. "These are people's lives you're fucking with, not just mine but every women I've been with, and every child that'll be born because of it. All facing added challenges they didn't expect and don't deserve."

"Pregnancy is a consequence of sex you and your lover both agree to. You knew that even with Prevent Conception there's a minute chance of conception."

"That's different and you know it, don't give me that bullshit!" He began furiously pacing. "Thanks to you I've knocked up, as far as I know, Ellui and Clover in Lone Ox, Zuri, Pella, and Linia, and that mermaid Trissela in Kov. Oh, and the fucking *Succubus that just sperm jacked me*, but at least had the grace to tell me the truth!"

"Don't forget the slime girls," his benefactor said cheerfully. "Normally they only split off an offshoot when they grow big enough or at certain other specific times. But with your fertility you triggered just about every large and regular sized slime you came inside into mitosis."

Fantastic. "Is there anything I didn't impregnate?" he demanded, growing even angrier at her casual tone.

She laughed. "Actually yes. If it makes you feel better, you didn't impregnate *me*. The forms I took to bed you are incapable of it."

"Do you think this is all a joke?" Dare shouted. He whirled back towards camp. "You're always fucking off when I need you, how about you go ahead and do that now?"

Her voice became stern. "Don't throw a tantrum and walk away, Dare. If you want me to take responsibility for not telling you this, when I've never told you *anything* without you asking me first, then shouldn't you be willing to take equal responsibility for failing to learn about and properly use the gift of high fertility I gave you? You've been so careful to think through and plan everything else."

Gods damnit, she kind of had a point. He resumed his pacing. "These are women's lives I've already affected, without realizing it! They deserve better than to be stuck with my children while I run off finding more women to screw. And I deserve better than to be stuck obligated to care for a bunch of kids I didn't know about or agree to, just because you wanted some entertainment."

The voice sobered. "What if I told you that all the women you've impregnated thus far are going to be fine, and so are the children? That they're well situated for a baby and eager to raise a child they'll love with all their hearts."

Her voice became warmer. "And the children will have me looking over them as well, because they're yours. Few are so fortunate as to have divine attention aiding them in their lives."

"That's something," Dare grumbled, actually a lot more reassured than he was willing to admit. "But those children deserve to have a father, don't they?"

"They will. Those women will all find good men willing to love them and be a father to your child. I swear it." She hesitated. "Well, except for the bunny girl and catgirl, since that's not really how they work. But you don't really need to worry about those children, they'll do great."

He opened his mouth, then shut it. "It's still fucked up. I don't want to be the auto pregnancy man, wandering around knocking up every woman I so much as smile at. It's going to ruin my sex life."

Her amusement returned. "Relax, my lover. Zuri is two levels away from learning the next rank of the Prevent Conception spell, which she'll still be able to use to make scrolls. That rank will work to a fertility stat of 60. Most people don't bother upgrading the spell that high, since the lower tier works for pretty much all circumstances so it's a waste of an ability point."

Dare rubbed his eyes wearily. "Every cloud has a silver lining."

Her voice turned almost teasing. "But you should probably ask Zuri if she'd be willing to spend one of her precious ability points to help you keep your raging virility in check. Ask very nicely, or maybe beg, or offer to make it up to her with very, very special treatment.

"Although in all honestly she'd probably offer to do it even if you didn't ask, she's that devoted to you." Her tone became stern. "You should just be sure you continue to be worthy of that devotion."

Somehow that sounded almost more like a threat than a suggestion; was his benefactor *fond* of Zuri?

Dare wouldn't blame her if she was, since he was very fond of Zuri too. Or more accurately head over heels for her. "I'll definitely do that." He glowered. "Although on the subject of Zuri's happiness, even though you seem to have an answer for all my objections, there's the fact that you not telling me has caused problems for the women I care about.

"Zuri and Pella may be overjoyed to have my babies, but we're going to struggle because I wasn't able to reach the point where I was powerful enough to farm wealth to provide for them and our kids." He glared into the distance. "I want you to admit that you screwed me long before you came to me as a shadow, and not just me."

"Ooh, well said." She laughed again. "Fine, I'll admit that I suspected this would complicate things, and I refrained from warning you because I wanted to see how it played out. But be honest . . . much as you complain, you know you're happy to have children with the women you've come to love."

Her voice turned teasing. "And you know seeing their flat tummies swell with your babies is going to make it impossible for you to keep your hands off them. I'm privy to your past life, I know how much you're turned on by big pregnant bellies and swollen breasts."

To Dare's annoyance he felt his cock twitch. She wasn't wrong; now that he knew Zuri's growing belly was due to her being pregnant, he was finding her even more appealing. And the thought of Pella's lush body eventually showing the same changes was something he looked forward to with great anticipation.

But after the fun pregnant sex came the childbirths and babies. He'd need to provide them a proper home, and all the basic comforts, and all the opportunities for success this world could provide, like gear and spellbooks and class tutors and . . .

And it was all more than he could ever hope to pay for at his current level. Which meant that instead of living his dream of becoming a godlike high level and having a harem of women from all the races, he was going to be scraping for a living.

A complete disappointment to the women who depended on him.

"Dare," his benefactor said gently. "My lover. I'm sorry that this happened because of the fertility I gave you. And that your ignorance and trust in Prevent Conception has caused you problems. I didn't withhold the information capriciously."

"Fine," he said, not really mollified but finding it harder and harder to argue any point with her. "Still, don't you think you should make it up to me? You say you want to watch what I do in this world for your entertainment. Then you put me in a situation where what I'll be doing is abandoning my leveling goals and struggling to farm gold, so I can pay for my lovers and our children. That sounds like it's going to be incredibly boring for you."

The disembodied voice's amusement had faded when she answered. "You have a point." She was silent for a long time, and Dare wondered if she was waiting for a prompt from him; she hadn't done that for a while.

Then she spoke. "All right. If you have a proper estate and sufficient savings then your women and children can be comfortable while you go on trips and continue leveling, exploring, and finding new romantic opportunities. I've already bent the rules in your favor in more major ways, I suppose I can give you a hint. One word." Her voice became severe. "But in return there's something I want."

Dare stiffened warily. Aside from this one instance she'd only helped him so far, and also given him literally mind-bending sex. In fact, he wouldn't even be here, alive after dying on Earth, without her.

He trusted her, but this bullshit she'd pulled with the fertility stat had shaken that. "And what's that?"

"Simple," she said with an easy laugh. "Grow your harem. It's fun to watch you find new and exciting women to sleep with on adventures, but more importantly fall in love with more women who'll fall in love with you in turn. Take them into your family, make a home with them, and have children with them. If you do that, I'll do my best to ensure you can provide for their needs."

Dare looked suspiciously at the sky. "So in other words, you'll help me if I do what I was planning to do anyway? What's the catch?"

His benefactor laughed even louder. "There is no catch, my lover. I want what you want." She hesitated. "And also, I don't like to think you hate me and no longer trust me because of this misunderstanding."

He blinked, surprised in spite of himself. Did she have genuine feelings for him? More than that, did she have feelings to begin with?

"Of course I have feelings," she said, reading his mind and sounding a bit hurt. "And of course I have feelings for you." Her voice became fond. "I have ever since I saw you on Earth, min/maxing obscure games and challenging yourself to beat them completely for the sheer love of them."

Her tone abruptly became brisk, as if she was a bit embarrassed by her confession. "In any case here's your one word hint: east."

Dare turned to stare in that direction, frowning. "East?"

"East. As in directly into the rising sun. Although that was more than one word. You're welcome."

The system command overlay abruptly disappeared as if she'd shut it down herself; she'd never done that before. Dare hurriedly opened it again and found it working as normal, but when he asked for information he only got text.

It looked as if she was done talking to him for now.

With a sigh he returned to camp, where to his surprise he found Zuri seated by the fire waiting for him. She silently threw herself into his arms.

"The others head to bed?" he asked, kissing her gently.

She nodded. "Pella wore herself out with her excitement, and Leilanna has just generally been tired as she's getting used to her new sleeping schedule." She rested her head on his shoulder. "I'm fine to stay up for a bit longer if you are, though."

Dare wasn't in the mood to make a meal, but he was hungry. So he carried her to his chair and settled down with her in his lap, where she cuddled him contentedly as he brought out some jerky and dried fruit he'd made a few days ago and shared it with her.

"You'll reach level 27 soon at the rate we're going," he murmured, affectionately rubbing her tummy; he could admit that now that he'd had a chance to get used to it a little, the thought of his child growing inside her excited him.

"Mmm," she said in agreement. "I'll get the next point in Prevent Conception as soon as I can."

Dare blinked, surprised that she'd thought of it without him even having to bring it up. "Thank you." He leaned down and kissed the top of her head, then began kissing and nibbling her pointy ears the way she liked. "I love you."

"I love you too, my mate." She swallowed a last bit of jerky and yawned hugely. "Ready for bed?"

He wouldn't have minded sitting out for a bit longer to sort through his thoughts, but he nodded and carried her to the tent.

Pella woke up just enough to drape herself over him, making contented noises, and Dare fell asleep tenderly holding the two women he loved.

The mothers of his children.

Man, that blew his mind. Back on Earth a part of him had wondered if he'd ever have children, or find someone who could love him and settle down to share her life with him.

And here he'd found two incredible women, with the prospect of more to come.

Dare was still angry at his benefactor for how she'd handled this. But even so, he was grateful that she'd given him this chance at an incredible new life.

And he was going to make the most of it. Not just for him but for the women he loved and the children they'd bring into this world.

Chapter Eight
Hint

The next morning Dare woke to Pella stirring against him.

"Time to head out with Leilanna?" he mumbled, squinting his eyes open. It was still dark outside.

"Soon," she murmured, kissing his neck. "Sorry for waking you up early, Dare, I'm just so excited."

"I am too." He kissed her golden hair, gently resting a hand on her tummy. Now that he was paying attention he thought it did have a slight bulge to it from the baby growing inside, which sent a warm glow through him. "I've been thinking about the best way to care for our children."

"I have too," she said, tail wagging. "We'll get a house, right? Or maybe build one? And little cradles. And Zuri can make baby clothes." She nuzzled his neck some more. "If it's a puppy, pregnancy lasts about 6 months, and of course the time you'd expect for a human baby. I think Zuri will probably have her baby in a couple more months, though, so we need to be ready by then."

"We will be," Dare told her solemnly. "I promise, our babies will have a home. And a comfortable one."

"I know." She lifted her head off his chest, and he got the sense she was looking at him intently. "I trust you to take care of everything. You know that, right?"

He felt a lump in his throat, hoping he'd be worthy of that trust. "Thank you," he said, voice husky.

Zuri stirred. "I trust you too," she murmured, taking his arm and pulling it around her. "So what do we do next?"

"Well first off, how long until Leilanna's rested enough to fill her mana pool?"

Pella cocked her head. "About another half hour." She had an almost flawless internal clock, either a trait of canids or just a unique talent.

Of course, thanks to his benefactor's gifts his internal clock was pretty much dead on as well. To the point he could even wake up when he needed, nearly as accurately as an alarm.

Dare nodded and began to sit up. "Okay, let's pack up and get ready to move out together. We can wake her up when she's rested."

His lovers perked up. "Where are we going?" Zuri asked.

"East," Dare said. "Into the rising sun."

"East?" Pella repeated, and he smiled slightly at how close she sounded to him when he'd been talking to his benefactor.

"Yes. There's something good in that direction. Something we need."

His dog girl lover looked up at him. "What is it?"

"I don't know," he admitted with a laugh.

Dare could feel their flat stares. "Then how do you know it's there?" Zuri demanded.

"Call it inspiration, after spending half an hour debating with the air about our situation."

"Ah." The goblin made a satisfied noise. "Good."

A half hour later, they were all packed up and ready to go. Even a sleepy Leilanna, who did her morning ablutions while they took down her tent.

Obviously tired and dragging at this early hour, the Mage looked almost eager to climb up on his back so she wouldn't have to walk wherever they were going. But Dare shook his head. "We'll all go on foot. We need to go slower so we can keep an eye out for what we're looking for."

"Which is what?" she demanded.

He chuckled. "I don't know, but hopefully we'll recognize it when we see it."

If Leilanna was disappointed not to get a piggyback ride, she was even more put out when she realized that his idea of a slower pace was going at her best speed. Which meant she could look forward to spending the morning jogging until she had to stop, hunched and panting, to rest before continuing on sooner than she would've liked.

She became even more salty when she realized Dare was going to carry Zuri. "Why does she get special treatment?" she demanded.

"Because she's two months pregnant," Dare said, affectionately kissing his little lover.

"You don't have to treat me like glass," Zuri protested, although she showed no signs of wanting him to set her down.

"I know, but we also don't want to push you too hard."

"No, just me," Leilanna said sarcastically.

Dare grinned at the curvy mage. "Tell you what. If we find what I hope we're going to, a horse is the first thing we'll buy."

As it turned out, he probably could've gotten away with carrying the Mage and going faster, because it took hours for them to get where they were going. And as he'd hoped, they recognized it when they saw it.

They'd made it into an area where the monster spawn points were Level 23-25, approaching a tall hill that was almost a mountain. And halfway up that hill was a yawning crack, an obvious entrance to a cave.

"There," he said, pointing.

Pella darted forward to investigate, sniffing, and he saw the hairs on the back of her neck rising at whatever it was she smelled. "Dungeon," she growled. "I can smell all sorts of monsters in there." She sniffed again. "Maybe even a wyvern or drake, probably a boss."

Dare believed her, although it looked nothing like the kobold mine dungeon he'd seen north of Driftwain. There were no guards, for one thing.

But no doubt it was higher level than that one, which had been around Level 21, considering the levels of the monsters they'd just passed; the monsters around the kobold mine had been in their mid 10s.

"Okay, stay here," he said. "I'll go inside and check the levels of the monsters." He started to step forward, then hesitated. "Unless there's some sort of instance barrier that'll pop up the moment I go in, until the dungeon is cleared?"

They all stared at him. "Why would there be a barrier?" Pella asked.

Leilanna nodded. "That would be fucked up, like the gods were trying to kill us."

Well that was a relief; Dare had never liked games where you got locked in. Although he supposed he could understand if it was for balance purposes or to prevent cheesing.

He edged into the cave mouth, new recurve bow ready. Then he stopped, amazed.

Back on Earth he'd had the opportunity to visit some amazing cave systems. A few of the bigger ones, like Meramec Caverns, Mammoth Cave, and Ruby Falls not too far from his home. And some cool ones practically in his backyard that weren't famous but still had beautiful features.

This cave, large enough to fit a plane inside and only the *entrance* cavern, put them all to shame.

Glittering curtains of delicate stone and crystal formations blanketed most of the walls, like waterfalls flowing to the cave floor below. Stalactites and stalagmites so big he wouldn't be able to fit his arms around them made a jagged maze towards a dark hole on the far side that led deeper into the dungeon.

A river flowed through the cavern from one side to the other, the water swirling with brilliant blues and greens with a bed of rainbow sand lined with bands of gold color.

His Adventurer's Eye alerted him to several enemies in the cave, giant bats hanging among the stalactites. They were colored in shades of stone, and so still they could've been stalactites themselves.

A nasty surprise for adventurers without his gift.

A view of their stats confirmed that even though they were all Level 22-23, they were far stronger than normal monsters of their level. Not quite as strong as a party rated monster, but close enough to challenge a party.

Especially if they came more than one at a time.

Dare backed out and returned to his companions, mind whirling as he considered the best way to approach this.

"Can we find treasure in dungeons?" he asked.

The three girls glanced at each other. "Of course," Leilanna said. "That's what dungeons are for. Treasure and levels and sometimes valuable items."

"Not all of them," Pella supplied. "My old master took me into one with a party and it was a huge disappointment. Just a few monsters and a bunch of junk in every sack and cupboard."

"Somebody probably visited that dungeon before you without fully clearing it out and making it respawn in another location," the dusk elf replied. "It's a dick move and has no benefit to anybody, but some adventurers are stupid and thoughtless."

Her pointed look in Dare's direction implied he could be included in that group; she seemed less inclined to forgive him for his mistake than his lovers. Which seemed a bit unfair since it didn't even affect her.

Dare turned back to the dungeon, frowning. "How much loot do you usually get from a dungeon at this level?" he asked. "Enough to buy an estate with healthy savings so we can raise our children in a safe and comfortable place?"

Leilanna laughed scornfully. "You think it would be that easy? A dungeon like this might earn us enough to live well for a month or so. Maybe more, if we sold the rare items instead of using them ourselves."

"Unless there's a legendary treasure chest at the end!" Pella said, tail wagging eagerly at the thought.

The elf snorted, sneering at the enthusiastic dog girl. "Don't be stupid. Those have like a one in ten thousand chance of spawning in a dungeon this low."

Dare glanced at the sky, a habit he'd adopted when thinking of his unseen benefactor. Somehow he had a feeling this dungeon was going to be that 1 in 10,000. "How much do those chests usually have?"

Leilanna rolled her eyes at him joining in the dog girl's silly optimism. "There's not going to be one, but it would have a Master quality item of the dungeon's level, one to three Exceptional quality items, a bunch of crafting materials and reagents, and-"

"Enough gold to buy a manor and servants!" Pella cut in, tail waving furiously. "Thank you, Dare! This is just what we needed!"

"Don't thank him, you idiot!" the elf snapped. The dog girl's smile faded and tail slowed to a stop, ears drooping. "We're *not* going to find a legendary chest in there," Leilanna continued. "And even if we did, it drops enough gold for at best one person to buy a small house and live comfortably for the rest of your life. It wouldn't last nearly as long stretched among four people, not to mention babies soon enough."

"But if we did find one, and wanted to get a manor and live well," Dare pressed. "How long would it last us?"

The elf threw up her hands and stalked away to inspect the dungeon entrance, refusing to answer. After a few moments Zuri cleared her throat. "Maybe a couple years. Five, if we continue to work hard farming gold or working at professions when we're not caring for the children."

"Good enough," he said, grinning and ruffling Pella's adorable floppy ears. "I'm not making any promises, but I for one am getting my hopes up."

"Me too!" she said, brightening again. "I know it'll have a legendary chest. I *know* it!"

So do I, he thought smugly. *Thanks, creepy shadow mannequin lover.* He straightened his shoulders. "All right, let's plan how we're going to crack this nut."

They all looked at him expectantly, even Leilanna coming back over to listen. "Can we clear it now?" she asked.

Dare hesitated. "Maybe, but it would be risky. Those entry monsters were 22-23, not quite as powerful as a party rated monster but close. And no doubt the deeper in we go the harder the enemies will get, if this dungeon is like many I've seen."

"How many could you possibly have seen?" the dusk elf demanded. "You've only been high enough level to even *do* dungeons for a few levels."

He didn't have any good answer to that aside from revealing the existence of video games, and he didn't need his benefactor's command to know his companions weren't ready for that yet.

So he ignored the question and began pacing. "I'd feel more comfortable about this if Pella was Level 30 and got her amazing new abilities, and me and Zuri got at least another level each." He nodded to the Mage. "And it goes without saying we should try to get you up to at least Level 18, and more ideally Level 20 for your own awesome abilities, so you can help us."

She snorted. "So what, you plan to hang around here for a month to make that happen? I just turned Level 15, and even if you've proven I can level faster than I expected, five levels is no joke."

Dare shook his head. "I don't want to risk anyone else finding out about this place and taking it from us, or even worse fighting us for it. So I say we give it a week, then go."

He gave the dusk elf a wolfish grin. "In other words, we'd better get to work."

* * * * *

Dare was both amused and gratified by how overjoyed Pella was to spend the next few days with him, pushing hard to level her to 30 and to get him as much experience as possible as well.

As the party's healer, Zuri could make do with being a bit lower level than the rest of them, so she'd agreed to go with Leilanna and help her with her leveling. Which meant she might end up being a level or so behind Dare for a while, but he'd make it up to her.

It took four days of hard work to get his dog girl lover her level, and Dare got to 26 and earned a third of the way to 27 as well. During that time Leilanna got two levels, getting them all closer to their goals.

What Pella got at 30 was pretty good, but not as spectacular as they'd all been hoping for.

First things first she got an ability called Intervene that was like a reverse Pounce, allowing her to leap to a friendly target and put herself between it and the nearest enemy. It also made her immune to the next attack she received.

The beautiful golden-haired woman broke down as she read her ability, needing Dare to comfort her. It turned out she was thinking of her old master's death, and how she'd been too slow to protect him.

"I could've saved him," she sobbed, huge tears rolling down her cheeks. "If I'd had this, he'd still be alive."

A bit helpless in the face of her misery, he could only hold her close and rub her back. "We can't dwell on the past," he said awkwardly. "It's always easy to think back on what you could've done better, but we have to keep moving forward."

Eventually she calmed, a bit embarrassed by her outburst, and most of her usual good cheer returned. As did her enthusiasm as she looked at what else she got for her level.

Where the big deal at 20 had been unlocking weapons and armor to use, at 30 it was a passive boost to all stats called Power Up that apparently everyone got at that level. As the name suggested it was a flat stat increase, giving +5 to Strength, Stamina, Agility, Constitution, Dexterity, Intellect, and Speed. As well as the noncombat stats like fertility.

Considering most people's stats were in the 20-30 range, it was a decent boost. Although it wouldn't have been as much of one to Dare, who thanks to the body his benefactor had given him was apparently ridiculously overstatted.

Also you got small stat increases throughout the course of leveling, particularly for stats your class benefited most from, but you'd have to get around 30 levels to add up to what Power Up gave, and they wouldn't be evenly distributed.

Not very dazzling, but cool enough. With it Pella was able to keep up with him better, without needing to use Run Down unless he was really sprinting full out.

They ended up testing it with a game of tag, his dog girl lover giggling in delight as she caught him again and again. Until finally she brought him down in an exuberant tackle and climbed on top of him for some celebratory lovemaking.

Which gave them a chance to appreciate another of her stat boosts.

His benefactor's words about the benefits of higher fertility were subtle but immediately noticeable. Pella was even more horny than usual, produced more copious nectar, and climaxed more easily and much more intensely. She was also ready to go for longer, putting him through his paces.

And since fertility affected both lovers Dare enjoyed it even more than usual as well.

Part of that might've been her excitement at reaching Level 30, but the +5 fertility made a clear difference. As evidenced by the fact that when his dog girl lover finally came down from an earth-shattering orgasm that rolled her eyes back in her head, she slumped contentedly on top of him, affectionately licking his sweaty chest.

"Wow," she murmured.

"Wow," Dare agreed, stroking her silky skin.

She giggled and looked up at him. "Promise me . . . when you hit 30 we're doing this again."

His cock, sated and limp against her well satisfied sex, twitched hard enough at that for her to feel it and giggle again. "Definitely," he said, sliding his hand down to her ass and squeezing it firmly as he pulled her harder against him. "In the meantime, ready to go again?"

She very much was.

The next day the group switched back to the previous arrangement, at which point Leilanna surprised him with an unexpected complaint about it. "How come I'm the only one who doesn't get to spend time with you?" she whined.

Dare stared at her in confusion. "I thought you'd be jumping for joy to not have to be near me."

Her ashen skin flushed darker. "I just think we should all spend equal time together." She gave him a hurt look. "Are you saying you don't want to spend time with me?"

"Of course not," he said hastily, and was surprised to mean it. He kind of enjoyed their verbal sparring, especially since a lot of the acrimony had faded in the time they'd been together, making it more like banter. He even found himself enjoying her passion in everything she did.

And it didn't hurt that she was beautiful, had a pleasant voice, and was an honest-to-god elf.

"I'll tell you what," he said. "When the crunch of getting the levels we need is over and we're done with the dungeon, we can spend a nice day together. We'll make it a date."

The Mage's cheeks flushed. "I never said I wanted to spend time with you romantically, idiot!" She grabbed Pella's hand and stormed off.

"She totally wants to spend time with you romantically," Zuri said, grinning. Her smile widened further when the dusk elf, still in earshot thanks to her elvish hearing, stiffened at that and glared back at them.

Dare shook his head with a sigh. "Let's not read anything into it that's not there." He patted her head. "Ready to go?"

His goblin lover nodded determinedly. "I need to catch up to you."

The determined focus they showed in leveling continued to the end of the week, with Leilanna getting up to 18, Zuri to 26, and Dare to 27. Then they encountered a group of five adventurers in their low 20s sniffing around the area, hunting monsters from a few well known spawn points, and Dare decided they shouldn't risk that group discovering the cavern entrance.

"Tomorrow we'll tackle the dungeon," he announced. "Get a good night's sleep tonight, and prepare however you can." He nodded to Leilanna and Zuri. "I'd like you both to only sleep four hours, so if needed we can take a break in the caves and you can sleep to restore your mana."

The curvy dusk elf shouldn't have been surprised at that, but she still scowled as she wolfed down a fruit cobbler he'd made. "Get a good night's sleep, he says," she muttered. "Wake up after four hours, he says. Make up your fucking mind."

Zuri patted her hand. "I'll keep you company, since we'll both be up anyway."

"Oh, that reminds me." Dare extended a party invitation to the dusk elf. "I won't look at your private information if you don't want me to," he added. Although he dearly would've liked to see if there was something in there that explained why she was such a pampered hothead.

"I don't," she snapped. "Not that that'll stop you, I'm sure." Still, she didn't hesitate to accept the invite.

True to his word, he left her information unlooked at.

As they prepared to sleep that evening Dare gently but firmly turned down overtures for lovemaking from his lovers, insisting they needed to be properly rested. And also since Zuri was going to be spending the night in Leilanna's tent.

In spite of Pella's disappointment she was mollified when he cuddled her for a while, stroking her soft ears, her fluffy tail, and up and down her back while whispering loving words until they settled down to peaceful sleep.

* * * * *

Torches, check. Rope, check. Extra wood for a fire or more torches, check. Food and water for up to three days, check. Packs empty of anything but bedrolls and necessities so they'd have plenty of room for loot, check.

Dare inspected his recurve bow, making sure the durability was good, and also his spear. He was aware of his companions eyeing him impatiently, already long since done with their own preparations, but he couldn't help feeling a bit nervous.

This would be his first dungeon, and although all of them but Leilanna out-leveled it he was still nervous. There were only four of them and they didn't have a proper tank, which was a concern.

He'd been part of countless parties tackling countless dungeons in games back on Earth, both parties of his own making and under his complete control in single player and with real people in multiplayer.

Good dungeon runs, bad ones, ones where he'd taken a backseat and ones where he'd contributed and ones he'd led. And not just parties but raids, sometimes with up to 50 people. He knew what he was doing here, and he trusted that he'd be able to judge if the dungeon was getting too difficult and they needed to turn back and try leveling more.

Or even, out of desperation, team up with that lower level party.

"All right," he finally said, nocking an arrow to the string and activating Rapid Shot to grasp four more in his bow hand. "Let's go."

They slipped into the entrance, Pella in front of the formation with Zuri just behind her, Dare off to one side, and Leilanna bringing up the rear. Dare quietly pointed out the nearest of the giant bats, imaginatively named "Nightmare Bats".

Which, admittedly, they were definitely the stuff of nightmares, with all the hideous creepiness of the small animals, but exaggerated in monster form.

Using his Eye, he told his companions the bats' exact stats and attacks, and formed a plan for how they'd deal with one, a few, or the entire room aggroing. That last being to retreat to the opening of the cave and use it as a choke point, having Pella use her crowd control on each one that came through until they could kill it.

Before pulling, Dare gathered his companions around him, expression serious. "One last thing. What's the most important thing in group fights?"

"Don't die," Zuri said immediately.

He smiled. "That's definitely the most important part of it, but not the rule that'll help prevent that from happening. What else?"

"Kill the monster," Leilanna said.

"Again, important but not the key rule."

"Oh!" Pella said, raising her hand. "It's protecting your teammates."

Dare chuckled. "You're all correct in part. The most important rule is *fulfill your role*." At their blank looks he smiled again.

"Leilanna, what's your role?"

"Kill the monsters," she said.

He nodded. "Right. So as soon as the fight starts, you blast the designated target nonstop until it's dead. Unless a monster is literally about to rip your head off, you keep doing damage. And once you're out of danger you go right back to damage." He turned to Zuri. "Your role?"

"Kill the monsters, and be ready to heal any wounded," she said.

"Good. And when it comes to doing damage, same applies to you. Drop everything if you need to heal or you're about to be attacked, but otherwise keep casting your Mana Thorns." He turned to Pella. "Your role?"

"Keep the enemies away from the rest of you however I can, while avoiding getting hurt," she said, grinning. "If I'm not doing that I can do damage."

"Exactly." Dare pointed at himself. "And I'll be doing damage and, if necessary, taking any monsters that get away from Pella. I'll also be leading the fight, so pay attention to my instructions. And try not to fill the air with chatter or give orders of your own unless it's an emergency."

He looked around at his companions. "Pay attention, be careful, protect each other, and *fulfill your role*. If we do that this dungeon will be a piece of cake."

Zuri brightened. "I have no idea what that means but I like the sound of it."

Chuckling, he motioned to the nearest Nightmare Bat. "Zuri, Leilanna, start casting your spells. I'm going to pull." Once they complied he drew and loosed an arrow at the monster, immediately nocking and drawing another to also loose.

As the first arrow buried in the monster's sternum it Screeched, the sound echoing around the large cavern with shocking volume. Dare staggered at the sonic attack, ears ringing and vision blurring. He'd expected it, but it still dazed him for a moment as the bat detached from the cavern ceiling, Screeching again as his second arrow slammed into its lower body.

It swooped toward them, wings outspread, and two more bats joined it. They were all Screeching, but the disorienting effects diminished as he got used to them.

Okay, three should be doable.

Just behind his second arrow came Zuri's Mana Thorn and Leilanna's fireball, the latter far more devastating than the former in spite of the eight level difference between the two women. The Nightmare Bat caught flame, putting negative effects on it that caused damage over time and disorientation.

Because of that the monster veered clumsily and slammed into a stalactite, taking minor impact damage and dropping to the ground below like a stone, temporarily out of the fight. That just left two coming at them.

Dare loosed the last three arrows in his bow hand at the next closest bat, then activated Rapid Shot again for four more arrows and the increased attack speed. At the same time more Mana Thorns flew out, hitting his target, while Leilanna cast a fireball at each of the remaining bats to apply the negative effects on them.

Being on fire disoriented the monsters, but neither one were so affected that they collided with anything. On silent wings they quickly closed the remaining distance, shifting into terrifying attack positions that on a dark night back on Earth would've made him shit his pants.

He used Pounce on the one he and his companions were damaging down, slamming it to the ground and rendering it unable to move or attack for 1 second. He used that time to stab his spear down into the meat of one of its wings, staggering slightly as it unleashed another Screech at point blank range.

Text appeared in front of him. "You have unlocked Wing Cripple in the Hamstring tree. Wing Cripple: Slow enemy flight speed by 25%. 5% chance per second for enemy to lose control and plummet for 3 seconds."

"Pella, slash their wing to unlock Wing Cripple!" he called as he activated Roll and Shoot, putting distance between himself and the recovering bat as he loosed another arrow at it. Since she also had

Hamstring she should be eligible to learn it, too.

The dog girl, who'd tackled the second monster and currently had it locked down with Subdue, called cheerfully, "I unlocked and maxed that out to my level ages ago . . . my master was pretty good about teaching me to optimize my Tracker build."

Dare danced out of the way of the first bat as it swooped past, slowed by his blow to its wing. It was nearly dead, and shortly after he thrust his spear into its chest a fireball from Leilanna fried the last of its hit points.

It convulsed and flopped lifelessly with a final Screech.

That gave him just enough time to leap aside from the first bat he'd pulled, which had recovered from its collision with the stalactite and subsequent fall. He was too slow, and Prey's Vigilance triggered to make him dodge away from a swift bite, narrowly escaping wickedly long fangs dripping with poison.

Fuck.

Dare Wing Crippled the monster as it passed, slowing it, then darted in behind and slashed its other wing. As he'd hoped, that removed its ability to fly and reduced it to skittering awkwardly on its wings.

He ran back, putting some distance between them, and began loosing arrows at the bat Pella had just been forced to release, and was now doing her best to slow with her lasso. Zuri and Leilanna were both targeting that one, and under their sustained attacks it quickly dropped.

Pella abandoned her target when it became clear the monster wouldn't be a further threat, rushing over to Overpower the bat chasing him. Then she caught its neck in her lasso and backpedaled, yanking it away from Dare.

With a shivering Screech the Nightmare Bat turned its wrath to her as she expertly kited it away.

So far so good. Dare joined the others in damaging down the remaining bat, feeling confident that their next fights with the remaining groups of bats would go more smoothly.

At least until his dog girl lover, straying a bit too far into the cavern as she led the bat away from the others, got too close to one of the monsters still hanging on the ceiling.

He first became aware of the threat as three more Screeches echoed through the cavern, pounding into his skull and making him stumble to one knee in spite of his best efforts. He looked up with dread to see three more bats swooping down towards Pella and felt sick to his stomach.

"Leilanna, Gale!" he shouted as he desperately kept shooting the nearly dead bat, trying to eliminate it as a threat before the aggroed adds arrived.

Pella, thinking quickly, used Run Down on the Mage, who was closest to the entrance. She managed to zoom out from under the swooping monsters just as they whooshed through the air where she'd been, and they were forced to wheel around after her, slowing their pursuit.

The curvy dusk elf, showing surprising courage, rushed right towards the fleeing dog girl, hands outstretched. They glowed storm cloud gray and a whirling vortex of wind flew out from her in a cone. It caught two of the bats, slamming them into each other with a loud *crunch* and then blowing them back to crash into a stalagmite with an even more sickening noise.

The remaining monster careened away, having to circle wide to avoid the spell and buying Pella more time.

Dare loosed a final arrow at the last of the original three bats, finishing it off, then motioned urgently for the entrance. "Keep doing damage but back up towards the entrance!" he called. "We'll use the choke point if we have to."

They focused on the single bat that had escaped the spell as they all backed away, Pella taking a position at the front of the group where she could deal with it when it reached them. They had a bit of luck, though, because one of Leilanna's fireballs hit the monster directly in the head, and like the first bat they'd aggroed it also veered to slam into a rock formation.

The fight stabilized from there, and they were able to kill the first bat while the other two were recovering from their crash. Leilanna hit them both with fireballs to make them even more manageable, and Pella was there with her lasso and abilities as they got close enough.

Somehow, in spite of the hairy complication, they managed to win without anyone taking any injuries. Dare thought that was worthy of celebration and gave out a round of hugs, including Leilanna in the spur of the moment. "You were amazing!" he said, grinning.

"You were!" Pella agreed. "You really came to my rescue."

Unsurprisingly, the fiery Mage flailed at his back and shoulders and grumbled until he let her go, although her ashen cheeks were flushed as she backed away muttering complaints.

The Nightmare Bats dropped a specialty leather, wing membranes, fangs, and eyeballs that were apparently a reagent. Considering the difficulty in killing them he would've hoped for more, but hopefully the real treasure was waiting farther inside the dungeon.

"Two groups down, four more to go," Dare said briskly, taking in the remainder of the cavern. "Once we finish them off we'll poke around to make sure there's no hidden goodies, then go deeper."

"Do you deliberately word things to sound obscene?" Leilanna demanded, biting her lip and blushing.

Pella snickered. "No, I think he's right that you just have a dirty mind."

The Mage scowled and quickly turned away. "Were we going to clear this dungeon or just stand around talking?"

The rest of the cavern went smoothly, Dare and his companions clearing the remaining bats without much trouble. There were no more near disasters like the first one, and the fact that they'd basically killed two groups one after the other gave them all confidence.

Then came the treasure hunt.

As it turned out, the beautiful rainbow stream bed glittered with more than just pretty colored sand. Leilanna was the first to discover an uncut gem, and that led to a lot of eager splashing around as they dredged every square foot of the underground river as it passed through the cavern, before becoming a torrent downstream and spouting from the wall upstream in the same torrent.

He had to admit that there was a special excitement involved in closing his fingers around a lump of rock, and raising it to find a raw ruby or emerald or sapphire glittering on his palm. Sure, the vast majority of the time he picked up a regular old pebble, and only found one small emerald, but it was still a blast.

Overall they found six gems total: his emerald, a ruby and two sapphires from Leilanna, and another emerald and a thumb-sized ruby from Zuri. To Pella's vast disappointment, in spite of her enthusiastic splashing around she found nothing.

The fact that there were two of each gem seemed to Dare like a clear pattern, and after another half hour or so of searching fruitlessly he convinced his companions that they'd probably found everything there was to be found.

Surprisingly, it was Zuri who was most reluctant to move on; he'd noticed before that even though his little lover had little interest in wealth aside from getting what they needed with it, and was very generous with those in need, she got a lot of enjoyment out of treasure hunting.

She'd been the most eager to search through Pella's loot cache, too.

The cavern ended in a crack in the stone so narrow that they had to squeeze a little to get through it. Dare wondered if it was some sort of deliberate barrier to prevent adventurers from bringing in horses or siege weapons or other advantages.

Then, inconveniently enough, the tunnel opened out into a series of small caverns and narrow tunnels infested with giant cave salamanders.

Thankfully the monsters only came one at a time, and were about as difficult as the bats. But those small benefits were vastly outweighed by the challenge that the confined spaces were awful for ranged classes, which all of them but Pella were.

Even worse, the salamanders aggroed before they even saw them,

142

so they'd be moving along the tunnels and one would suddenly burst around a corner, jaws snapping and claws slashing.

Their dog girl Tracker led the way, and was quick to keep the monster controlled when it attacked. Although once her abilities were all on cooldown there wasn't really enough room for her to kite the enemy, so she had to rely on evasion in the narrow confines while keeping herself between the salamander and the rest of the group.

While terrifying, the fact that Pella was 6 to 8 levels higher than these enemies meant they didn't do much damage to her. That, plus the fact that there was only one at a time, meant that she only got a few minor bites and scratches in the fights, most of which weren't even worth healing since there were no bleed effects and her hit points would gradually recover on their own.

Also the salamanders had no poisons, diseases, or curses, so she could afford to take some hits.

The salamander loot was more specialty leather, a gall bladder that was a reagent, and claws and teeth. But unlike with the bats there were no hidden treasures to be found in the small, winding caverns.

That, or they just weren't able to find what was there.

Disappointed, the party continued on to a large cavern dominated by a still, dark pool. It blocked their bath forward, aside from narrow paths to the far side on ledges running along either wall. The walls were covered by breathtaking curtains of calcite or whatever it was, flowing in delicate patterns over every surface.

Beautiful, but the entire "dark pool they had to cross" thing was suspicious as hell.

Chapter Nine
The Depths

Thus far they hadn't needed to use torches, since the ceilings were covered with a bioluminescent lichen or mold that gave of enough faint blue light to let them see by. Here that lichen was joined by small fish in the pool that glowed an eerie green.

Beautiful, in their own way, watching them dart about in the water chasing ripples made by droplets falling from the ceiling. Although Dare got less enjoyment out of the sight when their faint light revealed a larger shape moving beneath them in the murky depths.

Much larger.

"Fuck this," Leilanna said, also seeing it. "What the fuck are we supposed to do here? I bet the moment we step onto those ledges we're going to get grabbed and pulled into the water by tentacles."

"And not the good kind," he joked.

"The fuck kind of tentacles are good?" she demanded.

Dare couldn't help but laugh at the fact that after taking half of what he said as naughty, the dusk elf missed that one.

Still, her question had been a valid one. His companions were all looking to him for ideas, and he shrugged. "We aggro whatever's down there one at a time, I guess," he said. "I bet if we make a splash they'll come."

He found a good sized rock and tossed it into the water near their end, and they all spread out near the entrance and got ready. Sure enough, the water immediately rippled ominously. The fish all darted away in fear as a shape rose to the surface, making a beeline for them and quickly growing larger.

As it got closer it lit up with a livid red glow, illuminating its monstrous shape.

It was, indeed, some sort of kraken or squid, about the size of a yacht and sporting a dozen writhing tentacles. Dare inspected it with his Eye and quickly shouted out information as they braced for the attack.

"Lord of the Depths. Monster, Party Rated. Level 24. Attacks: Snatch, Submerge, Frenzy, Bite, Rip, Crush."

"It's a boss!" he called in warning. "About four times as tough as the salamanders, but its tentacles have separate hit point bars. Obviously we're going to want to hit the body if we can, but I get the feeling we'll have to kill the tentacles that catch us. Pella, can you handle that with your knife, and maybe grab and redirect tentacles with your lasso?"

"On it!" the dog girl shouted, running forward.

"Fuck this entire cavern!" Leilanna shouted, squealing and throwing herself to the side as two different tentacles shot for her. One caught her around the foot and her squeal turned into a scream as she was dragged slowly towards the water.

Dare and Zuri were focused on the body, while Pella hacked furiously at the slimy tentacle that had caught the Mage. Unfortunately the closer Leilanna was pulled towards the water, the easier time the other tentacles had reaching her, and soon she was caught between three. An even more wrenching scream tore from her throat as the tentacles began pulling her in different directions, trying to Rip her apart.

"Zuri, switch to tentacles!" he called desperately. "It looks like we'll have to kill them all before dealing with the body. And hope they don't regrow or something."

The dusk elf was frantically casting Ring of Fire, singeing the tentacles grabbing her and causing them to flinch back. She singed Pella as well, but the dog girl shrugged aside the pain with a growl and kept hacking.

Dare used Rapid Shot and quickly loosed arrows at the tentacle Pella was working on, and finally killed it.

Unfortunately, not before the slimy limb thrashed and clenched. Leilanna screamed again, in pain this time, as with a sickening *snap* the tentacle Crushed her ankle in its death throes.

Fuck, this was going to shit fast.

Zuri immediately swapped to healing, while Dare and Pella continued killing tentacles. Leilanna cast Gale to send several tentacles blowing away over the water, then switched to Wind Slash for its fast cast speed so her spells wouldn't be interrupted.

Also, she'd probably noticed that her fireballs were having less effect against the kraken's wet, leathery flesh.

Finally the Mage, battered and bruised by flailing tentacles and their Crushing death throes, was freed. She scrambled back towards the entrance with a whimper, pursued by half a dozen tentacles.

Were they going after her because she was the lowest level, or a caster? "Use Gale again!" Dare shouted, jumping between the tentacles and his companion so he could knock aside and slash at them with his spear.

The panicking dusk elf either didn't hear or chose to ignore him, continuing her headlong flight to safety. Dare grit his teeth and redoubled his efforts as Zuri got back to casting spells.

"Zuri, use Nature's Curse on this big bastard!" he shouted, ducking a blurring tentacle with the aid of Fleetfoot's speed.

"Right!" his little lover said, a bit chagrined; her spell that slowed an enemy and had a chance to paralyze it was perfect for a major fight like this.

She darted forward to where some kraken blood had splashed, then scrabbled around helplessly in search of mud to make a figure of the kraken. Dare bounded over to the narrow strip of rock beneath the water before the ground fell away into the depths, scrabbled around for a small crack where some silt had accumulated, and flung a handful to his lover. "Here!"

Zuri quickly got to work, and Dare turned back to hacking at tentacles.

Leilanna finally reached the entrance to the cavern and calmed down enough to get back into the fight. She began flinging more Wind Slashes, and even used Gale to bat aside three tentacles that went for Zuri.

The goblin woman finally got off her Nature's Curse, and they all breathed a sigh of relief as the kraken noticeably slowed, its tentacles becoming more sluggish.

There were only a few left, and almost simultaneously Dare and Leilanna severed two. Dare looked at where Pella was working on the final one, leaping around as it writhed in an attempt to catch her, and a sudden instinct warned him.

Boss phases. Fuck.

"Pella! Don't kill the last-"

His lover hacked a final time with her long knife and the severed tentacle flopped limply to the ground.

The Lord of the Depths roared, shivering the pool around it in violent ripples, then with a mighty thrashing motion hurled itself out of the water. Without tentacles its motions were a sort of violent undulation, but it was still able to make for Pella with its wickedly toothed maw gaping wide to swallow her.

The dog girl squeaked and bolted away, and Dare switched back to his bow and activated Rapid Shot, loosing arrows at the kraken's plate-sized eye.

Thankfully Zuri and Leilanna had spotted the obvious vulnerability as well and were loosing spells at it.

Pella desperately ran, keeping ahead of the giant flopping monster mainly thanks to Nature's Curse. Still, she had the presence of mind to flick the knot of her lasso at the giant squid's other eye as she continued to lead it around.

Tense as the encounter was, from there it was fairly straightforward. Sure, it probably would've been easier if they'd burned the kraken down while Pella wrestled with a single tentacle, but she was able to keep ahead of the thrashing monster.

It wasn't exactly a tank and spank since she was kiting the enemy, but they had all the room in the world to kill the monster without interruption. And so while it took a while, finally the kraken squealed and gave a final thrash, then went still.

Text appeared in the corner of Dare's vision. "Party rated monster

Lord of the Depths defeated. 12,000 bonus experience awarded."

"Completed 2/10 towards Achievement Protector of Bastion: Slay 10 party rated monsters in the region of Bastion."

"Trophies gained: giant tentacle x6, kraken beak x1. Loot body to acquire."

A loud rumbling shivered the entire cavern, and a walkway covered with dozens of shellfish rose into view, giving them a safer path across the pool than the narrow, sloping ledges to either side.

Leilanna, shaken but stirred out of her terror by their victory, was first to loot the kraken body. "What the fuck?" she demanded in a cheated voice, scowling furiously. "The only stuff on this big bastard are the trophies and a bunch of squid meat! Where's the damn treasure for killing a party rated monster?"

"If I had to guess?" Dare said, pointing. "In those."

She looked, missing his intent and frowning into the water. "What, the glowing fish?"

Pella walked over to one of the shellfish and picked it up. "You mean these?"

"Yup, freshwater mussels." Dare took the creature from her and used his knife to pry it open. Inside, sitting on a bed of flesh, lay a small pearl.

"Oooh!" the girls all said, gathering around him for a closer look.

"There's got to be over fifty of them!" Zuri said excitedly, looking at the mussels lining the walkway. "And this is one of the smaller ones!"

A new treasure hunt began as they raced to open all the shellfish. Disappointingly, not all of the mussels had pearls, and the larger ones didn't always have larger pearls, either.

Still, by the time they reached the other edge of the walkway they'd collected 37 pearls, varying in size and quality. The prize among them was one the size of an egg found inside a massive, ancient mussel in the center of the walkway. The shellfish also dropped meat, although that wasn't as exciting.

With all the loot squared away Dare did a quick tally of the party.

Leilanna was down to a bit over 10% of her mana, and Zuri had even less. Pella also needed a heal from accumulated injuries, and they were all weary from the fights they'd gone through so far.

"All right," he said briskly, drawing his companions' attention from their admiring inspection of the pearls. "Let's see what's waiting for us next. I'm guessing it'll be more easy monsters, not another boss, so I say we hunt them until our casters are out of mana, then stop to let them get their four hours of sleep. We can cook a meal at the same time."

Everyone agreed with that plan, so they left the Lord of the Depths behind in its cavern and entered a broad tunnel with a steeply sloping ramp downwards.

* * * * *

They finally had to break out the torches as the luminous lichen faded away on their way down the sloping ramp, which seemed to stretch on forever.

The eerie cave became even more unsettling in the flickering light, especially as the steep path opened into a dark cavern and they disturbed what felt like hundreds of giant, blind cave moths that immediately fluttered towards the torches.

They began aggressively swirling around the light, shooting strands of silk that bound Dare and his companions as the strands accumulated, then darting in to bite at them with small, vicious teeth. The comparatively silent beating of their wings became a deafening commotion with so many, especially as the sound echoed in the cavern.

The monsters were Level 18 and weak for that level, with half the health and damage, but there were so damn *many* of them. They'd overwhelm them with sheer numbers unless they retreated back to the ramp.

Or made use of their Mage.

"Protect Leilanna!" he shouted, crowding close to her on his side. "Leilanna, cast Ring of Fire!"

"We'll all get burned!" Zuri protested.

Bastion

Dare shook his head as the dusk elf began to cast. "At the last second I'll pick you up and Pounce to a moth out of the spell's range. Pella can Intervene to us."

"What if I don't kill them all?" Leilanna protested, pausing her casting.

"Weak as these are the Burn effect will seriously disorient and slow them, and you can get away," he assured her. "And even if not, they don't do much damage and Zuri can heal you."

The Mage growled and prepared to finish the spell. "Go!"

Dare picked up Zuri and Pounced a distant moth, the ability's effect of Tackling the bird-sized creature to the ground looking a bit ludicrous. Pella was right behind him, and together they all turned back to watch.

Leilanna's spell fanned out in a brilliant reddish-orange dome, catching most of the moths and lighting them on fire. The effect was horrifyingly beautiful as hundreds of monsters fluttered about wildly, burning bright, with the Mage standing in the center, hair and clothes lashing wildly as she was buffeted by the searing wind.

God, she was hot. Literally and figuratively.

Only about half of the moths died, but she immediately began casting another Ring of Fire as she stepped into the thick of their chaotically flapping swarm.

Her second spell killed the majority of the surviving moths, and Dare and his lovers rushed in to finish off the remainder.

"That was fantastic!" Pella shouted, practically tackling the weary Mage in a hug. "It would've taken forever to kill those things, and we would've all been tied up with silk and bitten all over before we managed it."

Leilanna smiled weakly. "Hurray for area of effect spells." She plopped to the ground, taking the dog girl with her. "I'm at like 3% mana and ready to sleep, so goodnight."

Dare thought they could've gone a bit farther and killed another group or two, but this seemed like a good resting spot. The cavern around them had only two small entrances, one of which they'd

150

already cleared.

Still, he ushered Leilanna over to a spot where the cavern made a deep corner, where they could defend from only one direction if necessary. Then he set up a tent for the beautiful dusk elf, lit a fire, and left her to sleep.

Dare sent Pella to keep watch at the far entrance while he and Zuri got to the laborious task of looting hundreds of moths.

The effort was of dubious value. About half of them dropped silk strands that Zuri could weave to make silk thread, then silk cloth. More valuable was the huge cluster of moth cocoons at the far end of the cavern, which not only netted them much more silk but also valuable reagents.

"So far everything we've killed has had a loot trove of some sort outside what we get from the monster corpses," Zuri said with a frown, inspecting the pile of materials they'd just gotten. "Should we go back to the salamander caverns and look again?"

"Maybe on the way out of the dungeon," Dare replied. He plopped to the ground beside her and pulled her into his lap, affectionately rubbing her tummy. "How are you and this little guy doing?"

"We're okay," she said, contentedly cuddling against him. "Some exciting times since we got in here, though." She shuddered. "Especially with the Lord of the Depths."

"Mmm." He kissed her softly. "You going to get some sleep too? You shouldn't push yourself."

"In a minute," his goblin lover murmured, hugging him tighter. "I missed you last night."

"Same here."

Zuri giggled. "Although sleeping with Leilanna was nice too. She's a great cuddler . . . like hugging a warm fluffy pillow. You'd love it." She looked up at him, yellow eyes sparkling teasingly. "And just imagine what it would feel like to mate someone that soft and bouncy."

Dare shook his head wearily; his wingman wasn't going to give up. "Get some sleep, you," he said, affectionately rubbing her pointy ears.

She pouted. "Fine, I'll go cuddle with Leilanna some more." She slipped out of his arms and made her way over to burrow beneath the covers against the curvy elf.

True to her claim, Leilanna *did* seem to be a good cuddler. She woke up just enough to wrap her arms and one leg around the little goblin and pull her close, murmuring contentedly as she fell back asleep.

Dare couldn't help but envy Zuri her position, then cursed himself for being an idiot; the fiery Mage had made it clear she wasn't interested.

Shaking his head, he walked over to join Pella, who was alertly staring into the narrow tunnel leading deeper into the cave. She'd found a crack in the floor to wedge her torch in, leaving her free to crouch with her weapons ready.

"How's it looking?" he whispered.

"No patrols or roamers yet," she said. Still apparently intent on her watch, she added casually, "Zuri's right that Leilanna loves to cuddle and is really soft. And she smells great." She giggled. "She's more naughty than you might think, too."

He gave the dog girl a sharp look, wondering what exactly *that* meant, but didn't rise to the obvious bait. "You guys are killing me," he complained.

Of course Leilanna was beautiful and probably felt great to every sense, and he would've given anything to fuck her. That didn't change their rocky relationship.

His golden-haired lover grinned at him. "Smart as you are, sometimes I wonder about you when it comes to women," she said wryly. "Didn't you have girls back home who'd throw dirt clods at you and yell that they hated you, then go home and rub themselves crosseyed while moaning your name?"

Dare was pretty sure *he* had never inspired that sort of feeling in women back on Earth. Not that he knew of at least. "They're called tsundere," he said wryly. "And I'm pretty sure Leilanna isn't one."

She sighed. "Well, she might not be there yet. I'm glad you're being so patient with her, though. I like her, and if she ever did make up her mind about you she'd be a great addition to our harem."

He shook his head wryly and rubbed his dog girl lover's floppy ears. "Come on, let's set up closer to the others. We can still keep watch just as well there."

Pella bounded to her feet, snatching up her torch as her tail wagged eagerly. "Can we cuddle during our shift?"

Dare was about to refuse, then he thought about the fact that they were going to be sitting around for four hours waiting for the spellcasters to wake up. "Sure, we can get a bit more comfortable," he said. "As long as we keep alert."

"Don't worry," she said with surprising solemnity. "I never let my guard down when it comes to protecting the people I love."

He leaned in and kissed her soft lips, looking deep into her beautiful brown eyes. "I sometimes wonder what I did right to get so lucky in finding you."

His dog girl lover kissed him back tenderly, then gave his lips a playful lick with her flat tongue. "You were yourself, of course," she said with a grin. She tugged on his hand. "Come on, let's go lay out the blankets to sit on."

* * * * *

"A puzzle," Dare said, grinning. He stooped to pick up a rock, tossing it up and down in one hand. "Awesome. I thought it was all going to be monster fights and bosses."

This world never disappointed. He casually flicked the stone far into the cavern, where it landed on Number 883.

The 3-foot square tile exploded in an incinerating column of flames for a good five seconds, then petered out. Leaving the tile as untouched as if the flames had never triggered.

"How are trapped tiles that burn hot enough for it to singe our eyebrows from twenty yards away *awesome*?" Surprisingly, it was Zuri who spoke, rather than Leilanna.

The Mage was intent on the numbers.

The cavern in front of them was square in shape, the floor a grid of 100 by 100 tiles of various colors. Or in other words ten thousand tiles, the numbers randomized with no apparent pattern that he could see.

Not that he'd had time to look over *ten thousand* variables.

It couldn't be a math puzzle, unless the creators of this world system thought they were geniuses or had access to calculators. And it wasn't a matter of starting at 1, then jumping to 2, then 3, and so on, because the numbers were too random.

Also the colors had to mean something: red, blue, teal, orange, green, yellow, purple, brown, white, and black. It wasn't as simple as individual colors corresponding with multiples of a number, or odd or even, or any other pattern he could see.

Dare became aware of his companions looking at him in anticipation. "Okay," he admitted. "Maybe not so awesome . . . I have no idea what the puzzle even *is*, let alone how to solve it."

"What if we just brute force it?" Leilanna suggested. "Use your idea of throwing rocks and going tile by tile in every row until we find the path."

"You want to find ten thousand rocks and spend hours throwing them?" Dare asked.

She shook her head and motioned eagerly. "It'll be easier than that, because once we find the first tile the next ones will have to be close enough to it for us to step or jump to."

He nodded thoughtfully. "Good point." He looked over the tiles again, scowling. "Okay, we'll try that while trying to figure this out."

It was a good idea. Unfortunately, after they threw four more rocks, triggering the columns of flame on the first four tiles on the left end, a familiar screech filled the air. Three Nightmare Bats boiled out of the tunnel on the far side and winged towards them, Screeching furiously.

"Shit, back to the tunnel!" Dare called.

The fight was familiar, and they were able to down the bats without more injury than Pella getting a deep cut from a wing claw, which Zuri was able to heal. Dare was about to grin wickedly and suggest that triggered defenders meant this would be a great place to farm monsters, even if the experience was average and the loot was sub-par.

Then he realized that the bats hadn't given experience, and couldn't be looted either.

Fuck. "Okay, new plan," he growled. "If triggering five tiles brings a wave of monsters, we're facing potentially 19 fights on the first row, and potentially one fight every row after that. Or around a hundred and twenty fights. That would take days, maybe even weeks, if you take mana into consideration."

"And all for fights that don't give us anything," Pella added. "We're supposed to solve this puzzle, not take the easy way out."

Not that brute forcing the puzzle would've been particularly easy. Dare scowled at the tiles some more.

He had yet to break his chilly silence with his benefactor since their last conversation, and she hadn't tried to contact him either, apparently giving him space. But even if he was about to give in and ask her now, he seriously doubted she'd help.

So. 100 by 100 rows making 10,000 tiles, of 10 colors and randomized numbers from 1 to 10,000. The only possible solution was there was a pattern in there somewhere, and they needed to find it.

"All right," he told his companions. "Time to sit back and just look at this thing until something pops out at us. Keep your minds open to any possibility."

Pella shuffled uncertainly, looking like she wanted to say something. She had by far the least education out of all of them, in spite of Dare's and Zuri's and now Leilanna's efforts to teach her the basics of writing and math at every opportunity. It was obvious the puzzle made her uncomfortable.

Still, she raised her hand. "Does it help that the black tiles don't smell like fire?"

Dare perked up. "That sounds like it would help a ton." He picked up a stone and tossed it at the nearest black tile.

It didn't trigger. At least, not until the stone bounced onto the nearby yellow tile and that one went off.

Grinning, he pulled his beautiful lover into a hug. "Good job."

"Yeah, good job," Leilanna agreed. "Aside from the fact that after the fifth row the black tiles are spaced enough that that not even an elite athlete could jump to the next one."

Zuri and Pella both cursed, their eagerness fading into disappointment.

But maybe not. Dare inspected the puzzle again, then picked up a rock and tossed it at a brown tile on the sixth row. As he'd hoped it bounced without triggering, and by good luck didn't even leave the tile and trigger another blast.

So far they'd triggered one blast since pulling the bats. That should give them some leeway.

"Okay," he said. "Here's what I think. The puzzle is that we follow the tiles ranging in shades from black to white, switching every five rows. Once we get to the center either the pattern resets back to black and descends again, or we do another row of white and go in ascending order."

They stared at him. "How the fuck did you get that from throwing one stone?" Leilanna asked.

Dare shrugged. "There has to be some pattern, and that one at least makes sense. Especially after I confirmed that brown comes next." He smiled. "Also, it helps that on the sixth row there's a brown tile within stepping distance of every black one."

He turned to the puzzle. "I'll go first and confirm it's safe. Stay here until I get to the middle and determine the order of the second half, just in case something goes wrong and we trigger more monsters. After that you guys follow." He gave them all a stern look. "And be very careful."

"As if you have to tell us that," Zuri said wryly, looking at the slagged remains of the nearby rock that had been caught in the column of flame.

Dare grabbed a handful of stones and stepped onto the first black tile, then dropped a rock on the next one, just to be safe. It didn't trigger, so he stepped to it and picked up the rock, dropping it to the next one.

His main worry was not knowing exactly which colors were classified in order of shade. They wouldn't follow the order of a rainbow, since red at the edge was obviously darker than yellow in the middle. Some were fairly easy to guess, like pink being lighter than red, but what about between blue and green?

Well, he had four wrong guesses before he had to bolt back to the entrance for another fight.

The next brown tile was safe as well, supporting his theory, and when he got to the eleventh row he did purple next and his guess was correct. He messed up on teal being next after red, but that was because the remaining colors all seemed equally light. It turned out to be orange.

After one last mistake on yellow he found himself standing on the first white tile in the center. That gave him a bit of a buffer to test for the next row, so the heat wouldn't fry him from close range.

The most logical option was that it would go back to ascending order, since that was more symmetrical and would appeal to a rational mind. Although reseting was also rational.

It turned out his guess was wrong, and it went back to black; two guesses left.

"All right!" he called over his shoulder. "I'll keep going to the other side and spot for you, keep an eye out in case you put a foot wrong or something. Be careful!"

About fifty steps later he was on safe ground on the far side, and he breathed a huge sigh of relief. Even though it had been more straightforward than he thought once he got the pattern, it was still nice that nothing had gone wrong.

It would've sucked if there were false tiles or some other bullshit.

Pella led the way, following the exact tiles Dare had used. At his urging all three women stayed a few tiles apart, and used rocks to check every tile before stepping on it even though the tiles had already been proven safe. He also made sure they stepped carefully into the center of each tile, not getting anywhere close to the surrounding ones.

He was far more terrified watching the women he loved in danger than he'd been for his own safety, and his heart was in his throat with every cautious step they took. He was there to catch Pella when she stepped to safety with him, and she sagged in his arms as if she'd just sprinted to the point of collapse.

"I'm glad you went first," she confessed. "Even going second that was terrifying."

Zuri made it to them, joining the hug, and surprisingly Leilanna also threw her arms around them. "Part of me is glad we didn't have to fight a bunch of monsters," she said. "Another part never wants to do that again."

As if the dungeon had been listening, a deafening rumble sounded and the cavern around them shook. They watched as the tiles all flipped in a cool rippling pattern, showing smooth and white on the opposite side with no sign of colors or numbers.

Either the puzzle was defeated and now the entire floor was safe to step on, or the creators of this world had just given them a giant "fuck you" with a floor they could no longer safely traverse.

Dare tossed his rocks randomly, confirming it was the former.

"Look!" Leilanna called eagerly from the wall near the door. She'd discovered an alcove with a small, ornately carved wooden chest inside. There was no lock on it, and as they hurried over to join her she flipped the lid open.

The interior was separated into padded spaces, each one filled with a small glass vial. Three rows of four, with three different colored liquids. His information screen identified them as healing potions, skin regeneration potions, and fire resist potions.

Dare chuckled as he picked up a fire resist potion, looking up at the ceiling. "Fuck you," he told the dungeon's creator.

Zuri delicately plucked the potion from his hand and returned it to its padded nook, then shut and latched the chest and gingerly slipped it into her pack. "I don't know what you're complaining about. Most alchemists can only craft potions that have minor effects until they reach a much higher level. You can only get potions this powerful in loot or crafted at a high price."

He grinned and mussed her hair. "I didn't know that, but anyway I was just laughing at the irony of giving us those potions after that puzzle."

"Actually," Leilanna said, "irony would be if you got fired from your job and your final wages were paid in fire resist potions."

Dare rolled his eyes. "Okay thanks, Lady Literal." He motioned to the large, grandly carved tunnel leading from the cavern. "Let's keep going."

Chapter Ten
Last Cavern

The next cavern looked like the inside of an amethyst geode, and was filled with prismatic winged serpents that were immune to magic and shot spines.

Those were a huge bitch to fight with Leilanna and Zuri effectively sidelined. Luckily the creatures had low hit points and no melee attacks, and they could only shoot spines at a range. The spines could also be dodged if you were on the ball, which was convenient for Dare with Fleetfoot.

The fight was almost a game of tag, with Pella trying to stay within the serpents' melee range and damage them with her knife, while Dare shot arrows at them from a distance and ducked behind stalagmites when threatened. Meanwhile Zuri healed any wounds they took from the spines, which were deep but not alarming, and darted in with her spear to help Pella with the humble damage she could manage.

Leilanna, with her low level and hit points, did her best to stay out of the fight entirely.

The serpents dropped prismatic scales that were apparently a crafting item, and among the chunks of amethyst on the walls (none of which could be mined, unfortunately) Pella found a clutch of eggs with beautiful shells crusted with semiprecious gems.

Although they'd likely be more valuable sold to a rare animal merchant.

The dusk elf wanted to keep one of the serpents as a pet, which seemed like a bad idea given the spines, but Dare supposed that was an issue for when or if the treasure eggs actually hatched.

The next cavern was knee deep in water and dotted with stalagmites with flat, smooth tops that you couldn't quite jump between. The water was filled with eels that could electrify their scales in a dangerous melee attack, and if you were in the water when they did would transfer that charge through it to you.

That made for a tricky fight where they had to stay out of the water whenever any of them were within melee range of an eel, causing it to electrify, and had to stay away out of melee range in general to avoid their shocking attack.

The shock wasn't fatal, but it was like getting hit by a taser, taking you out of the fight for a while and leaving you with serious jitters after that. Zuri could heal the damage, thankfully, but even so they all got shocked at least once, and were cursing soundly by the time they cleared the cavern.

On the plus side, Leilanna reached Level 19 during the fight. She got a new rank of Fireball, and put her other ability points in better damage and survival. Including giving Ring of Fire a little love, since she'd actually found a use for it.

The eels dropped Shock Cores, which were apparently a material for low level enchantments for shock resist and shock damage to weapons. Which would've been nice if they had an Enchanter. That was apparently enough loot as far as the dungeon was concerned, and aside from some reptile leather and meat they didn't find anything else in the flooded cavern.

They made their way through a long tunnel after that, lit with more of the blue glowing lichen along the walls and ceiling. Although the far end of the tunnel had a more ruddy glow coming from it that looked like fire.

Dare felt a sense of trepidation at the sight of it, thinking of movies he'd watched and games he'd played where a glow like that came from a dragon or something like it. And Pella had said she smelled something at the entrance to the dungeon.

Confirming his fears, his dog girl lover stopped, face paling. "Draconic stink," she whispered. "Probably not an actual dragon, since they're intelligent, but a monstrous variant."

"Stay here," he told his companions. "I'll check it out with my Eye."

He cautiously edged forward in the narrow tunnel, ready to

spring backwards if the enemy proved smaller than he expected and could get at him. He could hear the heavy breathing of a massive creature, as well as snorts and scraping sounds. Like the sounds of an animal sleeping restlessly, or perhaps lying in a relaxed pose.

Finally, he got close enough to see into the next cavern, and his breath caught.

This chamber was as large as the entry cavern, but the walls, floor, and ceiling had been smoothed by a large creature rubbing against them, and scored with the gouges of large claws. There was a small pool on one end, and in the middle a thick column where a stalactite and stalagmite had joined millennia ago. Those were the only features he could see.

Aside from the monster sleeping curled up on itself against the far wall, positioned protectively in front of a large chest next to a pile of loot.

Two legs, two wings, features similar to a dragon. Which made it a wyvern. It was the size of the chimera they'd fought in the Gadris mountains on their way into Bastion, as big as an elephant or maybe even bigger. And it looked dangerous as hell, with long, wickedly curved claws at the end of its powerful legs, teeth the length of daggers in a jaw that looked as if it crushed rocks for sport, and a bladed barb at the end of its long, whip-like tail.

If the sight of it was terrifying, its stats visible with the Eye were even more so. "Vile Wyvern. Monster, Party Rated Dungeon Boss. Level 25. Attacks: Fire Spit, Acid Spit, Barbed Claw, Blade Tail, Crushing Bite, Wing Gale, Trample, Bellow."

Hoo, boy. Dare backed up to where the others waited. "Got those potions handy, Zuri?" he whispered.

"You mean the healing, fire resist, and skin regeneration ones?" Leilanna asked, gulping. "Which ones will we need?"

"Let's just say they could all potentially come in handy."

The girls all cursed. "Just what are we looking at, Dare?" Pella asked.

He quickly described what he'd seen. "It's got about half again as many hit points as the kraken we fought, and does more damage," he concluded grimly. "That, and the higher level, are going to make this tough."

"Fire Spit *and* Acid Spit," Zuri said quietly. "Even with the potions, getting hit by those will be unimaginably painful."

"On the plus side, at least we'll be able to start the fight with it sleeping, like with the chimera," Dare said. "Still, we'll have to make full use of our defensive cooldowns. And if need be we can retreat into the tunnel for a reprieve. Even if it resets the fight, it might be worth it if things go badly."

They all stared at him blankly. "Reset the fight?" Zuri said. "What does that mean?"

"Something that doesn't apply here, it looks like," he said sheepishly. Apparently bosses didn't despawn and respawn with full health if you ran from the fight or the party wiped. Although no doubt the wyvern would have a chance to recover hit points at an accelerated rate or something.

He took a breath. "Okay, let's camp and get a good night's rest so we're all at our best. We'll tackle this in the morning."

"What if it wakes up by then?" Zuri asked worriedly.

"Then we wait until it goes to sleep again."

Leilanna snorted. "It's a wyvern, it might sleep for a month and stay awake for a month." She looked around at them. "I'm doing okay for mana, and I bet Zuri is too. I say we tackle this now."

Dare shook his head firmly. "We don't rush something like this. We'll rest, plan, and go into it fresh and prepared."

She raised no further protests, and they all gratefully settled in to rest and check their gear. Dare cooked up some of the meat they'd got from the monsters in the dungeon with seasonings and vegetables he'd brought from outside, and they had a good meal.

Considering the potential for danger he set a watch rotation, volunteering for one of the undesirable middle shifts. Which was sort of necessary since Zuri and Leilanna needed four uninterrupted hours of sleep to fill their mana pool.

Then they all settled in, resting up for what would surely be a difficult fight.

＊ ＊ ＊ ＊ ＊

Dare had another arrow with rope tied to it so he could collect blood from the Vile Wyvern for Zuri's Nature's Curse spell. She had the ingredients for the spell all gathered and laid out in front of her, ready to cast it as quickly as possible once she had the final reagent.

His companions were all spread out, prepared to immediately begin doing damage the moment he loosed the arrow. They were rested, fed, and fortified with a fire resist potion each.

Which, as he'd learned to his surprise, worked different from most potions of the sort he was used to; instead of having a steady effect over a set duration, the potion started off strong and its effects slowly waned over time as it was absorbed through the body.

So they didn't want to waste any time now that they'd downed the burning, vaguely cinnamon-flavored mixtures.

Dare raised his bow and turned a questioning gaze to each of his companions in turn. He got determined nods from everyone, and with a last deep breath drew the arrow and loosed.

It hit at the same time as a Mana Thorn and Fireball from his companions, and the dungeon boss snorted out of its slumber and began to stir.

Was that a bad sign, that their first volley hadn't even drawn a roar of pain from it?

He yanked the rope back, whipping the bloody arrow in Zuri's direction. She caught it and immediately began her spell, and Dare got back to shooting arrows. Leilanna was right with him, really blasting into the wyvern.

Pella used Run Down on the Vile Wyvern as it lumbered to its hind legs, wings flapping. She reached the huge monster before its wings could rise out of range, dagger flashing as she used Wing Cripple on the nearest one.

At which point the dungeon boss fully woke up, and it was pissed.

Nature's Curse went off just in time to slow the wyvern as its

164

bladed tail whipped around at the dog girl, giving her time to dive out of the way. At the same time the monster's huge head swiveled to Dare, maw opening so wide the creature must've unhinged its jaw.

He had an excellent view of two rows of long, wicked teeth, and two different orifices at either end of the mouth that flared wide. From one gushed a fist-sized gob of burning spit with the consistency of napalm, and from the other came a similar gob that seethed a sickly green and yellow.

They were moving fast. Like, faster than arrows fast.

He abandoned the attempt to dodge he'd been about to make and sprang for Roll and Shoot, hurling himself ten feet to the side with the speed of the ability. The gobs of burning and acid spit hit the wall, eating into the stone and painting the cavern with an even more lurid glow.

Dare came up to his feet and immediately went back to loosing arrows, although he was wary of more spit coming his way. But there must've been at least some cooldown period for the attack, because the wyvern turned its attention to Pella and began pursuing her, frustrating her attempts to apply more Hamstring and Wing Cripple effects.

The dog girl yelped as its jaws gnashed closed just behind her in Crushing Bite, then again when the blade on its tail whipped past where she'd been about to dodge, nearly piercing her arm.

But she was keeping the dungeon boss's attention, buying time for the rest of them to unload maximum damage on it.

The second volley of fire and acid spit went for Leilanna, and the mage shrieked and abandoned casting a Fireball to dive aside. The fire spit hit her anyway, scorching her flesh in spite of the fire resist potion, and her shriek turned into a scream of pain.

She frantically yanked off her cloak and tried to wipe the viscous burning surface off her side and arm, while Zuri switched to healing.

The wyvern's momentary distraction to go after the Mage gave Pella an opportunity to dart in and cripple its other wing. Dare was pretty sure that was keeping the monster from using its ranged wing attacks, which would've further complicated the fight.

Their damage had slowed a bit, but he was still shooting arrows as quickly as he could while his companions recovered. Pella was slashing at the monster's body with her knife as she maneuvered to get behind its legs for a Hamstring attack, dodging its flailing tail as she did.

But rather than turning its attention back to the dogged Tracker, the Vile Wyvern turned and bolted straight for Dare with the speed of a charging raptor, tail whipping up in preparation to attack.

Shit.

He sprinted away, ready to distract the enemy while the others kept up the attack. He was fast, and the wyvern was slowed with multiple effects, but even so it caught up to him before he'd gone twenty feet.

He messed up and was a beat too slow activating Roll and Shoot to throw himself to the side of the charging monster, and was rewarded with a line of searing pain across his ass as its bladed tail tagged him.

Gritting his teeth around a shout of pain, Dare completed his roll and raised his bow, shooting the wyvern as it rushed past. He was prepared to take off running again if it went after him a second time, especially when he felt Zuri begin healing the wound he'd just taken. Pella rushed by, shooting him a thumbs up as she flicked her lasso out to catch the monster's legs in a not completely futile attempt to slow it.

Unfortunately, the dungeon boss didn't go after either of them.

Surprisingly quick on its feet, the wyvern veered and went straight for Leilanna, tail lashing out. She managed to dodge the blade at its tip, but the heavy tail still clipped her and sent her flying. She slammed into the cavern wall, banging her head, and landed hard on her hands and knees. Her movements were sluggish and dazed as she tried to get back to her feet.

Zuri cried out and switched to healing the Mage, so distracted helping her companion she didn't notice the Vile Wyvern turning its head to send a volley of spit at her. Pella did, and with a cry used Intervene to leap to the small Healer, putting herself between Zuri and their enemy.

The dog girl's Intervene immunity saved her from the Fire Spit, but immediately afterwards the Vile Wyvern spat a gob of Acid Spit. Zuri was still casting, not realizing the danger with the taller woman blocking her view, and there was no time to get her out of the way.

Dare watched in dread as Pella, with a choice between leaping to safety and in so doing letting an unsuspecting Zuri take the hit, or protecting her friend and taking the hit herself, turned and gathered the little goblin protectively in her arms, bracing to accept the attack.

"No!" he screamed, desperately Pouncing to her.

He arrived a split second too late, forced to watch in horror as acid sprayed over his lover's back, swiftly eating through her cloak and armor and into her skin.

The scream torn from Pella's throat would haunt his nightmares as he desperately ripped off the ragged remains of cloth and leather on her back, along with the clinging gobbets of acid on them, and desperately rubbed his own cloak over her skin to try to soak up what was still there.

The contact tore another agonized scream from her, then she slumped to the ground, unconscious, Zuri borne down beneath her by her weight.

Dare choked down a sob as he picked the two women up in either arm and bolted for the cavern entrance. He could feel acid eating into his own skin but didn't care.

Leilanna was off to one side, bravely flinging spells at the Vile Wyvern to cover their retreat. Tears were streaming down her cheeks and it was a wonder she could see, but the moment she realized they'd reached safety she bolted after them, narrowly avoiding a gob of Fire Spit that splattered on the wall behind her.

He carried his lovers far enough down the tunnel that the monster couldn't reach them with its attacks, at which point Zuri began squirming. "Set me down so I can heal her," she shouted frantically, tears streaming down her cheeks. She squirmed out of his grip and immediately began casting.

Dare gently laid Pella on the ground and got back to work wiping the remaining acid off her with his ruined cloak. The horrifying sight of her burned and pitted back made him want to scream, but he held it together so he could help the woman he loved.

What had he done?

At the sight of the Vile Wyvern's power and dangerous abilities he should've thrown in the towel and left the dungeon, no matter how much treasure waited in the chest the last boss guarded. It wasn't worth the lives of the women he loved.

Agonizing guilt ripped through him as he looked down at Pella's pale, strained features. How could he put her and Zuri in danger like this? They were carrying his children, they were the entire world to him. More valuable than his own life.

Never again. He wouldn't risk them like this again.

There was a soft *pop* as Zuri opened one of the skin regeneration potions, pouring it down Pella's throat and coaxing the unconscious woman to swallow. It worked swiftly, miraculously even, the acid burns beginning to fade before his eyes.

Then his goblin over turned to him, reaching for another potion. "Save it," Dare told her, voice gruffer than he'd intended. "I'm not done yet."

"Dare-" she began anxiously.

He looked down at his burned, pitted hands; he wouldn't be able to properly use his weapons like this. "Please heal me," he said.

She wasted no time casting the spell, although his hands remained lightly scarred from the acid burns. He didn't care, wasn't even sure he wanted to heal the superficial damage with a potion.

It would serve as a reminder of how stupid he'd been. Of the risks he'd taken with the lives of the women he loved.

Teeth gritted in determination, he grabbed his bow and pushed to his feet. "Stay here," he told Zuri and Leilanna. "Take care of Pella." He used Rapid Shot to bring four arrows to his bow hand and nocked a fifth.

Zuri grabbed his hand. "Don't do this," she said. "It's not worth it." Her tear-filled eyes pled with him, terrified. "Let's just go."

Dare shook his head and gave her a gentle smile. "Don't worry,

I'll be fine."

Without waiting for a response, afraid he'd lose his resolve if he stayed, he turned and bolted for the wyvern's cavern.

They'd already gotten so far in the fight with the dungeon boss, worked so hard and risked so much. He wouldn't, *couldn't*, waste that. Waste Pella's sacrifice.

Even more than that, his family's future was in the cavern with that wyvern. The comfortable life the women he loved and their children deserved, and he was determined to provide them. He wouldn't risk them in pursuit of it, but he'd risk himself.

And he'd win. For them.

The Vile Wyvern greeted him with two gobs of fire and acid as he came in view, and he dropped into a slide beneath them, loosing an arrow as he went. He came up to his feet smoothly, loosing the others in his bow hand swiftly and steadily.

To Dare's relief, even though Zuri was in the tunnel and out of the fight her Nature's Curse ability was still in effect; he'd be screwed without that.

He had just enough time to shoot all the arrows in his bow hand before the wyvern recovered with another volley of fire and acid. Rather than dodging he used Pounce, leaping over the gobs of spit and Tackling the large creature. Then he whipped out his spear and sliced its nearest foreleg, applying Hamstring.

The monster used Bellow, making him stagger as it surged to its feet with a powerful flap of its wings. His Roll and Shoot took him beneath a Tail Swipe, planting an arrow in its eye, then he sprinted for the single pillar in the center of the room where a massive stalactite and stalagmite had joined.

Dare rolled behind it just in time to avoid another volley of spit attacks, coming up to his feet and using Rapid Shot. He popped out from behind the column and loosed the four arrows in quick succession.

The Vile Wyvern roared at him and charged forward with its Trample ability.

Some sixth sense warned him that the stone pillar, massive and thick as it was, wouldn't stand up to that attack. Both to avoid getting caught behind it and to hopefully preserve one of the only sources of cover in the room, he sprinted out from behind it and made for the nearest wall.

Acid whooshed past him moments before sticky fire splashed over the back of his armor, engulfing it in flames even though the attack was weakened by his fire resist potion. He broke into a roll without pausing to put out the flames, then came back to his feet and kept going.

Dare could feel the thud of heavy footfalls shaking the stone beneath him as the wyvern shifted directions in pursuit, and he pushed for every ounce of speed Fleetfoot could give him. Faster than he'd run in his race with Ilin, faster than he'd ever run, the wall of the cavern rushing towards him and the Trampling dragon just seconds behind.

He timed it right, and just before he slammed into the wall at speeds fast enough to break every bone in his body, or possibly even kill him, his Roll and Shoot cooldown finished. Using the ability behind and to the right arrested his forward momentum and tossed him to the side, just in time as the Vile Wyvern reached where he'd been.

The huge monster slammed into the wall hard enough to shake the entire cavern, with a deafening *crack* that made it seem certain either the stone or the wyvern's body had broken in the collision.

Dare came to his feet facing the monster and saw that one of its legs was twisted at an unnatural angle and it was on its side, momentarily stunned. He loosed an arrow at its neck, darted in to slash at its back legs with his spear and apply Hamstring, then as the Vile Wyvern Bellowed and began to stir back to its feet he sprinted sideways.

Rapid Shot popped and he activated it, loosing more arrows. The monster's health was at a sliver, and it had multiple bleed effects from his arrows and an effect he hadn't seen before that was apparently damage over time and restricted movement from internal injuries inflicted by the collision.

The Vile Wyvern twisted painfully towards him, draconic eyes murderous. In spite of its horrible injuries and the fact that it was near death it still opened its mouth to spit a volley.

Dare Pounced a final time, spear leading as he landed on its head, stabbing down at its eye. Then he backpedaled and fired a final arrow into the dungeon boss's open mouth.

With an almost confused roar the wyvern convulsed, folded in on itself, and died.

* * * * *

Text appeared in the corner of Dare's vision. "Party rated dungeon boss Vile Wyvern defeated. 15,000 bonus experience awarded."

"Completed 3/10 towards Achievement Protector of Bastion: Slay 10 party rated monsters in the region of Bastion."

"Trophies gained: Wyvern Head, Wyvern Tail Blade. Loot body to acquire."

"CONGRATULATIONS! You have braved the perils of the Glittering Caves of Kargorath and emerged victorious! May tales of your heroic deeds spread far and wide across Collisa. Dungeon will despawn upon your exit."

"Ascended Ancients," he heard Leilanna breathe from behind him in an almost reverent voice. "You did it. You fucking did it. And without a scratch on you, either."

Dare didn't feel unscathed. With the text still scrolling he broke into a sprint, leaving the dungeon boss behind unlooted and rushing past the awestruck dusk elf into the tunnel.

Part of his soul healed instantly at the sight of Pella on her feet and coming towards him, beautiful face beaming in a pained but genuine smile. With a cry he held out his arms as he met her, hugging her tight.

"Are you okay?" he asked, anxiously running his hands over her bare back. Visibly she looked fine, but he needed to hold her, needed to touch her, needed to prove for himself that the woman he loved was okay.

To his amazement her skin felt as smooth and perfect as ever, with no sign of the horrific acid burns he'd last seen her with.

"I'm fine," she whispered, hugging him tight. "It wasn't a bad wound, and Zuri and the potion together healed it."

"What about the baby?" he pressed. "It's fine, right?" *Please, let it be fine.*

"Of course," Zuri assured him. "That was the first thing I checked while healing her."

Dare felt the numb leaden weight in his gut begin to dissipate. "Thank the gods," he whispered, wrapping his arms around Pella protectively. Then he just held her, letting himself feel the woman he loved in his embrace, warm and healthy and safe.

She rubbed his back soothingly. "I'm fine, Dare," she repeated, nuzzling his neck. "We're all okay. It was scary for a second, but we did it." Her voice turned awed. "You did it."

He shook his head in amazement. "You did it, Pella. I just ran around shooting arrows, you stood in front of fire and acid to protect Zuri." He buried his face in her golden hair, breath catching. "I've never seen anything so heroic."

"It was one of the bravest things I've ever seen," Zuri agreed, voice thick with tears as she joined their embrace. "Thank you, both of you. I'm just so glad we're all okay."

The moment was interrupted by Leilanna's excited voice echoing to them from within the wyvern cavern. "Guys, you have to see this!"

Pella perked up. "What do you think she found?" she asked eagerly; while her face was still a bit drawn with remembered pain, her spirits seemed to have returned.

"A legendary chest, of course," Zuri said. "Dare guessed there'd be one."

He had, although he wasn't so sure now that they were here. "Let's go see."

They found Leilanna standing by the chest and pile of loot, dancing in place. The fact that she hadn't dived in and started searching was a testament to her excitement. "You were right!" she said, grinning. "It's a legendary chest."

"How can you tell?" Dare asked as they joined her.

"Like this, watch!" she waved her hand over the chest. "Shrink."

He and his lovers jumped in shock as the chest vanished. "What happened?" Pella asked, horrified. "What did you do?"

The Mage grinned. "Legendary chests don't just hold loot, they're loot themselves. Master quality! They can shrink in size to make it easy to carry all the treasure. Look!" She reached down and picked up an object about the size of a peanut, showing it off. It turned out to be a tiny version of the larger treasure chest, perfect down to the last detail. "It reduces the weight as well as the size, so this only weighs a couple pounds even though it's full of gold."

Dare looked at the chest's information, confirming that it was a Master quality item. Its value was probably off the charts, but its use as a storage and transportation device made it unlikely he'd ever sell it unless absolutely necessary.

And there were other potential uses for it that he was excited to explore. "Is it like a dimensional pocket?" he asked.

Leilanna rolled her eyes. "No, I just told you what it is. It's enchanted to shrink and become lighter. Dimensional pockets are completely different." She set it back down and stepped back. "Grow." The chest grew back to its original size, and she turned to them excitedly. "Okay, now that you're here let's open this and see what we got!"

He was curious about the loot pile and what was on the wyvern itself, but he could admit he was most excited about the chest. He flung it open, and they all made awed noises at the same time.

The chest was literally overflowing with treasure, so the moment the lid lifted high enough gold coins and the occasional truesilver coin and cut gem began flowing out. It had to be thousands of gold at the least, and that was just the coins themselves.

His companions cheered and dove into the chest, digging through the coins for gems and other precious items. Dare wanted to join them, since obviously who didn't dream of finding a chest full of treasure and just going nuts sorting through it all?

But he was more excited about the loot pile, which while humble in appearance had to have some good stuff in it if it was at the end of a dungeon.

His suspicions were confirmed when the first thing he found when he reached into the pile, and by far the best thing he could've found, was a Level 25 Master quality hunting bow.

This had to be the big loot item of the Glittering Caves. And if his benefactor had hooked them up with a legendary chest, she'd definitely done the same with this bow. Dare ran his hands over the pristine, carved and polished wood, unable to help the shit-eating grin that spread across his face.

This thing was *awesome*.

Nearly twice the damage of his current Good quality recurve bow, it also had way more durability, significantly higher range, and moderately better accuracy and speed. As would be expected for an item near the top of the quality rankings instead of smack dab in the middle.

But where it shone was the special item attributes. The bow was called Entangler, and it had a 10% chance to apply a snare effect and a 5% chance to apply a root effect with every arrow. It also did bonus nature damage.

Best of all, it had a use on cooldown ability of its own. "Vine Lash: Spawn a vine from the bow that can be aimed at a target up the 20 yards away, and the vine would then retract on command. 5 minute cooldown."

That ability was obscenely powerful in both offense and defense. He could use it to grab targets and throw them around or drag them to him, or to grab onto nearby branches or tree trunks and yank himself to safety.

Entangler was close to the ideal solo leveler's bow, and would also be extremely useful in group fights. High damage, crowd control, utility, and a quick escape.

Just for fun he used Vine Lash on the top of the column at the center of the cavern. The vine whipped out of the center of the bow, which would allow him to hold the weapon at either end with both hands for stability, and looped around the thick pillar of stone in a way that should've been physically impossible.

"Retract," Dare said, then whooped as the vine whipped him towards the column. Text appeared at the edge of his vision that said "Entangler Cooldown: 5 minutes." It remained there with a running countdown and an option to dismiss it or make it opaque.

The vine slowed him down to a stop just before he reached the column, then unwrapped and disappeared back into the bow. Unfortunately, that left him a good ten feet above the ground and hanging in midair.

"Shit," he muttered as he dropped, desperately using his enhanced speed to position himself to land softly.

Okay, so the vine would make sure he slowed down safely when he reached his destination, but if his destination wasn't a place he could stand on or hold onto then he could accidentally hurt himself. He'd need to practice, but he was still excited by the possibilities as he trotted back to the chest, admiring his bow as he went.

His companions all grinned as they watched him fawn over his new weapon. "Ladies, I'm afraid you'll be sleeping alone tonight," Leilanna said with a grin; even her usually sharp attitude had softened with the discovery of the legendary chest, and she was the closest to bubbly and cheerful he'd ever seen her. "Dare's going to be pleasuring himself to his new Master quality bow."

Disappointingly, most of the loot pile was reagents and crafting materials. Good ones, definitely, but there were only two other items hidden within it, both Exceptional quality.

One was a set of Level 24 cloth robes that either Zuri or Leilanna could wear, although of course only his goblin lover was high enough level to at the moment. Which on the plus side meant that once Zuri out-leveled the item they could give it to their Mage.

With a few alternations for size, of course.

The robes greatly improved defenses and gave small improvements to the damage of spells and to mana regeneration. They were also suitable for formal occasions thanks to the fine, well cut material and beautiful, detailed embroidering.

His tiny lover was overjoyed at her new gear, and stripped right where she stood to put the robes on. Dare had a feeling his benefactor had hooked her up, too; the unseen woman really did seem to have a soft spot for Zuri.

The other item was a staff that could only be wielded by shadow magic users. It would probably sell for a decent amount, but he'd kind of been hoping for something else for his party members.

Leilanna had followed his lead and abandoned the chest to sort out rest of the pile, which included Enchanting materials, some things that Dare could use for Leatherworking and Zuri could use for Tailoring, and the reagents. A few of those were for spells the two women could unlock, and while they didn't have those spells yet they held onto the reagents for when they did get them.

Pella was still going nuts over the fact that they'd actually found the chest, and was pawing through the impressive mound of gold inside to see if anything else was in there. Suddenly she squealed and pulled out a ring, holding it up triumphantly.

"Oooh, a gold and sapphire ring!" she cooed, admiring it. "It's so beautiful." She turned to Dare, tail thumping furiously. "Can I have it Dare, please?"

"Any special enchantments or anything?" he asked, coming over to admire it as well.

The dog girl shook her head. "Nope, just a stupidly valuable ring that will go well with my coloring." She slipped it on her finger. "Please can I?"

"It's fine with me," he said with a shrug.

Zuri shrugged too. "I'd vote for selling it so we can live in the manor that much longer, but if she wants to wear it until we need the money, if we ever do, I'm fine with that."

"Hey wait a second!" Leilanna protested. "I want a ring!"

"Not this one," Pella said, holding it protectively away from her. "It would look terrible against your skin and hair." She hesitated, ears drooping as she realized that had probably sounded mean. "No offense, I love you Leil, it's just the truth."

The dusk elf sniffed. "Well, I guess you did find it. And you turned out to be right about the chest, too."

"Yay!" Pella threw her arms around Dare in a crushing hug. "I can't believe we found a chest. You were right that it would be here, and you led us right to it! You even did most of the work killing the boss!"

She abruptly sprang away, bending over the chest again. He thought she was going to go back to searching for more items among the gold coins, but then he saw her holding onto the front of the chest and shifting to wave her athletic ass in his direction, tail wagging furiously.

Then, grinning impishly over her shoulder, the dog girl reached back and started tugging down her leather leggings and panties, exposing the top of her round ass. "You deserve a reward, my love," she cooed.

Leilanna made a displeased sound and turned away. "Gross, you want to do that here? Now?"

"Learn to celebrate in the moment, Leil!" Pella said cheerfully.

"But I'm *right here*," the Mage complained. "I don't want to see that."

The dog girl giggled. "Well I'll take your word for that."

"Leilanna's got a point," Dare said reluctantly, although he wanted nothing more than to celebrate with his dog girl lover. "It's not polite to just get naked and fuck right in front of her."

"Don't hold back on my account!" Leilanna growled. "I'll just go somewhere else until you're done."

"Unless you want to join us?" Zuri asked, grinning.

"Shut up!" the dusk elf snapped, striding away across the cavern and calling over shoulder. "Just don't squirt all over the treasure!"

"Ooh, now I want to do that!" Pella said, fluffy tail wagging as she finished tugging her leggings down to expose her glistening pussy. "Mark it and claim it as ours!"

Leilanna growled and disappeared around the far side of the wyvern to loot it. "Just hurry up, then. And don't make a bunch of noise!"

Dare was always eager to make love to his beautiful golden-haired lover, but after the previous scare he was even more happy for a chance to hold her. He freed himself from his pants and stepped up to her, positioning himself at her entrance and pushing between her silky folds.

She moaned and thrust back at him eagerly, curvy hips wiggling with joy. "Yes, this is just what I needed," she moaned. "A good memory to wash away a bad one."

He positioned for an angle that would stimulate Pella even more and fell into a steady rhythm of long thrusts, with the occasional quick one to change things up, luxuriating in her silky pink walls. True to her words her arousal flowed around his cock and dripped down their thighs onto the pile of coins that had fallen out of the chest, making them glisten even more brightly.

Dare reached around and rubbed at the dog girl's clit as he continued to mount her from behind, and she whimpered happily and tensed into a climax, tight walls rippling around him.

A few seconds later she giggled naughtily. "Honey," she whispered, "Leilanna's watching us."

He jerked in surprise, throwing off his timing, and she made a dissatisfied noise and pushed back at him more urgently until he regained his rhythm. "What?" he hissed.

Pella looked over her shoulder at him, brown eyes sparkling. "She's watching and rubbing herself like crazy," she mouthed, looking on the verge of delighted laughter. "Gods, she's so wet and she smells incredible."

Dare didn't want to risk checking for himself, but the mental image of the beautiful, curvy dusk elf pleasuring herself to their lovemaking pushed him over the edge. With a groan he bottomed out in his dog girl lover, grabbed her tail and pulled her tighter against him, and unloaded everything he had inside her.

If he thought he was done Zuri quickly disabused him of that idea. She'd shucked out of her new robes and was waiting eagerly, and the moment he pulled out of Pella, releasing a flood of their mingled juices, the little goblin moved in to sprawl on the pile of coins, legs spread wide.

Her beautiful little pink petals were flushed and pouting open in eager need, her arousal visibly flowing from her delicate entrance and down her ass to join their juices coating the coins.

Dare couldn't help but stare in awe at the erotic sight. The increasingly visible signs of her pregnancy made her sexy little body look even more lush and fertile than usual; he feasted his eyes on her round tummy, her already large breasts enlarged even more, with beautiful dark green nipples jutting out proudly, and her thickening ass and hips.

"Well?" Zuri asked with a laugh, blushing a bit at his frank admiration. She wiggled her hips. "You don't need to eye fuck me when you can actually fuck me."

True, but at the wondrous sight of the mother of his firstborn child he was more in the mood to make love. He ran his hands over her growing belly, and played with her large breasts that made a perfect handful, firm yet yielding. He lovingly kissed and sucked on her nipples, making her moan and squirm, and kissed his way down her round tummy to bury his face between her legs, making her gasp and buck her hips in delighted pleasure.

She tasted as wonderful as always, her sweet, honeyed juices rich with pheromones driving him wild. And not just him.

Pella joined them, lovingly caressing the beautiful goblin's body as he licked and sucked on her little pink pussy. "Leilanna just came again," his dog girl lover whispered with a soft giggle. "She seems to like you going slow and loving even more than fast and enthusiastic."

Zuri giggled and pushed Dare's head away. "Speaking of fast and enthusiastic," she spread her delicate folds, giving him a view deep into her tiny pink hole. "I need you inside me, my mate."

He wasted no time climbing up to position herself at her entrance, sliding into the impossibly small tunnel thanks to the world system letting larger and smaller races breed without difficulty or discomfort.

However, in that odd way of the system, even though there was no discomfort he could *feel* how crushingly tight the beautiful goblin was. So tight it would've been painful, but instead was incredible.

"Yeeeesss," Zuri moaned, squirming beneath him. "I'll never get tired of this."

Dare began moving in her as Pella got beneath him, soft flat tongue lapping at his balls and asshole, then down his shaft and over Zuri's obscenely stretched opening, then down to her asshole. His little goblin lover gasped and squirmed at the enthusiastic attention, which combined with his slow, patient thrusts brought her to a shuddering climax, squirting over his cock and the dog girl's eager face.

He grabbed Zuri's small hips and shifted position, pushing more eagerly inside her. Meanwhile Pella began a furious assault on the beautiful goblin's tiny rosebud. It didn't take much of that before Zuri was driven to an even higher peak, squeaking with delight and clawing at his back.

He abruptly realized he could hear another voice raising in climax along with his goblin lover, and it wasn't Pella. Leilanna's husky, melodic voice sounded raw and passionate, strained with pure lust, and he couldn't help himself.

Dare turned his head and saw the beautiful dusk elf leaning heavily against the dead wyvern, pants around her knees and delicate fingers furiously moving between her plump legs, tantalizingly preventing him from getting a good view of her pussy. Her skin was flushed almost charcoal gray, aristocratic features slack with pure lust.

It was sexy as fuck.

Her wide, dark pink eyes met his and filled with mortification as she realized she'd been caught. But rather than trying to hide or glaring at him in challenge, she simply closed her eyes with a shuddering moan of blissful resignation and her fingers mauled her flushed slit even harder.

She stiffened with a whimper and collapsed against the dead wyvern, her nectar flowing around her fingers in a flood as she gave in to a shuddering climax.

That incredibly erotic sight was more than Dare could take, and with a groan he turned back to Zuri and prepared to come inside her. He saw that she was also looking in Leilanna's direction, panting with lust at the sight of the climaxing dusk elf.

The little goblin reached down and rubbed her clit with a sweet whimper, viselike pussy clenching down so tightly she pushed him right out of her. "Now, my mate," she whined as her finger moved furiously. "Let's all come together."

Pella whimpered in agreement, also watching Leilanna while furiously rubbing herself, and with a grunt of effort Dare pushed his way back into Zuri's soft little tunnel as he followed their gazes over to the dusk elf.

Leilanna's mortification spread from her eyes to her whole body as she saw them all watching her. With a whimper she slumped to the ground on her back, hips thrusting furiously upward against her hand as she strained for a higher peak. She finally cried out and squirted hard in their direction, and Zuri's and Pella's moans of climax joined hers.

Dare felt his goblin lover's silken vise crushing him again, her nectar flooding around his shaft, and with a groan of his own bottomed out and began spraying her insides with his seed, spurting over and over as he watched Leilanna's beautiful thighs quiver as she squirted again, even farther this time.

The intense rush of pleasure took the strength from his limbs, and with a gasp he pulled out of Zuri, a final jet of his come painting her sexy pregnant belly. Then he rolled to one side facing Leilanna, gathering his lovers into his arms.

"Come over here," he invited the dusk elf, holding out a hand to her.

Instead Leilanna, sprawled obscenely on the floor panting as she came down from her climax, gave a start of surprise at his voice. She frantically yanked her pants into place, glaring at him with a furious expression.

"You, you just shut up!" she shouted, bolting for the tunnel. Her words drifted back to them as she disappeared, echoing in the cavern.

"This never happened!"

They stared after her. "Well, maybe next time," Pella said, tail wagging contentedly as she cuddled closer to him.

"Still, that was seriously hot," Zuri said, languidly stretching against his chest. "She'd be a great addition to our harem, wouldn't she?"

Dare shook his head. "She can find me attractive and still not want to be with me," he said. Which was a pity, since after what he'd just seen he was aching even more to get between those thick thighs and feel her soft body jiggle beneath him as he thrust into her sweet pussy.

With a sigh he reluctantly extricated himself from his two lovers and stood, rearranging his own pants. "Come on," he said. "Let's finish tallying the loot and go see where she ran off to."

Chapter Eleven
Home Town

In the end they counted 4,317 gold coins and 11 truesilver ones. Zuri guessed that the combined gems, pearls, semiprecious stones, and other treasure items probably added up to another 20,000 gold between them.

And that didn't count Entangler or Zuri's new robes, or the crafting materials and reagents. Or the value of the legendary chest, which was currently stuffed to bursting and shrunk down in Dare's coin pouch.

He could admit that it kind of freaked him out to be carrying 25,000 gold worth of treasure in a peanut-sized object on his person. He kept double checking to make sure it was still there, then checking again to make sure that checking hadn't made it fall out of the sealed pouch.

The Vile Wyvern had dropped the head and tail blade trophies, of course, as well as its teeth, claws, and a hundred or so scales. It also had so much meat on it that they were faced with the choice of either crafting more sleds to tow it all, or leaving it behind.

Dare was reminded of his miserable experience with eating poisonous meat from a basilisk runt soon after arriving on Collisa, and used his Forage ability Test Edibles. Confirming that the wyvern meat, too, was toxic.

No doubt it had some value and someone would be willing to buy it, but all things considered they decided to pass on a few dozen gold at best to save themselves the hassle of dragging sleds for days.

He assumed Leilanna had left the dungeon ahead of them, since they didn't encounter her on the way out. Then they reached the salamander caverns and saw signs of singed stone.

Eventually they found the Mage stalking through a tunnel ahead. She was venting her anger by systematically casting Ring of Fire so the spells just barely overlapped, obviously putting it to productive use trying to tease out whatever treasure they'd failed to find in this area.

Assuming there was one.

She either didn't see them behind her or pointedly ignored them, continuing on to the end of that section without finding any other secrets. "I guess we'll just have to accept that if there's something here, we aren't finding it," Pella said, looking disappointed.

Leilanna shot a single glance back at them, expression carefully neutral, then continued on through the rest of the dungeon until they reached the entrance. Dare and his lovers let her take the lead and gave her space; things were a bit awkward now that the passion they'd felt in the heat of the moment in the wyvern cavern had cooled.

Or at least they were for him, and obviously for the dusk elf. Pella and Zuri seemed cheerfully oblivious to any tension in the air, and even seemed to think that Leilanna jilling off in front of them had been a step in the right direction.

Hopefully the awkwardness would dissipate quickly, and they could do as the Mage had suggested and pretend it hadn't happened.

Outside the breeze was warm and smelled amazingly fresh after the often dank air of the caverns. They all turned to watch as the ground rumbled and the crack in the hillside closed, the dungeon despawning.

"Think we'll find another dungeon?" Leilanna asked, surprising them by breaking the silence. Her tone was flat and her expression carefully neutral, although a slight flush suffused her cheeks whenever she looked their way.

Dare shook his head. "Not any time soon," he said firmly. He still needed to talk to his lovers about being more cautious in their monster hunting, for their sakes and that of the babies.

Much more cautious.

"So what now?" Pella asked. "Back to hunting monsters?"

"Well, we've got enough gold now that we won't have to worry about the finances to start our family for a while," Zuri said, slipping her small hands into his and the dog girl's. "So should we find a house?"

Pella made a happy noise as she took Dare's other hand, making a triangle. "You're right, we should do that right away." She practically wiggled with excitement. "I can't wait to have a home and fill it with puppies! Can we have lots of soft carpets for them to play on?"

Dare couldn't help but laugh. "Of course. And all the other comforts we can find." Or make; he had some ideas for conveniences from Earth he could provide for his family. Assuming the world system let him.

He turned to Leilanna, who was looking a bit left out as she stared at the three of them. "Your people are wanderers and you've spent more time in Bastion than we have. Any suggestions about where would be best to buy a home?"

The beautiful dusk elf frowned thoughtfully. "I guess it depends what you want. There are plenty of spots in the wilds where you can raise a settlement, as many non-humans have. But it's usually only a matter of time before the local lord discovers them and either rousts them out or puts them under his heel. And none too gently, either."

"I'd say we want to buy or build a good-sized house on a good amount of land," he said. "In some secluded place where we would be close enough to civilization to be safe, but far enough that we'd be left alone." He motioned at the four of them. "Especially with our particular group."

Leilanna shrugged. "Terana seems the obvious choice, in the southeastern part of Bastion. It's a relatively small town, eager for settlers, and has a reputation for being the most friendly to other races."

Hmm. That would put them far from the dangerous northern border, where monsters were encroaching into the kingdom from the wilds. They'd also be near the goblin ravine, where they already had a friendly relationship with the Avenging Wolf tribe and which would offer them an easy path into Kovana if they wanted to return to that region.

Dare looked at Zuri and Pella. "What do you think?" he asked. "As a long term home where we can raise our children, what are you looking for?"

Pella shivered in quiet delight. "Say that again." At his blank look she grinned eagerly. "Our children."

He grinned, wrapping an arm around her and kissing her cheek. "Our children," he said gently. Then he got back on topic. "Where should we raise them?"

"Terana seems like a good place to start looking, at least," Zuri said. "And we can sell our loot and buy some horses while we're at it."

Dare looked around, getting nods from everyone, and squared his shoulders. "All right, Terana it is."

* * * * *

They were weighed down with enough loot that the fastest way to travel was to have Dare and Pella carry it while Leilanna and Zuri did their best to keep up.

That was a bit of a relief, honestly, since he would've felt awkward carrying the beautiful dusk elf on his back after watching her writhing around orgasmically on hers. Not to mention he doubted she would've gone for it, still clearly embarrassed about the entire thing; she even went out of her way to avoid him for the first day of their journey south.

Their progress was slow but steady, not stopping to hunt monsters unless they were close enough that they wouldn't have to go out of their way. Not to mention the ever-present animal predators that never passed up a chance to go after them.

It wasn't just haste that kept Dare from seeking out leveling opportunities. He was still shaken by Pella's close call and was far more cautious in their hunting, not only trying to go for lower level enemies but keeping the pregnant women back so there wasn't even a possibility they'd take damage.

If kiting or taking damage was required, he did it himself. And in the face of his lovers' remarks about coddling them he looked down at the few small, pale scars of acid burns on his hands and firmed his resolve to not let the women he loved and their children come to harm.

With Leilanna still much lower level, she was the best situated to gain experience from all the monsters they passed. When the monsters were closer to everyone else's level she'd stay part of the party and fight with them, but when they were closer to the Mage's level she'd drop group and do the full damage on the monsters while Dare kited her targets, so she could get full experience.

While leveling up wasn't a priority, Leilanna reached Level 20 and Zuri reached Level 27 in the four days it took to reach Terana. Both were exciting in their own way.

For Zuri, obviously, it was because she got the next rank of Prevent Conception, the one that she insisted would work even with his ridiculously high fertility. And of course she immediately got to work making scrolls for Dare to carry around with him just in case she wasn't around, which was a huge relief.

These ones will *work, right?* he sarcastically asked his benefactor, breaking his obstinate silence with her to toss out the barb. *I'm not going to spend a few months boinking with this spell only to find out I've knocked up another half dozen or so women?*

She sighed in his head. "It's good to hear from you, my lover. Even if it's just sarcasm, you finally talking is something." Her tone became playfully casual. "You're welcome for tweaking chance to make sure you got a legendary chest, by the way . . . I *did* give you a healthy helping of luck."

Dare scowled for a few seconds, then relented, feeling a bit guilty about his petulance. "I've missed you too," he admitted. "It's nice knowing I always have someone to talk to. Someone who knows every-"

He abruptly became aware his companions were giving him confused looks and realized he'd said that out loud.

Flushing, he shifted back to talking in his head. *Maybe you can visit again, and we'll talk things out.*

His benefactor laughed. "I'd very much like to talk things out.

But as for visiting . . . I think I'll hold off for now. It takes so much effort, and as much as I enjoy the results I have so many pressing things competing for my time." Her voice became playful. "Besides, I still have that surprise I told you about."

Hopefully it's more pleasant than the last surprise you sprang on me.

Dare could practically see her wince in her words. "It should be. I think. *I'm* certainly excited about it. And so is Ir-" she abruptly cut off.

Well that was reassuring.

"Anyway, need to go," his benefactor said hastily. "Love you."

As for Leilanna, her Level 20 was as big as it had been for the rest of them. Not only did she get access to staffs, wands, and spears, but she also got a choice of magic based subclasses, similar to how Dare had Leatherworking.

Apparently the Mage had already done her homework about her options, and chose the subclass of Ley Line Harvester. It allowed her to sense the presence of nearby Enchanting materials, as well as ley lines and other mana sources where those materials could be created.

As she put it, for people who picked combat main classes, picking some sort of harvesting subclass was superior to a crafting one. Crafter subclasses would always produce inferior items, but harvesters would be able to find the nearly the same quality items as harvester main classes, just at a level deficit. So, for instance, the things she found would be several levels lower than her, where for a harvester main class they'd be her level.

Harvesting lower level and quality materials wasn't an issue for Dare, since he had the ability to harvest leather and other crafting materials from animals as part of his Hunter class, and harvested those items as if he had a main harvesting class as a perk of being a Hunter. Although of course the items he crafted with his Leatherworker subclass would be inferior even if he had bothered to put points in it.

It wasn't an issue for Zuri either, since the quality of cloth dropped from monsters was based on their level and random chance, not her level or proficiency in her Tailor subclass. Although like him the items she crafted were subpar, as was any cloth she wove herself.

As for Pella, she had yet to unlock a subclass. Or at least not one she wanted.

Another thing Leilanna got was a choice between four elemental spells. Obviously the viable options for her were fire and air, and with her bloodline trait giving her bonuses to fire she went with that.

It was called Flame Needle. It wasn't flashy like Fireball with its massive damage and powerful status debuffs, but it was more mana efficient, faster casting, and had an armor piercing bonus that gave it less of a damage penalty against armored targets.

Dare immediately had her switch to Flame Needle for leveling, saving Fireball for an opener to apply its debuffs in harder fights. The Mage grumbled at that, not so much at the change but that he'd had the gall to tell her what to do with *her* class.

Still, the fact that she was losing her temper and giving him snark was an improvement from the embarrassed silence of the first day or so.

The last thing Leilanna got was Carve Staff, as she'd mentioned. They didn't have a good quality staff for her yet, of course, but she didn't want one right at the moment anyway. In fact, at her insistence Dare carved a dozen bow staves for her every night, using his shitty basic bow crafting ability, and she got to work increasing her Carve Staff proficiency so it would be maxed out when she got a high quality staff worthy of it.

The group was more excited to reach Terana than they usually were with the next town, since they had a lot more to do there than just sell loot, buy a few items to help them level, and maybe get a good meal at an inn.

They had gold to spare, lots of things to buy, and the women were leaping at the chance to do some proper shopping.

And Dare agreed fully. Along with the house and horses for all of them, he also wanted to equip them in the best possible gear for their level. And they'd need a lot of things for the house, and items to make living there more comfortable for his lovers, like the carpets

Pella had mentioned.

Also, Terana might end up being their home. Which put them a lot more in the mood to explore it and get to know its people than if they were just passing through.

Their first view of the town from a nearby hilltop showed a small but bustling place. The high, sturdy wall was reasonable for a frontier settlement, even a smaller one in the safest corner of Bastion. The buildings inside were neatly made and well maintained, the streets clean and the crowds orderly.

Dare judged that maybe five hundred people lived there, but the buildings were well spread out within the walls, with plenty of room to grow. The guards at the town's main gate looked well equipped and disciplined, alert in spite of the fact that there was little traffic coming in.

Considering their change in fortunes over the last week, the girls insisted they change into their nicest clothes and each get a clean with Zuri's Cleanse Target. "After all, we want to make a good impression if we're going to be tossing a lot of gold around," Leilanna said.

Their efforts seemed to have some benefit, given how the guards straightened at their approach. "Well met," the woman in charge called, taking in their levels, appearance, and gear and packs. She was a Level 30 Warrior, while the other guard at the gate was Level 26. "Welcome to Terana."

"Well met," Dare replied, smiling as they reached her and noting how her cheeks colored and she surreptitiously checked her uniform. "And thank you . . . it's a beautiful town." He might've let his tone imply it wasn't just the town he appreciated.

It wasn't just flattery, either; while the brunette guard was older than Pella and had a slightly worn look about her, there was still a tough beauty there.

Her flush deepened. "You and your companions can go right in. No taxes or checks for travelers and traders, especially not adventurers." She tried for a stern tone, but it came off as more playful. "Just keep the peace."

"Of course." But Dare lingered. "You know, a town like this seems like a wonderful place to live. Do you know of any homes for sale? Or good lots for property where we could build one?"

"Preferably out of town a ways," Zuri added. "A nice place, big enough for dozens of people if needed."

The guard looked surprised at the question, but smiled warmly. "You'll find no trouble getting land to build a house, of course. The Baroness has worked hard to grow the town and is always eager for new residents."

She tapped her cheek thoughtfully. "She handles a lot of the more important business personally . . . if you want a bigger manor on a good piece of land your best bet is to approach her. Assuming she can make time for you."

The lovely woman's tone was fond as she spoke of her lady, which seemed like a good sign. "You hold her in high respect," Dare observed.

"Absolutely," she said, expression becoming firm. "As should you . . . Terana prospered under the leadership of her husband, and she's managed things well since the Baron's death."

"It will be an honor to meet her, then, assuming I'm so fortunate."

The guard gave them directions to the baroness's manor, as well as to the market and a nice inn where they could stay. Although honestly the town was small enough that they could've found those places easily enough.

As they started through the gates the pretty woman caught his arm, looking a bit awkward. "By the way, my name's Helima. If you end up staying at the Mountain's Shadow I usually swing by there for a few drinks after my shift."

Dare smiled at her. "I'll hope to see you there then, Helima."

She blushed, gave him a shy smile, and hastily returned to her post.

"Wow," Leilanna said, rolling her eyes. "Do you fall dick-first into every woman you meet?"

"As many as I can," he replied with a grin, unapologetic. Zuri and Pella snickered.

True to the dusk elf's claim about Terana's welcoming attitude towards other races, the people in town seemed friendly enough towards his companions, not seeming to care that they weren't human. Although it probably helped that, given his interest in the town as a home, Dare made more of an effort than usual to greet people.

He even stopped to chat with a few friendly elderly women sitting on a porch enjoying the sun. They seemed more than happy to impart some of the town's gossip to the newcomers, all while complimenting him and his companions about what lovely young people they were. When he finally excused himself and they moved on, he felt like he'd get along well with the residents of Terana.

For the most part.

Just shy of the market they passed a man in laborer's clothes who gave them a dark look, muttering something less than complimentary about non-humans. Dare and his lovers, used to the hostility of townspeople in Kovana and knowing better than to cause problems over it, let the insult pass with barely a second thought.

Leilanna, not so much.

"Hey!" she shouted, making the roughly dressed man freeze in place. "You want to say that to my face, you shriveled pencil-dick?" As he turned in surprise she sneered at him and pressed a thumb to her ample chest. "You know what I did this week? Killed a Level 25 dungeon boss! What've you done lately aside from jack off thinking of women way less hot than me, who you'd still never have a shot in hell of getting with?"

A few passersby snickered, while others looked offended. The man reddened, but one look at their levels sent him scurrying away.

"You know you were his level when we met, right?" Dare asked, amused.

The beautiful dusk elf flushed darker gray. "Yeah, well I was never a bastard like him." With a sniff she kept going down the street.

The market, as they'd hoped and expected from towns in Bastion, had plenty of vendors and crafters catering to adventurers. The big problem they ran into was not finding people willing to buy their loot and treasure, but that what they had was so valuable most couldn't afford it.

Still, they could always hold onto things until they could get a better deal, or travel to another town with deeper coffers.

One thing Dare didn't try to sell, however, was the trophies. Apparently people on Collisa *did* make a big deal about those, and having them to show off made a difference to people's opinion of you. So while having them hanging on his wall wouldn't have been his first choice for decorations, he'd do it anyway for bragging rights.

As for purchases, he'd always enjoyed haggling and had a blast going around equipping himself and his companions with the best gear. Fiercely bargaining for every gold piece as he arranged to sell what they currently had, to replace with the upgrades.

Of course he found nothing that came even close to being as nice as Zuri's new robes. And especially nothing even close to Entangler, which came as no surprise.

He loved his new hunting bow; even in the little monster hunting they'd done on the way here, he'd absolutely obliterated everything they encountered. To the point that Leilanna whined about him leaving something for her to kill, and even Zuri looked disappointed about not having much to do.

It was getting harder to find gear of their level, even in a region like Bastion that drew adventurers. Most people didn't select a combat class and rarely reached Level 20 by the end of their life. Of the ones who did go with a combat class, less than half got higher than Level 30 and an even smaller number got above Level 40.

Considering the relative ease and speed with which Dare and his companions had leveled, he could only conclude that the absence of Adventurer's Eye really did make that much difference. He supposed when every pull could end in death, the longer adventurers stayed at it the more likely odds would eventually work against them.

Not so much laziness or cowardice, but a brutally unforgiving world where power was a battle of attrition. Hell, even with his Eye he and his loved ones had had some close calls.

Which was why even the Royal Guards Dare had seen were only in their 40s and 50s, and the heroes of Haraldar in their 50s and 60s. It made him wonder if the Level cap really was 100, or if Haraldar was just on the weaker side when it came to their adventurers.

Either way, crafters at higher levels were even more rare, and the things they made more difficult to find. Supply and demand. Which was why even with the best haggling in the world (which he couldn't claim) he paid a hefty chunk for all their new gear.

As they continued to level it might not even be a matter of expense, but traveling to places where high level crafters could be found. They might even have to join a guild or organization that had gone to the effort of leveling up their crafters.

Or more ideally recruit some of their own and power level them the way they were doing with Leilanna. Most crafters would probably leap at the opportunity.

Since Dare was finally in the mood to spend money to get things they'd needed for a while, he remembered that he'd been meaning to buy maps and translation stones so everyone in their group had them. The maps were just a matter of finding a parchment vendor and spending a few silver.

The translation stones he'd anticipated more trouble with. They were so cheap and so incredibly useful that if they weren't such a pain to get he already would've purchased more, but he recalled the hassle of finding one in Driftwain.

Fortunately, they were easier to find in Bastion. There were so many people of other races who spoke other languages coming into the region, not just north out of the wilds but from other parts of Haraldar, as well as from Elaivar to the east, that their demand was higher than in more peaceful regions dominated by humans who all spoke the same language.

Dare bought translation stones for him, Pella, and Leilanna, and spent a fraction of what he'd paid for anything else to get them. Since they were so cheap he bought several more just in case they needed them in the future for new companions, and was completely happy with the purchase.

Honestly, an enchanted item that allowed you to understand several languages, not just spoken but written, and to be understood in turn, seemed way too incredible to only cost 30 silver apiece.

He supposed prevalent magic and different priorities on what was important made the difference.

While he was busy selling what loot he could, and buying gear, Pella went in search of good horses for all four of them. She was the most qualified, having lived on a nobleman's estate and spent a lot of time around fine mounts.

Meanwhile Leilanna and Zuri were looking at furnishings for a house and luxury items that previously they couldn't afford or had no place to put. They didn't buy anything just yet, just familiarized themselves with what was available and compared prices.

In spite of that, they were fortunate that Pella was getting horses and tack because they ended up buying enough to need a beast of burden to carry it. Including a surprising amount of baby stuff; even though Zuri planned to make clothes for their children, the girls all went nuts at the sight of the little clothes and shoes and hats and insisted on buying some finer outfits. Along with cradles and carrying harnesses and other amenities.

Which Dare fully agreed with, of course. It was just cute to see the mothers of his children, who only hours ago had joined him in eradicating a nest of giant wasp monsters as seasoned adventurers, now gushing over tiny onesies.

Once they'd finished shopping and were fully outfitted as proper adventurers, for the first time since Dare had come to Collisa, they followed Helima the guardswoman's directions to Baroness Arral's mansion.

To say it was the nicest building in Terana would be a vast understatement. In fact, it looked far too nice even for the noblewoman who owned the town and the surrounding lands.

Set in one corner of town, it took up a good tenth of the total area. A vast, sprawling estate of gardens and orchards of fruit trees, with walkways lined with cherry blossom trees.

The mansion itself was three storeys for the main building and had two-storey wings on either side, probably over twenty thousand square feet in total. And it was opulently constructed of fine materials, with glittering rows of leaded glass windows.

And then there was the sprawling stables, and a multitude of other necessary outbuildings. All in all it spoke of major wealth and status, and Dare found himself wondering if they should even be here bothering the Baroness about something like buying a house.

"Holy shit," Leilanna murmured, staring at the mansion in awe through the wrought iron gates barring the drive. "How the hell do you afford something like this as lord of a little province like Terana?"

That was a good question, and one that he'd learned the answer to while chatting with vendors. "Apparently Baron Arral was a Level 41 adventurer. He and his party went out on monster hunts a lot, and made a fortune in their efforts."

"Until he died to monsters, I take it?" the Mage said dryly.

Dare put a a supportive arm around Pella, anticipating her pain at the reminder of her own master's similar death. "That seems to be what happened," he agreed.

The guard watching the estate's front gate seemed dubious of them in spite of their decent clothing and clear signs of wealth. Still, he reluctantly agreed to send up to the mansion and inquire about whether the Baroness would see them.

Honestly, it came as a surprise when the guard returned and began laboriously opening the gate. "Please, go right on up," he said politely.

They shared a relieved look and made their way through the gate, walking up the crushed gravel drive beneath the shade of cherry blossom trees.

At the entrance to the manor waited an honest to god maid, complete with the familiar black and white ruffled uniform from Earth. Dare wouldn't have believed it if he hadn't seen it for himself.

She was a human in her early 40s, handsome rather than pretty, with an efficient, no nonsense air about her. "Welcome to

Montshadow Estate," she said politely, offering a curt curtsy. "I have the honor of being the estate's Head Maid, Miss Garena." She motioned, and two boys from the stables trotted over briskly. "We'll provide the mounts the best care, I assure you."

"Thank you, Miss Garena," Dare said with a polite bow. He wasn't used to this sort of formality, but it felt appropriate.

Or maybe not, since he was bowing to a maid; on Earth etiquette usually didn't call for that sort of thing.

The severe woman's expression gave no hint about whether he'd been correct. "Please leave your weapons with your mounts along with your other things," she said as the stable boys collected the reins. "I am not comfortable with armed guests in the Baroness's presence."

That was a reasonable enough request, and Dare obligingly left his bow and spear behind, as his companions shed their own weapons. Besides, at their level they were probably dangerous enough with their fists to defend themselves if necessary.

And Leilanna and Zuri didn't need weapons anyway. Or Pella with her unarmed skill.

Miss Garena nodded in polite satisfaction and stepped towards the heavy wooden door, which opened at her approach as if by magic. That, or a curious canid maid peeking around the door, ruffled bonnet knocking slightly askew as she hastily yanked her head back at the Head Maid's stern look.

"We apologize for dropping in without prior notice," Dare said, taking in the opulent entry room with its twin staircases looping up to the second floor, a massive chandelier glittering overhead. "We can wait until the Baroness is available, or come back at some more convenient time."

"That will not be necessary. Please, come this way." Miss Garena glided gracefully to a set of doors tucked away beneath one of the stairways, where she rapped on the wood once with her knuckles.

"Bring them in," a refined, melodious voice said calmly.

The Head Maid opened both doors with a practiced move, leading the way into a comfortably appointed study with a table large enough to seat six set closer to the door. Farther back, tucked into a turret alcove, was a small desk overflowing with parchments surrounded by crowded bookshelves built up to the ceiling.

"The adventurers, my Lady," Miss Garena said with a curtsy. Then she retreated, closing the doors behind her.

They were left with a slim woman in her late 40s, age only beginning to dim her aristocratic beauty, who waited expectantly by the table. She was dressed in a plain but finely made gown, with a set of spectacles on a silver chain perched amidst the silver-streaked curls of a simple but elegant hairdo.

Shockingly, in spite of her age she was only Level 4. As if she'd rarely if ever needed to do anything that required increasing her ability proficiencies, and thus earned her experience.

Proof if ever any was needed that there were many kinds of power.

"Ah, the adventurers who've been stirring such a fuss in my humble town," she said with a wry smile. "Welcome to my home. I'm Baroness Marona Arral, although you may address me as Lady Marona."

Dare bowed low and his companions all curtsied. "My Lady," he said. "We're honored by your hospitality. I'm Dare, and these are my companions Zuri, Pella, and Leilanna." He motioned to each as he named them.

Smiling slightly, Lady Marona settled into a chair at the head of the table, motioning for them to join her. "Please, be seated."

He cautiously took the seat near hers, Leilanna sitting across from him and Zuri beside him, with Pella taking the seat by the dusk elf.

Once they were settled in Lady Marona motioned. Dare started with surprise as a maid by another door, who'd been standing so still and quiet he hadn't even noticed her, stepped forward and curtsied. "Drinks for our guests," the baroness said. She turned to them. "What can I offer? Tea, coffee? Wine or perhaps brandy?"

Given the formal situation and the nature of their business, alcohol was probably not the right choice. "Coffee, thank you," Dare said. His companions nodded and murmured their agreement of the choice.

The maid, a gorgeous petite blonde human about his age, with a plainly bombshell body even when covered by her prim ruffled uniform, curtsied again and disappeared through the door she'd been standing by.

"Now," Lady Marona said briskly. "I believe you've proven with your purchases in the last few hours that you have money to spend and things you wish to by. I've been informed that you wish to buy property in the Terana province. Is that correct?"

"It is," Dare said, surprised at the close eye she kept on her town; his respect for her went up another notch. "My preference would be a house that's already built, since I want to provide my family a home soon. But a good plot of land could also work. Something outside of town, isolated and secluded, large enough that my family has room to grow."

"I see." Her full red lips pursed as if she was trying not to smile as she took in the three beautiful women with him. "By family, I assume you mean a harem and the children your wives and consorts bear you?"

At his look of surprised discomfiture she finally did smile. "You see, I know something of the appetites of successful adventurers. And their financial and social ability to appease those appetites." She motioned to the manor around them.

Dare smiled sheepishly. "Yes, I intend to grow my harem if I'm able, and want to provide them the most comfortable lives possible. Which means I'd like to buy big in advance to save the need to expand in the future."

"Ah," the baroness said, expression thoughtful. "In that case, there is a place available that might be perfect for you. Depending on how sturdy your finances are."

He paused. "Let's say very sturdy. I've had some recent good fortune."

A tiny gnome maid with flowing pink hair down to her ankles bearing a tray over her head swept through the service door. She went to Lady Marona first and the stately woman took a cup of coffee and saucer. "Thank you, dear."

The maid curtsied smoothly, not even disturbing the coffee in the other cups, and hurried around to deliver drinks to Dare and his companions as well.

Charmed by the beautiful little gnome, he couldn't help but smile as he took his own cup and saucer. She was a bit shorter than Zuri, plump and curvy, with a cheerful round face and big blue eyes. "Thank you," he told her, and her rosy cheeks flushed as she smiled back, giving him an appraising look in spite of her downcast eyes.

Lady Marona cleared her throat, looking amused, and he hastily turned his attention back to her. "Yes, I'd love to hear more," he said, feeling his cheeks heat.

"It's a lovely manor set in the center of five thousand, seven hundred and sixty acres, or nine square miles, of pristine Terana Province land," the stately woman said, blowing on her coffee then taking a cautious sip. "Plains, woods, and a bit of foothills. Ideal for farming, grazing livestock, or harvesting lumber, with full water and resource harvesting rights. It's down near the southeastern corner of the province, and thus the Bastion region, with the Gadris Mountains to the south and the Tangle marking the border with Elaivar to the east."

Dare couldn't help but whistle. That was a large plot, three miles to a side. And it was actually nice that it was down out of the way, assuming no border incursions from the elves. "I like what I'm hearing so far."

"You'll like what you see even more, I assure you." Lady Marona smiled slightly, obviously reminiscing. "I visited there more than once, and it's as fine a house as you can imagine. Perfect for a young adventurer wishing to establish himself, and perhaps even take on tenants." Her eyes settled on his three companions and twinkled mischievously. "And of course a wonderful home for a growing family."

Pella giggled, and Dare blushed a bit and quickly sipped his coffee, wincing slightly as it burned his mouth. "May I ask why the manor is available?"

The noblewoman's expression fell, and he was afraid he'd said something wrong. "It was the property of a good friend of my late husband's," she said quietly, taking another cautious sip. "One of his adventuring companions. He fell fighting beside my husband, along with the majority of their party."

Ah. "I'm sorry," Dare said gently.

She waved that aside briskly, her stately facade falling back into place. "The price would be two thousand gold a year paid over ten years. A steal for that land and the manor sitting upon it, although I'm afraid to say they've fallen into disrepair over the last year in spite of my best efforts to maintain them. That, and their far-flung location, may explain why I've had such trouble finding a buyer."

That was generous of her to admit, given she was the seller in this negotiation. Although she seemed adamant about the price.

He rubbed his jaw, considering. Twenty thousand gold over ten years was a fortune, most of what they'd gotten in the dungeon. It was obviously more than he and his companions had been expecting when they'd talked about a manor and amenities.

But Dare didn't hate that. He liked to think big, not just for now but for the future. A place like that would allow room to grow, a comfortable home for a large harem.

And the baroness had admitted it was within his rights to take on tenants. Which meant at some point he'd be able to realize his dream of freeing slaves and giving them a home where they could live peaceful, prosperous lives.

"There are some specific details I should ask about," he asked, finishing the last of his coffee. "You'll pardon me if I seem ignorant, but I originally hail from a land other than Haraldar and am not certain on its specific workings in the case of land and titles."

Lady Marona chuckled. "Few outside the nobility are. And even some among them." She set down her cup with finality, even though there was some coffee remaining with it. "I like it when prospective vassals consider things carefully and ask questions. Please, what did you wish to know?"

"Well first off, I assume I'll need to pay taxes on the land on top of the asking price, as will any tenants or laborers I have on the land."

"Of course," she said. "But don't worry, Bastion's governor is lenient in these sorts of matters because he wishes to encourage settlement. The property taxes will add up to about one hundred gold per season, and will include those to me as Baroness of Terana and your liege, as well as those I pass on in turn to the regional government."

Another maid entered, a beautiful woman his Eye identified as draconid, with smooth, delicate dark green scales on her hands and her long thick tail, and pale whitish-green scales along her face, throat, and what he could see of her chest and small but shapely cleavage, beneath the ruffles that made up the bust of her maid outfit.

In spite of her scales and tail she looked human in appearance, slender but curvy, although rather than hair she had lacy green frills falling about her head like a bob haircut, and instead of ears small, smooth bumps. Also her golden eyes had oval pupils, somewhere between round and slitted like a reptile's. They had the sort of alluring, natural glisten that made her look as if she was giving you bedroom eyes or on the verge of bursting into tears, depending on her expression.

She bore a tray of various sweets, immediately catching Zuri's attention, and gracefully moved around the table placing plates and offering the tray to first her lady and then her guests.

Lady Marona picked out what looked like a donut covered with powdered sugar and a croissant filled with butter and jam, waving the exotic draconid on towards Dare as she continued. "There will be a one silver tax per season for each person living on your lands, as decided by yearly census, which you will be responsible for paying."

"Thank you," Dare said to the draconid, giving her his most charming smile as he selected out a few cream-filled pastries slathered with jam.

She blushed, scales shimmering in beautifully shifting shades of green, and returned his smile boldly, revealing sharp teeth similar to Zuri's and licking her full, glistening lips with a slender forked tongue.

Then, as if remembering herself, she curtsied hastily before hurrying on to his goblin lover. Who of course unapologetically took one of everything, filling her plate.

Dare turned back to the baroness. "What about operating my land? Do I have full autonomy over my tenants, traders, adventurers, and other travelers?"

"That's a rather broad question with a lot of specifics," she said. "But for the sake of simplicity yes. As long as you don't violate their rights as citizens of Haraldar, you may tax them as you wish, provided you give them the alternative of leaving your lands if they refuse to pay . . . no strong-arming or extortion."

The stately woman smiled apologetically. "Not that I believe you're the sort who'd do that, of course. It is also within your rights to evict anyone you please with the exception of tenants. You will be required to draw up a contract for each one, and if they feel you've broken the terms of the contract it is within their right to seek me for arbitration. You may also take on laborers with no contracts, and wages and housing are at your discretion pending their right to leave if they're unfavorable."

"What about crime?"

"It's within your rights to arrest anyone who's committed a crime, but you must bring them to Terana for trial. You'll be required to justify any violence, especially killing, that occurs because of an arrest."

"And it's within my rights to protect my tenants from being hassled by others?"

"Your right?" Lady Marona said, frowning. "That's an odd way to put it. It's your duty, of course. As any person has the right to protect themselves from unlawful attack, so a lord has the duty to protect his vassals who cannot protect themselves."

"Lord?" he asked, smiling.

She laughed. "Landed gentleman, in your case." Her eyes danced. "However, you'd be eligible to petition for knighthood if you wished. Although that comes with duties to Bastion and the kingdom."

"Anything else you wish, sir?" the draconid maid asked, coming back around to him. Her bold smile was inviting, and her gold eyes smoldered.

Dare noticed she hadn't paid a second visit to any of the others, even her mistress. "No, thank you," he said, offering her another smile. "An opportunity to experience your beauty is treat enough."

Lady Marona choked on her donut, and he felt his face heat as the maid scurried away with a pleased but slightly scandalized giggle. "Your pardon for my impropriety, my Lady," he said hastily.

She cleared her throat, hiding a smile. "It *was* a bit improper," she agreed. "Maids are generally expected to be ignored, part of the background of a household." Her lips twitched as she glanced at his companions. "Still, in most circumstances women like a compliment, especially as you seem to be a great admirer of beautiful women."

Dare risked meeting her eyes and smiling. "I am, my Lady."

The stately widow's cheeks turned ever so slightly pink and she cleared her throat again, more sternly. "Speaking of duties, along with taxes you'll also be expected to assist in law enforcement and protecting adventurers and travelers in the wilds around your lands, an area I'll designate on a map. In the event Bastion is invaded or the King calls for a mobilization of Haraldar's forces, you may be expected to answer the call as any landed gentleman would be."

That seemed reasonable enough. "It looks as though there's more details involved to owning land here than where I'm from," he admitted. "Thank you for your advice."

"Of course." Her stern exterior softened in a smile. "I'll admit it will be good to see the place thriving again, and I believe you'll be a good vassal." She abruptly straightened, expression brisk. "You will no doubt wish to go and inspect the manor and lands before making any decision. My Head Maid will give you directions to it, although more simply it is a day's ride east by southeast of here, and the walled manor is plainly visible."

Lady Marona stood, and Dare and his companions quickly stood as well. "I hope you'll excuse me," she said, "but pleasant as this conversation has been I have many duties. You're welcome to stay the night here, seeing as you're prospective business partners and vassals deserving of my hospitality. I'll have a maid show you to your room or rooms, as you wish, and feel free to use the sitting and dining rooms at your leisure."

She motioned, and as if by magic a catgirl maid appeared, bowing low. "If you'll follow me?" she asked politely.

Dare bowed to the baroness, who'd returned to her desk as if they were already gone. "Thank you again, my Lady. I hope to return quickly with my decision, but from the sounds of things I am inclined to make an offer."

"Until then, Master Dare," she said absently, looking at a parchment.

Chapter Twelve
Hospitality

Dare followed the catgirl maid out of Lady Marona's study and through the mansion, with Zuri, Pella, and even Leilanna all clustering close around him as they made their way through the opulent rooms and hallways.

"Dinner is at sunset," the maid said as they walked, peeking over her shoulder to give him and his companions curious looks, tufted ears twitching. She had dark red hair and very large, bright eyes of the same color that made her resting expression seem somewhat incredulous. "I'm afraid the Mistress will likely be too busy to attend, as she usually is. But we've been instructed to show all hospitality."

He had to wonder when exactly that instruction had been given. Before they'd even had their meeting seemed unlikely.

Some unspoken signal from the mistress of the house, maybe?

The redheaded woman was abruptly intercepted as another maid, the beautiful draconid, appeared as if by magic from behind a tapestry; a servant's hallway. "Thank you, Milin," she said curtly. "I'll see to our guests."

The catgirl stared at her, those huge eyes looking even more incredulous. "Um, what? You're a kitchen maid and I'm a housemaid. Why would *you* be assigned to this, Belinda?"

The draconid, Belinda apparently, blushed that scintillating range of green across her scales again; it was not only beautiful but also adorable. "I just am," she said sternly. "And seeing as I've worked here two years longer than you, *and* had the Master's favor before his passing, what would you know?"

Milin gave her fellow maid a smug smile as her incredulous eyes darted between the draconid and Dare. "Then I suppose I'm relieved of my duties for the next few hours, by your approval?" she purred.

Belinda hesitated, and he couldn't help but get the impression she was about to get herself into hot water. But she nodded firmly. "One hour. And don't leave the household."

The catgirl giggled and gracefully stepped aside. "Then have fun, *kitchen maid*. Hopefully your hands aren't too rough from peeling vegetables."

The draconid made a rumbling noise and swatted Milin's rump with a towel, and her fellow maid squeaked and darted behind the tapestry, disappearing from view.

Belinda turned to Dare and his companions and curtsied, scales still swirling with embarrassment. "Please forgive that improper display, master and mistresses. If you'll follow me to the baths?"

"Yes, please!" Leilanna said, grinning eagerly. "Cleanse Target is nice, but it doesn't compare to a proper bath." She looked wistful. "Too bad I haven't had mana to waste on heating water since you started my accelerated leveling."

The draconid faced forward as she led them, prim and proper, but from the stiff set of her tail Dare had the feeling she was listening eagerly. He wondered how often the mansion had guests, especially adventurers.

Soon they reached a pair of doors maids were scurrying around, bringing full buckets of water in and empty buckets out. About half were human but the others were a mix of other races, including the pink-haired gnome Dare had seen before.

They looked startled to see Belinda with the guests, but only curtsied at their approach.

The draconid maid ignored them and motioned to the first door. "You'll find everything you need within, mistresses, although please ask if you require assistance." She motioned to the other door, scales starting their mesmerizing swirl again as she flushed. "If you'll accompany me to your bath, master? I'll personally see to all your needs."

"I don't mind bathing with my lovers," Dare said hastily.

"*I* mind!" Leilanna said, scowling. "If you're trying to-"

"I just meant you can take the other room," he cut her off, cheeks heating.

"No no!" Zuri said hastily, shoving him towards the door where Belinda was waiting. "If I'm not mistaken, the kind maid has offered to help you bathe?"

All the maids in the hall stopped dead, staring with wide eyes.

Oh. Ooooh. Dare gave the draconid a questioning look, and felt a surge of excitement as she nodded in agreement, lowering her eyes and blushing harder. "It would be my pleasure, master."

The other maids tittered, but at Belinda's glare hurried back to their tasks.

Fuck yes. "You're okay bathing with Leilanna?" he asked Zuri and Pella.

They both grinned at him. "Have fun," the dog girl said, tail wagging.

Zuri surreptitiously slipped a scroll into his hand. "Just in case," she whispered with a wink.

Dare glanced sheepishly at the dragonkin girl, who by her furiously shimmering scales had obviously seen it and guessed what it was. But the maid just curtsied again. "This way, master."

Trying not to look too eager, Dare stepped into the room. Belinda stepped in after him and locked the door behind her with a decisive *click*.

"You're not afraid to go for what you want," he teased.

Surprisingly, her blush was settling into a warm dark green, and she gave him a wide smile to reveal her sharp teeth and delicate forked tongue. "I bear the blood of dragons, and our kind are covetous. If we see something we desire we take it for ourselves."

The maid abruptly lowered her gaze, acting abashed. Although the lack of more blushing belied her sudden return to propriety. "Your pardon, master," she murmured meekly. "Please, allow me to attend you."

Ah, so the bold draconid wanted to keep up the timid maid roleplay. Dare certainly wasn't about to complain.

210

Given the two bath rooms side by side, he wasn't surprised to see a shaving stand complete with mirror in this one. The room was dominated by a large sunken tub, easily big enough to accommodate several people and full of pleasantly steaming water.

Belinda gave the appearance of shyness as she undressed him, placing his clothes outside the door to be cleaned and taken to his room, although her golden oval eyes greedily devoured every inch of his body she revealed.

Her hands were warm, the pale green scales of her palms dry and with a texture that reminded him of an iguana he'd once held, although smoother and infinitely softer. She touched and caressed him more than was strictly necessary to remove his clothes, and he could hear her breathing quickening by the second, with a slightly sibilant hiss as the air passed around her forked tongue.

Dare couldn't help but notice that the scroll Zuri had given him didn't get put outside with everything else, but instead ended up on a table near the door. Hinting at future use?

Thanks to that possibility, and the draconid maid's gentle ministrations, Dare's cock had stirred to a half chub by the time she removed his underwear. She gasped at the size of it.

"Like what you see?" he teased.

She hastily looked away and her blush finally made a reappearance, rippling across her skin in a quick pattern before fading. "Your pardon, master."

Belinda gracefully led him over to the shaving stand and settled him on a stool, then got to work trimming his hair with a pair of sharp scissors. She wasn't quite as good as Pella, understandable given she was a kitchen maid, but she didn't butcher the job.

Dare got a bit more nervous when she lathered his stubble and picked up a straight razor, but her hands were steady and smooth as she shaved him.

When she was done she patted his face with a hot towel, then boldly looked down at his pubic hair. "Any other shaving you'd like me to do, master?" she asked, golden eyes dancing.

Fun as that sounded, he wasn't sure he wanted to go bare down there. Especially not without getting Zuri's and Pella's opinions about it first. "Thank you, no," he said with a laugh.

Giggling, the draconid took his hand and pulled him to his feet. "Then please come this way, master."

Dare followed the beautiful maid to the tub, allowing her to usher him into the pleasantly hot water. He settled down on a submerged ledge, the water coming up to his chest, and watched as she stood back.

The maid wasted no time untying her clean white apron and lifting it over her head before carefully folding it and placing it on a nearby table; it was obvious she meant to undress and continue attending him in the bath.

It was his turn to greedily observe her as she removed her ruffled bonnet, then untied her uniform's laces and let it slip off her shoulders, leaving her in a soft camisole and puffy, ruffled petticoats.

The petticoats came off next, with a slit to accommodate her long, thick tail, and finally she was left in just her camisole, small nipples poking prominently through the thin, clinging cloth. He also caught a brief, tantalizing impression of the garment molding around her slit as she shifted position.

Dare wasn't sure if that was as far as she'd intended to undress, or if she lost her nerve at the last second, but to his disappointment the camisole stayed on as she slipped into the water.

His dragon girl bath attendant brought soap and a towel with her, lathering up her hands as she moved him around on the ledge so he was sitting sideways. She sat behind him, her soft fingers running over his back as she soaped him up.

Her dry scales became smooth and sleek when wet, as well as somehow even softer, with a pleasant feel that made him want to turn around and run his hands over the rest of her body. But he was in no hurry, and instead closed his eyes and relaxed into her ministrations.

The draconid's touch was firm, almost like a massage, and he felt the tension of the last few weeks begin to bleed away. Along with the sharp edge of the fears he'd carried since learning that the women he loved were both pregnant, and he felt the looming responsibility of fatherhood.

If all went well with this purchase he'd have a house where his harem could live and raise their children, and land that could potentially support them. His benefactor had come through for all of them and the future was looking brighter.

Dare heard the splash of Belinda standing behind him. She cleared her throat, voice husky with nervous anticipation. "If you'll stand, master, I'll wash your lower half."

Much brighter.

He eagerly turned, and his breath caught at the sight of the beautiful draconid presented in all her glory.

The thin white camisole had become soaked in the bath and was now completely transparent, clinging to her lush body like a second skin. He could see that her coloring was dark green on her back, arms, and legs, with her entire front that beautiful whitish-green. The bath had brought out the color in her scales, the way a drab stone could become a beautiful gem when wet, and now she glistened like an emerald.

Her scales had been beautiful before, of course, but now they were absolutely transcendent.

The sexy draconid's small, pert breasts were pleasantly rounded, her nipples dark green and protruding proudly. Her tummy could've been sculpted by a god, toned but at the same time voluptuous, a narrow waist leading to wide hips, thick thighs, and at their junction a glorious pink slit, the cloth of her garment molding into every fold and curve. Her legs were powerful but with a feminine slenderness, her delicate feet sharing the same small, sharp black claws as her hands. Although her fingernails had been trimmed back.

Dare realized he was staring openmouthed, but he couldn't stop himself as she began to blush and coyly covered herself with her hands. "Gods, you're perfect," he murmured.

Belinda's golden oval eyes widened and she sucked in a sharp breath. "Do you really think so?" she whispered, sounding surprisingly vulnerable after her earlier boldness. Her blush became a kaleidoscope of shades of green flickering over her entire body in a beautiful pattern, as expressive in their own way as her aristocratic features.

He smiled as he admired the amazing show. "How can I not? A man would have to be crazy not to see how beautiful you are."

To his surprise her lovely features fell. "Then almost all men are crazy," she growled bitterly. "They seem to find my green scales and tail hideous. I can see the disgust in their eyes." She paused, looking away. "Lord Arral was one who saw differently. It's one of the reasons I loved him."

Dare gently rested a finger under her chin, lifting her eyes to meet his. "If those men can't see your beauty then they *are* crazy, I don't care how many of them there are."

The draconid's shoulders lifted proudly. "Thank you," she whispered, naturally glistening eyes brimming with tears. "I'm of a noble lineage, with the blood of dragons. They *should* see my majesty."

She abruptly seemed to remember she was playing the demure maid, and with a gasp lowered her gaze again and dropped into a clumsy curtsey. "If it please you, master," she said, voice trembling shyly, "shall I wash your manhood?"

He blinked; it looked as if she was done playing around and ready to go right for it. "Please," he said, smiling.

Belinda eagerly lathered her hands, then reached out and took his massive cock in both, lovingly stroking it. She began breathing harder, small breasts heaving, and her proud features relaxed in pure lust.

"Gods, it's beautiful," she gasped, tightening her grip and stroking him faster with her delicate hands. She looked up at him, glistening eyes glazed with need. "*You're* beautiful."

"Then I'm in good company." Dare leaned forward and pressed his lips to hers.

Contrary to his expectations they were soft and moist, with a sweet, smoky taste. Her mouth opened eagerly and her delicate forked tongue pressed into his, finding his tongue and teasing it like a serpent coiling around its prey.

215

The draconid maid moaned and started to pull his cock towards her, and he remembered himself just enough to jerk his hips back with a gasp. "Scroll," he panted.

"It's fine, I just want you to fuck my thighs first," she moaned against his mouth, soap-slippery hands struggling and failing to pull his throbbing cock to her. "I need to feel you against me right now or I'll go insane."

"Okay, but then you cast the spell on yourself," he said, giving in. "My fertility is so high I could impregnate you just by touching your pussy."

Belinda pulled back and looked at him with a giggle. "What, are you secretly a cunid?"

Dare smiled apologetically. "Even worse," he admitted. "My stat is 51."

Her golden oval eyes inspected him. "Scroll," she agreed solemnly. Then she playfully slapped his ass. "If your fertility is higher than a cunid's then even the gods must think you're a stud."

He wasted no time retrieving the scroll and handing it to her, and she stripped out of her clinging transparent camisole so she could press her hands to her lower belly as she cast it.

"I'm already loving this," he said, greedily staring at her pink slit.

"Oh?" The draconid's scaly tail lashed languidly, and she grinned at him. "Then this is going to blow your mind." She backed up until she was seated on the edge of the sunken tub, lifting and spreading her legs to part the pouting lips of her glorious pussy. Her interior glistened with a steady flow of her arousal, as sopping wet as her exterior.

Dare licked his lips at the sight and climbed into the tub, wading over and burying his face between her legs.

"Oh!" Belinda exclaimed again in surprise, powerful thighs clamping closed around his head. "Oh, this is new."

He wasn't sure how it was possible that no one had ever gone down on her before, because she tasted delicious. Like sweet melon with a sharp, smoky flavor and a powerful musk. He lapped at her silky lips, then buried his tongue deep in her tunnel.

That was all it took for the quivering draconid, and with another squeal of surprise and pleasure she squirted all over his face, tight folds eagerly milking his tongue as he continued to explore her depths.

Her orgasm continued under his ministrations, and when he brought his thumb in to rub her swollen clit she cried out and squirted again, drenching him in her fragrant nectar.

"Ah!" she gasped, forcefully shoving him away. "That's enough of that . . . I need you inside me."

Dare eagerly rose and began rubbing his throbbing tip along Belinda's pink slit and over her small pearl, while she wrapped her arms and legs around him and hugged him close, passionately kissing him.

"Your face is all covered with my juices," she moaned. "Fuck, that's so dirty." Although she didn't seem to really think so because her forked tongue snaked out and licked at his cheek, tasting herself.

He abandoned teasing her and lined up with her quivering entrance. "Ready?" he asked gently.

"Please!" the draconid maid nearly whined, hips rolling against him and nearly doing the job of penetration for him, although she tensed and stopped at the last second.

Dare kissed her gently, running his hands over her silky smooth back, then gripped her hips and gently pressed forward.

Belinda made a muffled sound against his lips, and her walls clenched down on his tip with shocking tightness. "Gods, you're huge," she gasped, sounding a bit nervous.

He kissed her again, stroking her tail. "I'll go slow," he promised.

She nodded, glistening eyes holding his with a smoky heat, and he began to press forward again.

He'd barely gone in a few inches before the beautiful dragon girl moaned, grabbed his back desperately with her small scaly hands, and hugged him tight with her powerful legs. Her silken walls clamped down on him again, and she squirted all over his crotch.

"Fuuuck," Dare panted, not just at the glorious sensation but at the knowledge he was bringing this bold yet demure maid so much pleasure. "I love how much you're loving this."

Her delicate scales shimmered with another blush. "I've only done this a few times, and it's been so long," she confessed. "You're making it so good for me."

That was the sort of thing any man loved to hear, especially since it seemed completely genuine.

As Belinda came down from her climax he began gently thrusting inside her, surprised to find how deep she was; he only had an inch or so outside when his tip kissed her core, and her tight walls were rippling deliciously along his entire length.

"You feel amazing," he told her. "*I'm* not going to be able to hold out long at this rate."

She giggled and hugged him closer, hips eagerly undulating against him as he pulled out to thrust again. "Then you'd better hold on, because I want this to last longer."

"I will," Dare promised with a grin. "But if you're worried about this ending too soon, just remember that I've got two lovers that I usually tire out long before I'm ready to call it quits."

The beautiful maid gasped as he began a long, slow thrust back into her. "Then do whatever you want," she moaned, tail writhing across the tiles behind her. "Just keep making me feel this good."

That was an easy request to fulfill.

Dare thrust into her for five minutes, using her cues to determine when she was ready for him to go faster, when to go harder, and when to slow down so she could tremble her way through another climax.

Which she did. A lot.

Some of it might have been that she'd been thirsty for so long, but he got the feeling that draconids just generally loved sex and had a blast with it. Which he certainly wasn't complaining about.

Finally one of her orgasms caught him by surprise as her short fingernails raked across his back and she squealed, soft pink pussy squeezing so tight it almost pushed him out. "I'm coming!" he gasped as he thrust in deep enough to bottom out.

"Yes!" Belinda squealed, squirting again as she reached an even higher peak.

Dare grit his teeth and twitched his hips to press against her cervix, spraying her sweet little dragonkin pussy as he emptied himself inside her.

They both clutched each other tight, panting as they came down from their shared climax. Dare kissed her again, running his tongue over the front of her smooth sharp teeth, and finally began to pull out.

"Nooo, keep going," the sexy draconid begged. "Please keep going, even though you just came." Her hips jerked against him, trying to keep him deep inside her quivering walls. "I need more."

Dare chuckled. "Don't worry, I'm not done yet." He flipped her over onto her stomach, making her giggle in surprise, and with her bent over the edge of the tub grabbed her tail as leverage and thrust back into her in one smooth motion.

"Eeeeeee!" she squealed, squirming back against him. "Gods, it's like you're fucking me with a completely different cock!"

That was the wonder of different positions, all right; he wondered how many ways she'd tried, if she'd only done this a few times.

Well, he'd have to see how many new ones he could introduce her to before he reached his limit.

As it turned out, Belinda ran out of steam long before that. Dare thrust into her from behind for several minutes, teasing a few more orgasms out of her before giving into his pleasure and releasing inside her sweet pink pussy again.

But as he shifted around to let her be on top, she clutched at him desperately, weak as a kitten. "Ancient Progenitor," she moaned. "I don't think I've ever been fucked so thoroughly . . . this was incredible." She began kissing her way along his jaw, tongue flickering teasingly across his skin. "Thank you."

He chuckled and slid back into the tub, pulling her with him and cuddling her soft body as the warm water lapped over them. "That was incredible," he agreed, stroking the lacy green frills that served as her hair; they were surprisingly soft. "You're incredible."

The draconid rumbled contentedly, tail swirling the water. "If you stay at the mansion for a while we might just have to do this again."

"Sounds good." Dare reached over and grabbed the soap, idly lathering his hands. "Since you already washed me, I feel like I should return the favor."

She giggled and looked down, the demure maid returning. "Please, master, that's my job. I'm here to serve your every whim."

"What if my whim is to run my soapy hands all over your sexy little body?" he teased.

Belinda's scales made that beautiful scintillating pattern again as she blushed. "Well then I suppose that's my duty," she said eagerly.

As it turned out, after working her up by caressing every inch of her body, paying special attention to her pink slit and little rosebud, she discovered she had one more fuck in her after all. In a surge of passion she mounted him in the tub, riding him in the warm water for several minutes until finally she slumped against him in a quivering climax, and he pumped one last load into her silken pussy.

After that the somewhat weak-kneed dragon girl dried herself with a towel and dressed, carrying her sopping wet camisole over one arm. She gave Dare a final passionate kiss, then leaned in close to his ear, tickling it with her forked tongue.

"The other maids can play with you if they want," she murmured in a sultry voice, "but only because I allow them to. As far as they're concerned you're *mine*."

Other maids, huh? He definitely liked the hint that Belinda wasn't the only one interested in him; hopefully that included some of the beauties he'd seen here, like the adorable pink-haired gnome and the incredulous catgirl. And that smoking hot blonde.

Chuckling, Dare stroked her smooth cheek with a finger. "Have I become treasure in a covetous dragon girl's hoard?"

Belinda gave him a coy smile. "Yes." With a lingering smoky look she slipped out the door, leaving him to get dressed himself.

Chapter Thirteen
Disrepair

The rest of the stay at Lady Marona's mansion was fairly uneventful.

Dare continued to get interested looks and subtle flirting from the numerous maids the baroness kept on staff, which he was more than happy to return in kind. But none approached him.

Dinner was quiet, just him and his companions around a table big enough to hold dozens. The maids serving them just giggled and looked scandalized when he invited them to eat with his party, and he hoped he hadn't gotten them in trouble.

He was proud of his ability to cook good food for his companions, and his experience with a lot of inns was that their food wasn't much better than what he could make.

Not so with the baroness's kitchens. Their cooks, Belinda included no doubt, were chefs in the truest sense of the word, creating course after course of gourmet dishes better than anything Dare had eaten on Earth. He and his companions ate eagerly, lavishing the embarrassed maids with praise when they frequently popped in to check on them and see if they need anything else.

After dinner they were escorted to their rooms, Leilanna seeming eager to duck through her door and enjoy the luxuries she'd missed in the wilds.

And the room Dare and his lovers were given was definitely luxurious. The bed was enormous, big enough for six so that he, Zuri, and Pella were nearly lost in its pillowy softness. As they settled in to sleep his lovers pressed him for details about his bath with Belinda, and immediately began planning how they'd join in next time.

Gods, they were almost talking like they assumed the dragon girl would be joining their harem. Which as far as he'd seen, the beautiful woman had shown no interest in.

Just good, clean fun.

The next morning they got up bright and early to set out. But before they could they were intercepted by the maids, who insisted they get a proper breakfast. Since Belinda was spearheading the charge he readily agreed, not that he'd been about to refuse another chance to enjoy the delicious food here.

Dare was enthusiastically digging into a plate of bacon and fried potato cakes when he felt someone coming up between his legs below the tablecloth. He nearly jumped out of his skin and looked down into a pair of big, mischievous blue eyes peeking up at him from beneath the hiding place of the long cloth.

It was the adorable pink-haired gnome, cheeks flushed with the naughty excitement of taking a daring risk.

She licked her plump rosebud lips and playfully pressed a finger to them, making a "shh" sound. Then her delicate hands went for the laces of his pants and freed his swiftly growing erection, her fingers soft and warm.

The pink-haired maid's already big eyes went huge when she saw the size of him. Compared to her small face his rock hard shaft looked monstrous, and she licked her lips again with an eager expression and lovingly kissed the tip.

Then with effort she took him into her mouth, lips stretched obscenely around his girth. She felt warm, soft, and deliciously wet, and Dare had to stifle a groan of pleasure as she took him in deeper.

In spite of the adorable gnome's best efforts she couldn't get more than the tip into her mouth, but she compensated by forming a fierce suction and working his pee slit aggressively with her little tongue, making him struggle not to squirm in his seat. Her saliva flowed freely down his shaft, lubricating it so her small hands could vigorously squeeze and pump him.

She was obviously trying to finish him off quickly, before they got caught, and in spite of his best efforts to hold off his orgasm and enjoy the sexy little maid's incredible blowjob, Dare eventually gave in and began pumping a torrent of his seed directly into her eager mouth. It took all his willpower to keep the incredible pleasure of his orgasm from showing on his face.

The daring gnome valiantly swallowed as much as she could, but thanks to the sheer volume a bit still leaked out of the corners of her mouth as she made contented noises.

When he finally shot his last spurt she pulled back, licking her lips in satisfaction. She produced a small soft cloth and daintily cleaned him off, then stuffed him back into his pants and retied the laces.

With a conspiratorial wink the little pink-haired beauty disappeared beneath the tablecloth.

Dare finally became aware of his surroundings again and leaned back, hastily looking around to see if anyone had noticed. The maids moved with their usual competence, beautiful faces showing only calm professionalism, and Leilanna seemed oblivious as she tore her way through a stack of pancakes.

Seated to either side of him, however, Zuri and Pella were doing their best to stifle laughter.

He got back to his breakfast, pretending not to notice as the sexy gnome appeared out from under the far side of the table. She took a second to smooth her maid uniform, gave him a last saucy look over her shoulder, then walked briskly towards the nearest door, ankle-length pink hair swishing adorably with every step.

After the meal they exited the mansion by the front entrance to find their horses already saddled and their gear loaded up. Surprisingly, the entire staff of fourteen maids had assembled to see their party off.

Although it seemed more like they wanted one last chance to see *him*.

In spite of Head Maid Garena's obvious irritation at the presence of the young women, Dare took the time to properly thank them for their hospitality. And subtly flirt with many of them, particularly Belinda and the cute little pink-haired maid. His companions also said their goodbyes and expressed their gratitude.

Finally he arrived in front of the Head Maid herself, bowing low. "Thank you for your hospitality. Please extend my gratitude to the Baroness as well, and assure her we'll return with a decision on the property as soon as we're able."

"It was a pleasure to have you, Master Dare, Mistress Leilanna, Mistress Pella, Mistress Zuri," she said; from her stiff tone it was hard to know whether she was being formal or hiding disapproval. "Lady Marona wished me to extend an invitation to visit her again, even should you decide not to purchase the manor. She enjoyed your conversation."

"It would be our pleasure," Pella said, tail wagging. "Thank you for your kindness, Miss Garona."

"Until next time, then." The Head Maid turned and shooed the other maids back into the house, then waited at the doorway to see them off. Half a dozen heads poked out around her to also watch.

Dare certainly looked forward to returning to the mansion, particularly if Lady Marona was willing to extend her hospitality for another night or even longer.

The place had a lot of gorgeous maids, and a lot of hidden nooks and crannies to duck into for some fun.

"Enjoy your breakfast?" Pella teased him as they mounted their new horses. "Or did it blow?"

He felt his cheeks heat. "It was very nice."

"I don't know, don't you think one of the maids sucked?" Zuri said, deadpan.

Leilanna looked between them suspiciously. "What the fuck are you two talking about? That was one of the best meals I've ever had."

Dare hastily cleared his throat. "We've got a long way to go, and I'd like to reach the property by nightfall."

* * * * *

In the golden light of sunset they got their first look at the manor, looking down from a rise that gave them a view over the high, solid walls.

The manor itself was two storeys and was perhaps half the size of Lady Marona's mansion, plain but well constructed and showing clear signs of disrepair. He judged it had maybe a dozen bedrooms, and had been constructed with room for expansion.

Dotted across the expansive yard, which was currently overgrown with weeds, ivy, and untrimmed hedges, were outbuildings such as a small servants' quarters to one side of the manor, a tiny caretaker's cottage near the front gate, stables, a barn, a shed, another building that might've been a smaller shed or an equipment locker, an outhouse, and finally a well.

"It's beautiful," Zuri, who'd abandoned her own little horse to sit with him in his saddle, said in awe, resting a hand on her belly as she took in the sight.

Dare wasn't sure he'd go that far in its current state, but it had the *potential* to be beautiful. He rested a tender hand on his lover's belly as well, and with a start of pleased surprise felt the baby kick. He shared a delighted smile with her and rested his cheek on her head as he continued to look around.

The monsters in the area were around Level 20, with the nearest spawn point only a few hundred yards away. But his lovers had assured him that by aggressively clearing the nearby spawn points every time the monsters within respawned, they'd steadily drive their level down even without needing to have enough people in the manor to constitute a proper settlement.

Apparently when over a hundred people lived within a mile of each other for over a year, it triggered the world system's process of dropping the nearest spawn points to Level 1, and having them gradually increase with distance from the settlement.

The land around the manor was beautiful, wild and untamed and brimming with possibilities. There were signs that the nearest fields had been cleared and cultivated at some point, but were now overgrown.

Dare could imagine himself exploring this land, taming it and making the most of its resources. Even encouraging settlers and forming a village of people who could live safe and free.

The prospect excited him almost as much as the view of the manor itself.

He looked at Pella and Leilanna as they reined in beside him on their own horses. "First thoughts?"

"It's a dump and we'll spend a month cleaning it and repairing everything," Leilanna said, scowling with displeasure.

"It's amazing and I can already see our puppies playing in the yard!" Pella countered, face glowing with happiness.

"We all have a say in this," Dare told the dusk elf. "So if you really hate it that will influence our decision."

She glowered for a few seconds, arms folded beneath her large breasts, before making a "hmph" sound. "It's got potential. And the disrepair will lower the price."

There was a light on in the caretaker's cottage, indicating the place wasn't completely abandoned. Although any signs of actual care-taking were few and far between. Dare led the way down to the front gate, rapping on the solid wood.

It took several minutes to coax out whoever was in the cottage, to the point that Dare was tempted to scale the wall and open the gate himself. But finally he heard the creak of poorly maintained hinges as the little cottage's door opened.

"Who's there?" a man called, voice quavering with age as much as fear.

"My name is Dare," he called back. "My companions and I were thinking of buying the place and Lady Marona invited us to come look it over first."

The gate hastily opened, an old but spry man in ragged laborer's clothes eagerly ushering them inside. "Welcome, welcome!" he said with a grin. "Please, come in and let me show you around."

The caretaker, who turned out to be named Volen and had been in the employ of the previous owner, led them to the stables and helped them care for their horses, chattering all the way. It turned out he'd been employed by Lady Marona after the owner's passing to keep an eye on the place, and had spent the last year in almost complete isolation.

He was clearly grateful for the presence of other people.

From the sounds of it Volen seemed to expect that he'd stay on after the purchase, continuing his job right until old age claimed him. Although after seeing the state of the place Dare wasn't sure he wanted to keep the man employed.

To be fair, though, maintaining the manor was an impossible job for one man, especially one who was getting on in years.

They were pleasantly surprised to find that the manor was fully furnished, which he supposed was no surprise if the previous owner had died with no heirs, leaving it in the hands of the Baroness of Terana. Some of the furniture showed signs of water damage, and the place was musty, but that could be fixed soon enough.

It was obvious Baron Arral wasn't the only one who'd grown rich from his adventuring; the manor was well appointed, if to more humble tastes than the richness of Montshadow Estate.

The girls were practically bouncing off the walls in excitement as Volen led them through the main room, living room, parlor, dining room, kitchen, study, and the rest of the first floor. They were already making plans, talking about what furniture to keep, what they needed to buy, how to move furniture around and redecorate to their tastes, and dreamily talking about what living here would be like.

Dare couldn't blame them for being so awestruck. Although he'd lived humbly on Earth thanks to his modest finances, he was no stranger to large houses that would seem like unimaginable wealth and luxury to the people of Collisa.

But his companions had lived very different lives. A goblin raised in a small village. A dusk elf who'd lived a nomadic life on the road, sleeping in a wagon house. Even Pella, who'd had a noble master and lived in a place even nicer than this, had been a pet there, with no sense of ownership. And before that she'd been raised and trained in a kennel.

The thought of being owners of a place like this, of making it their own and living their lives here, was a dream come true for the three women. As all of them said at least once as the tour progressed.

The upstairs bedrooms were small but comfortable, with a large master bedroom complete with a changing room and vanity for ladies. At the end of the hall was a room with a chamber pot adjacent to a small bath room, the tub inside barely large enough for one person.

Volen led the way out of the house and gave them a quick inspection of the outbuildings, although in the fading light and after a long, tiring journey Dare knew he wasn't the only one eager to finish the tour. He did take notice of the servants' quarters, however, a series of small rooms with a bed and clothing chest, sparse but not uncomfortable.

"How many servants did the previous owner have?" he asked.

The old caretaker rubbed his jaw. "There was me, of course, and the gardener and stable boy. And the cook and maid to serve him in the house itself." He grinned suggestively. "Although by the end both were as good as his mistresses . . . I tasted Deria's cooking a time or two, and I can tell you he didn't hire her for that. As for Helane, she swept more of the floor with her knees and her back than with a broom, if you catch my drift."

The girls giggled. Dare smiled politely, not really interested in old gossip. "Were the five of you sufficient to maintain the manor and yard?"

"Well enough," Volen said with a shrug. "Jori, the old master, wasn't fussy about the place not being perfect. Although he was particular about his horses, and his roses and the shrine to the Outsider he kept in one corner of the yard."

Dare noticed Zuri yawning and swaying on her feet, and turned to the old caretaker. "Thank you for your time. I think we'll call it a night and look over the property more closely in the morning."

"Of course." Volen motioned. "You're welcome to use the manor, just clean up any messes." With a bow he started back towards his cottage.

They filed back into the darkening structure, where Leilanna sent bright white flames burning over one hand, holding it in front of her for light.

"It's a good place," Dare said, looking around the manor in approval. "I think we could make it a perfect home by installing a few fixtures."

His companions gave him surprised looks. "Like what?" Pella asked curiously. "This manor is as luxurious as my old master's, if not even more so."

He waved. "Well the outhouse needs to go, first off."

"Seriously," Leilanna agreed, wrinkling her nose. "The hole is almost full and more than a little ripe. The sooner we cap it off and dig a new outhouse, the better."

"We won't be digging a new outhouse," Dare said firmly. "We'll turn the second pantry and the chamber pot room in the upstairs hallway into bathrooms."

They all stared at him blankly. "What do baths and pooping have to do with each other?" Zuri demanded.

He scrubbed his fingers through his hair in embarrassment. "I mean privies. Chambers to relieve ourselves in."

"You want to have a privy just off the kitchen, stinking up our food?" Leilanna demanded in disgust. "And how would that work on the second floor, just have a hole so it all drips down the side of the house?"

Dare ignored their revolted disbelief at her vivid descriptions as he quickly continued. "We'll bury a septic tank with a drainfield outside the walls on the downhill side. A perfectly sanitary way to dispose of waste. As for the privies, we'll make toilets with u-shaped pipes, to trap some water in the bowls so the sewage smell doesn't waft up, that connect to the septic tank to whisk away our waste with almost no smell. They'll flush by pouring water into them, at least until we can get proper plumbing."

As they stared at him in baffled silence he kept going enthusiastically. "And we can see if there's the magical equivalent of a water pump so we can get running water. And magical ways to heat and cool for refrigeration, hot baths or even a complete bath house, heating and air conditioning during the winter and summer, and all sorts of other uses." He turned to Leilanna. "You'd probably have some ideas about . . . ."

He finally read the room and trailed off into an awkward silence.

"Was that complete gibberish to everyone else, too?" the dusk elf finally asked.

"I understood most of the words," Zuri said. "It's just the ones I didn't understand and how he stringed them together that made it all nonsense."

"I heard hot baths!" Pella said, fluffy tail wagging happily.

"So hold on," Leilanna said, scowling. "You're claiming you can give us the equivalent of magical waste removal, running hot water, heating and cooling, and food preservation without going into ruinous debt?"

"Well I'd have to look into it to be sure," Dare said. "All those things are possible at this level of technol-that is, our level of innovation. And anything I design would go into the crafting system as a pattern so I could create more of them, making tasks like creating pipes for the plumbing system pretty easy."

"Okay," Zuri said, not quite doubtfully. "Well until you figure out how to do all that, my mate, we'll just have to make do with the luxuries this manor already affords us."

"Although definitely second the motion of moving the outhouse," Leilanna pressed. She turned to Pella. "You're with me there, right? With your sensitive nose?"

The dog girl shrugged. "Bad smells don't really bother me all that much."

"Okay, but we're about to have a house with two pregnant women, and in case you didn't know pregnant women are *very* sensitive to-"

"Nobody's arguing about moving the outhouse," Dare said, amused. "That'll be the first thing we do if we buy this place." He looked around. "Speaking of which, what does everyone think?"

"Buy it," Pella said quickly. "And next after the outhouse figure out the bath house you were talking about."

"Buy it," Zuri agreed. "It'll be a perfect place to raise our children, luxurious and isolated. We'll be left alone here."

"Buy it," Leilanna said. "It's better than wandering around in the wild pooping against trees."

"I'm for buying it as well," Dare said. "So I guess we'll take another look around tomorrow, make sure we didn't miss any red flags that would-"

"Any what?" Zuri cut in, wrinkling her nose.

"Any problems bad enough we decide not to buy it after all." He rubbed her head. "After that we'll head back to Terana and give Lady Marona our decision, then make the necessary arrangements."

"Sounds good." Leilanna yawned hugely. "Anyway, I'm going to pick the room farthest from the master bedroom. Good night." She hefted her bag and headed for the leftmost of the twin stairs in the entryway leading up to the second floor.

Dare watched her go. "Think she's really happy with all this?" he asked. "I mean, thanks to the Lifesworn Oath she has to stay with us, and this all sort of happened in a whirlwind with her on the outside. Does she want to make a life here?"

Pella wrapped her arms around him and put her head on his shoulder. "Honey," she murmured, "haven't you noticed that every time we talk about starting our family, we just naturally include her in the discussion as if she's already part of it? Leilanna herself does it. What does that tell you?"

He blinked. Was that true? He hadn't noticed. "Maybe she just doesn't feel comfortable expressing her true feelings," he said. "We should ask her more directly if there's anything else she would rather do with her life."

Zuri laughed lightly. "My mate, have you ever known Leilanna to have trouble expressing her feelings?"

"Aside from how she feels about you," Pella corrected. "But sometimes I'm not sure she even knows herself." She stroked his back. "She'll get there, though, and then all four of us will build our family here."

"Along with the other women we find to join our harem," Zuri added.

"That would be nice," Dare admitted, hugging his lovers. "But I'm not about to make assumptions until I hear from Leilanna that that's how she feels."

Zuri and Pella both stared at him intently. "What about you?" Zuri asked quietly. "Can you tell us how you feel about Leilanna?"

Wait, what? He shifted awkwardly at their expectant scrutiny. "I mean, she's very beautiful, and I like spending time with her."

"And?" Zuri asked.

Damnit. "I think I'd like to have a relationship with her," he admitted.

"Then you could love her?" Pella asked, kissing his neck. "The way you love us?"

Dare sighed in defeat. "I think so, yes."

The two beautiful women exchanged looks. "Let's go to bed, husband," Zuri said in a husky voice. "We need to test out the mattress and bedding and see if it needs to be replaced."

Somehow he could guess how they intended to test it.

* * * * *

Morning confirmed their impressions that the manor, while in need of work, was worth the investment.

Leilanna in particular seemed absolutely enchanted with the gardens and orchards, dragging them from one pretty spot to another and enthusiastically talking about all the changes she'd like to make. Dare wondered if she just naturally loved gardening, or if it was an elvish thing.

While the women continued browsing the yard and outbuildings he found himself drawn to one corner of the grounds, where an overgrown shrine that had obviously once been lovingly cared for stood.

The Shrine of the Outsider. It was a simple stone pedestal topped by a delicate iron globe worked with the shapes of Collisa's continents, a shape like a comet with a long tail hanging suspended from a wire above it.

If he hadn't already had it identified to him he would've thought it was some sort of astronomy thing. Pretty in its own way, and interesting. Not that he'd given much thought to this world's deities or his role with them.

He wondered if the Outsider had Noticed him, the way that demon lord who'd sent Ashkalla had. Or maybe he'd had the god's attention even before then; he thought of his and Zuri's visit to that brothel in Kov run by Adherents of the Outsider. How the way the bookkeeper/high priestess Ireni and mermaid Trissela had acted had made him and his goblin lover nervous enough to leave the capitol immediately afterwards.

"What do you think?" his benefactor's voice said, making him jump in surprise.

He looked up at the sky, then down at the shrine. "Friend of yours?"

She laughed richly. "We're as close as gods can be, yes." She made an impatient sound. "What do you think of the planet and comet sigil? You're one of the few on Collisa who can really appreciate its meaning."

"What they are, sure, although I have no idea what they're meant to signify. But as godly symbols go it's pretty cool." He looked up at the sky. "Good to hear from you, by the way."

"Well I figured since you were getting the opinion of all your companions about whether to buy this place, you might want to ask your first friend here and one of your lovers." His benefactor sounded more than a little miffed.

Dare winced in chagrin; he hadn't really considered that. "Okay yeah, sorry. What do you think?"

"*I love it!*" she squealed, her enthusiasm so powerful it made him stumble back a step. "I think this will be a perfect place for our family . . . I can already see all your adorable little children running around in Leilanna's gardens."

He couldn't help but chuckle. "You wouldn't happen to have had anything to do with us finding it, would you?"

"My lover, I don't meddle in *every* aspect of your life. I barely meddle at all, really."

Well, that was certainly true. "Are you going to give me my

surprise soon? I miss seeing you."

"You mean you miss the mind-blowing sex we have." His benefactor laughed. "Patience, my lover. It won't be too much longer." She paused. "Oh, it looks as if the girls are done. Pella's getting the horses ready while Zuri packs up and Leilanna's coming to get you. She's-"

"Praying?" the dusk elf said from behind him, making him jump. "You? I suppose I shouldn't be surprised you'd worship an outcast god like the Outsider, since you don't do anything normally."

He turned to find her standing with her hands on her voluptuous hips, tapping one foot. "I don't really know anything about the Outsider, actually, aside from that their adherents had a brothel in Kov that I visited." He motioned to the stable. "We ready to go?"

"Yeah, just waiting on you." She turned away with a huff. "Come on, let's get back to Terana and buy this unpolished gem before someone else snatches it out from under us."

Chapter Fourteen
Handshake

Miss Garena solemnly accepted the pouch with 2,000 gold that Dare had proffered, on behalf of her mistress who remained seated behind her desk.

"Excellent, Master Dare," Lady Marona said with a warm smile. "I'll admit it was an invigorating experience to see you and your consorts so excited about the property. It warms my heart to know I'm not the only one who sees its value."

He expected Leilanna to jump in and furiously protest that she wasn't his consort, but she kept silent. Maybe staying tactful during an important meeting.

"Thank you," he said. "We're looking forward to moving in as soon as possible."

"Ah." The baroness glanced at her Head Maid. "Of course we'll need to send to Redoubt to get approval of the sale from the Regional Governor, and arrange for all the proper paperwork. It should be a few weeks at the least."

She motioned. "You're welcome to stay here during that time, call it thanks for easing an old woman's heart about the future of Jori's manor."

Dare felt his heart leap at the prospect of spending weeks here surrounded by beautiful maids, and all the adventures they might have.

But in their plans for the future he and his companions had agreed that they should purchase some packhorses and return to Pella's hoard, collecting it and selling it along the towns back north to ensure they had every gold possible gathered to offset future expenses with the manor.

And, if he was being honest, he was looking forward to seeing Rosie the plant girl again, since she lived near there. Maybe this time her butterfly girlfriend would be back and they could have some fun.

So he reluctantly shook his head. "The offer is very much appreciated, but if we're not needed here during that time there's some business in Kovana we should probably see to, before finalizing the deal and moving in."

"I see." It might've been his imagination but he thought Lady Marona looked almost disappointed. "You'll be setting off right away, then?"

"I believe so."

She sighed. "A pity you arrived too late last night to enter the town, or I would've offered you at least the hospitality of one night."

Oh, Dare definitely regretted that as well. They'd gotten distracted helping Leilanna test out her new staff, which she'd finally completed carving to her satisfaction. It had been a good chance to get some experience, too, considering they'd been a bit lax about that since leaving the dungeon.

Safe experience, of course.

Unfortunately, the delay meant that by the time they reached Terana the gates were closed for the night. Some towns in Bastion were more welcoming about people arriving after dark, but with the increasing trouble with roaming monsters and tribes from the wilds fleeing into the territory, Terana followed the policy of hunkering down as the sun set.

"That's kind of you to say, my Lady," he said with a rueful smile. "We certainly would've been much more comfortable here."

Lady Marona gestured briskly, as if it was settled. "Then I hope you'll take the chance to visit and even stay the night more often in the future, even after we've finalized all the arrangements with Jori's manor . . . I'd like to speak to you and your friends more."

Dare would've been happy to accept that offer anyway. But the fact that the invitation meant a chance to have more enjoyable encounters with beautiful maids made him even more eager. "Thank you, my Lady. If we're not imposing I'm sure we'll take you up on that."

"Good." Her full lips pulled upward in the slightest smile. "I'm sure my staff will be excited about having company visit more often to liven the place up. It can get a bit dull with our established routine."

Something in her knowing gaze made him feel like she suspected what he'd gotten up to with her maids. Although if so it didn't seem like she minded.

He felt his cheeks heating. "Until next time, then."

The baroness gracefully stood and offered him her hand. "Congratulations on your new home, Master Dare. May you build many happy memories there."

Dare shook her hand firmly. Then he paused as she turned her face slightly, and with a start realized she was presenting her cheek for a kiss.

A bit hesitantly, he leaned forward and gave it a brief peck. "Thank you for all your help, my Lady."

She beamed at him. "Not at all. Business partners are a delight, but friends are a rare treasure."

It was a bit surprising to hear the elegant lady call him that after what basically amounted to two brief, business related conversations. But he would be proud to call her a friend, if that's how she felt.

Miss Garena escorted him and his companions out, past another farewell party of somewhat disappointed looking maids, and they mounted up and headed out into town to buy packhorses.

"Well," Dare said, feeling a surge of excitement. "That's it, we have our home."

His lovers cheered at that, although Leilanna was less impressed. "In a few weeks once the approval and contracts from Redoubt make it back here."

He chuckled. "Well, that just means we'll have something to look forward to when we get back from Kovana."

* * * * *

A day later, Dare and his companions and a train of packhorses entered the goblin ravine.

He was less worried about the danger than his last trip through. Back then he, Zuri, and Pella had out-leveled the goblins in the ravine by enough that they hadn't dared to attack even with overwhelming numbers, and now not only were they even higher level, but they also had Leilanna with them to make their party even stronger.

Besides, after helping the Avenging Wolf tribe they were now friends. Or at least not hostile. As long as the goblins didn't see a moment of weakness to tempt them into betrayal.

Dare looked around at the majestic peaks as they rode up the ravine. "You know, our new home is close enough to the mountains that they might be a great place to level."

Leilanna snorted. "Are you insane? With the sharp changes in elevation the spawn points get all wonky, and you can find Level 50s right next to Level 20s. Since you can't know which is which, trying to hunt monsters in the mountains is suicide. Especially since everyone realizes that and leaves them alone, so roamers tend to escape their spawns and wander around killing indiscriminately."

He smirked at her. "And what part of all of that is a problem for us? Randomized spawn points just means we might find good spawns closer to home than we'd otherwise find them, and closer together than usual too. Especially when we start out-leveling the monsters around our land, as well as driving down *their* level for safety's sake."

"Right, Adventurer's Eye," the dusk elf said, cheeks turning darker gray. "It turns everything on its head, huh?"

"I think it would be fun to hunt in the mountains," Pella said. "The terrain is a lot more exciting for running around."

Leilanna sniffed. "Especially if we're running away from a Level 50."

"Relax, we'll be able to-" Dare cut off abruptly at the sight of Chieftain Gar of the Avenging Wolf tribe and a dozen of his warriors rushing down the ravine towards them, clutching weapons and with fierce looks on their faces.

"Heads up," he murmured, checking his weapons. "Everyone got their translation stones?"

"I wear mine all the time!" Pella said. "It was a gift from you, after all."

He wasn't sure a somewhat unsightly piece of enchanted quartz he'd purchased for its utility really needed to be prized as a gift. But that was beside the point at the moment. "Keep your guard up," he said as he nudged his horse forward to meet the approaching goblins.

They didn't slow as they came within earshot, and Dare raised his voice. "Chieftain Gar'u'wek! I ask your leave to travel through your lands."

"Human," Gar said anxiously, sparing Leilanna and their new horses barely more than a glance. He looked on the verge of panic. "When last we saw you and your mates, you did us a service. Now we ask if you will be a champion of the Avenging Wolf tribe again."

Dare genuinely hadn't been expecting that. He exchanged glances with his companions as they reined in beside him, having determined that the goblins weren't a threat after all. "What is it?" he asked cautiously.

Gar made a soft keening noise, incongruent with the show of strength he usually tried to project. "The slavers have come again, human," he spat. "They waited until I and many of my warriors were away hunting."

The large goblin gnashed his teeth, yellow eyes blazing. "My people fled, but the humans captured many and slew many more. Now they have almost forty of our females, strong laborers, and young." His voice turned anguished. "Including two of my mates and three offspring."

"I'm sorry that you've suffered such a tragedy," Dare said sympathetically. "What is it you wish of me."

"Save my people from the slavers," Gar said simply.

Leilanna sucked in a sharp breath. "Are you insane?" she demanded. "Vile as they are, slavers are sanctioned by Haraldar, acting within the kingdom's laws. If you do anything to them it will be seen as a criminal act. We'll all become exiles or worse."

The goblin chieftain's heavy shoulders slumped, and he dropped to his knees. "Please, human. You do not know the horrors slavers inflict on their captives. And that's *before* they put them on an auction block for short, miserable lives of toil and degradation."

He hung his head, and his voice dropped to a whisper. "I can't bear to think of my mates and offspring suffering that fate."

Text appeared in front of Dare, along with the soothing, neutral voice of his benefactor as the world system. "Quest offered. Slaver Savagery: Rescue 41 goblin captives from a band of Kovana slavers. **Warning! This quest is for the Avenging Wolf tribe faction of the goblin race. Direct action against the slavers will result in loss of reputation for the Region of Kovana and the Kingdom of Haraldar if caught, and possible labeling as criminals.**"

Fuck. The last thing Dare had expected when passing through the goblin ravine was to face a dilemma between following the law or following his conscience.

But the chieftain's plea to help his family struck particularly close to Dare's heart as he imagined his own loved ones suffering that fate. Especially considering everything they'd already been through.

He looked at Zuri, who stared back with huge eyes, expression anguished. She'd suffered what these goblins were suffering, including horrors so terrible she wasn't comfortable sharing them with him yet. If she ever would be.

The silent pleading in her eyes was all the convincing he needed.

Taking a breath, he accepted the quest for his party. "I'll do what I can to rescue the goblins through peaceful, lawful means," he said solemnly.

"And if that doesn't work?" Leilanna challenged. "I won't become an outlaw for you, human." Her voice raised. "And think of Pella and Zuri, carrying your children. You want them to give birth while fleeing bounties, or as exiles out in the wilds?"

"Thank you, human!" Gar said, relief evident in his voice. "There are sixteen slavers, between Level 17 and 22 as far as my people saw. They've already fled the ravine and are headed south, but if they follow their usual despicable pattern they will set up camp early to-"

he cut off with a shudder and continued in a sick voice. "Just please, human, hurry."

"Are you listening to me, Dare?" the Mage demanded furiously. "We just bought a home! We're starting a new life! I'm not going to throw that away for a bunch of goblins!"

The goblin chieftain bristled. "You want to speak as if you're so much better, dusk elf? Your kind put up a guise of mending pots and acting as traveling entertainers, but it's just a cover for your thieving and kidnapping to sell your victims as slaves in the next town!"

"That's a fucking lie!" Leilanna seethed. "My people are an ancient and honorable-"

"Enough!" Dare snapped. "Come or don't come, Leilanna. But I'm not going to sit here squabbling while 41 innocent people are being dragged away from their home in chains."

Without waiting for a response he heeled his horse forward at a trot, the goblins hastily clearing the path for him. Zuri was right beside him, Pella bringing up the rear leading the packhorses. And after a few seconds he heard Leilanna curse loudly and urge her horse to a gallop to catch up.

"I won't make myself an outlaw," she repeated fiercely as she reined in beside Pella. "But I know you're not a fool. Hopefully you have some plan."

Unfortunately, he didn't. The best he could think of at the moment was buying the captive goblins from the slavers, or somehow intimidating them into letting them go.

But if he bought the goblins there was no reason to assume the slavers wouldn't just come right back and capture them again. Besides, the idea of enriching those scum didn't sit well with him. And intimidating them might get him and his companions branded criminals anyway, and *also* the slavers would probably just come back again.

He couldn't guard the goblin ravine 24/7.

Dare glanced back at his companions. "I accepted this quest, but we haven't committed to anything yet. I need to know what you think we should do."

"I think we should just ride on sout-" Leilanna started.

"We already know what you think!" Zuri said, voice surprisingly fierce. She turned to him, yellow eyes glimmering with tears. "I'd never ask you to do anything against your conscience, my mate, but please, help them if you can."

Pella nodded firmly. "I agree we should help them. I'll always love my master, but I've tasted freedom for long enough to know just how fucked up it was that I was raised in a kennel and trained to be a pet. No intelligent creature should have to suffer that."

She rested a protective hand on Zuri's shoulder. "And in many ways I was very fortunate compared to what my fate could've been."

"All right then," Dare said in grim determination. "Let's push the horses as hard as we can and try to reach the slavers before they stop for the night."

He dreaded to think what they'd do to their poor captives then.

Unfortunately, even though they pushed their horses to a lather they were too late.

Pella heard it first, whimpering as her face went pale. "Hurry!" she cried, leaping off her horse and breaking into a sprint, leading the laboring animal and the train of packhorses behind her.

Dare leapt off his own horse and followed, tugging the reins to encourage his horse to keep up. Zuri and Leilanna nudged their own horses to a final gallop, pulling up beside him and the dog girl as they ran south with the sun sinking towards the horizon to their right.

Finally after a tense minute he heard what Pella had: screams.

In spite of himself he slowed to a stop. He wasn't alone, Leilanna and Zuri also reining in with expressions of horror, forcing their dog girl companion to stop and come back for them.

"Ancient Spirits preserve us," his goblin lover breathed, looking sick.

It was the most awful sound Dare had ever heard: Over a dozen goblin voices raised in raw, ragged misery. And not brief but sustained and prolonged.

They reminded him of when he'd first met Zuri as she was being attacked by the panther, when she was wounded and thought she would die and cried out hopelessly for help she knew wouldn't come. Except instead of fear for their lives these goblins, most of them women by the sound, cried out in broken, hopeless torment.

People who'd given up resisting and were still being hurt, just for the amusement of their captors.

Dare swallowed, feeling sick. Zuri's and Pella's faces were pale with grief and fury, while Leilanna had her hands to her mouth and was visibly shaking. "What are they doing to them?" she whispered in a shaky voice.

Zuri answered, expression dull and voice empty. "Raping the women. Torturing the old who have little value and aren't worth feeding and transporting all the way to the block. Maybe doing both, just for the fun of it." She was obviously speaking from experience, and had hunched small in her saddle.

His heart broke for her, and he wished they were riding together so he could gather her up in his arms and hold her tight, comforting her from the demons of her past and the demons of the present.

Slavers were worse than bandits, as she'd told him. Committing the same atrocities bandits would, but with the full support of the kingdom. Riding through the streets of Haraldar's towns with their heads held high, as if they weren't monsters.

These might be the same people who'd captured Zuri's tribe. Who'd done such terrible things to her and her people. And it was obvious they meant to continue as long as they could get away with it.

The screams continued, heart-wrenching and sickening, and Leilanna bent out of her saddle and emptied her stomach at the sounds.

Dare wanted to do the same. Instead he grimly unslung his bow. "I was going to try to negotiate, maybe even buy the goblin captives," he said, surprised at how calm and flat his voice was. "But I won't deal with scum who'd do something like this. I'm going to kill every single slaver in that camp."

He looked at his companions. Pella, grim and determined, Zuri, shaken and grief-stricken. Leilanna, her usual belligerence nowhere to be seen. "I want you all to abandon this quest and leave my party. If there's some consequence for this, I'll suffer it alone."

"Like hell," Pella growled. "We'll only be in trouble if they report our actions." She drew her long knife, brown eyes burning with quiet resolve. "Not one slaver will get away from me to continue their vile trade."

"I'm going too," Zuri said, trembling but sitting straight in her saddle. "Some of my people will need healing as soon as possible, and comforting."

Dare wanted to protest, but his lovers' expressions suggested they wouldn't back down. "All right, but don't put yourselves in danger," he said. "Let them come after me, if they're in the mood to fight." He turned to Leilanna. "Drop the quest and party and wait here, we'll-"

"I'm coming," the young dusk elf said quietly. She'd sat up straight in her saddle, and although her face was almost white her dark pink eyes almost glowed with pain and fury.

He blinked. "I thought you said you wouldn't become an outlaw-"

"Then we'd better not get caught!" she snarled. They stared at her in shock as she angrily dashed tears from her eyes. "I can't stand the thought that people out there can get away with doing this." She looked at Zuri with anguish. "Those are people down there, people like Zuri. Innocent and defenseless, Ascendants damn it! What sort of monsters . . ."

Her hands blazed with blue flames, her eyes burning with equal intensity. "I'll fucking burn them all."

Well, that seemed to be that. And Dare wasn't about to waste another second while listening to those tormented screams.

Activating Rapid Shot, he looped his horse's reins around a nearby tree branch and sprinted forward. Behind him he heard his companions following at their best pace.

The camp came into view in a clearing through the trees ahead, a slovenly place full of piled possessions of dubious value, obviously looted from the goblins. Packs and bundles were strewn about, along with a few hastily erected tents and others abandoned in the process.

Dozens of goblins tied together huddled at one end of the camp, while the slavers crowded around a large fire drinking and-

They'd taken goblins from among the huddle of their captives and dragged them over to their vile celebration.

Dare didn't want to see the horrific specifics of what they were doing. Instead he laser focused on the slavers, determining which ones needed to die first to protect the goblin captives, and counting to make sure he had every enemy in camp identified.

Unfortunately there were only eleven slavers in sight. Gar had said there'd be sixteen, so some were either in the tents or out keeping watch in the trees. In which case hopefully Pella would get them.

Drawing his first arrow to his cheek, he sighted on the first slaver, who was tormenting an elderly goblin, and loosed.

That began the slaughter.

Dare felt no guilt about being up to ten levels above these scum, or that with Entangler he killed some of them in one hit. The ones who survived best were those who, like him, had an ability that protected them from an attack, but even that was small reprieve.

He loosed all the arrows in his hand in quick succession, then used Rapid Shot again and loosed four more in even quicker succession, killing five slavers with nine arrows.

As the camp erupted in chaos at his sudden and brutal attack, a slaver who'd been abusing a goblin woman drew the knife at his belt and raised it over his cowering victim. Dare wasn't sure what the piece of filth's reasoning was for murdering a helpless woman while he was under attack. Maybe afraid she'd try to run away while he was distracted, or justifiably try to bash him over the head with a rock while his back was turned.

Dare used Vine Lash, sending the vine whipping out of Entangler's grip to wrap around the slaver's throat. Then, bracing his feet, he shouted, "Retract!"

The man was yanked backwards several feet, knife dropping out of his hand, and the force slid Dare forward six inches in spite of his best efforts. The slaver continued to be dragged across the ground towards him, scrabbling desperately at the vine wrapped around his throat, until Dare released the lash so he could put an arrow in the man's chest.

Leilanna was launching Fireball after Fireball at the milling slavers, further adding to the confusion and chaos. Meanwhile Zuri was healing the most injured goblins, starting with the elderly the slavers had been torturing.

A slaver with his pants around his knees disappeared into the woods before Dare could loose an arrow after him, only to stumble back into view screaming, clutching his belly as his guts spilled around his fingers. Pella followed him, long knife flashing as she cut his throat.

Blood stained her clothes and her face was set in a fierce snarl as she went after one of the burning slavers. Although Dare and his companions were starting to run out of targets.

As he took down the last standing slaver Zuri ran into the camp, tending and comforting the goblin captives near the fire who'd been the targets of the slavers' cruelty. Pella joined her, expression immediately becoming gentle again as she cut bonds and spoke gently to the terrified, traumatized goblins.

Leilanna broke away from him and entered the camp as well, using her cloak to cover a goblin woman cowering beside the body of the slaver who'd been assaulting her. She gently helped the woman to her feet and led her over to Zuri.

Dare followed his companions into the camp, pained to see how the goblins shied away from him even though he'd put away his weapons. He began checking the slaver bodies, making sure they were all dead.

Many of the goblins bound together in a huddle had recovered from the shock of the attack and the terror of their situation, and now that they were beginning to believe their ordeal was over they'd begun weeping and keening in grief for lost loved ones.

Sticking around in this camp wasn't doing these poor people any good. They needed to get back to their tribe, where they'd be safe among friends and family and could get the help they needed to get over what they'd suffered.

Dare made his way over to where Zuri and Pella were huddled together discussing what needed to be done to help the freed captives, near where Leilanna stood staring off into space. "All right," he said briskly. "Zuri, if you and Pella want to lead the freed goblins back to the ravine, we'll take care of camp. Leilanna, I'm going to gather all the bodies together. Then can you burn them in a way that will come as close as possible to destroying all the remains, but won't produce a lot of smoke or a big fire?"

There was no response and he frowned, turning. "Leilanna?"

The dusk elf was standing in the middle of the camp, eyes glassy and expression distant and horrified.

He and his lovers exchanged concerned looks. "Lanna?" Zuri asked, resting a hand on the taller woman's arm.

"No!" Leilanna cried, sinking to her knees. She was breathing in short, fast gasps. "I can't . . . I have to hide. They'll find me, they'll hurt me." She made a keening noise and pulled her knees up to her chest, shaking like a leaf and breathing even more shallowly.

"Lanna?" Pella asked frantically, dropping down beside the panicking elf and wrapping her in a tight hug. "It's okay, sweetie. Calm down, it's okay. Just take a deep breath and calm down."

Zuri, looking frightened, hugged Leilanna's other side just as firmly. "Don't worry, Lanna, we're here," she said, voice anxious as she pressed the gasping dusk elf's head to her shoulder. "Don't worry, we're right here."

Rather than seeming reassured, Leilanna stopped breathing entirely and her face began to darken; she was about to pass out.

"Back off!" Dare snapped, tugging at his lovers' shoulders. "Give her some space." They gave him confused, wounded looks, but he paid no mind as he ushered them away. "Let me handle this," he told them.

He crouched in front of Leilanna, meeting her at eye level, and firmly took her shoulders. "Leilanna," he said calmly. "Focus on my eyes."

The frantic elf met his gaze, wheezing desperately. "Do you see what color my eyes are?" Dare asked in the same calm voice. "My eyes are blue. Keep looking into them, good. You're doing great. Now take a small breath but focus on my eyes."

Leilanna, tear-filled eyes desperately holding his, swallowed and took a small breath.

"Great, Leilanna, you're doing a great job. Keep focusing on my eyes . . . what color are they?"

"B-blue," she wheezed.

"Good." Dare squeezed her shoulders. "Now take another breath and repeat after me. Exactly what I tell you. And keep focusing on my eyes." She nodded, taking a slightly deeper breath. "Good, Leilanna. You're doing such a good job. Now breathe in and repeat after me . . . I'm in the woods."

"I-I'm in the w-woods," the dusk elf whispered faintly.

"The sky is blue overhead," he continued.

"The s-sky is blue overh-head," she repeated.

"The ground is solid beneath me."

"The ground is solid b-beneath me." Leilanna was breathing a bit easier, color returning to normal and trembling easing. Her words were coming out clearer and more confidently.

"Good, Leilanna, good," Dare said, gently patting her shoulder. "Feel the ground beneath you. It's right there, solid." Her fingers clenched in the dirt, grounding herself as she turned her focus to it. "Good, Leilanna, you're amazing, you're doing wonderful. Now say "I'm in the woods, the sky is blue overhead, the ground is solid beneath me."

"I'm in the woods, the sky is blue overhead, the ground is solid beneath me," she whispered. She abruptly threw her arms around him, holding him tight as if he was the only thing keeping her from drowning. But her breathing had become more even, and her wide, glassy eyes were becoming clearer and more alert.

"Great, you're doing great." He stroked her back. "Where are you?"

"In the woods."

"What's overhead?"

"The blue sky."

"What's beneath you?"

"The solid ground."

"And what color are my eyes?"

"Blue." Leilanna breathed in deeply, almost as if inhaling his scent, and her hands on his back began stroking him softly between the shoulder blades. "So blue."

To his surprise she abruptly gave a start, then pushed away from him and stood, glaring down at him. "Never speak of this."

Dare stood as well. "If you don't want me to," he agreed. "But I'm always willing to listen if you need someone to talk to."

She sniffed and looked around the camp, then shuddered and strode away purposefully in the direction of the horses.

Pella and Zuri were both staring at him. "How did you do that?" the dog girl asked. "She was about to pass out!"

Dare shook his head. "My friend when I was a kid used to have panic attacks like that. His mom would do something like that to help him." He stared after the dusk elf. "I'm just glad it worked . . . I've never done it before myself."

Zuri rested a hand on his arm. "Maybe you should go after her, keep her company," she said gently. She glanced significantly at the goblins who were still staring at him in fright. "You can do more good there."

Ah. Well, he supposed they'd just gone through a nightmare due to other humans, so he could hardly blame them for being cautious of him. Hopefully once they recovered from the trauma of this experience they'd realize he meant them no harm.

Until then, he followed Leilanna to where the horses waited.

She'd taken out the soft cloth blanket she'd bought in Terana and pulled it around her, huddling on her unrolled bedroll with her back against a tree.

"Want some company?" Dare asked quietly as he approached.

She didn't reply, eyes on the ground, but she did scoot over slightly to make room on the leather bedding. He settled down beside her, but kept quiet; right now it felt like she didn't need awkward conversation, just the comfort of not being alone.

After a few awkward minutes Leilanna cleared her throat sharply. "Thank you," she said in a subdued voice.

Dare nodded but said nothing, continuing to sit with her and give her a chance to gather herself; hopefully his presence was doing some good for her, while Zuri and Pella were busy helping and comforting the freed captives and couldn't be with her.

After a few minutes the pale dusk elf began speaking quietly, almost as if talking to herself. "I was seven when my family's caravan was destroyed. Orcs, coming west over the sea and raiding along Elaivar's eastern shore."

She began breathing more quickly as panic set in again, but after a few seconds of focus calmed herself and continued. "My mother was a skilled Illusionist. She cast a glamor over me and the caravan's other children, just big enough to cover us so we all had to huddle close." She snorted raggedly. "Which we were all doing anyway, in the terror of the moment."

Leilanna closed her eyes, tears slipping down her cheeks, and her voice became hollow. "She saved us, but we were hidden right next to the caravan throughout the attack. Forced to listen to the orcs slaughtering our loved ones. And what they did to the poor people they left alive.

"It might've been minutes or hours or days the attack lasted. It felt like an eternity of hell. Even after the screams and moans were replaced by the clamor of the orcs leaving, we kept hiding. And hiding, for the full six hours until the illusion spell ended and we got our first view of the horror they'd left behind, the blood and bodies of our loved ones."

She whimpered and huddled against him, and he did his best not to stiffen in surprise, reflexively putting an arm around her shoulders. "We fled the devastation and wandered for days, avoiding monsters and predators until finally a patrol of wood elves found us near death and left us with another dusk elf caravan."

With a shuddering breath Leilanna shifted to lie down with her head resting on his thigh, tears leaking from her closed eyes. "I was luckier than most, thanks to my heritage and bloodline trait. Elder Nirol took me in and treated me like royalty as he nurtured my class and helped me level. And over the years that horrible day became a fading memory, until finally I only knew it had happened by what others told me about it, as if I hadn't been there at all."

She turned haunted eyes back towards the camp. "Until the plight of the goblin captives in the slavers' camp brought those awful memories back."

Dare did his best to sit still, feeling like a timid and delicate bird was perched on his knee, until finally Pella returned. She leaned down and wrapped an arm around the haunted elf for a minute or so before finally straightening with a sigh.

"Zuri says the rescued goblins are ready to travel back to their tribe. The sooner we can get them away from here, the better." The dog girl's sad brown eyes silently added that it would be better for Leilanna, too.

"All right," he said. "I need to finish up in the slavers' camp, but maybe you and Leilanna should go ahead."

Pella nodded her agreement of that idea, and with his help gently helped their companion to her feet, getting her up onto her horse. His dog girl lover then wordlessly climbed up behind Leilanna and held her as she guided the horse towards the ravine.

Dare found Zuri helping the goblins, many of whom shied away at his approach. "Pella and Leilanna rode ahead," he murmured, taking her aside. "I'm going to stay behind with the horses for a while, but I'll catch up to you quickly."

She looked alarmed at the thought of him being away from her. "Why?"

"The slavers took a lot of the goblins' possessions, and I'd like to load them up along with all of the slavers' own stuff and take it back to the Avenging Wolf tribe to help them out." He hesitated, then added. "Also I need to destroy any evidence of the slavers' camp and our presence here, to help cover our tracks."

His goblin lover shook her head bitterly. "We shouldn't have to fear trouble for saving these poor people from those monsters."

"We shouldn't," Dare agreed wearily, "but this is the world we live in."

His goblin lover nodded and hugged him tight. "Thank you." She hurried back to the freed captives and began gently leading them back the way they'd come.

They wouldn't be able to make it all the way back to their tribe before nightfall, but at least they'd be away from this cursed camp.

With a sigh Dare got to work dragging bodies into a pile and loading everything in the camp worth taking onto the packhorses.

Chapter Fifteen
Goblin Friend

What looked like the entire Avenging Wolf tribe had gathered at the bottom of the ravine to reunite with their loved ones who'd been taken.

There was a lot of grief and tears and haunted expressions, but also quiet celebration that the goblin captives had been saved, and also that the slavers who'd been tormenting them would never bother them again.

At least that group of them.

Gar had gone so far as to offer Dare his hand, exchanging a fervent handshake. "Thank you, human," he said; in spite of his proud stance tears glimmered in his eyes. "We have little to offer you in reward for this great deed . . . most of our things were taken by the slavers when they raided us, and I know that by the rules of looting they're yours now. But what we have to give, we will."

Dare shook his head and pointed to the laden packhorses. "No, we brought your things to return to you." Honestly that stuff would have little value to him, and were items and tools the goblins needed to survive.

The Chieftain of the Avenging Wolf tribe looked stunned. "But if not wealth then what do you wish?" he asked. "I can offer you nubile maidens, as many as you desire. Or laborers, I have those in plenty."

Dare couldn't help but wonder what kind of scumbag would save a bunch of people from slavery, then demand slaves as a reward. "No, I do not wish slaves or mates," he said firmly. "I wish only to help the Avenging Wolf tribe."

Gar obviously couldn't understand such reasoning. At a bit of a loss, he held out his arms expansively. "Then at least accept the everlasting friendship of my tribe. You are always welcome in our lands, at our fires, in our huts. And may any female who offers herself to you as mate or for pleasure meet with your approval."

Dare coughed, feeling his cheeks heat at that last bit as behind him Zuri and Pella snickered. "I would be honored to have your friendship," he said. "But I would like to offer more."

At the large goblin's confused stare he pointed north towards Bastion. "I have purchased land in Bastion, and after my business in the south is done I'll be returning there. Rich lands, with good soil for tilling, lumber for building and fires, and perhaps even hills to mine. To say nothing of game and monsters to hunt. More than enough space for all your people to live, and far from other humans where you won't be bothered. I will also offer you my protection, so no more slavers, bandits, or adventurers will trouble you."

Gar gave him a guarded look. "You wish us to become your thralls?"

Dare shook his head firmly. "No. You will be free on my lands, to live your lives and prosper. My Lady in Terana will require a tax of all of us, yes, but it is a small one."

"And what do you get from this great generosity?" a sharp-eyed older goblin beside the chieftain asked.

Dare chuckled. "Believe me, it's not purely altruism. First off, with so many living on my land the nearby spawn points will become low level, ensuring the safety of my family. Secondly, I hope you will trade with me and any other tenants I bring onto my land, to our mutual profit. And lastly, you can help patrol my lands, keep the monster spawn points from releasing roamers, and defend against intruders."

"And he will require rent, according to a tenant/landlord lease," Zuri said firmly, surprising him. "It will be a generous one, but expected every season. You will also keep the peace, neither stealing nor raiding nor enslaving nor any other troublemaking in his lands or any other, or you will receive worse than merely eviction."

To Dare's further surprise, Gar almost seemed relieved by those stipulations. As if maybe they made the deal less suspicious. "I will speak to my tribe of this," he said. "You were passing through on business before you agreed to deal with the slavers?"

Dare nodded. "Yes. We'll return in a week or so."

The large goblin nodded firmly. "We will have an answer for you then."

Text appeared in front of Dare. "Quest completed: Slaver Savagery. 10,000 experience awarded. You have done a great deed for the Avenging Wolf tribe, which will surely be remembered."

He and his companions quickly unloaded the packhorses, further delighting the goblins when they realized that his party was giving them everything from the slavers' camp, not just the stolen possessions from the goblin camp.

It wasn't all altruism, of course; while some of the slavers' gear and items were valuable, and together they'd sell for a decent price, it was all evidence of the disappearance of the slavers. Not something Dare wanted to drag across Kovana and try to sell in towns.

He made sure the goblins knew to be careful with the slavers' things if other humans came sniffing around. Although honestly it was kind of a moot point, because most humans they encountered would probably try to rob or enslave the beleaguered goblins anyway.

Yet more reason for them to move up onto his land in Bastion.

Exchanging a few last farewells with the chieftain and other goblins of the tribe, Dare and his companions retraced their steps south.

With the captives safely returned they were able to make better time, although at his insistence they took a detour southwest to Yurin before going on to Hamalis and from there Pella's hoard in the nearby woods.

"Why are we going to Yurin?" Pella asked a bit worriedly.

He smiled at her. "Don't worry, we're just going to check the bounty boards in the garrison and adventurer's guild to make sure Braley kept his word." He paused. "And I might pay him a visit to make sure he continues to do so."

She shook her head at that. "Let me do it. I want to visit Ama anyway."

He hesitated, but his golden-haired lover was strong enough to handle herself if there was a problem. And he meant to be nearby just in case. "All right."

In Yurin Dare left his two lovers outside and entered with Leilanna. A goblin and dog girl were easier to identify than he'd be, although he had a feeling his appearance was eye-catching enough that he might end up being noticed anyway. So he kept his hood up and hoped for the best.

The guards at the gate didn't seem to have a problem with him, which was a good sign. Although one warned Leilanna not to steal anything while she was in town. The beautiful Mage darkened furiously, but with some effort managed to not cause a scene.

"Do dusk elves really have such a poor reputation that they'd accuse a Level 20 adventurer?" Dare asked. "Considering your honorable natures, you'd think more people would be aware you're trustworthy."

To his surprise Leilanna didn't bite his head off at the question, although she did give him a stiff look. "Are all humans the same?" she snapped. "Constant travel and mistreatment by those we meet takes its toll, and some of my people don't hold to their honor as well as they should."

He patted her shoulder. "Well, when you're a high level hero you can do more to repair your people's reputation."

"We don't hold to our honor to ingratiate ourselves to humans or any other race," the Mage said with a sniff. "Good thing, too." She sped up, clearly done with the conversation.

To Dare's relief there were no signs of bounties for him or his lovers at the adventurer's guild or guard barracks. A bit of subtle asking around also reassured him that Braley didn't have some secret bounty or search going for them.

Before leaving Yurin, Dare made his way to the inn he, Zuri, and Pella had used. He wanted to thank the innkeeper for not immediately ratting him out to the guards, as well as pay for any damage their hasty departure might've caused.

And while he was at it, he might as well order some hot meals for himself and his companions to take with them when they rejoined the others.

The innkeeper seemed surprised to see him, and a bit worried, but Dare quickly assured him that he'd cleared up the previous misunderstanding. The man seemed happy to accept a few gold for his trouble and quickly went off to arrange hot meals for them to take.

While they waited the cute redheaded serving girl who'd flirted with Dare before came to chat. Which he was definitely happy about, since he'd had to run off before being able to take her up on her offer to fool around.

To Leilanna's disgust, he used the time while they waited for the food to be prepared to let the slender woman drag him to a secluded spot.

When he showed the cute redhead the Prevent Conception scroll, reassuring her they could safely do whatever they wanted, the lusty serving girl threw herself at him with almost zero inhibitions, hungry mouth finding his while her hands trailed over his chest and rock hard abs, moaning appreciatively.

After a few minutes of passionate kissing and heavy petting the petite redhead eagerly raised her skirt, and he wasted no time lifting her up against the wall and thrusting into her while she bit into his shoulder to stifle her cries of pleasure. In spite of their haste she orgasmed twice, drenching his crotch with her arousal, before he emptied his balls inside her soft little pussy.

"Gods, I needed that today," the serving girl said as she quickly wiped them both down with a cloth. "Any time you want to come back and give me another good dicking with that behemoth of yours, you're more than welcome."

He grinned. "I'll probably take you up on that."

After a final fierce kiss they slipped out of the nook they'd found, her to return to her duties around the common room while he rejoined Leilanna, who gave him a disgusted glower as she eyed the flushed, happy woman across the room. "You really do fuck every woman who's interested, don't you?"

"You haven't figured that out by now?" he asked with a laugh. "Jealous?"

The beautiful dusk elf flushed. "Don't be stupid." She motioned to a cloth-wrapped bundle on the table. "By the way, the food was done a while ago. It's probably cold by now."

They wasted no more time meeting up with Zuri and Pella, giving them the good news as they ate that they had no bounties out on them as far as he'd been able to find.

His dog girl lover sniffed around him as he ate, giggling. "You had a good time in Yurin," she said with a wink. "Do I possibly smell that serving girl with red hair from the inn where you gave me that bath?"

Dare blushed. "It turned out she was very friendly, even after the way we had to leave."

"Oooh, did you two have fun?" Zuri asked. "What sort of things did you do?"

"Can you guys not?" Leilanna complained, blushing. "I'm trying to eat."

In spite of the good news Pella still wanted to check at the manor, leaving them behind as she went on alone. She returned after an hour or so to report that she'd managed to intercept Amalisa outside doing chores, and had a joyful reunion with her.

Amalisa had been over the moon to learn that Pella was pregnant, and that she and Dare and the others had bought a manor in Bastion where they planned to settle down. Pella had invited the young noblewoman to visit when she could, and Amalisa had seemed eager at the prospect.

More importantly for their purposes, during the visit Pella had learned that she, Dare, and Zuri were still in the clear.

Braley was still being an ass, of course, but it seemed as if he was taking his spite over the confrontation out on his younger sister with cold treatment and cruel words. Dare felt bad that the poor girl was paying the price for Pella's freedom, but Amalisa seemed optimistic that eventually her brother would get over his pique and things would go back to normal.

Since there wasn't much they could do to make the situation better, being the cause of the problem in the first place, they left the manor behind and continued on south.

* * * * *

It went without saying that their first stop when they reached the section of woods where Pella had lived for four years was the grave of her old master, to pay respects.

Nature had already begun to reclaim the garden she'd created in the clearing, even in the short time they'd been gone. So as the dog girl continued to kneel by the grave Dare and his other companions got to work clearing away weeds, trimming flowering plants, and cleaning paths.

Leilanna especially threw herself into the work. She knew her way around plants, too, which was a bit of a surprise for someone who'd lived a nomadic life. She also seemed to love the work and was clearly determined to leave the garden looking better than ever.

Dare and Zuri eventually left the two and led the packhorses on to Pella's camp, where she'd dug a hole for her hoard beneath a nearby tree. The plan was that once the dog girl finished paying respects she'd go visit Rosie, taking Leilanna with her so the dusk elf and plant girl could meet. Meanwhile he and Zuri would get to work packing up the loot for a while, then meet up with the others at Rosie's flower.

Dare's first impression of the cavern Pella had dug was one of relief that no one seemed to have disturbed it or stolen anything. His second was disappointment.

They'd taken the most valuable of the loot when their dog girl companion had joined their group and left with them, creating sleds to drag as much as they could carry. It had been worth 120 gold in the nearby town, which at the time had been a fortune for them.

Now, however, the sight of all the broken or Trash quality gear, scraps of metal, cloth, and leather, crude baubles and trinkets, cheap crafting materials and reagents, and other sundry items was less than impressive.

It might be worth four or five hundred gold at best. And even if they loaded all the packhorses, their own mounts, and loaded their packs they'd still have to leave some of it behind.

Worth the effort since they'd already come all this way, but still kind of discouraging.

Dare carted his first load out of the cavern, then got to work hobbling the horses and turning them out to graze. This job was going to take a while, but the sooner they got going on it the sooner they'd be done.

A few minutes later Zuri climbed out of the hole that led to Pella's cavern full of loot, looking disgruntled as she dusted her hands off. "Is it just me, or did this hoard seem a lot more valuable last time we were here?"

Dare chuckled and finished closing the hobbles around the legs of the last packhorse, dusting his own hands off as he straightened. "We were a lot poorer and lower level back then."

"Maybe so, but now it all just looks like junk!" She scowled at the ramp leading down beneath the tree, then at the packhorses. "It wasn't even worth the trip down here to get it, honestly . . . we could've made more farming monsters in Bastion."

He hastily made a shushing noise and glanced in the direction of Rosie's clearing. "I know," he said quietly. "But don't forget Pella spent four years farming this stuff. Aside from caring for Lord Kinnran's grave and standing vigil over it, this was her main accomplishment during that time. It'll make her happy to get all this stuff sold and put the money towards our new lives back at the manor."

"I guess." His goblin lover sighed. "Still, it's going to be a pain in the ass lugging all that stuff out of the cave and loading it. And even more of a pain to sell it."

Dare picked her up and kissed her soundly, rubbing her back. "Well, just remember that it wasn't our only reason for coming here. We also wanted to visit Rosie, and give Pella a chance to visit Lord Kinnran's grave." He playfully gave her pointy little nose a butterfly kiss. "Speaking of which, now that we've had a look at the treasure, wouldn't you like to go meet Rosie?"

Zuri brightened. "Of course." She giggled and pointed at the horses. "We can also check if she wants us to tether our mounts close enough for them to fertilize her flower."

He found the idea gross and ludicrous for a moment, then realized that for the plant girl it was logical and might actually be something she'd want to help her grow more healthy. After all, animals ate plants and produced poop, but plants did the exact opposite. And horses and cows and other grass eaters did produce good fertilizer.

Although it was still a bit off-putting.

"I suppose we can ask," he said.

Pella came bounding into the clearing, Leilanna puffing to keep up. "How was your visit?" Dare asked them. "What did you think of Rosie, Leilanna?"

The dusk elf beamed. "She's very friendly and absolutely gorgeous. Which is exactly what you'd expect from a plant girl, of course. And one of the reasons I'm always so happy to visit one. Also it was sweet to see how close she and Pella are."

"Forget Leilanna's first meeting with Rosie, it went fine and the two get along great," Pella said, fluffy tail wagging enthusiastically. "More importantly, Rosie wants to see you, Dare!"

"Well that's part of the reason we're here, to say hi to her," he replied, smiling at the thought of the friendly plant girl.

Although part of him was steeling himself to be around the little floran without ogling her gorgeous naked body and thinking naughty thoughts. Especially since she seemed open to the idea of having some fun with him, except she was in a committed relationship and didn't want to do anything unless her girlfriend was okay with it.

"Just Dare?" Zuri asked, sounding hurt.

Pella winked at her. "Well, for a little while at least. Hint hint."

"Oh. Ooooh." The goblin grinned mischievously.

Dare stiffened in excitement. "You mean . . ."

His dog girl lover laughed. "Let's just say there are two

absolutely stunning girls in that clearing who have pollination on the mind, and could use a little help from your stamen."

Zuri clapped her hands in delight. "In that case maybe the three of us should get to work loading this treasure, and give Dare a chance to have a reunion with Rosie and meet her girlfriend."

"How come he gets to have fun while we have to work?" Leilanna complained.

The other two women rolled their eyes. "Come on, a little manual labor will do you good," Pella said, looping an arm around the curvy dusk elf.

"Are you guys sure you don't want to join us?" Dare asked.

Zuri shook her head firmly. "Plenty of time for that. You know we like to let you enjoy women for the first time without us distracting you. Especially when there's already two waiting for you."

"I don't mind the distraction," Dare said hastily. "And I know you really wanted to sleep with Rosie too. Didn't you love her soft skin and how she smelled?"

His tiny lover grinned at him. "Plenty of time for that," she repeated. "Right Pella?"

"Well we *will* probably spend the night in Rosie's flower," the dog girl admitted, tail wagging eagerly. "As long as she doesn't mind."

Somehow Dare didn't think the sexually adventurous plant girl would. Especially since she'd seemed so fond of Pella when they first met, and disappointed that the dog girl would never agree to leave her master's grave behind and come live with her and her girlfriend.

Of course, Rosie's butterfly girl lover might be less than enthusiastic about having four unexpected guests crowding their home.

Oh gods, butterfly girl. He felt his heart racing with excitement and his cock stirring in anticipation at the prospect of meeting Enellia. Especially if she was as beautiful as Rosie made her out to be.

He couldn't wait to have both of them.

Before he could make a beeline for Rosie's clearing Zuri hurried over, hands glowing. "Don't get too ahead of yourself, my mate," she said with a wide smile.

Right, Prevent Conception. An important thing if he was about to engage in some wild pollination with a plant girl and a butterfly girl.

Dare kissed Zuri and Pella, waved goodbye to Leilanna, and hurried through the woods to Rosie's clearing.

The plant girl was standing at the base of her huge, tulip-like flower that grew in the center of the open meadow. She looked just as he'd last seen her, barely five feet standing on tiptoes with all the lean curves of a gymnast. She was the pale green of new leaves in spring, her long, silky darker green hair like the soft shoots of new vines, with flowers growing among the strands as if woven in. She had a thick stem growing from just above her cute little butt like a tail, stretching up to disappear inside her flower.

Rosie was contentedly embracing a slightly taller woman as the two exchanged deep, languid kisses. They seemed to simply be enjoying themselves while they waited for him to arrive so the fun could begin.

The plant girl was naked, of course, but Enellia was as well; as she shifted slightly, giving Dare a better view, he stopped in awe at his first sight of a butterfly girl.

If he had to describe her in one word, it was ethereal. Her hair was like a flame or a sunrise, starting deep red at the roots and descending into burnt orange, then pale yellow, and finally yellow-white at the tips. It flowed in a silky wave all the way to her feet, so light and fine that it floated with her every movement, wreathing her body.

Which was lush and inviting: a perfect hourglass figure, with an incredibly narrow waist that would be physically impossible for women of most other races. Her skin was a warm golden caramel, smooth and perfectly flawless, and like Rosie she didn't have even a hint of body hair. Her dark nipples were the very picture of fertility, and as she squirmed against her plant girl lover her legs parted and he caught a glimpse of her tantalizing pink slit, framed by plump labia glistening with arousal.

Enellia's face was perfect. There was no other way to describe her other than the ideal of feminine beauty, such as he had never seen before in real life or even in art from the most talented artists. As if she didn't quite belong in reality, delicate and strong and flawlessly symmetrical.

Her eyes were the same colors as her hair, dark red at the center fading to whitish-yellow around the edges, large and expressive yet at the same time mysterious. Her lips were luscious and full, glistening in a way that made him desperate to taste them. High on her forehead she had two thin, delicate antennae, which instead of looking out of place instead seemed to complement the pristine beauty of her features.

But her impossibly sexy body and even her ethereally beautiful face paled in comparison to her wings.

They spread from her back like a butterfly's, rounded at the top with a graceful taper at the base. They were a brilliant pattern of all the same colors as her hair, swirling and blending into eye-pleasing forms as if the masterpiece of the most skilled artist ever to live. They looked too impossibly delicate to hold any weight, moving subtly in small expressive flutters as Enellia lovingly kissed and caressed her girlfriend.

Dare had seen many beautiful women since coming to Collisa. All his companions fell in that category, of course, as did most of the women he'd had the pleasure of sleeping with. And it went without saying that Rosie herself was absolutely stunning.

But for the first time he found himself looking at a woman and feeling like he had no place touching such delicate perfection.

Was it really possible she wanted to make love to him? That such an angelic creature could even enjoy such a carnal act?

As if in answer Rosie, who'd been caressing her lover's plump hairless mound, abruptly slipped a finger down through the butterfly girl's delicate folds to begin rubbing her clitoris.

Enellia's back arched, and she moaned in pleasure against the plant girl's mouth. Her voice was as perfect as the rest of her, clear and musical like the most precisely crafted chimes. Which made the sounds she continued to make as she pressed herself into her lover's fingers all the more erotic.

Dare's cock throbbed in his pants, and he was overcome with an urge to run his fingers over that flawless caramel skin. To see if his hands were large enough to circle her narrow waist, and trace the delicate expanse of her majestic wings. And finally to hold her close to him as he tenderly made love to her perfect body.

Rosie abruptly broke the kiss, giggling mischievously. "I think we've turned him on enough, honey," she cooed. "Should we invite him to join the fun?"

The butterfly girl looked over at him with those enchanting sunrise eyes, and he found himself almost hypnotized as a very naughty smile curved those perfect lips. "I think so," she said, musical voice husky with lust. "It's so much funner to pollinate when we don't have to use our fingers or a toy."

She crooked a long, slender finger at him, and he found himself walking forward as if in a trance. "I'm Dare," he said, embarrassed at how hoarse his voice was. He swallowed. "It's a pleasure to meet you, Enellia."

"And you, Dare." She tapped her plump lips with her finger, expression speculative. "You look as if you've come straight out of an artist's best work. Absolutely majestic."

Dare couldn't help but chuckle. "I was just thinking the same about you."

"And me?" Rosie asked, mock pouting. Although her eyes sparkled; she was obviously smug about this confirmation of her claim that her girlfriend was the most beautiful woman in the world.

Or at least the most beautiful he'd ever seen. He grinned at her. "Of course, you're absolutely adorable."

Both women laughed, but to his disappointment Enellia fluttered away as he got close, flying up to sit on the edge of one of the large petals of Rosie's flower. Her movements were unimaginably graceful, in a way that shouldn't have been physically possible given the laws of aerodynamics.

Was there some sort of magic involved in her ability to fly?

Rosie grabbed his hand and pulled him over to where her vine hung down like a rope, beginning to climb and motioning for him to follow. "Come on," she said cheerfully. "We want to talk before we start the fun. There's something we want to ask."

"That's right," Enellia said, lazily kicking her legs over the edge. "Kind of a favor, depending on how you want to look at it. We can share the nectar I've gathered from some of the best flowers to be found, including the Yellow Passion Orchid and the Firebud."

"They're delicious!" the plant girl agreed happily.

Dare gave her a curious look as he climbed after her, unable to stop himself from admiring the tantalizing view of her from below. "I thought you didn't need to eat."

"I don't *need* to," she said, grinning down at him. "But I *love* nectar, and Enellia always brings the best stuff."

He couldn't help but chuckle. "Isn't it a bit naughty for you to be drinking nectar from other flowers?" he teased.

Both women burst out in peals of laughter. "Don't be silly!" Rosie said. "Nectar is the treat flowers leave out to entice creatures to come pollinate them. And the ones Enellia finds are the perfect aphrodisiac for our own pollination." Her green eyes danced. "We plan to get a lot of use out of your stamen, and we want to make sure you keep up your strength."

Gods, that was what he liked to hear.

Inside the giant flower they made their way down the gently sloping petals to where they met to make a surprisingly soft floor, like a giant mattress. Rosie and Enellia settled down with their backs to a petal, cuddling together affectionately.

Dare was fascinated to see that rather than having to be careful of her gorgeous wings, the butterfly girl was able to fold them gracefully so they tucked tight to her back, almost like an elegant half cape. Even like that their colors and patterns were breathtaking; she was a work of art, all flawless grace and beauty even while lounging inside a giant flower.

Next to Enellia was a leather bag bulging with filled waterskins, and as he sat down across from them the ethereal woman rummaged inside it and withdrew one. "Essence of Passion Orchid," she said, mesmerizing multi-colored eyes dancing as she popped the cork and took a sip, then passed it to her lover.

Rosie took a deep drink, making a contented noise, then replaced the cap and tossed it across to Dare. It was filled with nectar, as promised, refined in some way to make it more of a thin syrup.

It was delicious, light and sweet with multiple floral tones and a deeper flavor that had a strong musk to it. It refreshed him from the first sip, and he also noticed that his semi-rigid cock began to stiffen again with a pleasant surge of sensation.

The plant girl had mentioned it was an aphrodisiac.

He stoppered the waterskin and tossed it back to the girls. "So what did you want to talk about?" he asked, trying to keep his eyes on their faces rather than their perfect bodies reclining in front of him.

The women looked at each other. "Go ahead," Enellia said. "You know him better."

"Not much better," Rosie said with a nervous giggle. She reached for the nectar and took another gulp. "Besides, you're so beautiful and perfect . . . no one could say no to you."

The butterfly girl sighed. "Fine." She turned back to him, golden brown skin flushing shyly. "You know that we're lovers, and we enjoy pollinating together." As if to demonstrate she reached over and playfully cupped her girlfriend's small breast.

Dare felt his own cheeks heat, cock twitching; these two would drive him crazy just sitting there if this conversation lasted too long. "Rosie mentioned that," he said with a smile. "She's absolutely head over heels for you."

"Yep!" the plant girl said, nuzzling her lover and making happy little sounds.

Enellia patted her leg fondly, but remained all business. "Well as you might guess, there are certain things two females can't do while pollinating." She hesitated. "Like, um, actually pollinating."

Rosie cut in eagerly. "That's why we want you to pollinate both of us!"

Chapter Sixteen
Flower and Butterfly

Dare stared at the plant girl and butterfly girl in shock.

Were these two beautiful women saying they wanted him to impregnate both of them? They had to mean just some fun sex, right? "By pollinating you mean . . ."

"We want you to give me a baby and Rosie a seed," Enellia confirmed, blushing even harder. The sight of her showing such human emotions made her seem more approachable in spite of her ethereal beauty.

"We want to have fun with you too, of course," Rosie added, bouncing up and down on her knees and looking at him with glowing anticipation. "But it's been ages since I've produced a seed and I'm longing to feel one growing inside me."

Enellia nodded. "I've traveled far and wide on the Shalin continent, and never seen a man as beautiful as you. I want to have an even more beautiful baby with you."

Part of Dare was not only eager at the prospect of the pleasurable sex involved in impregnating these two beautiful women, but happy at the thought of having a plant girl daughter and a child with a butterfly girl. Especially when they were so eager for it.

But another part of him hesitated. "This is . . . a bit sudden."

"There's no need to worry about any responsibilities," Enellia said hurriedly. "You should already know that plant girls are like cunids . . . you stumble across one in the wilds, have some fun sex with her, and walk on confident that any child you have together will be just fine."

She somewhat bashfully fluttered her gorgeous wings. "Well butterfly girls are the same. We travel far and wide looking for suitable mates, and when one gives us a child we go back to the Lepid Flower Fields far to the south to raise it. It's a paradise, beautiful and safe, and our children grow well there in a community of lepids and their offspring of other races."

Still Dare hesitated, and Rosie patted her lover's shoulder to get her attention. "Lia," she whispered, "remember what Pella told us."

"Right." The ethereal butterfly girl fluttered her wings again, this time taking flight and flitting over to settle down on her knees beside him, resting a hand on his knee.

The proximity of such a perfect woman, her touch, were hugely distracting. Dare felt his cheeks heat in a way he hadn't experienced since he was a shy kid trying to talk to his crush.

"I understand you're concerned for the welfare of your children," she said, brilliant sunrise eyes holding his intently. "And that you wish to be part of their lives if possible. That is good, and a pleasant surprise from most who are eager to fuck me and then go their way without a second thought."

She smiled and stroked his leg. "Well rest assured, my people have a good relationship with the Kingdom of Marogia on our border. They boast some of the finest schools on the continent, especially for students of magic, and we have a mutually beneficial arrangement to send our children there."

The beautiful woman leaned forward, eyes pleading. "We can also arrange for visits. You might make your way down the Flower Fields some day and are welcome to spend time with us there, and for the first few years when the baby's light enough I plan to fly up with it to visit Rosie and can visit you at the same time. And if our child is a lepid we can fly up whenever we want once it learns to fly at about five years. Perhaps it can even stay with you and its siblings for a time."

That was about as accommodating as he could hope for, and honestly a relief to have those assurances so plainly laid out.

The question remained: Did he say yes? It seemed almost surreal to have two beautiful women begging him to give them children. Although if he thought about it, Zuri and Pella were eager for the same thing.

But this situation was different than with his harem in a lot of ways. Rosie and Enellia were willing to take responsibility for the children he gave them, aside from any responsibility he was willing to offer.

There wasn't much to debate here. The two women wanted his children, those children would have good lives, and he could admit the thought of them having his children was an appealing one.

And the thought of the act of *giving* them those babies was definitely an appealing one.

He rested his hand atop Enellia's, quietly delighting in the feel of her impossibly soft, smooth caramel skin, and smiled. "All right," he said solemnly. "I would be honored to pollinate you and Rosie."

"Yay!" The plant girl bolted to him and threw herself onto his lap, hugging him enthusiastically. Her skin was smooth and warm, and her soft, naked little body pressed against him felt incredible.

Especially when she shifted to straddle him, small pussy pressed against his rock-hard shaft through his pants. He felt her already copious arousal swiftly soak through the cloth, coating his throbbing erection, and his senses were filled with the delicious scent of wildflowers, honey, and a fresh musk heavy with floran pheromones.

Rosie enthusiastically ground her pink petals against him, small face right in front of his and eyes holding his eagerly. "Can I go first, Dare? Please?"

Dare laughed. "I would love that, if Enellia doesn't mind."

The butterfly girl laughed. "I'm happy to wait my turn." She gave the petite plant girl a look of pure adoration. "Besides, I can't refuse my sweet little flower anything."

"Yay!" Rosie shouted again, bouncing eagerly on his cock. "This is going to be so fun!"

"It is," Enellia agreed. "I can't wait to see his cock stretching your cute little pussy. Especially if it's as big as Pella said." Giggling, she climbed onto Dare's lap to straddle him behind her lover, pressing herself against the petite woman's back.

He could just feel the pressure of the butterfly girl's beautiful sex,

274

slick with her own heady arousal, pressing against the base of his shaft, and had to bite his lip and fight the pressure to explode right then and there.

He was a more than experienced lover, but these two ridiculously sexy women were immediately testing his limits. At this rate he was going to blow before he had a chance to pollinate either of . . .

Oh.

Rosie had risen up enough to begin working on the ties to his pants and he gently took her hands, pausing her efforts. "I, um, forgot that I've got Prevent Conception for the next six hours," he said sheepishly.

The two women looked at him with blank impatience. "So cancel it," Rosie said.

Dare stared at her in surprise. "You can cancel effects?" he blurted.

Now their looks were even more blank. "Pella mentioned you were from some place where things were a bit different, but really?" Enellia said, grinning. "Yes, of course you can. Beneficial spells voluntarily placed upon you can be canceled, along with many temporary beneficial effects you get from food or items. Usually only negative effects need to be removed or require you to wait out their time limit."

Good to know. Although he'd played plenty of games where that was the case, so he should've thought of it sooner. In his defense it had never really come up that he'd needed to remove a buff; it wasn't something that happened often.

He opened his command screens, went to his character sheet, and with only a bit of fiddling around figured out how to remove Prevent Conception. Then he grinned at his two lovers. "Okay, good to go."

"Then let's gooooo!" Rosie exclaimed. She eagerly finished freeing his cock, then without the slightest hesitation rose up, positioned him at her tiny entrance with her small soft hands, and began lowering herself onto him.

Dare grit his teeth at the sensation of pure pleasure as the plant girl's tight lips stretched obscenely wide around his tip. He went in without the slightest effort, her constantly flowing nectar easing his passage in spite of the fact that she was almost as tight as Zuri. Her walls rippled and caressed him in a way no woman he'd been with before was normally able to, and he tensed with the herculean effort of holding back his towering climax.

"Hold in there, Dare, she's just getting started," Enellia teased, reaching around to play with her lover's small breasts and pinch her little dark green nipples. "Think of ogres, and ice wraiths, and-"

"Oh gods!" he gasped, making a startling discovery.

In spite of Rosie's tiny body and even tinier pussy, he was past the point where he'd bottom out in Zuri and reaching the point where he'd bottom out in Pella. And she showed no signs of stopping.

Right, the plant girl had mentioned before that she was basically one big sex organ for her flower, and her orifices were all connected and she could be impregnated through any of them.

Was she able to take his full length, like pretty much no woman he'd met could? And with such a petite body, too?

Dare looked down to watch his length disappearing inch by inch into her warm, crushingly tight tunnel, her lips straining to stretch around his girth. Then he spotted the outline of his cock making a bulge in her flat tummy, moving upward with no sign of stopping, and it was too much.

"Fuck," he grunted. Grabbing Rosie by her slender waist, he pulled her downward the final few inches until he was balls deep, then with an eager thrust of his hips began emptying himself inside her.

"Oooh, I can feel him!" the plant girl squealed. "You're giving me your seed so we can have *our* seed!" She squirmed against his twitching cock, her warm tunnel continuing its delightful massage as he spurted again and again. Finally with a cry of pleasure her tight walls crushed down on him, rippling in a violent orgasm as her tiny body stiffened and shuddered in Enellia's arms.

"Good girl," the butterfly girl cooed, dropping one hand down to rub Rosie's little clit while the other continued to tease her nipples. "Don't drop from the peak, rise higher and higher. There we go." She leaned in and began kissing and nibbling the base of her lover's neck.

"Yesssss!" the petite woman squealed, and a flood of her sticky nectar flowed over Dare's crotch, finishing the job of soaking his pants. She trembled harder in Enellia's arms, small hips grinding against the base of his cock with desperate circular motions.

Dare's cock twitched a final time, letting out a last dribble after what had to have been one of his most intense orgasms. Since he'd let out what felt like a gallon of his seed he expected it to start flowing out of her pussy as their juices mingled, but he continued to only see her own pale nectar.

Enellia saw him staring and giggled. "Expecting a white flood from her little pussy?" she teased. "Plant girls are very jealous of the seed they're pollinated with . . . they soak up every drop of it."

"Lia!" Rosie abruptly blurted, voice excited. "Dare's not getting soft! I must be making him feel really good!"

He chuckled and cupped her small ass with both hands, kneading the smooth, warm flesh. "You're making me feel incredible," he assured her. "But don't worry, I can usually fuck right through the first couple orgasms. And with you two ridiculously sexy girls, probably even more than that."

"Well in that case . . ." The plant girl lifted herself off his cock, panting in pleasure, and with a playful giggle threw herself down on her back on the mattress-like petals of her flower's floor.

She coyly spread her slender legs, stretching them into a split and then beyond with a flexibility even an elite gymnast would envy. Her flushed petals glistened with her nectar, opening up like a flower in invitation to reveal her beautiful pink walls.

Enellia fluttered her wings to rise gracefully off his lap, settling down straddling Rosie's face with her beautiful plump lips pressed firmly to the plant girl's mouth. The petite green girl gave a muffled sound of delight and eagerly began kissing and licking her beautiful lover, small hands holding the butterfly girl's perfect thighs tightly.

"Well?" Enellia asked, sunrise eyes sparkling as she gave him a playful grin while grinding against her girlfriend's face.

Dare didn't need a second invitation. Climbing atop Rosie's beautiful petite body, he positioned himself at her entrance and smoothly pushed inside, causing her to squeal against her lover's pussy and undulate her hips eagerly against him.

As he went balls deep inside the plant girl Enellia pulled his face towards hers and pressed her open mouth against his in a passionate kiss, tongue swirling around his. She tasted like nectar and sunshine and a hint of the ambrosia he'd savored from his benefactor in her alabaster dream form.

Had his benefactor gotten inspiration for the heady flavor of her arousal from butterfly girls? If so did that mean their taste was the most alluring to be found on Collisa?

Gods, Dare wished it was his face Enellia was sitting on. Although he contented himself that by the time they were done, he'd find a chance to taste the ethereal butterfly girl.

Enellia broke the kiss and trailed her luscious lips across his cheek, making his skin tingle delightfully, before pressing them to his ear. "Go ahead and be as rough as you want with Rosie," she purred. "She may be soft and sweet but she's also as resilient and springy as a sapling, and can stretch as much as needed to accommodate a cock of any size. And the rougher the sex the more plant girls enjoy it, so she'll love whatever you do."

The petite green girl made a muffled noise of agreement, hips twitching eagerly and pussy rippling and squeezing his cock even more intensely.

Damn, that was awesome.

Dare pulled back and thrust into her hard and fast, and both women squealed as Rosie took out her pleasure on Enellia's pink pussy with her tongue. He thrust again, faster and harder, and the plant girl's hips pushed back eagerly.

So soon after he'd just come, his frantic pace made his sensitive tip throb with a pleasure bordering on pain. Or maybe vice versa. He did his best to ride it out, and after a while the sensitivity receded.

Again and again he pounded into the plant girl, going faster and faster until he was vigorously pistoning his petite lover's tiny pussy in a way he'd been afraid to do with any other woman, given the size of his cock. Aside from slime girls and his benefactor's alabaster form, that was.

And no matter how hard he went Rosie continued to egg him on with muffled cries of pleasure, not to mention her hips and the massaging walls of her pussy. As if racing to see which broke first, her or the pole impaling her.

Enellia grabbed his head and pulled his face down between the pillowy mounds of her perfect breasts, and he savored the delicate scent of her perspiration as he ravaged her lover.

Rosie gave a muffled squeal and climaxed again, flooding his cock with another gush of sticky nectar as her sweet walls again tried to crush him. A moment later her butterfly girl lover rose a few inches over her face and squirted all over her as the ethereal woman orgasmed as well.

Then the plant girl wiggled out from beneath Enellia and began pushing at Dare's chest to pause his frantic thrusts.

"Your turn, Lia!" she panted, small chest heaving. While he was still processing the statement she scrambled off his cock and pushed him onto his pack, giving Enellia a fierce kiss before rolling away.

That left the beautiful butterfly girl. "Want to see something neat?" she teased, nibbling her lip in shy eagerness as she straddled his thighs. She teasingly inched forward, sliding her delicate lips along the length of his throbbing shaft with an almost musical moan of pleasure.

"Gods yes," he panted, grabbing her wide hips and lovingly stroking the silky caramel skin.

Grinning, Enellia positioned herself over his tip and, like her lover had, began lowering herself onto him. She almost immediately gasped, eyes widening as she paused her motion.

"Okay, I might need to take a second," she admitted sheepishly. "I need to get used to this monster before I'm ready to show you." She twisted her head to grin at Rosie, antenna waving playfully. "I don't have an infinitely elastic, bottomless cunt like some people."

The plant girl giggled, leaning forward to teasingly slap the

280

ethereally beautiful woman's perfect ass, making it ripple hypnotically. "Take your time, I get off just watching you."

Enellia snickered. "You get off doing just about anything."

"Says the sunflower to the marigold." Rosie moved to sit behind Enellia like her lover had for her, reaching up to toy with her dark nipples and kissing along her delicate wings.

"Okay then." The beautiful butterfly girl took a deep breath, curvy thighs rippling in a subtle flex, then gently began lowering herself onto Dare's cock.

It didn't stretch her quite as obscenely as it had the plant girl, and it didn't feel quite as crushingly tight, and yet it was obvious she had more of a struggle to adjust to it. "Sun above and suns below," she breathed, musical voice husky, "you've got the best cock I've ever felt. Because we're close to the same size the ##### ####### doesn't affect it as much as it would for a larger race with the same size, and that makes this *incredible*."

"You're taking it like a champ," Dare told her with an encouraging smile. He'd been about to ask her how she was holding up before she said that, but she seemed to be doing okay.

He'd let her keep setting the pace until she adjusted and gave him the okay to take part, though.

"Of course she is," Rosie said proudly, stroking the tips of her butterfly lover's beautiful wings "She's the best at everything, and she's so gorgeous doing it, too."

Dare felt a fresh surge of pleasure as Enellia finished sliding down his tip and her delicate folds wrapped around his shaft. He didn't know exactly how to describe it, but her pussy felt unlike any he'd ever been inside. Even though she wasn't nearly as crushingly tight as Rosie or Zuri, there was something about her pink interior that felt amazing.

Maybe it was the incomparable softness, or the perfect warmth. Or some specific ridges or rippling of her walls. But her perfect beauty was reflected by the feel of her sex, and as she continued sliding down his length he twitched in delight.

"You're incredible," he said, reaching back to rub her perfect ass.

It yielded just like it should, firm but pliant, and he couldn't help but give it a good squeeze as she squirmed and giggled on his cock.

She seemed to like it, because she moaned deliciously and her tight walls relaxed enough to take him deeper in one smooth motion, until he bottomed out against her cervix.

Enellia wasted no time rising back up, silky walls stroking his shaft as she slipped off him, lips gripping him as if reluctant to let go. She rode him for a minute or two, moving more quickly as she adjusted to his size, before finally dropping down until he was bottomed out in her again.

"Now," she panted, brilliant sunrise eyes sparkling. "Time for the surprise. Can you give me some room, honey?"

"Yay!" Rosie squealed, backing up until she was perched just below his knees, her soft little pussy rubbing eagerly against his shin as she looked on. "I can't wait to see this!"

Dare was about to ask what when Enellia's gorgeous wings snapped out to their full size and began fluttering gently. Then, to his absolute amazement, she began slowly lifting herself up his cock on just the power of her wings alone.

That allowed her to raised her knees up to her large breasts and hug them to her, then squeeze her thighs together tightly, increasing her delicate pussy's pressure around his cock.

"Gods above," he panted at the intense sensation of her fluttering up his shaft paused, and then she started back down in the same smooth motion. "This has got to be one of the most incredible things I've ever seen. Ever *felt*."

"You're telling me," she moaned. "And what makes it hotter is that at the end of it our baby will be growing inside me." Her walls tightened eagerly at the words, and Dare groaned as his cock twitched in response.

Gods, the thought of this perfect woman's belly growing with his child was amazing.

The butterfly girl's beautiful wings were hypnotic as they fluttered behind her, expertly moving her up and down his shaft as she moaned in rapture. Her arousal poured down his cock, the ambrosia scent turning his head, and he began pushing his hips up to match her as she descended, sliding his hands over her perfect caramel skin, up her thighs and over her hips to grab her heavenly ass.

Her fluttering abruptly became erratic as she gasped, eyes widening and warm pussy clamping down. "Yeesssss!" she moaned, sliding down onto his chest and clutching him as she climaxed. Her incredible walls caressed his cock in a series of rippling motions, and her nectar flooded out to soak his crotch, belly, and thighs.

"That's it, honey!" Rosie said, leaning over her lover and vigorously flicking Enellia's bud with one finger while she mauled the butterfly girl's breasts with her other hand. "Ride it out!"

The sight of the ethereal woman having the mother of all orgasms on his cock, the feel of her quivering climax, pushed Dare over the edge. He gripped her ass tightly and released inside her in a torrent, closing his eyes against the overwhelming surges of pleasure.

Enellia lay limp across his chest as she came down from her peak, and Rosie squirmed up to press up against her side atop Dare's arm, making a contented sound as she cuddled them both.

He shifted to wrap both arms around the beautiful women, luxuriating in the feel of their soft bodies as his cock gradually softened in the butterfly girl's pink pussy, but remained inside her as they lay contentedly.

After a few minutes to recover their strength Rosie finally stirred and poked her girlfriend, who seemed almost drowsy in her post-orgasmic bliss. "It's getting close to dark, honey. Want to fly over to Pella's camp and introduce yourself to Zuri, then invite them here to play a bit more before we stay the night in my flower."

"Do I have to?" Enellia mumbled, kissing his neck and shoulder and making contented noises. "I could just go to sleep like this."

The plant girl pouted. "Come on, you want to play with Pella, don't you? And Zuri is so adorable and soft. And think of how comfy it would be to snuggle with Leilanna's pillowy body."

"Fine." The butterfly girl sighed and rose, Dare's mostly softening dick finally slipping out of her with a quiet *plop*.

A torrent of their combined juices flowed over him, and with an eager noise Rosie got to work lapping them up as Enellia fluttered out of the flower and disappeared in the direction of Pella's camp.

"Mmm," the plant girl moaned in delight. "Nothing tastes better than Enellia, but your flavor is great too." She giggled. "And it never hurts to absorb more of your seed, just to make sure."

Right, the plant girl had mentioned that she could get pregnant through all her orifices, including her mouth. Which made her contentedly lapping up his seed even hotter.

Dare ran an affectionate hand over his petite lover's flat belly. The thought of it swelling with his child delighted him, and he felt his cock twitch and begin to harden again as he imagined it all big and round, her adorable little innie belly button popping out into an outtie.

"Oooh," Rosie giggled, grabbing his stiffening shaft in both her small hands and lovingly stroking him. "What're you thinking that's got you hard again so suddenly?" Her green eyes danced impishly. "Imagining me all big with our seed?"

"Yeah, actually," he admitted with a grin. "You're going to look so sexy."

She giggled again. "I know." She abruptly sobered, biting her lip. "Can I ask you for something else, Dare?"

In his blissful state he probably would've done anything the adorable plant girl asked. "What is it?"

Rosie released his shaft and squirmed around to perch on his chest, elfin face only inches from his. "It takes about two months for florans to produce a seed after pollination." Her eyes held his soberly. "Will you come back then?"

Dare blinked in surprise. Unlike Enellia's careful explanation of how their child would be cared for, Rosie hadn't said much about the fate of their seed other than that as a plant girl she would be fine. Was that because she'd planned to discuss it more with him when she produced the seed?

"It would be my honor to return," he said, kissing her flower-strewn hair, then burying his face in the fragrant curls and breathing deep of their sweet perfume. "Thank you for giving me the opportunity."

"No, thank you!" Wiggling her soft little body, she slid down him until the wet lips of her pink slit were pressed against his tip. "Pella said you can go enough times to tire her and Zuri out, right?" she asked with a playful smile.

He grinned. "Over a dozen times in one session, especially if the girls give me some rest while they play with each other."

Her green eyes danced. "So if we go again now, you'll still have enough energy to play with me and the others when they get back?"

If it meant more opportunities to be with the beautiful plant girl, Dare would go until he passed out if he had to.

So in answer to her question he grabbed her hips and thrust upwards into her wet warmth, making her gasp with delight. She rose up above him, back arching in pleasure and small breasts jutting out proudly, and he reached up to play with them as she began enthusiastically bouncing on his shaft again.

* * * * *

They spent a few lazy days with the plant girl and butterfly girl, unhurriedly loading up the horses with Pella's stash and taking frequent breaks in Rosie's flower to make love with the beautiful women.

Unsurprisingly, the couple had as much fun with Zuri and Pella as they did with Dare. And he certainly had a lot of fun watching them.

What *was* a surprise was that Leilanna insisted on taking part, especially if he wasn't there. Although at night when they couldn't avoid all sleeping in the flower together, he and the dusk elf ended up basically making love with the other women on opposite sides of the room from each other.

In spite of Leilanna's unwillingness to do anything with him, he noticed she eagerly watched while he fucked the others, playing with herself the entire time. And when she noticed him looking at her naked, curvy body writhing in pleasure as she rubbed herself to the sight of him thrusting into one of their lovers, she didn't fly off the handle at him.

If anything, it seemed to arouse her even more.

Dare could only assume that when it came to their group she wanted to be with Zuri and Pella, but not him. Also that she was an exhibitionist, and while she wasn't interested in him she didn't mind his presence.

On the morning of the third day since their arrival Dare and his companions finally prepared to set out. He could admit he'd been worn out by the attentions of four women, but in a good way, and was in a good mood as he looked over the horses to make sure they were ready.

Rosie surprised him by jumping into his arms in an enthusiastic goodbye hug, wrapping her legs around his waist and pressing her pussy to his crotch as she showered his face with kisses. "Remember to come back in two months!"

"I will," he promised solemnly as he hugged her soft little body close. "Thank you for your amazing hospitality."

"And thank *you* for the wonderful visit! Love you!" She gave him a final fierce kiss on the lips, slipping her small tongue into his mouth for a few seconds, then with a giggle hopped off him and ran over to give the others their own goodbye hugs and kisses.

Enellia was close behind her girlfriend, ethereal features lit up in a brilliant smile as she wrapped him in a warm embrace, pressing her naked body close.

"Thank you for giving me a child," she murmured, kissing him tenderly. "And of course for giving me and Rosie such a wonderful time. I'll bring the baby north to visit as soon as it's old enough to travel, I promise."

"I can't wait to meet our child, and of course see you again." Dare hugged her back for a few seconds, then took the opportunity to stroke her delicate wings one last time before she stepped away and went over to embrace Zuri.

The plant girl and butterfly girl stood waving and calling out final farewells as he and his companions led the laden horses away,

Leilanna and Zuri riding while Dare and Pella walked.

The trip up north was mostly uneventful, the highlights when they stopped in Hamalis and Yurin to sell as much of their junk loot as they could. And, at the insistence of the women, fill up the freed space on the horses with carpets and small furniture and other amenities they shopped for in the towns.

Although one big exception to the uneventfulness was the fact that Leilanna had apparently gotten used to sleeping with them, and on the first night insisted that he make a larger tent that could fit all of them.

She still didn't show much interest in him, although she was eager to keep making love to Pella and Zuri, and usually cuddled with one or the other when they settled down to sleep, using the other women as a buffer between her and him.

It felt a bit petty to be jealous, but at times it was hard not to be. Almost like Leilanna was invading not just his tent but his relationship with Zuri and Pella, and stealing the women he loved away from him.

Although his lovers seemed confident it was only a matter of time before Leilanna wanted to sleep with him, too, and were always quick to reassure him of their love for him.

Still, he sourly wondered if Leilanna was going to invade his bed when they moved into the manor, too. And not in a good way.

Chapter Seventeen
Dark Pink

When Dare and his party passed through the goblin ravine, he was pleased to see a greeting party of over a hundred goblins waiting for him. Which possibly meant a positive answer to his offer for the Avenging Wolf tribe to move onto his lands.

"Human," Gar said solemnly.

Dare nodded to him. "Chieftain Gar'u'wek. How fares the Avenging Wolf tribe?"

"Well. The slavers have not returned since you dealt with them." The large goblin got straight to the point. "My tribe has deliberated on your offer."

Dare perked up. "What have you decided?"

Gar was slow to answer, looking at him gravely. "My tribe is split. My warriors and I wish to stay in the mountains and hunt, grow stronger for the tribe. And most of our mates wish to stay with us, along with many of our offspring."

"I see." Dare couldn't help but be a bit disappointed; as the chieftain went, so did the tribe. Especially with the warriors behind him.

But the large goblin surprised him. "Over a hundred of my people, however, wish to accept the peace and safety of your lands. The weak and timid, and most of those taken by the slavers and rescued by you." He motioned curtly behind him. "My son Rek'u'gar will lead them."

The crowd of goblins parted as one head and shoulders above the others strode forward. A hobgoblin, hybrid of a human and goblin.

Dare couldn't help but be interested at his first view of a hobgoblin. Rek's face was more rounded and human than a goblin's sharp features, although his skin was the same green tone. His ears were longer than a human's but with rounded edges, and he was more sturdily muscled than most goblin men. And rather than the inky black hair goblins usually had, his was light brown, and he had a beard of the same color.

Most goblins topped out at four feet, with Gar an obvious exception, but Rek stood even taller at above five feet. Dare's Adventurer's Eye identified him as adolescent, and he judged the young man as sixteen or seventeen, nearing adulthood. He bore a claymore on his back, and in spite of his youth seemed confident and bold.

"Human," Rek said, voice lower than most goblins. "You have my gratitude for rescuing my mother from the slavers. She wished to go to a place where the slavers cannot come, and I will go as well to protect her."

Dare nodded politely. "You and your people are welcome."

"That is our hope. But there must be negotiations. And first of all, an agreement to bind us in friendship and ensure peace with my tribe." The hobgoblin raised his fingers to his lips and let out a piercing whistle.

Another figure emerged from the goblin crowd, also standing taller, although not quite as tall as Rek.

She was a female hobgoblin, her features similar to Rek's, obviously a few years older and his Eye identified her as adult. She had the same brown hair, and her large eyes were such a pale yellow they were almost white.

Her rounded features were soft, with just enough sharpness to give her face an exotic air. Unquestionably beautiful, with a plump, curvy figure hidden beneath a tunic and breeches that were above average in quality for the goblins.

The hobgoblin woman approached with downcast eyes, looking shy and clearly nervous. Rek glanced questioningly at Gar, but the chieftain had stood aside, clearly ceding the meeting to his son, so the hobgoblin youth pulled the woman up to stand beside him.

"This is my sister Se'weir'u'gar," he said. "I offer her to you as mate, that my people may be as family to you."

289

Well shit . . . how exactly did Dare navigate this minefield? He looked questioningly at Zuri, who nodded solemnly. "You should accept, my mate," she said with a grin. "Marriage is a great way to foster peace and friendship, and works toward your goal to grow your harem and be with women of all races." She motioned to the hobgoblin woman. "And Se'weir is very beautiful, isn't she?"

"She is very beautiful, yes," he said awkwardly, drawing a shy, pleased smile from the hobgoblin.

Rek grunted in satisfaction. "Then you will mate her, and become one of the tribe."

The idea wasn't an unpleasant one, certainly. It would be very tempting to accept, take Se'weir to his tent, and explore that sexy body of hers. But Dare held up a hand. "My people don't do things quite the same as goblins, and a formal joining such as this is not so simple as just bringing a woman to my bed."

"How is it not simple?" Rek asked, a bit suspiciously. "You mate her and our tribes are joined. I trust you know how this is done?" Several of the goblins snickered, and Gar laughed outright.

"First off, I'm not comfortable with arranged marriages," Dare said firmly. "It's too easy to force a woman into such an arrangement, and I don't want an unwilling mate."

"I am willing!" Se'weir blurted, then blushed and looked down again.

"Why wouldn't she be overjoyed to be your mate, Dare?" Zuri asked, frowning.

He chuckled ruefully. "Believe it or not, not every woman wants to jump on my dick," he told her for her ears only. He shot a significant look at Leilanna to prove his point, earning a scowl from the dusk elf. "And she might be especially hesitant if it means being taken away from her people and living with me for the rest of her life."

"Your pardon, human," the hobgoblin woman said, stepping forward with her eyes still downcast. "My sisters and I competed fiercely for the honor of being your mate. In fact, we tried to convince our father to let several of us present ourselves to you."

Dare blinked. That was unexpected. "I'm a stranger to you, why do you desire me so much?"

Apparently hobgoblins turned pink rather than darker green when they blushed, because her flawless pale green skin did so now. "Do you wish for compliments? You are very pleasing to the eye, and strong enough to defend your mates and offspring. And we see how happy Ge'welu is with you." She looked at Zuri a little enviously. "We all wish for that, to bear your children and have the fine things you offer."

When he still hesitated she took another bashful step forward. "I will be a good mate to you, I promise. My body is yours, to please you however you wish, and I will work hard in your household. And all who know me speak well of my sweet disposition and submissive nature."

"My mate, stop embarrassing her and just accept," Zuri hissed.

Dare shifted uncomfortably. "As my people's customs dictate, I will agree to marry Se'weir in one year, as a courtship period. We will have time to get to know each other better, decide whether we both truly wish to be joined."

An awkward silence settled. "And in the meantime Dare will offer gifts to win your favor," Zuri said hastily.

"I don't understand," Se'weir murmured, crestfallen. "Do I not please you?"

"Sister, bare yourself so he can better see what you offer," Rek said curtly.

"No!" Dare blurted, blushing furiously. He wasn't about to allow the poor woman to be humiliated like that. "That's not necessary, I can see how beautiful she is."

"Then is it her hobgoblin heritage?" Rek asked, frowning. "I would think that would make her more pleasing to a human, but if not I can offer another of my goblin sisters that would be more to your liking. More than one, if you wish. They are all beautiful and fierce, daughters of the great Gar'u'wek."

"No, it's not that either," Dare said hastily. "I just don't want to force Se'weir to rush into a decision she may regret later." Out of the corner of his eye he saw Zuri shaking her head in bafflement.

Rek also looked baffled, and starting to get irritated, but before he could say anything Gar cut in. "The human is overly concerned with the feelings of females, my son, as I've seen before. It's a wonder he's found any mates at all."

There were more snickers among the goblins. Although not from the women, Dare noticed.

"Then you desire me?" Se'weir asked hopefully.

He smiled at her. "I desire you very much," he said gently. "Allow me to properly court you, and marry you in a year."

"A wife is higher status than a mate for humans," Zuri added. She gave Dare a hard to read look. "Even I'm not married to him."

"Well I mean, not officially," Dare said, abashed. "I think of you that way, though."

She gave him another look. "We will speak of it later, Dare. With Pella."

"Sure, absolutely." He had a feeling he was going to be in hot water by offering to marry another woman ahead of his own lovers, even though he hadn't meant to hurt their feelings. Which, admittedly, probably made it even worse, that he'd been that thoughtless.

Se'weir still looked doubtful. "I don't wish to wait that long, but if it is what you require . . ."

"Very well," Rek said, seeming relieved to have the issue settled. "If we are agreed on this, let's continue with the negotiations."

The discussion with Gar, Rek, and a handful of goblin elders ended up being surprisingly lengthy and detailed. They were clearly wary of trusting a human, even after what he'd done for them, and wanted to make sure they addressed every possible issue.

For her part Zuri wanted to make it very clear that the goblins were expected to be peaceful and productive, paying their rent and taxes in full and on time. Dare hastened to assure them that he'd help however he could to raise their standard of living, and he had a few ideas, but he couldn't argue the points his lover brought up.

Finally, after hours of debate, Dare shook hands with Gar and Rek, and once again reassured them that the engagement with Se'weir was still on. The goblins who'd be moving to his land needed time to prepare, and he needed time to prepare for them as well, but they agreed to make the move in two weeks.

Before continuing on towards Terana, Zuri insisted that he make his farewells to Se'weir. "She's going to be your wife in a year, after all."

"I was planning to," he said stiffly. "Or at least, I wanted to. I wasn't sure exactly what to do in this situation." He did his best not to scowl. "And I'm not a fan of arranged marriages, so this entire thing has thrown me off balance."

"So you've already said," she replied, rolling her eyes. "You don't have to be an ass about it."

"I'm not," Dare protested. "I just want to make sure we really love each other before we get married. And that Se'weir will really be happy with me. If it turns out that's not the case, this way we'll have time to make some other arrangement."

"As long as you marry me and Pella and Leilanna before her," his goblin lover insisted.

"Do you know something about Leilanna I don't?" he asked, throwing up his hands. "Because last I checked she doesn't even want to touch me."

Zuri also threw up her hands. "Just go and say goodbye to Se'weir. If you want to know whether you love each other, you should be doing your best to convince her to love you."

Dare found the young hobgoblin woman surrounded by goblin girls, most likely her sisters. Although she quickly excused herself to come talk to him. "Are you leaving?" she asked, lovely round features full of disappointment. "I could come with you."

"I'll visit you soon," he assured her. "We need to go get your people's land prepared for the move."

He smiled. "We also need to fix up the manor, but when it is you're welcome to visit me as well."

294

Se'weir blushed. "I'd like that." She shifted, looking equal parts hopeful and nervous. "Is it true?" she blurted. "Do you really think I'm beautiful and wish to mate me? That wasn't just something you told my father and brother as part of the negotiations?"

He felt his cheeks heating again. "I wouldn't lie as part of a negotiation, Se'weir," he said gently. "I think you're very beautiful, and more importantly gentle and kind. I would be very honored to marry you and have a life with you."

Her face lit up with happiness, and he wished he could leave it at that. "Now it's my turn to ask you something," he said gently, stepping closer so he wouldn't be overheard. "I want you to be happy in whatever life you choose, with me or on some other path. So if this arrangement makes you uncomfortable, if you'd rather not leave your people to be with me and you're only doing it out of duty or because you're being compelled to, I'll understand. I'll tell Gar and Rek that I've changed my mind, and take any blame for their displeasure."

The beautiful hobgoblin looked at him with big eyes, obviously fighting not to be devastated. "Why are you so certain I wouldn't want to be with you?" she whispered in a small voice. "Do you think *I'm* lying when I say I wish to be your mate?"

She looked so sad and vulnerable that Dare wanted to wrap his arms around her and hold her close until she felt better. He gave her his warmest smile. "That's not it at all, Se'weir. I just believe that people should be free to live their lives in the way that'll make them happy. I want that for you, whatever you choose."

"Then let me use the time you've given me to prove that I'll be happy with you!" Se'weir said fiercely. "Give me a chance to be part of your household and your family."

He looked into her eyes and felt some of his reservations lift. "Of course I will, Se'weir," he said. "And if I'm lucky enough to earn your love, I promise I'll do my best to make you happy." He reluctantly looked over at where his companions were waiting, surprised to find that he wanted to spend more time with the beautiful hobgoblin. "I should go, but I look forward to seeing you again."

"So do I, my, um, soon-to-be mate." She shifted in shy

anticipation. "Do your people's customs allow me to hug you goodbye?"

Dare chuckled and held open his arms, and the plump little woman threw herself against his chest, soft body pressing eagerly against him. He held her tight for a few moments before finally pulling back.

She looked up at him, pale yellow eyes uncertain. "I hope I'll prove to you I can be a worthy mate," she murmured. "I would like to be yours, heart and body, and give you many children."

"I would like to be yours as well," he said. "But we have a year to get to know each other and make that decision."

"If that's what you require," she said a bit wistfully. She threw her arms around him in a last spontaneous hug, then with a furious blush hurried back to her sisters, who all gathered around her giggling and speaking quickly, shooting him frequent glances.

It seemed like no matter the race, some things were the same.

* * * * *

Although Dare and his companions pushed on hard for Terana, they were still half a day away as the sun sank towards the horizon on the second day.

He wanted to push for a few more miles, but Zuri disagreed; he got the feeling it was because she was hoping they'd encounter some of the small, cow-like animals with delicious meat that roamed this area.

For her sake he went out hunting while the others made camp, although the best he was able to find was a roaming boar. Which Zuri liked almost as much.

They spent a quiet evening working on their individual abilities, then the girls put their heads together to talk about expanding the manor and building guest houses. As well as houses for the women of his harem who preferred more solitude, which Leilanna admitted she may want.

"Not that I'm part of your harem!" she said furiously.

"Yet," Pella teased.

The beautiful dusk elf blushed even more furiously. "I'm going to bed," she snapped. "Want to come with me, Zuri?"

The little goblin patted Dare's leg fondly, then wrapped an arm around Leilanna's waist and walked with her into the tent. The noises the fiery Mage soon started making seemed almost deliberately loud and enthusiastic, as if to make some kind of point.

"I honestly have no idea what's going on," he confessed to Pella.

She just grinned at him. "You will soon," she assured him, moving over to cuddle up with him.

As it turned out, that happened sooner than he'd expected.

Late that night Dare was awakened by one of his lovers aggressively cuddling him, one leg hooked over his as she ground her pussy against his hip. Soft, moist lips trailed over his shoulder and across his neck, sucking hard enough to give him a hickey.

He found himself quickly stiffening and sleepily wrapped an arm around her curvy body, pulling her closer against him as he buried his face in her soft hair, inhaling her sweet scent.

Then he froze when he realized that, incredible as she smelled, her scent wasn't Pella's or Zuri's. She didn't feel like them, either.

As it turned out, though, his lovers had been absolutely right about how soft and cuddly their companion was.

Dare looked around desperately, realizing that Pella, who'd been lying between them, must've gotten up to relieve herself. Leilanna had sleepily pressed into that space and cuddled up to his side, seeming to be half awake as she continued to grind against him, moaning and nibbling his neck with her obscenely plump lips.

Fuck, she felt incredible.

A bit reluctantly, he tried to pull away. But the beautiful dusk elf just held him tighter and murmured drowsy protests. So he bit the bullet, preparing for her fury, and firmly shook her shoulder. "Leilanna," he whispered sharply.

She froze, pink eyes flying open and gleaming up at him in the darkness. "What the fuck?" she moaned.

"Pella got up to pee or something," Dare whispered. "I think you woke up enough to cuddle up to me while she was gone." He paused, then quickly added. "I only just woke up myself and realized it was you, so I woke you up."

"Oh," Leilanna said. Then, sounding resigned, added, "Fuck it."

To his shock she scooted up and kissed him, mouth open and plump lips hungrily devouring his.

She tasted like sweet blackberry wine, heady and welcoming. After a moment he relaxed and kissed her back gently, wrapping his arm back around her and luxuriating in her soft, curvy body.

The beautiful dusk elf moaned and began grinding against his hip again. Her hand slipped between them, sliding down his bare chest and stomach towards his erection straining to be free of his underwear.

Then the tent flap rustled and Pella ducked inside.

Leilanna threw herself backwards as if struck by lightning, and Dare's clumsy attempt to reach after her was interrupted by his dog girl lover cuddling up to his side again.

"Ohh," Pella cooed with a giggle, feeling his rock hard cock pressing against her thigh. "Is that for me?" Without waiting for a response she freed him and straddled his hips, guiding him into her wet heat and enthusiastically beginning to ride him, moaning with pleasure as she bottomed out.

He felt inexplicably guilty as he looked over at Leilanna. She'd scooted all the way over to press herself against the side of the tent, back to him like a wall.

Fuck.

With a resigned groan Dare grabbed Pella's firm ass and enjoyed the ride, wondering what the hell had just happened and whether he should talk to Leilanna about it.

Probably, although he had no idea what to say.

* * * * *

Leilanna avoided him like the plague the next morning, while Pella and Zuri seemed oblivious to what had happened.

298

Dare spent the trip to Terana trying to figure out a way to approach the Mage and talk about it, but before he could come up with anything the town's walls came into view.

Well, he'd find a chance soon. Maybe he could tell Zuri and Pella what had happened and ask their opinion; considering he'd watched them going down on the beautiful dusk elf and fingering her to squirting climax on numerous occasions, there weren't many secrets between them.

Just a wall that for some reason kept him and Leilanna from being intimate with each other, like they were with their goblin and dog girl lovers.

He recognized one of the guards at the gate as the tough but pretty woman he'd spoken to before, Helima. It seemed she remembered him, too. "Well, if it isn't the guy that stood me up for drinks a couple weeks ago," she said dryly.

Dare shifted awkwardly in his saddle. "Sorry about that."

She smirked. "I suppose it can't be helped if you got an invitation to stay the night at Montshadow Estate. I can hardly expect you to snub the Baroness just to grab a drink with some lowly town guard." She gave him an inviting look. "Although the offer's still available any time you want to swing by. I'm there most evenings."

"I'll take you up on that if I get the chance," he said with a smile as he rode through the gate.

The woman smirked again. "Good, because I've got a pair of manacles with your name on them."

Ooh, kinky. And a little terrifying.

While Dare was eager to sell the rest of their junk loot and be done with it, he was even more eager to see if the man Lady Marona had sent to Redoubt had returned with approval for their purchase and the necessary paperwork. He wanted to get the title to the land already and get to work improving the place.

Also, he had to admit, he was eager to see if he'd be lucky enough to have more exciting encounters with the maids of Montshadow Estate while he was visiting there. Maybe even an invitation to stay the night again in comfort.

But to his disappointment, when they arrived at the mansion the guard at the wrought iron gate met them outside. "I'm afraid the Baroness and her staff have traveled to Redoubt for an official function," he said. "However, she bade me tell you that the deed to your new land is waiting for you at the counting house. Also, she extends her regrets she wasn't here to conclude the deal in person, and requests that you meet with her when she returns to conclude the final formalities."

"All right," Dare said. "Thank you."

The man nodded and returned to his post.

"I guess that means no cute maids," Zuri said, sounding disappointed.

Pella turned to him. "Should we split up again? You can grab the deed and see about hiring the laborers we need, and we'll sell the rest of the loot and buy some things for the manor."

"Sounds good." Dare saw an opportunity to finally get Leilanna alone for a conversation. "What about if Leilanna came wi-"

"Not a chance!" the Mage said hastily. "I want to shop!"

Damnit. He watched as they rode away, leading the packhorses, then shook his head and went in search of the counting house.

He'd expected a bank, but rather than a room with tellers behind counters and everything else he would've expected, instead there was a small waiting room with a clerk in a uniform who took down his name and other information. Then he was lead down a hallway and seated in a small room, where eventually a well-dressed man bustled in to shake his hand.

"Master Dare," he said as he settled into the chair across the table from him. "We've been expecting you. I'm Norril, owner and proprietor of the Terana Counting House."

"Well met, Master Norril," Dare said, settling back into his own seat. "I trust everything's in order?"

"Indeed." Norril reached into a satchel and produced a sheaf of paperwork. "Everything's mostly sorted out and ready to go, but we need you to sign a few things in front of a witness and give you a few details."

Now that was more like Dare remembered from Earth. The paperwork may have used different terms and conditions than he was used to, but bureaucracy seemed to be bureaucracy wherever you went.

The laborious process of reading through fine print and getting signatures took about an hour, but finally he was given a scroll of thick vellum with the words written in beautiful calligraphy.

The deed to their new home. An end to his constant wandering, or at least a place to return to between adventures.

Dare produced his legendary chest and grew it to full size, then paused when he saw the well-dressed man's surprise. "Sorry, I should've asked."

Norril waved that away. "Not at all, we're here to offer a secure and discreet location to handle wealth. I was just surprised to see such a rare and valuable item. It's unusual to see anyone but nobles, wealthy merchants, and high level adventurers with them. Although given your obvious wealth it shouldn't come as a surprise after all."

Dare carefully placed the rolled scroll in its protective case in the chest, then quickly shut it and shrank it to return to his coin pouch. "On the subject of handling wealth, let's say I wanted to store gold here in the future?"

"Our prices are very reasonable, and we have yet to suffer a robbery," the counting house proprietor said. "If such were to happen, our main office in Redoubt would dispatch bounty hunters to retrieve the wealth, and failing that would reimburse the losses if possible."

Fair enough. "I'll consider you should the need arise." They exchanged another round of handshakes, then Dare headed out and made his way into the laborer's section of town.

After a bit of asking around he was able to find two brothers and a cousin who shared the last name Jorrin who were a Mason, a Woodcrafter, and an Architect, all classes available on Collisa. He talked through his plans for the manor a bit with them, discussed what they could do and what materials and other laborers they'd need, then got a handshake deal for them to swing around to the manor in a week to check it out and get to work.

"You'd be well served contracting an earth Mage to build a road from Terana to your lands if you mean to do a lot of hiring labor," the Architect he spoke to said. "A lot of people would be leery of traveling a day into the wilds on a job. Although thankfully I helped build the manor in the first place so I know a safe route."

Dare wasn't sure he wanted a trail leading potential criminals straight to his doorstep. Which might've been the reasoning of the previous owner, since there wasn't already a road.

However, he *did* want to talk to an Earth mage. "Do you know a good one?"

The men exchanged glances. "Our friend Morwal is sturdy enough," the Mason said. "He digs cellars for us every now and then."

Dare sorted out a few final details with the builders, then followed their directions to a simple workshop filled with pottery and a bit of stonework.

So far a good sign.

A powerfully built man straightened from a project he'd been working on in a corner of the workshop, the black glow of what Dare presumed was earth magic fading from his hands. He was a Level 19 Mage, and judging by his workshop seemed competent enough.

"Well met, good master," the Mage called, hurrying over. He dusted off his hand on his thick leather apron and proffered it. "I'm Morwal the earth Mage. How can I help you?"

Dare returned his crushing grip. "Well met. I'm Dare, recently moved into the area. I purchased a manor in the southeast corner of Terana Province and I need some work done there."

Morwal brightened. "Then I'm you're man. And you'll find my prices very reasonable. What do you need?"

"Well first off, how are you with pipes?"

"Ah, pipes for smoking?" The man motioned to a side table that displayed an array of clay pipes of different lengths.

Interesting, but not what Dare was looking for. "I was thinking more along the lines of ceramic or metal pipes for carrying water through a house. An inch or two in diameter, interconnected and waterproof, with ones that bend so I can change the direction of the pipe line. And then larger ones, maybe three or so inches, for sewage, and some specific ceramic work for a custom privy."

The earth Mage frowned thoughtfully. "I'm not aware of a setup like that. It doesn't sound like the magic system used for plumbing and sanitation that the wealthy usually commission."

Oh. That might be even better. "Can you make something like that yourself?"

The man laughed. "Fuck no. Nobody in Terana could, assuming you had a hundred thousand or so gold to spend in the first place. That's usually work for high level Enchanters or Voidcasters anyway."

Well, that was that. "Okay then, pipes. And preferably some sort of sealant to make the connections watertight."

Morwal pulled out some slates and chalk, as well as paper and a stubby pencil, and Dare quickly sketched out the specific pipes he wanted, as well as a diagram for a toilet.

Once he was finished the man looked them over, scratching his chin. "Nothing like these in the crafting system," he admitted. "I'd have to develop a new design, which will more than double the cost."

Dare prepared to go into haggling mode. "If I could prove how convenient these are, it might be worth your time just to have the pattern."

The earth Mage wasn't having any of it and laughed outright. "Or I could wait until you find someone else waiting to create the pattern and I'll get it anyway once it goes into the system."

Right. That really had a huge impact on things. "Guess the system giving everybody your designs kind of dampens the enthusiasm for invention."

"Meh, it puts your name in the pattern details. Immortality after a fashion." Morwal shook his head dourly. "Nothing I'd go out of my way to seek."

Dare nodded reluctantly. "Okay, well I'll bankroll you designing the patterns I need." It would still be cheaper than using whatever magic plumbing the wealthy used, and he wanted his family to have proper bathrooms.

"All right then, I'll get started making the patterns and creating the pipes you need. Anything else?"

"Lots, actually," Dare admitted with a laugh. "I'd also like tanks that can hold cold and hot water, sturdy and light enough to be mounted on a roof. And I need to commission pumps such as those used to bail water out of a ship, if you know someone who can do it. Also I have an idea for a sewer system."

"Sewage is always a trick," the earth Mage agreed. "All sorts of methods for disposing of it, none of them ideal. What did you have in mind?"

"Back home we call it a septic tank. What I need is a a large hole and connecting drainfield dug, as well as two waterproof tanks large and strong enough to hold several hundred gallons of liquid while buried underground."

The Mage rubbed his jaw thoughtfully. "The digging's no problem. Most of the jobs I take on are digging cellars and latrines, plowing fields, digging ditches and trenches, and helping with irrigation. The tanks, though, that's a tougher request."

Dare frowned . The hole for the septic tanks and the drainfield could be done by laborers, and probably for cheaper. But from what he'd seen of crafting in Haraldar he was going to have trouble finding a potter, stonemason, or other crafter who made containers anywhere near that big.

"Walk me through the problems," he said.

Morwal shrugged. "It requires a lot of finesse. I'm more of a brute force guy. You want to bury a monster in mud or raise an earthworks, I'm your man. You want me to craft a hollow tank several feet across made of some tough, reinforced material capable of holding in water and then being buried underground, that's a bit outside my usual skill range."

He rubbed his jaw. "You could try an earth Mage who specializes more in delicate craftwork, but there again they might not have the raw power to make something this big. Or, for that matter, the experience to try it."

Hmmm. Dare could maybe try several smaller containers with some sort of overflow or branching outflow system. Or just keep looking. "Assuming I sent a request to the region capitol, do you think there'd be someone there I could hire to make the tanks and ship them here, or better yet come and do the job on-site?"

"I'm sure there would," the Mage said. "The school for earth magic that my master was educated in has a chapter house there." He chuckled. "Hell, Gerar himself might be available if he's taking a break from leveling."

"Okay." Dare offered his hand. "I'll find a courier and send out a request. In the meantime, I have plenty of work a man of your skills would b-"

"Dare?" a familiar voice behind him called. "Peace and balance, my friend, is that you?"

Chapter Eighteen
Reunion

Dare spun around with a surge of excitement at the greeting.

A shorter man with a cleanly shaven head and the build of a gymnast who could shatter boulders with his fists was heading their way down the street, smiling broadly. A companion Dare and Zuri had left behind far to the south; he hadn't expected to see the man here in Terana, or maybe ever again.

"Ilin!" he shouted with a grin, rushing forward to pull his friend into a hug. "What brings you to Terana?"

"The same thing that brings you, I wager," the Monk replied, giving him a solid clap on the back. "Trouble along Bastion's northern border." He nodded politely to Morwal. "Well met again, my friend."

"Ilin," the earth Mage said with a polite nod. "I've got those estimates for your orphanage."

Dare wasn't surprised to learn his friend was working on a charitable project. Between traveling from place to place to level and farm gold, he found ways to use that gold to help those in need. "Building an orphanage in Terana?" he asked.

The Monk grimaced. "Trying to. Tragedies happen in the best of places, leaving children behind with no one to care for them. But in a dangerous region like Bastion there are many orphans needing aid who are often overlooked and left on the streets to fend for themselves. Especially children of other races. And finding those willing to lend aid is even more difficult, with everyone focused on their own survival"

Dare dug in his coin pouch and produced a truesilver coin as well as a handful of gold. "In that case, as a new land owner in the province allow me to offer a donation."

Ilin solemnly accepted the coins, making them disappear in his own coin pouch. "For the sake of the children, I won't be so proud as to refuse a sincere offer from a friend. It is much appreciated."

"Good. And keep me in mind with your charitable efforts in the future."

"I will." His friend abruptly grinned. "Especially as it seems your fortunes have greatly improved since last I saw you." He whistled in clear disbelief. "As have your levels, beyond what seems humanly possible even for a man of your talents. I'd forgotten how effective your methods are."

"Thank you." Dare didn't have the heart to comment on Ilin's progress; the man had been Level 20 when they parted, and remained that level.

A slightly awkward silence settled, as if his friend was well aware of what he was thinking. Then Ilin brightened. "What of Zuri, how does she fare? I'm surprised not to see her with you, but I suppose if she's your same level she has less to fear of harassment. Especially in a more tolerant town like Terana."

"She's doing well," Dare said, grinning. "Very well . . . as it turns out we're having a baby. She's due in about a month."

"Congratulations, my friend!" The shorter man pulled him into a fierce hug, slapping his back. "We should go and share some drinks to celebrate your good fortune, and also catch up on everything we've been up to since we parted." He glanced over at Morwal. "After I take care of business here, of course."

"Sure." Dare nodded to the earth Mage. "I'm hiring your friends the Jorrins for this job. They're coming to the manor in a week to see what needs to be done, if you want to come with them."

"That should be doable." The man gave him another crushing handshake. "I look forward to working with you, Master Dare."

A few minutes later they were on their way to the Mountain's Shadow inn, Ilin pressing him for more news about Zuri's welfare; he'd grown fond of the little goblin during their travels together.

"Actually, I have two more companions now," Dare admitted. "Pella and Leilanna."

"Oh?" The bald ascetic grinned at him. "You two always talked about having a harem. Are they the newest additions?"

Dare felt his cheeks heat. "Pella is our lover, yes. Leilanna is . . ." Complicated. "A friend." He sheepishly scratched the back of his neck. "And Pella is also carrying my child."

"You certainly didn't waste any time," his friend said with a chuckle. "I thought you and Zuri were carefully using Prevent Conception last time I saw you. Change your mind about that?" He frowned. "Actually, doing the math, if Zuri's only a month from . . ." He trailed off as if realizing he was prying.

Dare shook his head. "It's complicated."

Ilin nodded solemnly. "Generally what people say when they *could* give a quick explanation, but would rather not."

Now seemed like a good time to change the subject. "Anyway, we had wildly good luck in a Level 22-25 dungeon and got a legendary treasure chest, which earned us enough to purchase a manor in Terana province. We're making preparations to move there now."

"Then even more congratulations are in order," the Monk said, clapping him on the back. Although his expression was carefully neutral. "Just to be clear, I know you have ways of taking the danger out of leveling, but does this Leilanna happen to be a tank, or Pella someone who can cast protection spells?"

"No, Leilanna's a Mage and Pella's a Tracker."

"Then you're saying you took two pregnant women through a dungeon without anyone to draw aggro and take hits for your party, or prevent them from taking damage?" Ilin was obviously trying for curiosity, but a hint of judgment was creeping through.

And well deserved. Dare dropped his head. "I did," he admitted. "And it nearly ended in disaster. A mistake I've learned from and won't be repeating. I've limited us to fighting weaker enemies, and I'm the only one who goes anywhere near them."

The bald ascetic clapped him on the shoulder. "That's good to hear, my friend. I'm awfully fond of Zuri, and I'm sure Pella and Leilanna are wonderful people as well. I'd spare you the pain of losing a loved one."

From the man's tone, it was a pain he obviously knew.

Dare gripped his shoulder in turn. "What would you think about joining us again?" He smiled slightly. "As I recall, you have such high evasion that you could almost serve as a tank in most cases."

Ilin brightened. "I'll admit I sort of hoped you might make that offer." He shook his head ruefully. "I've missed leveling with you."

Dare couldn't help but laugh. "Or at all?"

His friend joined his laughter. "I'm halfway to 21. By most standards that would be more than respectable, but just coming away from a meteoric rise with you and Zuri it certainly feels disappointing." He shook his head in mild disbelief. "That skill you seem to have of guessing how dangerous monsters are is absurdly powerful, you realize?"

Dare grinned. "I realize."

The Monk grimaced. "Without you there, I went back to the spawn points we cleared on the way to Kov. It was more challenging on my own, certainly, especially since I had no Healer and had to take more precautions not to get hurt. But I was able to do it.

Another sip of water. "But it felt so *slow*. I was really missing you and Zuri, and the way you could always figure out almost clockwork systems for farming monsters quickly and safely. But I figured that since you seemed to be long gone . . ." The man trailed off and gave him a sharp look. "Without even saying goodbye, by the way."

Dare chuckled. "We had a worrying encounter and decided to move on." He quickly described his encounter with the Adherents of the Outsider in their brothel.

Ilin frowned. "I've worked extensively with followers of the Outsider, Dare. They're one of the most openminded and charitable religions out there. I've never seen or heard about them doing anything more sinister than trying to convince people to improve themselves through learning and hard work, or seek out new experiences in the world."

"All I know is I got a seriously strange impression from the ones I met in the brothel," Dare said with a shrug.

"And I'm wondering if it was a bad strange or a good strange," the Monk pressed. "I helped the Adherents of the Outsider in Kov in helping slaves who were being mistreated. I even visited the brothel you speak of and met Ireni. I never saw anything but kindness and compassion from her."

Interesting. It was possible they'd been needlessly paranoid in Kov. "Well, if that's true then the worst that came of the misunderstanding is I missed the chance to visit the brothel again, and possibly have a date with Ireni."

Ilin laughed outright. "Given your fervently expressed goal to sleep with as many women of as many races as possible, I would think you'd be sadder about the missed opportunity." His smile widened. "Especially if Ireni wanted to get to know you better. She's a very beautiful and charming woman, in case you've forgotten."

Dare did his best not to scowl; he hadn't forgotten. "You were talking about your struggles leveling?"

"Right." His friend grimaced. "Well since the leveling was going so slow, I decided I'd try to fight higher level monsters that gave more experience. So I asked around and found rumors of a spawn point with Level 20 monsters . . ." He trailed off with a wince.

Dare groaned in sympathy and reached across to clap his friend on the arm. "How badly did they kick your ass?"

The Monk scowled. "I had to open my Fourth Lock and I still got mauled. I might've handled just the one I aggroed, but its range for pulling adds was higher than I expected." He absently rubbed his leg. "I barely managed to drag myself back to Kov, and even with healing from Ireni I spent a week recovering. Most of that from the damage I'd done my own body opening the Fourth Lock."

"So you didn't know Level 20s and higher would be tougher, either?"

Ilin's mouth worked sourly. "I knew, and the man who told me about the spawn point warned me, too. But I underestimated just how much stronger." He chuckled, although it had the faintest tinge of bitterness. "Half the reason I came north was to try to find you and Zuri again, both because I was worried about your abrupt disappearance and, I'll admit, to see if you wanted to team up again."

Dare gave him a lopsided grin. "Well, you found us."

"Right." His friend barked a laugh and looked around. "And you're now seven levels higher than me, Zuri's about to give birth, and you have two new companions, one another lover who's also carrying your baby. And you'll all soon be living luxuriously in a manor fit for a nobleman, while you continue your meteoric rise to high levels."

"It's a good thing Monks are too enlightened to feel jealousy," Dare teased. "But you don't have to talk like you're on the outside . . . join our party and level with us. You're welcome to stay at the manor, or I can get you a plot of land to build your own house on."

The Monk mock scowled at him. "You're talking long term here, my friend. To a man who's spent most of the last decade wandering." He chuckled ruefully. "I never really considered it my destiny to serve as a retainer to another man's harem."

Dare grinned. "That's why I immediately thought of you, the whole celibacy thing. And I bet you'd make a great babysitter. Also you're one of the most educated people I know."

His friend was silent for a while, seriously mulling over the proposal. "It's worth considering," he finally said. "I need to take care of a few final matters in Terana before I came to join you, and I'll need to be here regularly to oversee the orphanage."

Dare clapped him on the shoulder. "In the meantime, Zuri will be happy to see you again. And I'm eager to introduce you to Pella and Leilanna."

Happy was a bit of an understatement. The moment the little goblin saw Ilin she squealed for joy and literally dropped everything she'd been holding, running over to throw her arms around him. "Ilin! What are you doing here?"

He laughed as he dropped to one knee to more properly hug her. "The same thing you are, I'd guess . . . hunting monsters." He drew back enough to take her in. "You look beautiful, my friend.

Motherhood suits you."

Zuri blushed. "Thank you. I can't wait to have the baby."

The Monk stood and turned to Pella and Leilanna, who'd approached at a more sedate pace. "Ilin, this is Pella," Dare said, putting an arm around the beautiful golden-haired woman's waist. "And this is Leilanna."

The man bowed. "Charmed, ladies." He smiled warmly at Pella. "And I hear congratulations are in order for you as well, miss."

The dog girl brightened, tail wagging. "Thank you! I'm so excited to have Dare's puppies." She showed little shyness as she also hugged the bald ascetic, although more briefly. "Dare and Zuri have told me about their time with you, and I'm glad I finally got to meet you."

"Well they haven't told *me* anything," Leilanna said, scowling. "Who is this strangle little bald guy?"

Little was a bit ungenerous, since Ilin was taller than anyone but Dare and Pella, and only slightly shorter than the dog girl. But the Monk greeted the question with warm equanimity. "It's a pleasure, Miss Leilanna," he said, pressing his palms together and bowing low. "My name is Ilin, a Monk of the Order of the Flowing Palm. A seeker of enlightenment and balance with the world and its people."

"He's also going to be the one leveling with you while the rest of us fix up the manor," Dare added. "I'll scout out all the best spawn points near our land and think up a good leveling pattern for you."

The beautiful dusk elf scowled. "You expect me to level with this bald creep? What if he tries something while we're alone together?"

"Lanna!" Zuri said, stepping protectively in front of Ilin. "You're being really rude to our friend right now."

"It's quite all right," the Monk said, although his expression had tightened slightly. "Some learn kindness at an early age. To others the lesson is longer in coming. And some learn a different lesson entirely."

"Don't act like you know me!" Leilanna snapped, furious. "You have no idea what I've been through!"

Dare stepped in quickly. "Leilanna, he's taken a vow of celibacy. If you can't trust the fact that he's our good friend, trust in his discipline." He frowned. "Also be more polite to people. I don't want you picking fights with everyone who joins us."

She seethed for a few seconds, then pointedly changed the subject. "Did you get the deed?"

He nodded and patted his coin pouch where the legendary chest was stowed. "And I've talked to craftsmen and builders about work on the manor. They'll be coming in a week."

"In that case we've got our work cut out for us," Zuri said.

"Look what we found, Dare!" Pella burst in eagerly, pointing to a few laden horses. "All of these beautiful carpets! They'll be so great in the manor!"

"And seeds!" Leilanna said, forgetting her pique in her own enthusiasm. "All sorts of flowers and sweet-smelling herbs, and fruits and vegetables too. I'm going to make the garden beautiful! And productive! Lots of healthy food for the babies and their mommies."

"We're both carnivores, Lanna," Zuri pointed out. "And judging by the rate of our pregnancies, our babies are going to be too."

The beautiful dusk elf looked a bit crestfallen. "Oh. Well you should still have a little. And it'll be good for the other people who join us."

Dare had to admit he was charmed by the dusk elf's uncharacteristic excitement; if gardening brought her so much joy, he was more than happy to leave it entirely in her hands.

Ilin cleared his throat. "Before you all head off to your manor, I'd love to catch up at the Mountain's Shadow inn. Share some drinks for those of us not expecting children, and some desserts for everyone."

"You had me at "catching up," Zuri said, grinning.

The Monk laughed. "I think we all know what caught your interest with that suggestion, my friend."

Leilanna smirked. "I guess you do know Zuri."

* * * * *

It was almost like old times, gathering around a table to enjoy a meal and drinks with Ilin.

Dare and Zuri shared their adventures since they parted, and Pella chimed in enthusiastically, seeming to take right to the Monk. Even Leilanna warmed up to him a bit, although she showed it in her usual thorny way.

As for Ilin, his own story was less exciting. Fighting lower level monsters, trying to fight the Level 20s and getting owned, making his way north to Bastion doing good deeds as he went. And finally his arrival in Terana and his work to find donations and help for the orphanage he wanted to open.

The time flew by, and all too soon their friend announced that he needed to get back to his labors.

"I'll join you at your manor as soon as I'm able," he promised as they all stood from the table. "A week at the latest, so I can travel with the craftsmen."

"Speaking of the manor," Leilanna chimed in, "shouldn't we name it something? It's a bit clunky calling it "the manor" all the time."

"What about Dare's Den?" Pella asked, tail wagging.

"But it's all of ours!" the dusk elf complained. "Besides, no offense but that name sucks. It's not grand or romantic at all."

"How about New Beginnings Hall?" Dare suggested.

To his chagrin the girls immediately shook their heads. "Too clunky," Zuri said, patting his hand apologetically. "We want something short that gets the point across."

"Like you!" Pella said, affectionately wrapping her arms around the little goblin.

"What about Nirim Manor?" Leilanna suggested. At their blank looks she hastily continued. "The Nirim flower only grows in rare and special places, or in gardens cultivated by skilled elves. It never loses its petals, and as the ages pass regularly grows a new ring of petals. The oldest ones are enormous and breathtaking."

That was actually really good. Poetic, symbolic, and romantic all at once. Not to mention short and easy to say. "I like it," Dare said.

Pella and Zuri both nodded. "So do I," his goblin lover agreed. "It's like our harem, always growing."

The dusk elf looked pleased that her suggestion had won their approval. "Nirim Manor it is, then," she said, wrapping her arms around Zuri and Pella and kissing them both.

* * * * *

By the time they were ready to leave Terana it was late enough in the afternoon that Dare suggested they rent a room. Although he had to admit that part of his motivation was seeing if the pretty guardswoman showed up for a drink.

It seemed the girls had a different idea, though, because they all adamantly insisted on traveling as far as they could before dark. "We want to get started on the manor as soon as possible," Zuri said. "Not an hour to waste."

He was sure that was true for all of them, but part of him wondered if there was something more.

The girls had been acting oddly ever since Ilin left. Huddling together whispering and shooting him looks, smiling and giggling as if at their own jokes, then going sober and blank faced whenever he got close.

Dare wasn't sure what it was about, but it was no fun feeling left out. Especially considering how close the girls had been getting ever since Leilanna started sleeping with Zuri and Pella.

Maybe it was unreasonable, but he found himself withdrawing in a bad mood as they rode for Nirim Manor, listening to them talking and laughing behind him. It brought his mind uncomfortably back to his life on Earth, when so often he'd been alone watching others happy together.

Especially when it came to the opposite sex.

"Quit wallowing in self-pity," his benefactor said, making him jump.

Dare glared at the sky. "Oh, you're taking their side too?"

315

"I'm taking all of your sides, my lover. Now get your head out of your ass. Do you honestly think Pella and Zuri or even Leilanna would deliberately exclude you?"

"What are they doing right now?" he demanded.

She didn't answer.

It was almost a relief to spot the cow-like creatures Zuri loved in the distance, which he'd learned were called epinds. He was more than happy to have an excuse to leave the others to continue towards Nirim Manor while he headed out to hunt, promising to catch up.

The girls looked almost relieved that Dare was excusing himself, probably so they'd be able to talk easier without him overhearing. He tried to keep his head out of his ass like his benefactor had suggested, but it was hard.

Instead he focused on gathering tender, flavorful, better than beef meat, potato-like tubers, onions, peppers, mushrooms, and other quality ingredients to make an amazing meal. That, plus the cooking ingredients he'd purchased in Terana to make desserts, had him excited about treating his girls.

It was better than dwelling on how they were treating him.

By the time he caught up the others had stopped and begun to make camp. Dare noticed that the tent was already set up, and candles in holders glowed in the corners, framing the made-up bed looking more comfortable and inviting than usual.

Zuri and Pella looked excited to see him, quickly latching onto his sides as he got started with dinner. For her part Leilanna looked impassive and remote, although after much throat clearing from the other two women she finally stepped in front of Dare to confront him.

"We need to talk, Dare," she said stiffly. "I may be bound to serve you, but as the holder of my Lifesworn Oath you have responsibilities too."

He tensed in spite of himself; fuck, this had to be about last night. She was probably going to tell him to keep his dirty paws off her.

At his side Zuri sighed and began stroking his arm, almost as if soothing him. Pella just shook her head and lay it on his lap.

The beautiful dusk elf grimaced and crossed her arms even tighter, shoulders hunched as she glowered at him. "It's time you were informed of them . . . for too long you've claimed ignorance of my people's customs as an excuse to mistreat me."

"Mistreat you?" Dare repeated with an incredulous laugh. "You live in the exact same conditions as the rest of us. Aside from the fact we usually have to prod you to do your share of the work."

Her glare intensified. "First, you are obligated to provide adequate shelter," she said through gritted teeth. "Second, you are obligated to provide me with clothes suitable to protect me from the elements and provide suitable decency and social status. You are also obligated to provide me with armor and gear suitable for my level, to protect me from monsters, animals, and predatory humanoids."

Leilanna's voice rose as she continued. "You are required to provide me with whatever items are needed for comfortable day to day living, as well as adequate food of sufficient quality. You are also required to provide me regular opportunities to bathe and launder my clothes. You may not compel me to do anything illegal, immoral, or harmful to myself or others. You must provide me adequate care from a healer should I become injured or be stricken with illness."

Zuri sighed again, while Pella's ears were drooping. "Leilanna," Dare said slowly. "Do you think I haven't done any of these things?"

"NO!" she said hastily, then flushed. "You've done all of them and more, very satisfactorily. I'm just clearly stating the responsibilities of the holder of a Lifesworn Oath."

The beautiful woman paused, giving him a quick glance, then threw back her shoulders defiantly and spoke in a quicker tone. "Finally, you are required to regularly bed me."

Dare made a strangled noise. "What?" Pella had sat up straight, and Zuri was leaning forward intently.

Leilanna blushed a darker gray than he'd ever seen her and continued in a rush. "You are required to regularly bed me. Also you must ensure I am sufficiently pleasured when you do, and take care for my wants and needs in coitus."

Was this a joke?

Her words tumbled out of her as she finished. "Finally, when I decide I am prepared to carry and raise your offspring, you must ensure I take your seed without any preventive spells. And you must act as a suitable father to those children, providing for their needs and giving them due attention and affection as-"

Dare had been struggling his best to hold it in until she finished, curious how far she'd push, but at that he burst out laughing, forcing her to trail off.

Leilanna glared murder at him. "Is there something funny about my people's customs?"

Zuri and Pella were also frowning at him, and he had a feeling he was getting himself in hot water, but he couldn't help it; he couldn't talk for a full half a minute, he was laughing too hard.

And all the while the dusk elf stood there with her arms crossed, beautiful face flushing darker and darker. Not just with wrath, he thought, but also embarrassment.

He finally managed to speak between guffaws. "Your people's Lifesworn Oath requires me to regularly pleasure you in bed?" he gasped. "And have children with you and be a good father to them?"

"It does," the dusk elf snapped, voice unconvincing.

"Are you sure you're not trying to use my ignorance of your customs to trick me?" he teased, wiping tears from his eyes as his laughter finally died down.

"Will you never stop insulting my honor?" Leilanna shouted. "The Lifesworn Oath is sacred, and yet you'd so casually accuse me of twisting it to my own ends?"

Dare finally sat up, turning suddenly serious and shooting her a firm look. "Don't try to catch me with twisty speech . . . you never specifically said that the responsibilities you listed were those required by the Lifesworn Oath." He crossed his feet in front of him and leaned over to stir the food. "Maybe you should consider giving up on treating me like I'm a complete fool."

"I will when I see evidence to the contrary!" the dusk elf shouted. "Are you completely blind to what's happening right now?" He stared at her blankly, and with a furious screech she turned and stomped away into the deepening gloom.

To his dismay, when he turned back from the departing Mage he saw Zuri and Pella both glaring at him. "Why would you do that to poor Lanna?" his goblin lover demanded furiously.

Dare's confusion deepened. "What?"

"Seriously, you were a complete ass," Pella growled.

"*I* was a complete ass?" he repeated incredulously.

"Yes, you were!" Zuri snapped, leaping to her feet with her fists clenched at her sides. "She was confessing her feelings in the only way she felt comfortable with."

He blinked. "Wait, what?"

His dog girl lover joined the smaller goblin, looming over him. "How can you be so insensitive, Dare? You spend weeks refusing to tell her how you feel, pretending it's what she wants, and when she finally gathers the courage to tell you herself you insult her honor?" Her soft brown eyes were filling with tears. "Did you see how devastated she was?"

No. If that was true then . . . "That's what was happening?" he whispered. "I didn't know. I didn't . . ."

Zuri began tugging him to his feet, expression fierce. "Go after her right now and make this right, before it's too late."

"Yeah!" Pella agreed, manhandling him after the departed elf with far more ease. "We're going to be very cross with you if you don't. We didn't spend all day helping her build up the courage to talk to you only to have you ruin everything."

Of course Dare was going to go after Leilanna. Damnit, had he really been teasing her while she tried to confess her love? He had to be the world's biggest dipshit.

To his relief he found her waiting just out of sight of the camp, sitting on a log in a small stand of trees. He approached cautiously. "Leilanna?"

"Go away!" she said, staying turned away. He could hear the tears in her voice, though. They broke his heart.

"If you really want me to, I will," Dare said. "But I feel like we've avoided talking about things we need to, and I'd like to fix that."

Leilanna didn't answer.

With a sigh he settled down on the far end of the log. To his relief she didn't immediately jump up and storm away, although her back stayed firmly turned to him. "Listen, Leilanna," he said gently. "We had a rocky start, I'll admit. And maybe we've gotten a bit too used to needling each other, trying to get a rise out of each other. Because it's safer and more comfortable than talking about how we really feel."

She made a "hmph" noise.

Dare risked scooting a little closer. "And I'll admit I misread how you feel, and because of that I might've pushed you away without realizing it, thinking it was what you wanted."

The beautiful dusk elf made another "hmph" noise and wiped at her eyes, but her back straightened.

He got close enough to touch her shoulder, turning her towards him. Her big pink eyes were luminous with tears, her expression unexpectedly vulnerable. There was no hint of her usual fiery temper.

Dare tenderly brushed a tear from her cheek with his finger, then took her hand as he held her gaze. "Because the truth is, Leilanna, I've had feelings for you for a long time now."

Leilanna's breath caught, eyes shining with wary hope. But she shook her head. "You just want to fuck me like every other woman you've met," she said in a small voice.

Ouch. "I do think you're beautiful and desire you," he admitted. "But it's more than that, and if you feel the same way I do then I think you realize it." He squeezed her hand. "I love everything about you, Leilanna. All your soft curves, and your rough edges too."

"Like what?" she challenged.

Dare smiled fondly. "Like your fiery disposition, and I'm not just talking about your bloodline trait. Your passion in everything you do, and how you're not afraid to fight for yourself and the people you care about.

"I love your fierce intelligence, and your sharp wit." He chuckled. "Even when you're using it to take digs at me. I love your pride in your ability and your hard work to improve yourself, and how you hold to honor no matter the sacrifice."

He scooted a bit closer so he could wrap an arm around her, close and intimate. "I love how when you finally let down your walls, you give everything of yourself. It's been wonderful to see it with Zuri and Pella." He hesitated, then added quietly, "And I hope I can be a person you can feel safe opening up to like that, too."

Leilanna's face crumpled, and she buried her head in his shoulder. "Damnit," she whispered. "Why couldn't you have said all this a long time ago?"

Dare chuckled wryly. "Because I'm an insensitive, oblivious ass. As has been pointed out to me very clearly."

She stayed pressed against him for a few minutes, saying nothing. Until finally he felt her tense as if readying herself and she spoke in a small voice, "I love you too, Dare. I think I loved you when I watched you charge in and solo a dungeon boss to keep us safe. And when I saw you show your love to Zuri and Pella every day, and hold them close to stand beside you. And how you started to do the same for me."

The beautiful dusk elf hiccuped. "And I love you for holding me together when I fell apart."

She finally looked up, eyes soft and open and full of quiet passion. "I want to be with you. I want to be part of the family you're making with Zuri and Pella, and share your love and one day have your children."

With a tremulous smile Leilanna took his hand in both hers. "I think you've figured out by now I'm a mess. I can't make it as easy as Zuri and Pella . . . even when I try my best I mess it up half the time. But if you can be patient with me we'll create something beautiful together. All of us."

"All of us." Dare leaned forward and gently pressed his lips to hers.

She melted against him, body soft and welcoming as she kissed him back with the same hungry heat he'd felt from her last night. It felt incredible. It felt warm and comfortable and passionate.

It felt right.

Then the beautiful dusk elf pulled back with a gasp and stood, hands smoothing her dress and fiddling with her snowy hair. "Dare, can-can you stay here?" she asked, sounding almost shy. "Just for a few minutes? Zuri and Pella helped me prepare everything, but I need to go make sure it's all ready."

Dare's breath caught at the implication. Was she saying she wanted to make love to him tonight? Was that why they'd set up the tent with the bed prepared extra nice and all the candles?

"All right," he said, throat dry. "As long as you need."

Leilanna shot him an enchanting smile, nervous and excited and happy all at once, then turned and rushed back towards camp.

Chapter Nineteen
Dream Come True

It was finally happening.

Dare's dream from the first, what he'd longed for since coming to Collisa. He was finally going to be with an elf.

Although honestly that excitement took a backseat to his happiness that he'd finally confessed his love to Leilanna, and he'd heard her confess her love in turn. That the fiery, passionate, beautiful, often difficult women who'd been driving him crazy for weeks wanted to be with him, not just as a lover but as a partner for life.

She wanted to have his children when she felt ready.

Dare settled back on the log, then after a few minutes of waiting in nervous anticipation gathered a bunch of rocks to juggle to distract himself. After an interminable half hour or so of waiting he finally heard a rustle, and straightened eagerly to see Zuri and Pella approaching.

His goblin lover wasted no time dumping a pitcher of water over him, then casting Cleanse Target to clean him. Then she held out a towel. "Here, dry off. I've brought your nicest clothes to change into."

To his chagrin he hadn't even given much thought to making himself presentable. He assumed his lovers had helped Leilanna with the same preparations, although likely even more in depth.

Once Dare was dried off and changed Pella held out a plate of the food he'd made. "Eat up," she said with a wide smile. She was practically dancing in place, tail wagging furiously. "You're going to need your strength."

"You sure are." Zuri clasped her hands in front of her, eyes shining. "It's finally happening!"

He was too excited and nervous to be hungry, but he shoved a few forkfuls of meat and potatoes into his mouth, barely tasting the deliciously spiced dish. Then he set the plate aside and turned toward camp. "Okay, let's go."

"Oh, we're not going to be there for your first time," Zuri said.

Pella nodded her agreement. "In fact, we set up the other tent to sleep in so you two can have the whole night together!"

Dare hesitated. "Are you sure? I know you guys like to give me some space so I can fully enjoy being with a new woman, but Leilanna's already your lover. Besides, wouldn't it make it easier for her if you were there with her for this?"

"Maybe," Pella said. "But this is what you two need." At his confused look she sighed. "She's not just *our* lover, Dare. She's *your* lover. Or at least she's ready to be. She needs to be with you and just you, allowed to be vulnerable and express her love and make that deep connection."

Zuri nodded. "Don't you want your first time together to be just the two of you, all about your feelings for each other and sharing that precious moment?"

When they put it like that, Dare very much wanted that. "All right," he said. He gave them both a brief but fierce hug. "Thank you."

As he turned away to start for the tent, a bit nervous about his first time with the beautiful dusk elf, Zuri caught his hand urgently to turn him back towards her. "One more thing, Dare, and listen carefully. Leilanna had plenty of reasons for hesitating to be with you, but one of the big ones is that she's a virgin and she's a bit scared about her first time."

"Especially since she's seen the size of your cock," Pella agreed frankly.

Shit, that didn't do much for his nervousness. Dare had never deflowered a woman before, aside from the alabaster mannequin his benefactor had fucked him with. Although he felt like that didn't really count.

But he knew you had to be especially gentle. And proud as he was of his monster cock, it wasn't exactly the tool for a job like this.

Seeing his expression, Pella gently patted his hand. "Relax, she might be a virgin but you're not. You've had plenty of experience by this point. So just pay attention to her reactions and be extra slow and gentle. That shouldn't be hard for you."

"Yeah," Zuri agreed, eyes twinkling. "I usually have to coax you to fuck me as hard as I want. For all your size you're the gentlest lover I've ever had, always patient at first and slowly building up to the rough stuff."

"Except no rough stuff with Leilanna this time, obviously," his dog girl lover said with a laugh. She began eagerly pushing at his back. "Come on, quit stalling and go make our family whole by filling hers."

Dare couldn't help but chuckle at the turn of phrase as he allowed himself to be ushered towards the tent. "I love you two."

"We love you back," Zuri said as she joined Pella's pushing. "Now love her."

He left them behind and made his way to camp, self-consciously running his fingers through his hair. The campfire was abandoned, leading him to conclude that Leilanna was already waiting in the tent.

Heart pounding in his chest, he walked towards it until he finally got his first view through the wide open flaps. Then he stopped, staring openmouthed.

Maybe it was a bit ridiculous to be so amazed at the view before him. After all, by this point he'd seen Leilanna naked numerous times. Heck, he'd seen her with her delicate pink pussy gaping open obscenely, arousal pouring from her as Zuri or Pella or Rosie or Enellia pleasured her to climax.

But it was different this time because she was waiting for him.

She was lying on her side across the bed, wearing a pink nightie that matched her eyes, transparent enough to see everything without quite seeing everything. Beneath it he saw only tantalizing curves.

Her hair had been arranged in a snowy waterfall over her shoulder and down her back, bound by thin twin braids that made an elegant circlet around her head. Her pale gray cheeks were flushed dark with excitement, eyes wide and inviting, and her large breasts heaved with every eager breath, charcoal gray nipples already erect and poking out the wispy cloth.

Dare was vaguely aware he was staring at them, lost in a fantasy of burying his face in the glorious valley they created and just losing himself in her softness.

The beautiful dusk elf rested a hand on her voluptuous hip, raising a delicate eyebrow. "Gratifying as it is to see you struck speechless, I wasn't planning on posing like this all night." She patted the bed in front of her. "Come here."

He started to step forward and she raised her eyebrow again. "Although don't you think you should lose the clothes first?"

Grinning, he peeled off his shirt and pants, leaving his underwear for now. He would've been more self-conscious about doing so if they hadn't already seen each other naked and having sex with their companions so many times.

Although Leilanna must've been thinking some of the same things he'd been about her first view of him as a lover, because her eyes greedily devoured every inch of him as he revealed it. "Ascendants," she murmured, thighs subconsciously rubbing together, "I can't believe I finally get to touch you."

"The feeling's more than mutual," he said, climbing onto the bed and gathering her in his arms.

At first she was a bit tense, nervous and maybe even shy, and he contented himself with holding her and luxuriating in her curvy body pressed against him. Holding her really was like cuddling warm pillowy softness, as his lovers had said.

Dare found himself idly running his hand up and down her arm through the thin cloth of her nightie, cheek pressed against her head as he breathed in her clean scent, which brought to mind a garden in full bloom.

"Gods you're beautiful," he murmured, kissing her soft hair.

Leilanna lifted her face to him, plump lips parted and quick breaths brushing his skin, and he leaned down and kissed her, tasting the heady savor of blackberry wine on her tongue as it emerged to meet his.

Phoenix

For a time they kissed deeply, bodies moving against each other with hungry passion. Dare ran his hands up and down her back, then down to her round ass and began kneading the pillowy flesh with his fingers.

His beautiful dusk elf lover moaned and lifted a leg over him, grinding desperately against his thigh as her hip pressed against his erection through his underwear. He felt her arousal on his skin and was overcome with the desire to taste her.

Breaking their intense kiss with a gasp for breath, he trailed his lips down her neck, kissing and sucking her flawless skin. "Ooh, keep doing that," she moaned.

Dare grinned up at her. "Are you sure?" he teased. "Because I could be doing this." He dipped his head and pulled one of her nipples into his mouth, sucking it hard through the thin cloth of her nighty.

"Ascendants, yes!" she gasped, pushing her chest against him and grinding her silky folds more desperately against his leg. "Keep doing *that*!"

Part of him wanted to tease her again and keep going south, but he was in no hurry. So he kept playing with her luxurious breasts through the thin cloth, moving to her other nipple and latching on.

Leilanna abruptly stiffened against him with a whimpery noise, trembling, and he felt her nectar flood his leg as she climaxed.

Dare buried his face between her pillowy breasts and hugged her close as she came down from her peak. He felt like he was in a dream, which only became more pleasant as she began pushing his head down and squirming upwards at the same time, until finally his face was buried between her plump thighs beneath her nighty.

He eagerly moved the final distance and kissed her glistening pink sex, trailing his lips over her plump folds.

If her lips tasted like blackberry wine, her arousal tasted like blackberry brandy, heavy and sweet and rich enough to turn his head, with a musk that reached right to his most primal brain and made his cock pulse with an urgent need to be inside her.

He buried his tongue between the beautiful dusk elf's lips, eager to taste more of her, and with a delighted squeal her soft thighs clamped tight around his head and she squirted almost directly into his mouth.

"Yes, Dare, yes!" she cried, grinding harder against his face, her juices making her glide over him easily, slippery with desperate need. "I've wanted this for so long."

Dare did his best to keep stimulating Leilanna's eagerly moving pussy, at least until with a final squirt her thighs abruptly fell away. She gripped his hair with both hands and began tugging him upwards again, while at the same time squirming to get underneath him.

"Now, Dare!" Leilanna gasped, beautiful face flushed with arousal. She pushed him away enough that she could squirm out of her nightie, then lay back with her legs spread wide and her arms raised in invitation. "I'm ready."

He swallowed, heart pounding, and quickly skinned out of his underwear. Then he positioned himself over her, the throbbing tip of his rock hard cock brushing her glistening pink folds, warm and inviting against him.

Then he hesitated, wondering if there was some special way he should do this.

Leilanna impatiently reached down to her pussy and gathered up some of her juices, slathering them over his shaft in a way that made him groan with pleasure. Then, for good measure, she spit on her hand and rubbed that on his shaft too.

"Well?" she asked, biting her lip in nervous anticipation. "You going to rub against my the entrance all night? Go slow, but actually go!"

Dare leaned down and tenderly kissed her as he ever so slowly began to push forward.

He wondered if she almost immediately regretted her demand as he began to stretch her tight lips, which spread obscenely around his girth and formed a crushing ring around his tip. She moaned and tensed slightly, and he stopped for a while as she adjusted and relaxed.

"Go," she gasped. He pushed in a few millimeters, then quickly paused at her grimace of discomfort until she irritably slapped his ass. "Go!"

Dare kept going, slowly and gently, until finally his head slipped past her entrance and was inside. He stopped there, letting her pant and clutch the blankets beneath her as she adjusted to his girth.

This was just the first hurdle, though. Next came slowly pushing deeper to give her a chance to gradually adjust, before finally reaching her maidenhead.

"You know, maybe I should work on you a bit with my fingers," he suggested. "Get you ready."

Leilanna grinned at him. "You might've suggested that before putting your cock in me." She twitched her hips against him impatiently, then winced as if regretting it. "Keep going," she panted.

So Dare did. Slowly and tenderly, millimeter after incredible millimeter of her sweet tunnel opening up to him and caressing his throbbing shaft. Until finally he felt a barrier stopping his progress.

His lover bit her lip. "Here we are," she whispered. "My maidenhood. We're about to become lovers in truth." She looked up at him, pink eyes shining with love. "I'm ready, Dare. Keep going."

He leaned down and kissed her softly, teasing her pillowy breast and playing with her thick nipple with one hand until he felt her relax even more and open up to him. Then he withdrew slightly and began carefully easing his way forward against her hymen.

Leilanna gasped against his mouth, and the barrier was gone. "Now we're one," she said with a sigh.

They lay like that for a minute or so, holding each other and exchanging soft kisses as they both got used to the feeling of him inside her. Then she twitched her hips, looking up at him with a nervous but eager smile. "Keep going."

Dare did, slowly easing his way in until he bottomed out, then just as gently withdrawing. The delayed gratification of going so slow was tantalizing in its own way, leaving him panting with pleasure as her tight virgin walls squeezed him.

He knew it was possible to open up a hymen without tearing it, but unfortunately in spite of his best efforts he didn't manage it with Leilanna. As he looked down at his massive girth leaving her stretched lips, he saw that her nectar glistening on his cock was tinged faintly pink.

Just a little, hopefully not a big tear, but he kind of regretted that it was his huge manhood that had taken her cherry.

Maybe part of their foreplay should've been an average-sized dildo. Too late now, though.

Dare pushed in again, just as slowly and gently, while her breathing slowed and her expression calmed. She was starting to adjust. "Just a bit more of this and then I'll start to enjoy it, right?" she asked, pale red eyes looking up at him hopefully.

He hesitated; he actually didn't know the answer to that. "I'm not sure. Maybe not your first time."

"I see." Leilanna sighed. "All right, come."

"What?" Dare asked, blinking in surprise.

She wiggled her hips impatiently. "Go ahead and come. We'll do more next time and I'll enjoy it."

Good to know his new lover cared so much about his pleasure. Although he supposed her first time *should* be more about her.

On the other hand, he'd been so focused on going slow and careful for her that he'd barely even let himself feel or enjoy the sensation of being inside her warm, crushingly tight pussy. "I'm not quite there yet," he admitted. "Can I at least get fully inside?"

His curvy dusk elf lover sighed again, then her face became focused. "Does this help?"

Dare bit back a gasp as her tight, slick walls began clenching and loosening around his girth. Not in orgasm, but as if she was doing some sort of pelvic floor exercise. With surprising control.

As it turned out, it *did* help. After about fifteen seconds of the beautiful dusk elf's patient onslaught he groaned, braced himself, and in a rush of pleasure began spurting into her silky pussy.

"Yeesss!" Leilanna moaned, virgin walls still twitching rhythmically around him. "Ascendants, it feels so hot inside me. I can't believe you'd be making a baby in me without Zuri's spell." She giggled, almost giddily, and hugged him tight with her arms and legs. "It's kind of sexy to think about."

With effort Dare kept his position over her, letting his orgasm sweep over him until he finally finished emptying inside her pink tunnel. "Gods, Leilanna," he gasped when he finally finished, carefully pulling out and collapsing beside her. "You're incredible."

She cuddled up to him, panting and beaming with pleased satisfaction. "Thank you for making my first time so special, Dare. I love you."

"I love you," He kissed her forehead, glowing with perspiration, then her nose, then her plump, glistening lips.

They spent the next half hour basking in the warmth of their new intimacy, exploring each other's bodies the way they'd longed to for weeks. Then Dare guided her to another gentle climax with his fingers, kissing and sucking her beautiful breasts at the same time, luxuriating in the feel of her sexy body responding to his touch.

Last of all he finally got to see Leilanna's almost obscenely plump lips wrap around his cock, the way he hadn't been able to keep from imagining from the first moment he saw them, as with effort she took him into her mouth. She could barely get his tip in, and her blowjob was probably the most inexpert one he'd ever been given, but he couldn't help but buck his hips in pleasure and run his fingers through her snowy white hair as she clumsily but enthusiastically sucked him while jerking him off with her soft, elegant hands.

Maybe it was those big, dark pink eyes staring up at him lovingly as she did her best to make him feel good.

"I'm going to come," he warned her after a few minutes. But rather than stopping she just sucked him even more eagerly, squeezing and stroking him hard. With a groan he grabbed her head and emptied his balls down her throat, while she made breathless whimpering sounds of enjoyment and swallowed everything.

"Ascendants, I've wanted to taste you for so long," his dusk elf lover murmured with a dreamy smile as she climbed back up to rest her head on his shoulder, soft body half draped over his.

It was hard to imagine that the hostile young woman he'd first met could ever have become this open and affectionate, which made it all the more incredible.

Dare gently caressed her body while she nuzzled his neck, until finally he felt her breathing deepen in sleep, her beautiful face relaxed and peaceful. He did his best not to disturb her as he pulled the blanket over them both.

In spite of his efforts he felt Leilanna stir. She sighed, and while he thought she'd been relaxed in his arms she somehow molded even more softly against him. "You know what," she murmured, "I was going to ask Zuri to clean us up when we were done, but I changed my mind. I want to fall asleep feeling your seed inside me."

God, that was hot. And he could admit he didn't mind the thought of falling asleep covered in her arousal, either. Especially when this intimacy obviously meant so much to her.

So he gently kissed her silky white hair and settled back, giving in to his exhaustion as he listened to her breaths become soft and even in sleep.

Epilogue
Homecoming

The next morning Dare and Leilanna were awakened by an excited Zuri and Pella, who eagerly burrowed beneath the blankets with them, wanting to know all the details of Leilanna's first time.

Before long the two women were kissing and caressing him and his new lover. Although not for long before they pushed him and the blushing dusk elf together, wanting to witness them finally being intimate.

He was only too happy to go along, once again luxuriating in Leilanna's soft warm body as he kissed and caressed her. Zuri and Pella squirmed against them, doing their best to increase their pleasure, and after a few minutes the little goblin's hands glowed in healing over the dusk elf.

"There, that should take care of any soreness from last night," she said, eyes dancing. Then she eagerly tugged on Dare's cock, not sensually but more as if trying to pull him along with it. "I want to see you put it inside her!"

"Ooh, me too!" Pella squealed. "I bet it looks so hot!"

Leilanna bit her plump lip, blushing. "I'd like that too," she admitted.

So he rolled onto his back and let his new lover lower herself onto him, whimpering with mingled effort and pleasure as her arousal dripped down his length. Zuri and Pella helped out by licking and kissing around where they were joined, adding their saliva to lubricate his entry until he bottomed out in her warm core.

The beautiful dusk elf was slow and cautious at first, but after a few minutes she began riding him more confidently, while the other two women oohed and aahed at the sight of his massive cock disappearing inside her.

They did their best to make the experience more pleasurable, Zuri planting her dripping pussy on Dare's face and kissing Leilanna fiercely, while Pella stimulated the snowy-haired woman's clit with her fingers.

Before long the dusk elf collapsed in a quivering climax, and Dare gave in to Zuri's and Pella's urging and released inside her earlier than he'd planned, so the two women could watch their combined juices flowing out of her.

Needless to say, they weren't done after that; it was nearly midmorning before the party ended up breaking camp and preparing to set out.

The entire time Leilanna stayed at his side, pressing close to him and seeming reluctant to end their new intimacy. In fact, after he finished saddling his horse she shifted awkwardly and blurted, "Zuri said that now that we're lovers, it wouldn't be seen as amiss if I rode with you."

Dare blinked. "You want to do that?"

"I wouldn't be asking otherwise!" she said, blushing.

He chuckled, seeing nothing wrong with the idea. "That sounds nice."

Brightening, the beautiful dusk elf eagerly climbed up into the saddle, and he climbed up behind her and held her close to his chest while he handled the reins. It felt nice.

Zuri and Pella thoughtfully took the leads of the packhorses, mounting up as well, and they all set out, the two women falling behind to give him and Leilanna space.

At which point Dare realized that he hadn't had too many conversations alone with his new lover. Especially as lovers, obviously. Any small talk and banter seemed ridiculous, but as the awkward silence stretched and the beautiful dusk elf began shifting against him, he finally blurted, "Soooo."

Smooth.

His curvy lover looked back at him over her shoulder and grinned at his discomfiture; she seemed completely relaxed. "Thanks for arranging for me to level with Ilin. I promise I'll work hard to catch up to you guys." She grimaced. "Even if it means sleeping four hours at a time."

Dare chuckled and kissed her pale gray cheek. "I can't wait. If you blow things up now, you'll nuke them when we're even level."

She frowned. "Nuke? Zuri's right, even with the translation stone some of the stuff you say is nonsense."

Probably best not to explain what a nuke actually was. "A really high level Mage spell."

"Ah." Leilanna settled back against him. "Anyway, it would be nice to be part of the group without you having to drag me around as useless weight."

Dare grinned and playfully toyed with her large breasts. "I don't know, I like the weight you're dragging."

She twisted around to glare at him, long elvish ears quivering in outrage; there was the quick temper and passion he knew and loved. "Care to rephrase that?"

"No need to rephrase a compliment." He affectionately kissed her nose. "No need to be self-conscious when you've got the body of a fertility goddess, either."

"Hmph." The beautiful dusk elf turned forward again and pointedly pushed his hands off her chest, folding her arms to take their place.

Dare just grinned wider and brushed her silky hair aside to kiss her neck, stroking her lush thighs. "Oh, suddenly you can't take a bit of teasing? I thought that was our thing."

"Only if you're ready to get the same treatment in kind," she said, plump lip extended in a pout. "Also you must be a moron to bring up a woman's weight . . . aren't you supposed to be a smooth womanizer with three lovers in your harem?"

She had a good point. He laughed and caressed a bit higher up her thigh. "Okay, you win. I'll avoid the off-limit topics with our playful banter."

Leilanna blew out her breath irritably, then grabbed his hand and shoved it firmly between her legs, treating him to the feel of her soft mound and delicate folds through the thin cloth of her slit silk riding dress. "If you're going to tease me, you might as well do the job properly," she said with forced casualness, although her cheeks were flushed and her breathing quickened.

Grinning, Dare began gently exploring her sex with his fingers, following her cues as she melted back against him, gasping and moaning when he found a spot she liked. He wrapped the reins around the pommel to free his other hand and cupped one of her pillowy breasts with it, kneading the soft flesh and grinding the heel of his hand against her quickly stiffening nipple.

It took only a few minutes before Leilanna shuddered her way to a quiet but intense climax. Afterwards she idly stroked his thighs with her hands, head pressed back against his chest. "You know," she murmured reflectively, "maybe it's not the worst thing that you ended up saving my life."

Dare couldn't help but laugh at that particular phrasing. "Still regret that you had to swear a Lifesworn Oath to me?"

"That depends on how well you take care of me." His beautiful dusk elf lover awkwardly squirmed around in the saddle, pulling up her skirts to give her more ease of motion, until finally she was straddling him with her panty-clad crotch pressed against him through his pants.

Her gorgeous dark pink eyes looked up at him, glazed with lust, as her nimble fingers got to work on the ties of his pants. "You know," she said in a low, husky voice, "I used to get off sometimes in the saddle if I put my horse to just the right pace. It can almost feel like sex."

Dare could believe that from his naughty lover. His cock, already swelling eagerly, twitched sharply at that mental image. Leilanna felt it against her quickly dampening pussy and giggled, brushing his ear with her lusciously plump red lips. "Just imagine what it would feel like to ride at that pace while *actually* having sex," she purred.

He didn't need to imagine, because he found out soon enough as he slid into her silky warmth, and at her urging nudged his horse into a trot then a gallop while she bounced up on down on him solely from the motion of their mount.

She finally collapsed against him with a cry of pleasure, tight walls clamping down and flooding their crotches and the saddle with her nectar. He gave in to the pleasure and released inside her as the motion of the horse continued to move them against each other, until finally the sensations grew too intense and he had to rein in to a stop.

Zuri and Pella quickly caught up to them, taking in their flushed, sweaty faces and joined bodies. "We're totally doing that next," his dog girl lover said, Zuri nodding emphatically.

* * * * *

They reached Nirim Manor in the early afternoon, Volen hurrying into view to open the gate for them. Or at least, hurrying as much as an elderly man could.

"Back again?" he called, looking a bit anxious but trying to hide it. "I suppose that means you bought the place?"

Dare nodded and produced the deed. "I hope you'll consider staying on in your role as caretaker," he said; he wasn't sure how much use the man would be, but if he'd been faithfully tending this place for decades of his life then it seemed heartless to turn him out with no more than a "k thanks".

Besides, he doubted his lovers would be particularly impressed by such a dick move.

Volen looked intensely relieved as he stood aside to clear the path. "I will indeed, Master Dare. Thank you."

The caretaker followed them up to the manor and helped them unload the horses, then joined Pella in leading them away to the stables to care for them. That left Dare and Leilanna to begin carrying things in, while Zuri busied herself pulling dust cloths off the furniture.

After all their traveling it would've been nice to be able to arrive home to a clean and welcoming manor, ready to eat a hot meal and fall into a soft bed. But that would have to be something to look forward to in the future.

For now they had work to do.

They spent the rest of the day cleaning, moving furniture, laying out rugs, and making plans for the future. Dare disappeared for a half hour to look at the rooms he planned to turn into proper bathrooms with indoor plumbing and hot and cold water, figuring out the best way to lay out pipes. Then he headed outside to find the best spot for the septic tank and drain field.

Inside he heard the bustle of his lovers continuing to work, while around him birds chirped in the trees as the first night insects made themselves heard. The sunset to the west was a brilliant splash of colors across the horizon, reminding him of Enellia's gorgeous wings.

He wondered how she was doing.

Although Dare had come outside to see about the septic tank he found himself drifting through the overgrown gardens, somehow eventually finding his way to the Outsider's shrine. He stared at the representation of Collisa with its circling comet, thinking that it wasn't so long ago when he'd been an outsider, too.

His life had changed completely when he'd died on Earth and come to this world. And it was changing again.

He had a home now, land he was responsible for, with three beautiful women depending on him and children on the way. He was going to be a husband and father, in a way he'd half expected he'd never have in his old life.

Which reminded him that he needed to look into the process for legally marrying Zuri, Pella, and probably Leilanna too. And of course his marriage with Se'weir was coming up in a year, assuming their relationship worked out. And doubtless he'd be meeting more women before then, and hopefully falling in love with some.

Speaking of Se'weir, he needed to go out and find a spot for the goblins who'd accepted his offer, and also talk to Lady Marona to make sure she approved of it. Or at least ask her forgiveness, since he'd failed to ask her permission.

And he needed to prepare for the arrival of the craftsmen so he could put them to work right away. And Ilin would be arriving at any time, so he needed to scout out the nearby spawn points to find a good leveling plan for him and Leilanna.

Eventually he'd need to get back out there and start leveling again and earning gold so they could pay for all this. Zuri probably wouldn't be able to join him and whoever else came along, so close to her due date or after the baby was born, and someone would need to stay back with her.

For that reason he couldn't be gone for too long at a time and would have to plan his leveling trips carefully. And as Pella got closer to her due date she'd need to stay as well, and he'd have to find women to grow his harem without their help as his wingmen, and . . .

A lot to plan for. A lot to do. A life brimming with challenges and opportunities.

And it was just starting.

End of Bastion.
The adventures of Dare and his harem
continue in Nirim, fourth book of the Outsider series.

Thank you for reading Bastion!

I hope you enjoyed reading it as much as I enjoyed writing it. If you feel the book is worthy of support, I'd greatly appreciate it if you'd rate it, or better yet review it, on Amazon, as well as recommend it to anyone you think would also enjoy it.

As a self-published author I flourish with the help of readers who review and recommend my work. Your support helps me continue doing what I love and bringing you more books to enjoy.

About the Author

Aiden Phoenix became an established author
writing stories about the end of the world.
Then Collisa called, a new and exciting world to explore,
and like the characters in his series he was reborn anew there.

Made in the USA
Monee, IL
12 January 2024

51672105R10199